SUBMERGED

" *Reads like an approaching storm, full of darkness, dread and electricity. Prepare for your skin to crawl.* "
—Andrew Gross, *New York Times* Bestselling Author of *15 Seconds*

CHERYL KAYE
TARDIF

SUBMERGED

http://www.cherylktardif.com

SECOND EDITION TRADE PAPERBACK

Imajin Books – www.imajinbooks.com

March 12, 2020

ISBN: 978-1-77223-389-6

Cover designed by Juan Padron: www.juanjpadron.com

Praise for SUBMERGED

"*Submerged* reads like an approaching storm, full of darkness, dread and electricity. Prepare for your skin to crawl." —Andrew Gross, *New York Times* bestselling author of *15 Seconds*

"From the first page you know you are in the hands of a seasoned and expert storyteller who is going to keep you up at night turning the pages. Tardif knows her stuff. There's a reason she sells like wildfire—her words burn up the pages. A wonderful, scary, heart pumping writer." —M.J. Rose, international bestselling author of *Seduction*

"Tardif once again delivers a suspenseful supernatural masterpiece." —Scott Nicholson, international bestselling author of *The Home*

"From the first page, Cheryl Kaye Tardif takes you hostage with *Submerged*—a compelling tale of anguish and redemption." —Rick Mofina, bestselling author of *Into the Dark*

"Cheryl Kaye Tardif's latest novel *Submerged* will leave you as haunted as its characters." —Joshua Corin, bestselling author of *Before Cain Strikes*

"*Submerged* will leave you breathless—an edge of your seat, supernatural thrill ride." —Jeff Bennington, bestselling author of *Twisted Vengeance*

"Cheryl Kaye Tardif's latest novel SUBMERGED will leave you as haunted as its characters." —Joshua Corin, bestselling author of *Before Cain Strikes*

To my father, who has always supported me.

Acknowledgements

A very special thank you to my longtime friend, Mike, without whom this novel wouldn't be possible. Mike, thank you for sharing your own story of addiction, of how it affected your life, your marriage, your career and those around you. Your quiet courage is inspiring. And your life now proves there *is* a chance for redemption, if one lets go of old ways, grabs onto hope and rises to the surface.

Thanks to Sharon DeVries of Yellowhead Regional Emergency Communications Center, for all the invaluable information regarding emergency services and practices in the Hinton/Edson area. As with all fiction, sometimes truth has to be bent in order to fit a plot and to rev up the pace, so if there are any mistakes made, these are completely my own, though I do strive to create believable scenes and characters.

Many thanks to Laurent Colasse, president of ResQMe, and Melissa Christensen, for allowing me to use their product and brand in my story. I am hoping this will bring more awareness to this important safety device. And my sincere appreciation for their donation of a dozen ResQMe key chains, which will be given away during the launch of this book. You can learn more about this device at www.resqme.com

And to Christopher Bain, senior manager of product planning and development at BioWare ULC, a division of Electronic Arts Inc., for allowing me the use of their company name in this novel. www.bioware.com

Thanks to John Zur, a valued reader and fan of my novels, for allowing me to turn you into a character—and a good one, at that. I have plans for Detective John Zur, and I believe he'll make another appearance in another novel sometime in the future.

Thanks to a very special teen fan, Gabbie Gros, who allowed me to immortalize her within these pages. Gabbie, I truly hope you realize you can be whatever you want to be. Your future is in YOUR hands. You are a gift to the world! Never, ever, forget that.

And thanks to fellow author, Luke Murphy, who won a contest I held a few years ago—one in which the winner supplied me with the first line of a new novel. The first sentence of the prologue is Luke's, and I think you'll agree it provokes gruesome images...and an elusive scent that might linger in your mind.

Prologue

You never grow accustomed to the stench of death. Marcus Taylor knew that smell intimately. He had inhaled burnt flesh, decayed flesh…diseased flesh. It lingered on him long after he was separated from the body.

The image of his wife and son's gray faces and blue lips assaulted him.

Jane…Ryan.

Mercifully, there were no bodies tonight. The only scent he recognized now was wet prairie and the dank residue left over from a rainstorm and the river.

"So what happened, Marcus?"

The question came from Detective John Zur, a cop Marcus knew from the old days. Back before he traded in his steady income and respected career for something that had poisoned him physically and mentally.

"Come on," Zur prodded. "Start talking. And tell me the truth."

Marcus was an expert at hiding things. Always had been. But there was no way in hell he could hide why he was soaked to the skin and standing at the edge of a river in the middle of nowhere.

He squinted at the river, trying to discern where the car had sunk. He only saw faint ripples on the surface. "You can see what happened, John."

"You left your desk. Not a very rational decision to make, considering your past."

Marcus shook his head, the taste of river water still in his throat. "Just because I do something unexpected doesn't mean I'm back to old habits."

Zur studied him but said nothing.

"I had to do something, John. I had to try to save them."

"That's what EMS is for. You're not a paramedic anymore."

Marcus let his gaze drift to the river. "I know. But you guys were all over the place and *someone* had to look for them. They were running out of time."

Overhead, lightning forked and thunder reverberated.

"Dammit, Marcus, you went rogue!" Zur said. "You know how dangerous that is. We could've had four bodies."

Marcus scowled. "Instead of merely three, you mean?"

"You know how this works. We work in teams for a reason. We all need backup. Even you."

"All the rescue teams were otherwise engaged. I didn't have a choice."

Zur sighed. "We go back a long way. I know you did what you thought was right. But it could've cost them all their lives. And it'll probably cost you your job. Why would you risk that for a complete stranger?"

"She wasn't a stranger."

As soon as the words were out of his mouth, Marcus realized how true that statement seemed. He knew more about Rebecca Kingston than he did about any other woman. Besides Jane.

"You know her?" Zur asked, frowning.

"She told me things and I told her things. So, yeah, I know her."

"I still do not get why you didn't stay at the center and let us do our job."

"She called *me*." Marcus looked into his friend's eyes. "*Me*. Not you."

"I understand, but that's your job. To listen and relay information."

"You don't understand a thing. Rebecca was terrified. For herself *and* her children. No one knew where they were for sure, and she was running out of time. If I didn't at least try, what kind of person would I be, John?" He gritted his teeth. "I couldn't live with that. Not again."

Zur exhaled. "Sometimes we're simply too late. It happens."

"Well, I didn't want it to happen this time." Marcus thought of the vision he'd seen of Jane standing in the middle of the road. "I had a…hunch I was close. Then when Rebecca mentioned Colton had seen flying pigs, I remembered this place. Jane and I used to buy ribs and chops from the owner, before it closed down about seven years ago."

"And that led you here to the farm." Zur's voice softened. "Good thing your hunch paid off. *This* time. Next time, you might not be so lucky."

"There won't be a next time, John."

A smirk tugged at the corner of Zur's mouth. "Uh-huh."

"There won't."

Zur shrugged and headed for the ambulance.

Under a chaotic sky, Marcus stood at the edge of the river as tears cascaded from his eyes. The night's events hit him hard, like a sucker punch to the gut. He was submerged in a wave of memories. The first call,

Rebecca's frantic voice, Colton crying in the background. He knew that kind of fear. He'd felt it before. But last time, it was a different road, different woman, different child.

He shook his head. He couldn't think of Jane right now. Or Ryan. He couldn't reflect on all he'd lost. He needed to focus on what he'd found, what he'd discovered in a faceless voice that had comforted him and expressed that it was okay to let go.

He glanced at his watch. It was after midnight. 12:39, to be exact. He couldn't believe how his life had changed in not much more than two days.

"Marcus!"

He turned…

Chapter One

Edson, AB – Thursday, June 13, 2013 – 10:55 AM

Sitting on the threadbare carpet in front of the living room fireplace, Marcus Taylor stroked a military issue Browning 9mm pistol against his leg, the thirteen-round magazine in his other hand. For an instant, he contemplated loading the gun—and then using it.

"But then who'd feed you?" he asked his companion.

Arizona, a five-year-old red Irish setter, gave him an inquisitive look, then curled up and went back to sleep on the couch. She was a rescue hound he'd picked up about a year after Ryan and Jane had died. The house had been too damned quiet. Lifeless.

"Great to know you have an opinion."

Setting the gun and magazine down on the floor, Marcus propped a photo album against his legs and took a deep breath. *The photo album of death.* The album only saw daylight three times a year. The other three hundred and sixty-two days it was hidden in a steel foot locker that doubled as his coffee table.

Today was Paul's forty-sixth birthday. Or it would have been, except Paul was dead.

Taking another measured breath, Marcus felt for the chain that marked a page and opened the album. "Hey, Bro."

In the photo, Corporal Paul Taylor stood on the shoulder of a deserted street on the outskirts of a nondescript town in Afghanistan, a sniper rifle braced across his chest and the Browning in his hand. He'd been killed that same day, his limbs ripped apart by a roadside bomb. The IED had been buried in six inches of dust and dirt when Paul, distracted by a crying kid, had unwittingly stepped on it.

One stupid mistake could end in death, separating son from parents and brother from brother. Resentment could separate siblings too.

"I wish I could tell you how sorry I am," Marcus said, blinking back a tear. "We wasted so much time being pissed at each other."

As a young kid, he'd hidden his older brother's toy soldiers so he could play with them when Paul was at school. In high school, Marcus had hidden how smart he was, always downplaying his intelligence in favor of being the cool, younger brother of senior hockey legend Paul Taylor. Marcus had learned to hide his jealousy too.

Until his brother was killed.

He stared at the warped dog tag at the end of the chain. It was all that was left of his brother. There was nothing to be jealous of now.

He glanced at the gun. Okay, he had that too. He'd inherited the Browning from Paul. One of his brother's war buddies had personally delivered it. "Your brother said you can play with his toys now," the guy had said.

Paul always had a warped sense of humor.

"Happy birthday, Paul."

He knew his parents, who were currently cruising in the Mediterranean, would be raising a toast in Paul's honor, so he did the same. "I miss you, bro."

Then he dropped the tag and flipped to the next set

of photos in the album. A brunette with short, choppy hair and luminous green eyes smiled back at him.

Jane.

"Hello, Elf."

He traced her face, recalling the way her mouth tilted upward on the left and how she'd watch a chick flick tearjerker, while tears steamed unnoticed down her face.

Marcus turned to the next set of photos and sucked in a breath. A handsome boy beamed a brilliant smile and waved back at him.

"Hey, little buddy."

He recalled the day the photo had been taken. His son, Ryan, a rookie goalie on his junior high hockey team, had shut out his opponents, giving his team a three-goal lead. Jane had snapped the picture at the exact second when Ryan had found his father in the crowd.

"I love you." Marcus's voice cracked. "And I miss you so much."

He couldn't hide that. Not ever.

There was one other thing he couldn't hide.

He had killed Jane. *And* Ryan.

For the past six years, whenever Marcus slept, his dead wife and son came to visit, taunting him with their spectral images, teasing him with familiar phrases, twisting his mind and gut into a guilt-infested cesspool. The only way to escape their accusing glares and spiteful smiles was to wake up. Or not go to sleep. Sleep was the enemy. He did his best to avoid it.

Marcus glanced at the antique clock on the mantle. 11:06.

Another twenty-four minutes and he'd have to head to the Yellowhead County Emergency Center, where he worked as a 911 dispatcher. He'd been working there for almost six months. He was halfway through five twelve-hour shifts that ran from noon to midnight. He worked them with his best friend, Leo, who would undoubtedly be in a good mood again. Leo liked sleeping in and starting his day at noon, while Marcus preferred the midnight-to-noon shift, the one everyone else hated. It gave him something to do at night, since sleeping didn't come easily.

He closed the photo album, stood slowly and stretched his cramped muscles. As he placed the album and the gun and magazine back in the foot locker, a small cedar box with a medical insignia embossed on the top caught his eye, though he did his best to ignore it.

Even Arizona knew that box was trouble. She froze at the sight of it, her hackles raised.

"I know," Marcus said. "I can resist temptation."

That box had gotten him into trouble on more than one occasion. It represented a past he'd give anything to erase. But he couldn't toss it in the trash. It had too firm a grip on him. Even now it called to him.

"Marcus…"

"No!"

He slammed the foot locker lid with his fist. The sound reverberated across the room, clanging like a jail cell door, trapping him in his own private prison.

Behind him, Arizona whimpered.

"Sorry, girl."

One day he'd get rid of the box with the insignia and be done with it once and for all.

But not yet.

Shaking off a bout of guilt, he took the stairs two at a time to the second floor and entered the master bedroom of the two-bedroom rented duplex. It was devoid of all things feminine, stripped down to the barest essentials. A bed, nightstand and tall dresser. Metal blinds, no flowered curtains like the ones in the house in Edmonton that he'd bought with Jane. The bedspread was a mishmash of brown tones, and it had been hauled up over the single pillow. There were none of the decorative pillows that Jane had loved so much. No silk flowers on the dresser. No citrus Febreeze lingering in the air. No sign of Jane.

He'd hidden her too.

Stepping into the en suite bathroom, Marcus stared into the mirror. He took in the untrimmed moustache and beard that was threatening to engulf his face. Leaning closer, he examined his eyes, which were more gray than blue. He turned his face to catch the light. "I am *not* tired."

The dark circles under his eyes betrayed him.

Ignoring Arizona's watchful gaze, he opened the medicine cabinet and grabbed the tube of Preparation H, a trick he'd learned from his wife Jane. Before he'd killed her. A little dab under the eyes, no smiling or frowning, and within seconds the crevices in his skin softened. Some of Jane's "White Out"—as she used to call the tube of cosmetic concealer—and the shadows would disappear.

"Camouflage on," he said to his reflection.

A memory of Jane surfaced.

It was the night of the BioWare awards banquet, nineteen years ago. Jane, dressed in a pink housecoat, sat at the bathroom vanity curling her hair, while Marcus struggled with his tie.

He'd let out a curse. "I can never get this right."

"Here, let me." Pushing the chair behind him, Jane climbed up before he could protest. She caught his gaze in the mirror over the sink and reached around his shoulders, her gaze wandering to the twisted lump he'd made of the full Windsor. "You shouldn't be so impatient."

"*You* shouldn't be climbing up on chairs."

"I'm fine, Marcus."

"You're pregnant, that's what you are."

"You calling me fat, buster?"

Five months pregnant with Ryan, Jane had never looked so beautiful.

"I'd never do that," he replied.

She cocked her head and arched one brow. "Never? How about in four months when I can't walk up the stairs to the bedroom?"

"I'll carry you."

"What about when I can't see my toes and can't paint my toenails?"

"I'll paint them for you."

"What about when—"

He turned his head and kissed her. That shut her up.

With a laugh, she pushed him away, gave the tie a smooth tug and slid the knot expertly into place.

He groaned. "Now why can't I do that?"

"Because you have me. Now quit distracting me. I still have to put on my dress and makeup."

Marcus sat on the edge of the bed and waited. Jane always made it worth the wait, and that night she didn't disappoint him. When she emerged from the bathroom, she was a vision of sultry goddess in a designer dress from a shop in West Edmonton Mall. The baby bump in front was barely noticeable.

"How do I look?" she asked, nervously fingering the fresh gold highlights in her hair.

"Sexy as hell."

She spun in a slow circle to show off the sleek black dress with its plunging back. Peering over one glitter-powdered shoulder, she said, "So you like my new dress?"

"I'd like it better," he said in a soft voice, "if it was on the floor."

Minutes later, they were entwined in the sheets, out of breath and laughing like teenagers. Sex with Jane was always like that. Exciting. Youthful. Fun.

After dressing, Jane retreated to the bathroom to fix her hair and makeup. "Camouflage on," she said when she returned. "Now let's get going."

"Yes, ma'am."

He heard her whispering, "Six plus eight plus two…"

"Are you doing that numerology thing again?" he asked with a grin.

Jane had gone to a psychic fair when she'd found out she was pregnant, and a numerologist had given her a lesson in adding dates. Ever since then, whenever something important came up, she'd work out the numbers to determine if it was going to be a good day or not. She even made Marcus buy lotto tickets on "three days," which she said meant money coming in. They hadn't won a lottery yet, but he played along anyway.

"What is it today?"

She smiled. "A seven."

"Ah, lucky seven." He arched a brow at her. "So I'm going to get lucky?"

"I think you already did, mister."

They'd been late for the awards banquet, which didn't go over too well since Jane was the guest of honor, the recipient of a Best Programmer award for her latest video game creation at BioWare. When Jane had stepped up on the stage to receive her award, Marcus didn't think he could ever be prouder. Until the night Ryan was born.

Ryan…the son I killed.

Marcus gave his head a jerk, forcing the memories back into the shadows—where they belonged. He picked up the can of shaving cream. His eyes rested, unfocused, on the label.

To shave or not to shave. That was the question.

"Nah, not today," he muttered.

He hadn't shaved in weeks. He was also overdue for a haircut. Thankfully, they weren't too strict about appearances at work, though his supervisor would probably harp on it again.

The alarm on his watch beeped.

He had twenty minutes to get to the center. Then he'd get back to hiding behind the anonymity of being a faceless voice on the phone.

Yellowhead County Emergency Services in Edson, Alberta, housed a small but competent 911 call center situated on the second floor of a spacious building on 1st Avenue. Four rooms on the floor were rented out to emergency groups, like First Aid, CPR and EMS, for training facilities. The 911 center had a full-time staff of four emergency operators and two supervisors—one for the day shift, one for the night. They also had a handful of highly trained but underpaid casual staff and three regular volunteers.

When Marcus entered the building, Leonardo Lombardo was waiting for him by the elevator. And Leo didn't look too thrilled to see him.

"You look like your dog just died," Marcus said.

"Don't got a dog."

"So what's with the warm and cheerful welcome? Did the mob put a hit out on me?"

Leo, a man of average height in his late forties, carried about thirty extra pounds around his middle, and his swarthy Italian looks gave him an air of mystery and danger. Around town, rumormongers had spread stories that Leo was an American expatriate with mob ties. But Marcus knew exactly who had started those rumors. Leo had a depraved sense of humor.

But his friend wasn't smiling now.

"You really gotta get some sleep."

Stepping into the elevator, Marcus shrugged. "Sleep's overrated."

"You look like hell."

"Thanks."

"You're welcome." Leo pushed the second floor button and took a hesitant breath. "Listen, man…"

Whenever Leo started a sentence with those two words, Marcus knew it wouldn't be good.

"You're not on your game," Leo said. "You're starting to slip up."

"What do you mean? I do my job."

"You filed that multiple-car accident report from last night in the wrong place. Shipley's spent half the morning looking for it. I tried covering for you, but he's pretty pissed."

"Shipley's always pissed."

Pete Shipley made it a ritual to make Marcus's life hell whenever possible, which was more often than not. As the day shift supervisor, Shipley ruled the emergency operators with an iron fist and enough arrogance to get on anyone's nerves.

The elevator door opened and Marcus stepped out first.

"I'll find the report, Leo."

"How many hours you get, Marcus?"

Sleep?

"Four." It was a lie and both of them knew it.

Marcus started toward the cubicle with the screen that divided his desk from Leo's. Behind them was the station for the other full-timers. He waved to Parminder and Wyatt as they left for home. They worked the night shift, so he only saw them in passing. Their stations were now manned by casual day workers. Backup.

"Get some sleep," Leo muttered.

"Sleep is a funny thing, Leo. Not funny *ha-ha*, but funny *strange*. Once a body's gone awhile without it or with an occasional light nap, sleep doesn't seem that important. I'm fine."

"Bullshit."

They were interrupted by a door slamming down the hall.

Pete Shipley appeared, overpowering the hallway

with angry energy and his massive frame. The guy towered over everyone, including Marcus, who was an easy six feet tall. Shipley, a former army captain, was built like the *Titanic*, which had become his office nickname. Unbeknown to him.

"Taylor!" Shipley shouted. "In my office now!"

Leo grabbed Marcus's arm. "Tell him you slept six hours."

"You're suggesting I lie to the boss?"

"Just cover your ass. And for God's sake, don't egg him on."

Marcus smiled. "Now why would I do that?"

Leo gaped at him. "Because you thrive on chaos."

"Even in chaos there is order."

Letting out a snort, Leo said, "You been reading too many self-help books. Don't say I didn't warn you." He turned on one heel and headed for his desk.

Marcus stared after him. *Don't worry, Leo. I can handle Pete Shipley.*

Pausing in front of Shipley's door, he took a breath, knocked once and entered. His supervisor was seated behind a metal desk, his thick-lensed glasses perched on the tip of a bulbous nose as he scrutinized a mound of paperwork. Even though the man had ordered the meeting, Shipley did nothing to indicate he acknowledged Marcus's existence.

That was fine with Marcus. It gave him time to study the office, with its cramped windowless space and dank recycled air. It wasn't an office to envy, that's for sure. No one wanted it, or the position and responsibility that came with it. Not even Shipley. Word had it he was positioning himself for emergency coordinator, in hopes of moving up to one of the corner offices with the floor-to-ceiling windows. Marcus doubted it would ever happen. Shipley wasn't solid management material.

Marcus stood with his hands resting lightly on the back of the armless faux-leather chair Shipley reserved for the lucky few he deemed important enough to sit in his presence. Marcus wasn't one of the lucky ones.

Bracing for an ugly reprimand, his thoughts drifted to last night's shift. A drunk driver had T-boned a car at a busy intersection in Hinton, resulting in a four-car pileup. One vehicle, a mini-van with an older couple and two young boys, had been sandwiched between two vehicles from the impact of the crash. The pileup had spawned numerous frantic calls to the emergency center. Emergency Medical Services (EMS), including fire and ambulance, arrived on scene within six minutes. The Jaws of Life had been used to wrench apart the contorted metal of two of the vehicles. Only three people extracted had made it out alive. One reached the hospital DOA. Then rescue workers discovered a sedan with three teenagers inside—all dead.

They'll have nightmares for weeks.

Marcus knew how that felt. He'd once been a first responder. In another life.

He straightened. He was ready to take on Shipley's wrath. At least this time it would be done privately. Plus, if he was honest, he had messed up. Misfiling the report was one of a handful of stupid mistakes he'd made in the last week. Most he'd caught on his own and rectified.

"Before you say anything," Marcus began, "I know I—"

"What?" Shipley snapped. "You know you're an idiot?"

"No. That's news to me."

Pete Shipley rose slowly—all two hundred and eighty pounds, six feet eleven inches of him. Bracing beefy fists against the desk, he leaned forward. "I spent three hours searching for that accident report, Taylor. Three hours! And guess where I found it?" A nanosecond pause. "Filed with the missing persons call logs. Whatcha think of that?"

"I think it's ironic that I filed a missing report in the *missing* persons section."

"Shut it!" Shipley glared, his thick brows furrowed into a uni-brow. "Lombardo says you've been sleeping better, but I don't believe him. Whatcha got to say about that?"

"Leo's right. I slept like a baby last night."

Shipley elevated a brow. "For a baby, you look like shit. You need a haircut. And a shave." He wrinkled his nose. "Have you even showered this week?"

"I shower every day. Not that it's any of your business. As for the length of my hair and beard, sounds like you're crossing discrimination boundaries."

"I'm not discriminating against you. I simply do not like you. You're a goddamn drug addict, Taylor."

Everyone in the center knew about Marcus's past.

"Thanks for clarifying that, *Peter*."

Shipley cringed. "All it'll take is one more mistake. Everyone's watching you. You mess up again and you're out on your ass." His shoulders relaxed and he folded back into the chair. "If it were up to me, I would've fired you months ago."

"Good thing it isn't up to you then."

Marcus knew he was pushing the man's buttons, but that wasn't hard to do. Shipley was an idiot. A brown-noser who didn't know his ass from his dick, according to Leo.

"This is your final warning," Shipley said between his teeth. "We hold life and death in our hands. We can't afford errors."

"It was a misfiled report. The call was dispatched correctly and efficiently."

"Yeah, at least you didn't send the ambulance in the wrong direction." A smug smile crossed Shipley's face. "That was the stunt that got you knocked off your *high* horse as a paramedic. Got you fired from EMS."

Marcus thought of a million ways to answer him.

None of them were polite. He moved toward the door. "I think our little meeting is done."

"I'm not finished," Shipley bellowed.

"Yes you are, Pete."

With that, Marcus strode from the office. He left Shipley's door ajar, something he knew would tick off his supervisor even more than his insubordination.

He tried not to dwell on Shipley's words, but the man had hit a nerve. Six years ago, Marcus had been publicly humiliated when the truth had come out about his addiction problem, and his future as a paramedic was sliced clean off the minute he drove that ambulance to the wrong side of town because he was too high to comprehend where he was going.

That's when he'd taken some time off. From work…from Jane…from everyone. He'd headed to Cadomin to clear his mind and do some fishing. At least that's what he'd told Jane. Meanwhile, he'd secretly packed his drug stash in the wooden box. Six days later, while in a morphine haze filled with strange images of ghostly children, he answered his cell phone. In a subdued voice, Detective John Zur revealed that Jane and Ryan had been in a car accident, not far from where Marcus was holing up.

That had been the beginning of the end for Marcus.

Now he was doing what he could to get by. It wasn't that he couldn't handle the career change from superstar paramedic to invisible 911 dispatcher. That wasn't the problem. Shipley was. The guy had been gunning for him ever since Leo had brought Marcus in to fill a vacant spot left behind by a dispatcher who'd quit after a nervous breakdown.

"What did Titanic have to say?" Leo asked when Marcus veered around the cubicle.

"He doesn't want to go down with the ship."

"He thinks you're the iceberg?"

Marcus gave a single nod.

"I got your back."

Leo had connections at work. He knew the center coordinator, Nate Downey, very well. He was married to Nate's daughter, Valerie.

"I know, Leo."

As he settled into his desk and slipped on the headset, Marcus took a deep breath and released it evenly. The mind tricks between him and Shipley had become too frequent. They wreaked havoc on his brain and drained him.

Because Shipley never lets me forget.

The clock on the computer read: 12:20. It was going to be a very long day.

In the sleepy town of Edson, it was rare to see much excitement. The center catered to outside towns as well. Some days the phones only rang a half-dozen times. Those were the good days.

He flipped through the folders on his desk and found the protocol chart. Never hurt to do a quick refresher before his shift. It kept his mind fresh and focused.

But his thoughts meandered to the misfiled report.

Was he slipping? Was he putting people's lives in danger? That was something he'd promised himself, and Leo, he'd never do again.

Remember Jane and Ryan.

How could he ever forget them? They'd been his life.

The phone rang and he jumped.

"911. Do you need Fire, Police or Ambulance?"

Marcus spent the next ten minutes explaining to eighty-nine-year-old Mrs. Mortimer, a frequent caller, that no one was available to rescue her cat from the neighbor's tree.

Then he waited for a real emergency.

Chapter Two

Rebecca Kingston folded her arms across her down-filled jacket and tried not to shiver. Though May had ended with a heat wave, the temperatures had dropped the first week of June. It had rained for the first five days, and an arctic chill had swept through the city. The weatherman blamed the erratic change in weather on global warming and a cold front sweeping down from Alaska, while locals held one source responsible. Their lifelong rival—Calgary.

"Can we get an ice cream, Mommy?" four-year-old Ella said with a faint lips, the result of her recent contribution to the tooth fairy's necklace collection.

Rebecca laughed. "It feels like winter again and you want ice cream?"

"Yes, please."

"I guess we have time."

They hurried across the street to the corner store.

"Strawberry this time," Ella said, her blue eyes pleading.

Rebecca sighed. "Eat it slowly. Did you remember Puff?"

Her daughter nodded. "In my pocket."

"Good girl." Rebecca glanced at her watch. "It's almost five. Let's go."

Her cell phone rang. It was Carter Billingsley, her lawyer.

"Mr. Billingsley," she said. "I'm glad you got my message."

"So you've decided to get away," he said. "That's a very good idea."

"I need a break." She glanced at Ella. "Things are going to get ugly, aren't they?"

"Unfortunately, yes. Divorce is never pretty. But you'll get through it."

"Thanks, Mr. Billingsley."

"Take care, Rebecca."

Carter had once been her grandfather's lawyer and Grandpa Bob had highly recommended him—if Rebecca ever needed someone to handle her divorce. In his late sixties, Carter filled that father-figure left void after her father's passing.

Her thoughts raced to her twelve-year-old son. Colton's team was up against one of the toughest junior high hockey teams from Regina. With Colton as the Edmonton team's goalie, most of the pressure was on him. He was a brave boy.

She bit her bottom lip, wishing she were as brave.

You're a coward, Becca.

"You're too codependent," her mother always said.

Rebecca figured that wasn't actually her fault. She'd been fortunate to have strong male role models in her life. Men who ran companies with iron fists and made decisions after careful consideration. Or at least worked hard to provide for their families. Men like Grandpa Bob and her father. Men who could be trusted to make the right decisions.

Not like Wesley.

Even her grandfather hadn't liked him. When

Grandpa Bob passed away two years ago, he'd sent a clear message to everyone that Wesley couldn't be trusted. Grandpa Bob had lived a miser's lifestyle. No one knew how much money he'd saved for that "rainy day"—until he was gone and Colton and Ella became beneficiaries of over eight hundred thousand dollars from the sale of Grandpa Bob's house and business.

Grandpa Bob, in his infinite wisdom, had added two major conditions to the inheritance. Money could only be withdrawn from the account if it was spent on Ella or Colton. And Rebecca was the sole person with signing power.

Wesley moped around the house for days when he heard the conditions. Any time she bought the kids new clothes, he'd sneer at her and say, "Hope you used your grandfather's money for those."

Once when he'd gambled most of his paycheck, he begged her for a "loan," and when she'd voiced that she didn't have the money, he slapped her. "Lying bitch! You've got almost a million dollars at your fingertips. All I'm asking for is thirty-five hundred. I'll pay it back."

She'd refused and paid the price, physically.

Rebecca wanted him out of her life. Once and for all. But for the sake of the children, she had to find a way to forgive Wesley and deal with the fact that he was her children's father. He'd always be in their lives.

Every time she looked at Colton, she was reminded of Wesley. Unlike Ella's blonde hair and blue eyes that closely resembled her own, both father and son had dark brown hair, hazel eyes, a light spray of freckles across their noses and matching chin dimples.

She'd met Wesley at a company Christmas party shortly after she started working as a customer service representative at Alberta Cable. The son of upper-class parents, Wesley had created his independence by not joining the family law firm, as was expected. Instead, he went to work at Alberta Cable as a cable installer. At the party, he'd been assigned to the same table as Rebecca. As soon as Wesley realized she was single, he poured on the charm. He was a master at that.

The next morning she'd found Wesley in her bed.

After nearly four years of dating, he finally popped the question. Via a text message, of all things. She was at work when her cell phone sprang to life, vibrating against her desk. When she glanced down, she saw seven words.

"Rebecca Kingston, will U marry me?"

She'd immediately let out a startled shriek. "Wesley just proposed."

This sent the entire room into a chaotic buzz of applause and congratulatory wishes. The rest of Rebecca's shift was a blur.

"Is Daddy gonna be at the game?" Ella said, interrupting her memories.

"No, honey. He's at work."

At least that's where Rebecca hoped he was.

Wesley had left Alberta Cable six months ago, escorted from the building after being fired for screaming at a customer in her own home and shoving the woman into a wall. It hadn't been the first complaint lodged against him. He'd been employed off and on since then, but no one wanted an employee with anger management issues.

When Rebecca had asked what had happened, he mumbled something about an accident, arguing that it wasn't his fault. "No matter what that ass of a supervisor says," he said.

She'd given him a look that said she didn't believe him. She paid for that look. The black eye he gave her kept her in the house for nearly a week. That's when she filed for separation.

Since leaving Alberta, Wesley had wandered from one dead-end job to another. For the past two months he'd hardly worked at all. She hoped to God he wasn't sitting at his apartment, surfing the porn highway.

Last time she saw him, Wesley had blamed his unemployment situation on the recession, which had, in all fairness, wreaked havoc with many people's lives and crushed some of the toughest companies. But the economy, or lack of a strong one, wasn't Wesley's problem. The problem was his lack of motivation and the inability to handle his jealousy and rage.

Perhaps Wesley was experiencing a midlife crisis.

Maybe she was too.

It was getting more and more difficult to keep it together. But she did it for her children. Besides, she'd endured worse than uncertainty when she lived with Wesley. Much worse.

Rebecca glanced down at her daughter. Ella was a petite child who'd been born two months premature. Wesley had seen to that.

She shook her head. *No. What happened back then was as much my fault as his. I stayed when I should've left.*

"Hurry, Mommy!" Ella said, tugging on her hand.

The hockey arena was a five-minute walk from where she'd parked the car, but with the ice cream pit stop, Rebecca was glad they'd left early.

"Ella, do you think Colton's team will win today?"

Her daughter rolled her eyes. "Of course. Colton is awesome!"

"Awesome," Rebecca agreed.

Tamarack Hockey Arena came into view, along with the crowds of hockey fans who gathered outside the doors to the indoor rink.

Rebecca took Ella's hand and drew her in close.

In Edmonton, hockey fans bordered on hockey fanatics. It wouldn't be the first time that a fight broke out between fathers of opposing teams. Last year, a toddler had been trampled in a north Edmonton arena. Thankfully, he'd survived.

"Stay close, Ella."

"Do you see Colton?"

"Not yet."

"Becca!"

Turning in the direction of the voice, she scoured the bleachers. Then she spotted Wesley near the home team's side. He wasn't supposed to be there. The terms of their separation were that he could see the kids during scheduled visitations. Once the divorce was final, those visits would be restricted to visits accompanied by a social worker—if Carter Billingsley, her lawyer, came through for her. She hadn't given Wesley this news yet.

"I saved you some seats," Wesley hollered. The look he gave her suggested she shouldn't make a public scene. Or else.

Rebecca released a reluctant sigh. *Great. Just great.*

"Are we gonna sit with Daddy?" Ella asked.

"Yes, honey. Unless you want to sit somewhere else." *Anywhere else.*

Despite Rebecca's silent plea, Ella headed in Wesley's direction, pushing past the knees that blocked the aisle. Rebecca sat beside Ella and tried to tamp down the guilt she felt at placing their daughter between them.

"There's a seat beside me," Wesley said.

Her gaze flew to the empty seat on his right and she winced. "I'm good here. Thanks for saving the seats."

Looking as handsome as the day she'd married him, Wesley smiled. "You look lovely. New hairstyle?"

She touched her shoulder-length hair. "I need a trim."

"Looks good. But then you always do."

She stared at him. He was laying on the charm a bit thick. That usually meant he wanted something.

Wesley chucked Ella under the chin. "So, Ella-Bella, how's kindergarten?"

"We went on a field trip to the zoo yesterday."

"See any monkeys?" he asked, his arm resting over the back of Ella's chair.

"Yeah. They were so cute."

"But not as cute as you, right?" He caught Rebecca's eye and winked. "You're the cutest girl here. Even though you have no teeth."

"Do too!" Ella opened her mouth to show him.

After a few minutes of listening to their teasing banter, Rebecca tuned out their laughter. Sadness washed over her, followed by regret. If things had gone differently, they'd still be a family, and the kids would have their father in their lives. But Rebecca couldn't stay in an abusive relationship. Her mind and body couldn't endure any more trauma. And she was terrified he'd start lashing out physically at the kids.

So she'd made a decision, and one sunny Friday afternoon, she'd summoned up the courage to confront Wesley at his current *job de jour*.

"We need to talk," she'd told him.

"This isn't a good time."

"It's *never* a good time." She took a deep breath. "I want you to move out of the house, Wesley."

He laughed. "Good joke. What's the punch line?"

"I'm not joking."

His smile disappeared. "You're serious?"

"Dead serious. It's not like you couldn't see this coming. I want a separation. You know I've been…unhappy in our marriage."

"I'll try to make more time for you."

"It's not more time that I want, Wesley. Neither of us can live like this. Your anger is out of control. You're out of control."

"So this is all my fault?" Wesley sneered.

"You nearly put me in the hospital last week."

"Maybe that's where you belong."

She clenched her teeth. "Your threats won't work this time. I've made up my mind. I'm leaving tonight, and I'm taking the kids with me."

There was an uncomfortable pause.

"Seems to me you're only thinking about yourself, what *you* want. Have you even thought about what this'll do to the kids?"

"Of course I have," she snapped. "They're all I think about. Can you say the same?"

"You're going to turn them against me. Like your mother did to you and your father." His voice dripped with disgust.

"Don't bring my parents into this. This has nothing to do with them and everything to do with the fact that you have an anger problem and you refuse to get help."

"What'll you tell the kids?"

She shrugged. "Ella won't understand. She's too young. Colton's getting too old for me to keep making excuses for you. He's almost a teenager."

Wesley didn't answer.

"You know what he said to me last night, Wesley? He said you love being angry more than you love being with us. He's right, isn't he?"

She stormed out of his office without waiting for a reply. She already knew the answer.

That evening, Wesley packed two suitcases.

"I'll be staying at The Fairmont McDonald. I still love you, Becca."

His actions had stunned her. She'd been prepared to take the kids to Kelly's. She was even ready for Wesley to try to hurt her. What she hadn't expected was his easy submission. Or that for once he'd take the high road.

"You're leaving?" she said, shocked.

"That's what you wanted," he said with a shrug. "So that's what you get."

For a second, she wanted to tell him she'd made a mistake. That she didn't want a separation. That she'd be a better wife, learn to be more patient, learn to deal with his rages.

Then she remembered the bruises and sprains. "Good-bye, Wesley."

"For now."

She'd watched him climb into his car and waited until the taillights winked, then disappeared. Then she let out a long, uneasy breath and headed down the hallway. She wandered through their bedroom and into the en suite bathroom, all the while trying to think of the good times. There weren't many.

She stared at her reflection in the mirror, one finger tracing the small scar along her chin. Wesley had given her that present on Valentine's Day two years earlier. He'd accused her of flirting with the UPS delivery guy.

"You deserve better," she said to her reflection. "So do the kids."

Now, sitting two seats away from Wesley at the arena, Rebecca realized that her husband was still doing everything in his power to control her.

"Penny for your thoughts," he said.

"You're wasting your money."

"What money? You get most of it."

"That's for the kids, Wesley, and you know it."

She dug her fingernails into her palms. *Don't fight with him. Not here. Not in front of Ella.*

She caught his eye. "Next time Colton has a game, I'd appreciate it if you didn't bother showing up."

"Wouldn't miss it for the world." He gave her an icy smile. "That's *my* son down there."

"What part of 'scheduled visits' don't you—"

Cheers erupted from the stands as both hockey teams skated out onto the ice and joined their goalies. Everyone stood for the national anthem, then a horn blasted.

Rebecca released a heart-heavy sigh.

The game was on.

After the game, the arena parking lot was a potpourri of car exhaust and refinery emissions, and a breeding ground for irritation. Everyone wanted to be first out. Especially the losing team.

Rebecca was glad she'd parked her Hyundai Accent down the street.

"Mommy, are we going home now?" Ella asked.

"Yes, honey. It's almost supper time."

"Is Daddy coming home too?"

"No, honey. Daddy's going to his own house."

As they made their way through the parking lot, Rebecca was sure Wesley would veer off toward his van, but he stayed at her side. Doing her best to ignore him, she reached for Ella's hand as they crossed the street. Behind them, Colton lugged his hockey bag and stick.

When they reached the sedan, Rebecca unlocked the doors, sank into the driver's seat and started the engine, while the kids said good-bye to their dad. Stepping out, she moved to the back door and wrenched on it, gritting her teeth as it squealed. Colton climbed in back. Ella looked up at her with a hopeful expression.

"Back seat," Rebecca said.

Ella obediently climbed in beside her brother, and Colton helped her with the seat belt for her booster seat.

Rebecca shut the door using her hip. Catching Wesley's eye she said, "You always said we should use the sticky door, that if we did it might not stick so much. Hasn't worked."

Wesley studied the exterior of the car. "Can't believe you haven't bought a new car."

The Hyundai *had* seen better days—and today wasn't one of them. They'd bought the used car back in 2003, when they'd gone from a two-door Supra— Wesley's toy—to a four-door vehicle that wasn't so "squishy," as the kids had called the Supra. The red paint was now worn in places, the hinges of the trunk groaned when lifted and the back door on the passenger side stuck all the time, making it impossible for either of the kids to open. The latter was a result of an accident. Wesley had been sideswiped by a reckless teen texting on her cell phone. Or at least that's the story he'd given her.

"This works fine," she said. "I don't need a new one." *And I can't afford one.*

Colton cracked the door open and poked his head out. "Dad said he's getting me a cell phone for my birthday next month. One that does text messaging."

Rebecca shut the car door and turned icy eyes in Wesley's direction. "You what?"

"Before you say anything, hear me out. Colton's old enough to be responsible for a phone. Besides, I'm taking care of it, bills and all. When he's old enough to get a job, he'll take over paying for it."

"I told you a while ago that I do not agree with kids walking around glued to a cell phone. It's ridiculous." She walked around to the driver's side.

"What if there's an emergency and Colton needs to call one of us?" he asked, following her.

"Then he uses a phone nearby or has an adult call us. It's not like he's driving any—"

"Rebecca, this is *my* decision. As his father."

"Well, I'm his mother, and I say no cell phone."

She scowled at him, mentally cursing herself for falling into old habits—childish habits. Truth was, she'd been thinking of the whole cell phone argument ever since Wesley had first brought it up. But her pride wouldn't let her back down. Not now.

"I think you're being a little unfair," Wesley said.

"Unfair? You really want to go there?"

She turned when she heard the whir of the power window.

"Did you tell her, Dad?" Colton asked.

"Hey, buddy, give me a second—"

Rebecca frowned. "Did you already tell him he's getting a cell phone?"

"Let's table the phone idea for another time."

"Fine."

Wesley shuffled his feet. "Becca, I have a favor to ask."

She held her breath. *Here it is.*

"I want Colton to stay with me in July."

From inside the car, Colton nodded. "Say yes, Mom."

She was livid. Motioning for Colton to roll up the window, she turned to Wesley. "What are you doing? This is something you should've discussed with me first."

"I *am* discussing it with you."

"You should've called me, not mentioned this right in front of him." She tried to ignore Colton, who had his grinning face pressed up against the window. "Why didn't you call me so we could discuss this?"

"I tried calling. I left you two messages last week."

Rebecca blinked. She checked the answering machine every day, and there'd been no calls from Wesley.

Wesley's mouth curled. "I'm not lying."

"Maybe I accidentally erased them."

"Probably. You always had problems with technical things. And managing money."

"For the last time," she snapped, "our financial mess isn't my fault. We both overspent."

"But you've got your secret stash, don't you?"

"You know that money is for the kids' college funds," she said.

When Wesley had found out about the money that had been set aside for the kids, it had enraged him to the point that he deliberately drove his van into the side of the bridge on the way home from dinner at a restaurant.

Rebecca hadn't come away unscathed. She suffered a multitude of scrapes and bruises, easily explained by the crash. The doctor had no idea Wesley had beaten her after pulling her from the wreck. She barely recalled that incident. But she remembered the others that followed in the days after the crash. The broken wrist. The bruises on her back and hips.

Every day afterward, Wesley had said he loved her. But love wasn't supposed to hurt physically. Was it?

She eyed him now, thankful he had never touched the kids. At least she'd done that right, gotten out before he was tempted to unleash his fury on Colton or Ella.

"Becca, why are you staring at me like that?"

"I'm reminding myself of why you'll soon be my *ex-*husband."

Wesley flinched, and she knew her words had hurt him.

Good. He deserves it.

"Do you think it's possible to be civil to each other?" he said.

She glanced over her shoulder at Ella and Colton. "If you're willing, I am."

"For the kids' sake, right?"

She caught his eye. "For all of us."

Silence.

"Look, Becca," he said in a contrite tone, "I've been seeing a psychologist, and I've taken an anger management class. I'm doing everything I can to show you I can be trusted with the kids. I would never hurt them."

"Like you'd never hurt *me*?"

He looked away. "I've apologized for my past. I'm not like that anymore."

She mulled over his words, her heart conflicted with such a heavy decision. If she was wrong and something happened to Colton, she'd never forgive herself.

But what if he's telling the truth? I can't keep him away from the kids. They need him.

She peered over her shoulder at Colton. He had a smile on his face and his hands clasped in front, pleading. How could she resist that?

Finally, she said, "How long do you expect Colton to stay with you?"

"One week. In the middle of July."

She bit her bottom lip. "I'm not sure…"

"I know it's not what we agreed on, but I'm taking that week off and I was hoping to spend it with my son."

"Just you and Colton?"

He rolled his eyes. "And Tracey."

Tracey Whitaker used to be a receptionist at his father's law firm. Wesley and Tracey had started seeing each other a few months before Rebecca had asked him to leave. She'd found out about the "other woman" when she'd called her father-in-law one day. Walter revealed to her he hadn't seen Wesley in weeks. Then he asked if she'd called Tracey's place. Everyone at the law firm, including her father-in-law, knew about Tracey and Wesley. Her husband hadn't bothered to keep his affair secret.

Except from Rebecca.

Wesley's father had been supportive enough to fire the woman after Rebecca stormed into his office, accusing him of trying to break up his son's marriage. She'd heard Tracey had resumed an earlier career as a caregiver in a senior's complex.

"So you're still with Tracey," she said.

"I'll dump her in an instant if you let me come home. We can rip up that separation agreement and make our own agreement." He arched his brows suggestively.

"How come she didn't come to the game?"

Wesley shrugged. "Tracey has a cold. Picked it up from the old folks. She didn't come because she didn't want to pass it on to Colton."

"How considerate of her," Rebecca sneered.

"Becca…"

She ignored the warning in his voice. "You two planning to tie the knot?"

As soon as the words were out of her mouth, she wished she could take them back. Why had she asked him *that*, of all things? It made her sound like she was jealous.

Am I?

Wesley smiled, as if reading her mind. "I'll be sure to send you an invite when we do."

She reached for the car door handle. "Don't bother."

"You haven't answered my question, Becca."

With a heavy sigh, she faced him. "Fine. You can have Colton for the week. But not a day more." A grin spread across his face and she scowled. "And please don't go getting any ideas about changing the custody agreement after that, Wesley. The kids need stability."

"Thanks," he said.

"You can thank me by making sure you look after him." She hesitated. "I guess I should tell you I'm going away for a couple of days. The kids will be staying with my sister."

"When are you leaving?"

"Tomorrow evening. After supper. I'll be back Monday afternoon."

"That's kind of last minute, don't you think?"

Her eyes narrowed. "I decided to do it today. And I do not owe you any advanced notice. I'm telling you now."

He held up his hands in surrender. "Okay, okay. So where you going?"

"Cadomin. You know I always wanted to see the

bat cave."

"I was going to take you."

She shrugged and climbed into the car. "But you didn't."

"I could." He regarded her with suspicion as he held onto the door. "Why aren't you taking the kids?"

"They have school on Monday."

"Who are you going with?"

"Me, myself and I." She scowled. "I'm going alone, Wesley. I need a break, so I'm taking a few days off."

"I'd babysit the kids, but I'll be busy this weekend."

She resisted the urge to tell him it wasn't *babysitting* when the kids were his own. "It's already arranged, Wesley. Kelly's expecting them."

"Doesn't she already have her hands full?"

Wesley was right. Her sister did have her hands full. Kelly was happily married with four kids—eight-year-old Evan and five-year-old triplets, Aynsley, Megan and Jacob.

"Kelly can handle it. She's a great mother."

Rebecca wouldn't admit it, but she envied her sister. Kelly was married to the perfect man, an electrical engineer who doted on her and their kids. Steve was highly respected, financially stable and he would never lay an angry hand on anyone. Except maybe Wesley. More than once, Steve had offered to help Rebecca *"toss that bastard out on his ass"*—or words to that effect.

"Well, I'll have Colton's visit to look forward to this summer," Wesley said.

She was starting to have second thoughts about that.

Grasping the door handle to close it, she eyed him. "We have to go."

"Have fun in Cadomin." He didn't sound too sincere.

She aimed a tight smile at him. "I will."

As she pulled the car away from the curb, Rebecca peered into the rearview mirror. Wesley stood on the sidewalk, watching her drive away.

"Did you say yes, Mom?" Colton asked.

"Yes."

In the back seat, her son did a seated jig and jabbed Ella in the side.

"Mommy, Colton's poking me."

"Don't worry, Ella," Colton said, "I'll be outta your hair for a whole week."

Rebecca peered into the mirror. "How did you know it was for a week?"

"Dad told me last weekend he was gonna ask you."

Her lips curled. "You should've said something to me."

"Nah, Dad said he'd ask you himself. And I didn't wanna jinx things."

Colton stuffed two ear buds into his ears, then sat back with a grin. She watched for a minute as he bobbed his head to whatever tune he was listening to on the iPod his father had bought him for his birthday last year.

It was going to kill her to be away from her son for an entire week.

You'll still have Ella.

As if on cue, her beautiful daughter giggled in the backseat.

Come July, Rebecca would keep busy with Ella and enjoy some real mommy-daughter time. But that wouldn't stop her from missing Colton. A week was a long time.

Too long.

Depressed, Rebecca pulled onto Whitemud Drive and headed for home, all the time wondering if she should cancel the summer plans with Wesley.

"You can do this," she whispered. "It's only a week."

It would be the longest week of her life. After it was over, she'd convince Wesley to go back to their original summer plan. Alternating weekends during the summer holidays. There was no way on earth she was ever going to be separated from either of her children for longer than that.

Colton and Ella are my life and soul.

"Can we get pizza to celebrate?" Colton asked.

"Sure. Pepperoni and mushroom?"

"Yeah."

"With double cheese?" Ella piped up.

"With double cheese."

Somehow, pizza made the world seem right again, and Rebecca smiled. She was in the proverbial driver's seat, in control of her life again.

She should have realized that life is never predictable.

Chapter Three

Edson, AB – Thursday, June 13, 2013 – 4:55 PM

The afternoon had crawled past at worm speed. Using the Kindle application on his iPhone, Marcus downloaded an eBook on sleep disorders and spent the time between calls reading about somniphobia—the fear of sleeping—something Leo was adamant Marcus had.

He yawned and stretched his legs beneath the cramped desk. Three calls had come in during the first three hours of his shift, and neither had warranted emergency vehicles.

"Pussy Willow's back home," Mrs. Mortimer said when she called in the second time. "One of my neighbors was kind enough to coax her down from the maple tree. They bribed her with—"

"Thanks for calling back," Marcus cut in, "but 911 is for emergencies, Mrs. Mortimer."

"This *is* an emergency. I didn't want you to trouble yourself by sending out a fire truck."

Marcus gritted his teeth. "Thank you, Mrs. Mortimer."

"You're welcome, dear. You have a nice day now."

He couldn't help but grin.

The third call had been a false alarm. Some kid had pulled the fire alarm at the elementary school. School staff had conducted a thorough check of the school and found nothing. No smoke, no fire. That was one of the good calls.

"Supper time," Leo said behind him.

"You read my mind."

Leo and Marcus preferred to take the five-o'clock slot, while the casuals—Carol and Rudy—took the six-o'clock supper break. That way there were always two people on the phones. They alternated the two fifteen-minute breaks the same way. Of course, if there was a major emergency during that time, Leo and Marcus would rush back to the phones.

Marcus followed Leo into the cramped break room with its bare walls and mismatched chairs. He grabbed a plastic container from the bar fridge, popped the lid and placed it in the microwave.

"Got anything good today?" Leo asked, eyeing him hungrily.

"Leftover lasagna."

"That's three days in a row, Marcus."

"I thought Italians were supposed to love pasta."

Leo scowled. "Not three-day-old lasagna. Besides, I was hoping you made one of your fancy dinners."

It was no secret that Marcus enjoyed cooking. He spent hours flipping through the cable channels on the prowl for the next great recipe. He watched Gordon Ramsey, Jamie Oliver and a few others, then concocted his own recipes using fresh herbs and lots of vegetables. He'd cook, day or night, depending on his shift. There was something almost magical about cooking up something delicious in the early hours of the morning, when the sun hadn't even made an appearance yet and his neighbors were all sleeping soundly in their beds.

With the container of hot lasagna in hand, he sat down at the single table in the break room, a warped slab of melamine with deformed metal legs, one of them propped up by a bent piece of cardboard. As Leo sat down in the chair across from him, Marcus rocked his chair back and forth, waiting for the legs to settle into the grooves in the old linoleum.

He took a bite of lasagna. "What about you, Leo? What's on the menu?"

"KFC." Leo held up a crispy drumstick.

Marcus laughed. "Again? Haven't you had *that* the past three days?"

"It's KFC."

Fried chicken was Leo's weakness. Marcus was concerned that one day all the grease would catch up to Leo and his arteries. The man was already overweight. And *exercise* wasn't in Leo's vocabulary, unless it was picking up the phone to order take-out on the way home.

But Leo did love Marcus's cooking.

At least someone does, Marcus thought.

"You and Val should come over for dinner Monday. Before work."

"Maybe. We might be busy that night."

"What, you got a hot date planned?"

"Naw, man."

"Why's your face so red? What's going on?"

"Val wants to try again."

"Try what?"

Leo leaned close. "She wants a kid."

"Ah, and Monday is D-Night."

"Yeah. De night for love."

Marcus chuckled. "Then how come you don't look too happy about it?"

"It's so…I don't know…planned. You know. Feels like the damn doctor is standing over us, telling us where to put what and for how long."

"You mean you haven't figured that out yet?"

Leo took an angry bite of a drumstick. "Hey, stop

laughing. This ain't funny. Trying to have a kid puts a lot of pressure on a guy."

"At least you're getting laid."

A rumble of laugher came from deep within Leo's burly chest. "Yeah, there's that."

Marcus scraped the last bite of lasagna from the container. "You're a lucky man, Leo."

"And don't I know it."

Marcus studied his friend. Leo would make a great dad. The kind that would always be there, always be cheering his kid on.

And God forbid anyone dumb enough to bully his kid.

"Why you staring at me like that?"

"I'm trying to imagine you with a teenage son."

Leo beamed. "A son? That what you think I'll have?"

"Yeah, a big, burly kid who looks just like you. Talks like you too. We'll call him Smartass Junior. What do you think?"

"You talkin' to me?" Leo said in his best De Niro.

Marcus laughed. "Yeah, I'm talkin' to you." Unfurling his long legs, he walked over to the sink and washed the empty container.

"You coming to the meeting tonight?" Leo asked, licking greasy fingers.

"I'm not sure."

"Marcus…"

There was a piece of onion stuck to the bottom of the plastic container, and Marcus spent a minute trying to scrape it off with his fingernail. It kept him from having to see the disapproval he knew was in his friend's eyes.

Leo grunted. "This'll be the second week you've missed. That's not good."

"So who's counting? Except you, Leo."

"*You* should be."

Marcus placed the container on a dish towel to air dry, then glanced at Leo. "Hey, don't look so pissed. I'm still good."

"Are you? Like I said before, you don't look too hot."

Marcus let out an exaggerated sigh. "Fine, I'll go. Happy now?"

"Yeah, happy as a snitch in concrete blocks."

"Careful, Leo. Your inner mobster is showing."

"And don't you forget it." Leo threw the empty KFC carton in the garbage can and let out a loud belch. "I'll drive tonight."

"Great," Marcus drawled. "I'll call ahead to the traffic cops. I'm sure they can use the extra ticket money." He turned abruptly as footsteps approached.

Carol Burnett entered the break room. Though allegedly named after the witty television comedian from the '80s, that's where the resemblance ended. Carol was a scrawny-looking gray woman—gray in hair color, pallor, attire and personality. There wasn't much evidence of a sense of humor either.

"It's 6:05," she said, unsmiling.

Leo gave Marcus a look of mock horror. "Good God! We're late."

"We've got a date…with *destiny*," Marcus said in an overdramatic tone.

Carol glared at them, then shook her head and wandered over to the fridge.

"One day we'll make her laugh," Marcus said to Leo.

His friend responded by taking a low bow, which showed off his butt crack in Carol's direction.

"Funny, Leonardo," she muttered. "Very funny."

Leo winked at her. "Someone around here has gotta be."

"You're the class clown of 911," Marcus said as

they made their way back to their desks. "The guy who always gets a laugh."

Leo pouted. "From everyone except Carol. She's ruining my mojo."

"Hey, even Shipley thinks you're funny, which is pretty damned amazing considering he rarely cracks a smile for anyone."

"Taylor!"

Marcus grimaced. "Shit. Speak of the Devil."

Shipley stood in the doorway to his office. He raised a hand, and at first Marcus wondered if he was going to wave. But he didn't. Instead, Shipley pointed two fingers at his own eyes, then pointed at Marcus.

Marcus nodded. *Got it. You're watching me.*

He strode to his desk while his supervisor's stare followed him. He knew exactly what the man was thinking. Shipley was praying he'd mess up again. But he'd already messed up enough.

Marcus's addiction had led to countless lies, theft of drugs and forging doctors' prescriptions. And though he didn't feel he deserved their support, his EMT-P platoon had gone to bat for him, defending him to the higher-ups. The powers that be agreed to rehabilitation and counseling, as long as Marcus promised to abide by the rules. It was a fair deal. He would serve no prison time for the theft of the drugs and had to abide by other conditions, and in exchange he'd work at the center as part of his rehab.

He recalled the day he started at the center five years ago. The first time he'd stepped into Shipley's office he knew he'd have problems with the man.

"So you're a druggie," Shipley said, referring to a folder in his hands.

"A recovering addict."

Shipley's eyes narrowed. "A druggie. I have no use for people who refuse to value life. Our job here is to save lives." He stared at Marcus. With a sigh, he slapped the folder on the desk. "But my hands are tied, and you've been assigned the job. Don't screw it up."

"I won't."

The man's mouth lifted in a sneer. "We'll see. Won't we? Personally, I doubt you'll make it a month here."

Marcus had smiled then. He knew an alpha male when he saw one. He also recognized a challenge. "I don't give a shit what you think, Mr. Shipley. I'll do my job."

"Don't forget the mandatory drug testing every week."

"I know the drill."

Yeah, he knew the drill well. He adhered to the rules, pissed in a plastic bottle on demand and stayed away from his old dealer haunts. It was the price he had to pay. Whenever the cravings teased him—and some nights they hit with a vengeance—he pictured Jane and Ryan. He recalled the look of despair and disappointment in her eyes when she'd first learned of his addiction.

Everything had started out so innocently. As a paramedic he was surrounded by drugs. He'd administered them to victims when needed. He stocked them, counted them and restocked them. After three grueling multiple car accidents and an apartment fire, both claiming dozens of lives and injuring dozens more, he'd suffered from burnout and back and shoulder pain.

The first time he used, he convinced himself it was only going to be that one time. He popped a couple of misappropriated Vicodin, and the rest of his day was a productive fog of pain-free activity. In the beginning, it was easy to "accidentally misplace" the drug when he needed more. On one occasion, he faked dropping a bottle so the pills spilled out on the ambulance floor. As he and Ashton Campbell, his partner, cleaned up the mess, Marcus furtively pocketed every other handful.

Not one of his proudest moments.

When Ashton began to notice the missing Vicodin, Marcus resorted to Tylenol 3s, an easy prescription to get. He broke them down in cold water and separated the codeine, an opiate used for pain relief. The concentrated codeine numbed the pain and had the added effect of making him high. Unfortunately he liked the feeling a bit too much. He tricked himself into believing he was more efficient as a paramedic when he was high. It made him feel more confident, alert, in control.

Who the hell was he kidding?

Over time, his addiction became more demanding. Codeine stopped working, and he returned to Vicodin and Percocet. Occasionally, he'd inject himself with morphine, when the pain became unbearable. Soon his dilated pupils gave him away.

Jane broached the subject one evening, but he walked out of the house, pissed that she'd accused him—a paramedic, for God's sake—of being an addict. Then Ashton told Marcus he knew about the pilfered drugs.

Within days, Marcus's deep, dark secret was out. He was exposed, humiliated and ashamed. He was given a choice—rehab or jail.

Wasn't much of a choice.

Jane had stood by him. She was wonderful that way, always forgiving. She even supported his decision to take off to Cadomin for a week, without her or Ryan. Fishing, he told her.

In actuality, he'd gone there to contemplate his life and the terrible choices he'd made. The box with the insignia had gone with him. It would be his last time using, he promised himself. Then he'd bury the box and be done with it all. He swore he go to meetings, get clean, whatever it took, as soon as he returned home. But he spent most of the time in the cabin high on morphine and sleeping. That was back in the days when he *could* sleep.

He remembered sitting in the candlelit cabin, a hypodermic needle in his arm. He was dozing, embracing the flow of lightness, when his cell phone rang.

"Marcus, it's John Zur." The detective went on to tell him Jane and Ryan had been involved in a serious car accident.

Marcus ripped the needle from his arm and jumped to his feet. "Where?"

"Not far from Cadomin."

"I'm on my way."

"Marcus, you should—"

Marcus shifted into autopilot. He hung up the phone before Zur could finish what he was saying, grabbed his coat and ran from the cabin to his car. It was raining, freezing rain, but he barely noticed. All he could think of was his wife and son, hurt and dazed. They needed him.

He sped down the highway until he saw the police cars and fire truck. He pulled up behind an ambulance, parked, then leapt from his car.

Zur strode toward him. "Marcus, I don't think you should—"

Ignoring the detective, Marcus skidded down the muddy embankment toward the water-filled ditch.

Then he saw it. Jane's car. It had flipped over and was half submerged in deep, murky water.

"Jaaaane!" he screamed. "Ryan!"

Two rescuers using the Jaws of Life ripped open the side door, the metal grinding and squealing in rebellion, water pouring to the ground. In the driver's seat a body hung upside-down, water up to the waist.

Marcus recognized Jane's jacket immediately. *"Nooo!"*

The remainder of that night was a blur of flashing lights and sirens.

And death.

He had a lot to make up for. Penance was his middle name.

The phone rang, tearing him from his dark thoughts. Over the next few hours he filed paperwork, forwarded a suspicious arson call to Fire and Police and sent an ambulance to a possible home invasion, while doing his best not to think of the meeting he'd promised Leo he'd attend.

There was a brief second when he stared at the computer monitor and thought of why he went to the meetings in the first place. To make amends. To help assuage the guilt.

To be forgiven?

Was that even possible?

Chapter Four

Edmonton, AB – Thursday, June 13, 2013 – 6:24 PM

When Rebecca pulled up to the house, the first thing she noticed was the garage door. It was open. She parked the car on the driveway and muttered a curse beneath her breath.

"You forgot to push the button, Mom," Colton said.

"Maybe it hit something and bounced back up."

She jabbed the remote button and watched the door close. It stayed closed. She pressed the button again and watched the garage door open.

"Nope, Mommy was a twit," she said in a cheery voice as she pulled the car inside and lowered the garage door once more.

"What's a twit?" Ella asked.

Colton snorted. "It's what you are, twit."

"Mommy, am I a twit?"

"No, honey." Rebecca turned in the seat and pointed a finger at Colton. "Stop teasing your sister."

She eyed the garage and the door into the house. She never locked that door, except at night. It made her nervous, knowing the house had been left unsecured. There had been a couple of break-ins in the neighborhood lately—mostly the larger, newer homes. But even though her open garage was an invitation to every thief and vandal in the area, she doubted anyone had bothered. The outside of the house was plain and unassuming, and with few luxuries, the inside screamed "hockey mom." Not exactly the best place for delinquents to shop for electronics, drugs or money.

She opened the car door. "Wait here. I'm going to check the house. Then I'll come get you."

"Aw, Mom," Colton said with a groan.

"Colton, watch your sister. I'll be back in a minute."

"Okay, but I'm timing you." He grinned. "Starting now."

Rebecca went inside the small bungalow that Wesley had convinced her to buy. "A great fixer-upper," he'd called it. She'd grown accustomed to calling it "the money pit," even though her husband had promised he'd handle all the repairs and finish everything the previous owners had neglected. Like baseboards. There wasn't one to be found anywhere in the house. Who lived in a house with no baseboards?

On the main level, the master en suite toilet was a constant annoyance, plugging the instant anyone flushed more than three sheets of toilet paper. And the fireplace in the living room leaked into the window casing, causing tiny puffs of smoke to enter their home. This was of great concern to Rebecca since Ella had been recently diagnosed with asthma.

"Note to self," she mumbled. "Get fireplace leak fixed next week."

Then there was the family room in the basement, which had no ceiling. Wesley had insisted that the raw wood beams and pipes made it feel rustic, like a "man cave." She'd told him he was welcome to it.

As Rebecca walked through the rooms, she looked about for anything missing. She hesitated near the table by the living room window. The family photos appeared disturbed. She frowned, examining the dust trail on the table. Was she imagining it, or had the photo of her and the kids been moved?

She repositioned the picture, stared at it a moment, then gave a nervous laugh. *One of the kids probably knocked it over.*

Shrugging off her paranoia, she hurried back to the garage and waved at the kids. Colton climbed out on the side with the good door, while Rebecca fought with the damaged door and helped Ella with her seat belt.

"Why'd we have to wait in the car?" Ella asked, scowling.

"Case there were burglars," her brother answered.

Ella's eyes grew wide and fearful. "Burglars?"

"You know, bad guys. Like The Fog."

"Colton," Rebecca warned. She turned to Ella. "There are no burglars in our house, honey."

"What about bad guys?"

"Nope. None of those either."

"You sure?"

Rebecca nodded and took her daughter's hand. "I checked everywhere."

"Everywhere?"

"Yes, honey. Even in the fridge."

Ella laughed. "He'd be pretty cold."

"And stupid," Colton said. "Maybe he's hiding under Ella's bed."

"Nope," Rebecca said. "I checked there too." Over her shoulder, she threw her son a scolding look. *I'll deal with you later, mister.*

"It's just us chickens," she said. "Cluck, cluck."

This set Ella off into a round of clucking and flapping her arms.

Rebecca grinned. "Homework before pizza. Go! Both of you."

The "chicken" raced down the hall, her scowling

brother plodding behind.

Rebecca ordered a pizza for the kids.

Not in the mood for such high carbs, she pulled a container from the refrigerator, lifted the lid and sniffed. "Good God, what *was* this?"

Whatever it had been, it wasn't identifiable anymore, and she scooped it out into the garbage can under the sink. On the bottom shelf of the fridge, she found the leftover Greek salad from last night. *That'll do.*

She settled into the armchair in the corner of the living room and polished off the salad while taking in the chaos of the living room. Wesley had always loathed coming home to a messy house, so she'd spend hours tidying up before he came home. Since he'd moved out, she'd become lax in her housekeeping. It was kind of liberating.

"We gotta clean sometime," she muttered, strolling into the kitchen and setting the empty salad container in the dishwasher.

Back in the living room, she gathered up Ella's sweater and Colton's hockey uniform and threw on a load of laundry. She put away Colton's Xbox and gathered up Ella's half-naked Barbies that were scattered over the sofa. She also wiped what looked like dried peanut butter off the coffee table.

Then she turned on the laptop that sat on the desk in the corner of the living room. Planning to pay the electricity bill, she logged into the joint checking account. "What the—"

The account showed a negative balance. *Wesley.*

Rebecca wanted to cry. Next week the mortgage payment was due. That meant they'd be going into the overdraft again.

She clicked to view the check for two thousand dollars that Wesley had written. It had been made out to Jeffrey Dover, one of the guys her husband played cards with every week. It wasn't the first time he'd owed someone money.

Suddenly, she didn't feel like crying. She wanted to strangle Wesley.

The phone rang.

Seeing the name on the call display, she muttered, "Damn."

"Hey, Rebecca," Wesley said when she picked up.

"To what do I owe the pleasure?" She was being snide, but she doubted he'd pick up on her sarcasm.

He didn't. "I wanted to thank you for being so agreeable about Colton."

"Yeah, that's me. Agreeable."

There was a pause.

"You sound pissed," he said.

"I am."

"What's up?"

"There's no money in the bank account."

"Oh yeah. I was going to mention that check, but I forgot."

"How could you forget two thousand dollars?"

"I'll make it back next week. We're playing double stakes."

"Jesus, Wesley! You can't guarantee you'll win at poker. Besides, where are you going to get the money to play?"

"Mike said he'd front me the money."

"And what if you lose?"

"You sure have a lot of faith in me. No wonder I feel so shitty all the time. I can't win with you."

"Don't make this about me. You're the one who put us in the hole again. I'm doing everything I can to keep us afloat."

At least until the divorce comes through, she thought. *Then I can save my own money.*

"Oh yeah. You're so wonderful to be supporting us all." There was acid in his voice.

"What are *you* doing to provide for your kids?" she snapped. "My lawyer and I would like to know."

There was a low growl on the other end of the line. "Rebecca, we managed this separation without a lawyer interfering. That's because we're reasonable adults, and we're thinking of our kids' best interests. I should move back. We can work things out. I'll go see someone—a shrink, if you want."

Her eyes watered. *Why does life have to be so hard?*

Part of her wanted to beg him to move back home. Maybe she *was* contributing to Wesley's employment problem and anger. How good could his self-esteem be if she kept nagging him? She should be more supportive. Her husband was a proud man who'd hit a crossroads in his working life. The economy wasn't helping either. Up one week and down the other. It made finding full-time employment very difficult. Wesley wasn't the only person looking for work. As for his anger issues, counseling could help.

But he won't go. She'd tried before.

"Leave things as they are," she said, drained of all energy.

"But how can we fix this if—"

"We *can't* fix this, Wesley. Our marriage is over."

Silence.

Rebecca juggled the phone and wiped a sweaty palm on her hip. She heard a clock ticking somewhere in the house and the kids giggling down the hall.

"Wesley?"

No reply.

"Wesley!"

"I've got a lead on a job," he said finally, his voice icy. "It's up north. Fort McMurray."

"Did you go for an interview yet?"

"I'm heading up there tomorrow morning. I won't be back until Sunday. How about we talk about everything when you get back from Cadomin? By the way, how's everything at work? I heard they were laying people off."

Tell him you're going to quit Alberta Cable and start a business of your own. Don't be such a coward!

For the past year or so, she'd been playing with the idea of owning a bed and breakfast outside of Edmonton yet close enough to the highway that she could advertise to travelers. Every time she'd considered bringing it up with Wesley, she froze.

What I do doesn't matter now. Not to him.

"Everything's fine," she said. "We'll talk later."

"Becca?"

She sighed. "Yeah?"

"Enjoy your little holiday." *Slam.*

She was left holding a dead phone.

At 8:50 Rebecca poured a small glass of white wine and sank into the faux suede recliner in the living room. She released a soft groan and mentally shook off the remnants of her day.

The kids were in bed. Ella was probably already asleep, dreaming of fairies and flowers. Colton had been playing Jade Empire on his Xbox 360. She'd given him until nine, then lights out. Of course she'd have to remind him more than a few times. That came with the territory of being a mom. She recalled reading with a flashlight under the covers when she was about Colton's age.

She smiled at the memory.

Thinking of her upcoming holiday, she began her nightly ritual. First she turned on the TV for noise. It comforted her to hear someone else's voice besides her own. Some nights she listened to music. Anything other than listening to the house breathe and creak and groan. She also turned on a light in the kitchen and bathroom, plus the lamp by her chair. She didn't like the shadows or walking into a pitch-black room. One never knew what was lurking in the dark.

Or in the fog.

Back in 2007, a serial child abductor had terrorized Edmonton. Reporters had dubbed him "The Fog" because he struck on foggy nights. She'd cried when she heard about the children's bodies found in the woods.

The Fog was gone now, yet when she thought of the open garage door, she shivered. *Forget about it, silly.*

At night, it was difficult not to think of her life with Wesley. She'd at least felt safe in her home.

Really, Rebecca? Safe?

One of the most difficult things she had to get used to after Wesley moved out was being alone. It wasn't easy. She'd depended on him to at least be there. Most nights.

Sipping the wine, she flipped through the channels and paused on an episode of *Law & Order.* A wife was being grilled after the suspicious death of her husband. Rebecca wondered if the husband had driven the wife to do it. *Had he abused his wife the way Wesley abused me?*

Abuse. A nasty subject. Even in today's world it was one of those hidden secrets that no one wanted to talk about it. Before meeting Wesley, she had always thought women who didn't speak up were merely weak. Now she knew better. It wasn't weakness that kept them from telling; it was fear. Especially if there were children involved.

She'd stayed with Wesley for the kids' sake—in the beginning. It was her father who had opened her eyes to the life she'd created. The make-believe one.

"You're too smart to make stupid choices," he said, not long after he returned home after his heart surgery.

"What stupid choices?" she asked.

"Staying."

She didn't ask him what he meant by that.

"You never liked him, did you, Dad?"

"No, I didn't."

"Why not?"

"Because I could see it in his eyes."

"See what?"

Her father turned away. "The same look I used to have in mine. An anger so consuming that it destroys everything in its path."

His admission had stunned her. She'd never known the side of him he was describing. Her father had always been funny and proud. He'd seemed happy most of the time, though she knew he and her mother had argued at times. What couple didn't?

"But you never hit Mom," she said.

"No…but I came close a few times."

"And that's why you divorced?"

Her father patted her hand. "That was *one* reason we got a divorce. Honey, it's not easy going through life with a strong woman like your mom. She's got her own ideas of what she wants to do with her life. I had mine."

"And they weren't the same," she guessed.

He nodded. "I was busy following my path, and your mother was following hers. I guess, after a while, we started to veer away instead of cross. Some people's paths are on a collision course for disaster."

Two months later, her father had suffered a fatal heart attack. But she'd never forgotten those words. *A collision course for disaster.*

Well, that certainly summed up her marriage.

Tonight as she sipped her wine, Rebecca thought about her own life path. She had no idea where it would lead, and that scared her. She'd detoured so far from Wesley now that she hoped their paths would remain far apart. She feared if they crossed paths again, it would result in a collision that would submerge her once more in a life of fear. She couldn't go there again. Not when she was finally learning how to breathe on her own.

Somewhere in the house something clanged.

Setting down the wine glass, she walked around, listening as the house settled for the evening. She heard a soft scratching sound behind the door to the garage. *Damn mice!*

She opened the door and flicked on the light. Nothing moved. No scurrying of little feet. She'd have to remember to get some mouse traps in the morning. She dreaded finding their lifeless bodies, but it couldn't be helped. If she didn't eliminate them, they'd leave droppings and rip open garbage bags. Not to mention they'd propagate like Gremlins.

She closed the door and locked it. Then she went back to the recliner and her wine. She finished another glass and found one of her favorite movies on Movie Central. *Sleeping with the Enemy.* It was about a woman, played by Julia Roberts, who ingeniously escapes her husband's abuse and starts a new life with a new name.

Rebecca could relate. She often wished she could start a new life.

I guess in a way I have.

The more she thought about it, the more she realized that she wasn't that different from Julia's character in the movie. She was starting over, and that meant anything was possible. Even another love.

She ran a finger over the rim of the wine glass. What would it feel like to be touched by another man? To be kissed with tenderness? To make love? It had been so long, she was afraid she'd forgotten how to go about it.

She let out a laugh and muffled it with her hand. She could imagine Kelly telling her, "It's like riding a bicycle. You never forget how."

Her sister had been her lifeline through all the turmoil of the past months. Kelly was always there for her, even when Rebecca had pushed her away at times when defending Wesley.

She let out a sigh and returned her attention to the movie. Julia was stealing apples from the tree in the yard next door—and she was about to get caught by her ruggedly handsome neighbor.

Rebecca pulled a blanket from the couch and snuggled into the chair. Though she'd seen *Sleeping with the Enemy* a dozen times or more, it still filled her heart with a strong emotion. Hope.

Chapter Five

Edson, AB – Friday, June 14, 2013 – 12:35 AM

Seated in rows of chairs before Marcus, his fellow addicts and Leo smiled and offered a greeting, welcoming him to the weekly midnight meeting of Narcotics Anonymous. He was the last person to speak because he was late as usual, but he'd make it short and sweet as usual.

"My name's Marcus, and it's been a few weeks since I've been to an NA meeting. But I haven't used."

Clapping erupted.

He cleared his throat. "My friend Leo convinced me to come tonight, and even though I was doing okay, he was right. I needed to be reminded of why I'm here in the first place. Thanks for listening." He gave a nod, then sat down.

No one seemed surprised at the brevity of his statement or at the lack of details. They were used to it. To the group, he knew he was a bit of a mystery. No one knew his whole story. Not even at the center. Shipley knew the bare bones, but only Leo knew about all the skeletons in Marcus's closet.

The rest of the meeting passed with the standard

meet-and-greet over coffee and cookies, though Marcus didn't feel much like socializing. He wanted to go home and curl up on the couch with Arizona, some pasta and his guilt.

On the drive home, Marcus did his best to breathe normally as Leo steered his rusty old VW down the empty main street. When Leo drove through a four-way stop without stopping, Marcus shook his head.

"What?" Leo barked. "There's no one else on the road this time of night."

It was morning actually. Almost one. Regardless, Leo was right about the lack of traffic. It still frustrated Marcus though. His friend was so nonchalant about disobeying traffic laws. Didn't he know that people were killed every year because some idiot drove through a stop sign?

"Why didn't you tell them your story?" Leo asked.

"I'm not ready to share it."

"One day, you're gonna talk."

"Maybe."

Leo stared at him with concern. "You can't keep it all locked up inside. It's not healthy. It won't help you recover."

"I don't think I'll ever recover, Leo."

"I know that's what you think, but I believe one day you will."

Marcus shrugged. "Perhaps."

"Look, man, just talk about it. Share. Admission is good for the soul."

"You want me to admit what I've done? Tell everyone I killed my son and wife?"

Leo released a heavy sigh, then crossed his massive arms over his chest. "You didn't kill them, Marcus. That accident wasn't your fault. One day you'll *get* that."

There was an awkward silence before Leo changed the subject. "Wanna stop at my place for a coffee?"

"Can't," Marcus replied. "I've got a date tonight."

"With who?"

"Not *who*. More of a what. I'm trying a new recipe tonight. Whole wheat linguine with shrimp, red peppers and a non-alcohol white wine cream sauce." Marcus saw the wishful look in his friend's eyes. "You want to join me for dinner?"

Leo shook his head. "Can't. Val's waiting."

Five minutes later, they pulled up in front of Marcus's house. The passenger door of the VW squealed in defiance as Marcus pushed it open. He stepped outside. "I'll bring some leftovers to work."

Leo grinned. "I can always count on you, Chef Taylor. You should have your own TV show."

Marcus watched Leo drive away and pondered his friend's comment. Maybe he *should* start looking into a new career. He wouldn't have a choice if he slipped up any more at the center. Shipley would keep pushing to get him ousted.

Maybe a change of career *was* in Marcus's future.

An hour later, he sank into the recliner, his fingertips balancing a plate heaped with his linguine creation on his fingertips. The dish smelled heavenly and his stomach rumbled. He'd even tossed in some finely chopped chilies to give it a kick, and he'd sautéed a handful of asparagus spears with a sprinkle of sesame seeds as a side dish.

For the past month he'd been on an asparagus kick. Sautéed asparagus in sesame seeds and olive oil. Or with fresh lemon juice and dill. Or rolled in egg whites, cracker crumbs and parmesan. Blanched asparagus, chilled and seasoned with orange juice, tossed in green or pasta salads. Yeah, there wasn't anything he couldn't do to a spear of asparagus.

Arizona lumbered into the room, eyeing his half empty plate wistfully.

"Hey, girl. We'll go for a walk later. Okay?"

Arizona barked once and spun in a circle. She dutifully sat down in front of him, waiting.

"Okay, but I gotta warn you. It's got a bite."

He pulled a strand of linguine from his plate and fed it to the dog. She swallowed it in one gulp. He went through the ritual "one for me and one for you" until his plate was empty.

After their meal, Arizona settled on the rug by Marcus's feet and quickly went to sleep. Ignoring her soft snores, he flipped through the television stations. One channel was showing a marathon of *Flashpoint* reruns. Man, he missed that series. He'd gone through *Flashpoint* withdrawals for weeks after.

He settled on a Clint Eastwood movie. One could never go wrong with Eastwood. It was one of the more recent films, produced by and starring the acclaimed film legend.

Halfway into the movie, he fell asleep.

And there was Jane and Ryan. They were laughing, playing on a coral pink beach with sand as soft as satin.

Marcus could feel the sand between his toes as he approached them, warm waves lapping at his feet as he strolled close to the surf.

Bermuda, he realized.

He recalled the day Jane had pleaded with him to go.

"We haven't had a real holiday since Ryan was born," she'd said, "and you could use a break. We both could." She giggled and leaned close to his ear. "Besides, we could have vacation sex. Lots of it."

How could he say no to vacation sex?

That night Jane appeared in the bathroom doorway, wearing some black slinky thing. "Do you like? I bought it online at Victoria's Secret. For this trip."

"Victoria's Secret, huh?" He could see her hardened

nipples through the lace. "I'm not sure it's working."

Her smile wavered. "What do you mean?"

Marcus tugged her against him. "It's not keeping your secret. I know exactly what you're thinking. And what you want."

"You do, do you?"

Jane turned her face and he captured her lips.

"I do," he said when he pulled away.

He'd spent the rest of the night showing her. Twice.

Now, in his dream, he watched them on the beach. Jane, all tanned and carefree, chased Ryan along the waterline. Ryan ran backward, taunting her. "You can't catch me!"

Marcus started running after them, even though he knew it was a dream.

"You can't catch us, Dad," Ryan hollered.

Marcus ran faster, his heart pumping erratically. Gasping. Faster. Pulse racing. But no matter how hard he ran, the distance between them grew.

"Wait!" he cried out. "Wait for me!"

Still running, Jane grabbed Ryan's hand. "You can't catch us, Marcus."

He watched in horror as their bodies faded in the sunlight and the waves washed away their feet. Then their legs and arms. When they disappeared completely, he let out a gut-wrenching howl of anguish.

He woke up, howling. "Don't leave me!"

But he was alone, with the exception of Arizona, who sat on the floor beside the recliner and rested her head on his lap.

"I'm okay," he said, stroking the dog's silky fur.

The soulful look in her eyes suggested she disagreed.

"Yeah, I know. I don't believe me either."

From the clock on the mantle, he estimated he'd dozed off for nearly an hour. The Eastwood movie was still on, and good old Clint was loading up some deadly looking guns. The hero of the movie was out for revenge, and someone was about to pay.

"I know how you feel, Clint," he muttered.

He'd give anything to be able to hunt down the person responsible for making his life a living hell. Except he had no one to blame but himself.

The flickering red light of the answering machine caught his eye. He'd forgotten to check it when he got home. Not that his phone was ringing off the hook these days.

"Marcus, it's Wanda." His mother-in-law. "Are you coming to Edmonton next month? For the…you know, the get-together? Give me a call when you can, dear." There was a protracted pause. "Marcus, take care of yourself."

He knew exactly what get-together Wanda was referring to—the annual memorial party for Jane and Ryan. Wanda had done the same thing every year since the death of her daughter and grandson's death. She always held it around June twenty-third, Jane's birthday. Once when he'd asked her why she didn't hold it in May, the month Ryan and Jane had died, Wanda had told him she couldn't function in May because of Mother's Day. She didn't consider that Jane's birthday was close to Father's Day.

He had attended the first two memorial parties. Three generations of family had gathered at Jane's parents' house, half of them drinking from morning to night, while the other half walked around in a grief-stricken stupor. Marcus had joined both halves, and everything had gone fine until one of Jane's uncles shoved him up against a wall in the upstairs hallway.

"I can't understand why you're here," the old man spat. "You killed 'em just as if you drowned 'em yourself. Where were you when they needed you? If you hadn't been so selfish going off to that damned cabin by yourself so you could get high, they never would have driven out there. They were going to see *you*, you worthless piece of shit!"

Tormented by self-blame, Marcus had driven off into the night. He found himself in a downtown alley inhabited by dealers and hookers. Sex didn't interest him, but the drugs did. So he drowned his sorrow in a drug-induced fog that left him passed out on the floor in his bathroom. In his own vomit.

He hadn't gone to the last three memorials. He couldn't face the condemnation in their eyes. He'd told his mother-in-law he was working and couldn't get the time off. It was a lie, of course. Even Shipley wouldn't be so heartless as to deny such a request.

Marcus considered Wanda's invitation. *No, I can't do that again.*

He deleted the message.

Behind him, Arizona barked twice. When he glanced in her direction, she had the leash in her mouth.

"Okay, okay. I get the hint. I'll get off my lazy ass and take you for a walk."

Arizona wagged her auburn tail and dropped the leash by his feet.

The residential area Marcus lived in had few houses. Most were separated by decades-old trees and spacious yards. In the shadows, nothing moved. No cars, no people.

"Looks like everyone's asleep," he said to Arizona. "So no barking."

The air was cool, no breeze.

As Marcus neared the end of the road where it opened into a wooded ravine, he glanced at the charming two-story Victorian on the corner. There was a *For Sale* sign on the front lawn.

Old Mrs. Landry's house. She'd lived there, alone, up until a week ago when she died in her sleep. He'd seen the ambulance parked in front. The paramedic said she died from a heart attack. Poor woman. No family that anyone could find, but more friends than the mayor himself. Yeah, Mrs. Landry could charm the stinger off a wasp.

Prior to her death, the ninety-seven-year-old woman had been a gem of a neighbor, always friendly to anyone who passed her house, and she'd talk up a storm to anyone who listened. She hired neighborhood teens and foreigners to keep her yard the envy of the neighbors, but mostly, Marcus guessed, so she had regular company. It wasn't uncommon to see her sitting on her front porch sipping lemonade with the unwitting prey of the day. Though, in her defense, her visitors seemed happy to oblige.

Marcus had obliged a few times and was regaled with stories from the Second World War and her late husband, Richard, a recipient of one of the highest honors for a Canadian war veteran—the Victoria Cross.

He inhaled deeply. The air was fragranced by the numerous pine and lilac trees that lined Mrs. Landry's property. Jane would have loved that house. And the yard. She probably would have adopted Mrs. Landry too.

Arizona eyed the ravine, her tongue lolling to one side, and he debated on letting her go off leash. They could cut through the ravine. It opened up near a small strip mall with a 7-Eleven, and he had a craving for a bag of chips.

The ravine offered more than a shortcut. It presented a complete immersion into nature, and it was often used as a meeting place for local drug dealers, something Marcus had zero tolerance for. It wouldn't bode well to have temptation just outside his door. He'd taken to scaring off any of the young hoodlums he came across, threatening to sic Arizona on them.

He looked at his dog. "I know you want to go in there."

Arizona would be one happy dog. She'd also end up being one big tangled mess. Did he really want to spend the next hour brushing twigs, leaves and dirt from her fur after she dove into the brush and rolled around on the path?

"Sorry, girl," he said, patting her head. "Not tonight. We'll take the long way around."

Seemed like that was what his life had amounted to—taking the long way around everything.

Chapter Six

Edmonton, AB – Friday, June 14, 2013 – 1:49 AM

Rebecca awoke to a dark house. It left her disoriented. Hadn't she left the lights on? Had the power gone out? Wait, that couldn't be. The TV was still on, but the movie was long over. The clock on the TV read: 1:49.

She stood, stretched, then reached for the lamp. She flicked it on, and light filtered into the room. *Must have been a power outage.*

Wesley had always looked after anything electrical or automotive. Now that he wasn't around, she had to call a handyman and mechanic to fix those problems. She was useless around anything mechanical. She'd never even changed a flat tire, though she could stop on the exact penny in one shot when filling her car with gas. Not exactly something she bragged about. Except to Kelly.

She wandered into the kitchen, turned on the light, then set her glass on the counter. Fastened to the fridge by a peacock magnet was her latest To-Do list. *Have someone check circuit breaker,* she added to the bottom.

She turned off the light, left the living room lamp

on and headed down the hall. Her bedroom was at the far end, and as she stepped inside, she shivered at the cool air. She'd left a window open that morning and had forgotten to close it. She cranked it until it shut, then locked it. She'd become more vigilant with door and window locks after the whole Fog thing.

She resisted the urge to check on Ella and Colton. They were safe. She knew that. She had to shake this weird feeling that had come over her. It reminded her of the time she'd found Wesley skulking around in the pitch black. She'd been to Bingo with Kelly and they'd gone for a drink afterward at Boston Pizza. It was after midnight before she'd arrived home, and all the lights were off. She assumed Wesley was in bed. Instead, he was waiting for her. In the dark.

That was one of the very bad nights. One that solidified the divorce.

She shrugged off the cobwebs of old memories and climbed into bed. She had a trip to look forward to. Some time alone to heal emotionally. It was long overdue.

Shutting her eyes, she slipped into a troubled sleep. She dreamed she was swimming in the ocean, trying to escape someone, trying to reach the lights of the shore. If she could reach them, she'd be safe. She took in a mouthful of salty water and gagged. Her muscles ached with exhaustion.

Swim, dammit!

Rebecca was so tired. If only she could stop, close her eyes, sleep for a bit.

With a sigh, she gave in to exhaustion. Her head slipped beneath the water.

And she slept.

Chapter Seven

Edson, AB – Friday, June 14, 2013 – 12:02 PM

"Glad to see you finally made it," Shipley said the second Marcus stepped from the elevator.

"I'm two minutes late, not an hour." *Asshole.*

"Late is late."

When Shipley wanted to bust someone's ass, Marcus knew damned well he couldn't argue.

"Fine," he said, staring his supervisor straight in the eye. "Dock my pay by two minutes."

Shipley twitched. "Don't think I won't."

Marcus caught sight of Leo leaving the break room. "Sorry, Pete. I don't have time to chat with you."

"I'm watching you, Taylor."

Marcus pasted a smile on his face. "I hope you like the view then." With that, he strode toward his cubicle, clenching and unclenching his hands.

When Leo saw him, he gave Marcus a pained look. "Why do you always have to goad him?"

"Goad?" Marcus snickered. "I see you've been reading the dictionary again."

"Thesaurus actually." Leo grinned. "Did you know there are, like, four dozen synonyms for the word *idiot*?"

"Did you find Shipley's name on the list?"

"You aren't getting my not-so-subtle message." Leo folded his arms across his chest. "Marcus, you are heading for trouble if you keep this up."

"Lombardo!" Shipley barked behind them. "Cut the chitchat. I'm sure you've got paperwork to file."

Leo rolled his eyes at Marcus. "The Almighty has spoken. Do *not* piss him off."

"No more than usual."

Marcus sat down at his desk and stared at the computer monitor. He picked up the headset. The second he set it on his head, the phone rang.

"Nine one one. Do you need Fire, Police or Ambulance?"

"Help me," a woman shrieked. "There's been a terrible accident."

"Ma'am, do you need Fire, Police or Ambulance?"

"Send them all!"

"What's the address of the emergency?"

"Twenty-five—" A loud explosion cut her off.

"Please repeat the address, ma'am."

The woman stammered out an address in an older residential neighborhood.

"It's a house," she cried. "Two floors."

"What's the number you're calling from?" When the woman gave him a cell phone number, he said, "And your name?"

"Addison. Addison Lane.

"Ms. Lane, tell me exactly what happened."

"I'm not sure. I just got home from works and my...my house is on...fire. I don't know where my kids are." The woman choked back a sob.

"Okay, Ms. Lane, I'm notifying Fire and Ambulance right now."

Marcus typed in the code 69-D-6t—structure fire, residential single, with trapped people. He immediately paged emergency crews and dispatched fire and ambulance to the address.

Behind him, Leo took over the radio work with the crews. "House fire," he heard Leo confirm. "Possible children inside."

"Ms. Lane?" Marcus said. "Are you at the location now? Do you see flames or smoke?"

"Both."

"How many kids do you have, ma'am?"

"Three. Amanda, James and Bryan."

Marcus's fingers stumbled over the keyboard. "Ryan?"

"Bryan."

Marcus's heart slowed.

"My babies!" The woman screamed.

"Ms. Lane?"

The line was muffled, but in the distance he heard sirens. Finally, the woman came back on the line.

"My babies are okay," she said, weeping. "They were at the mall."

"I'm glad to hear that."

He talked to her until the emergency crews arrived.

"Thank you," she said repeatedly.

"You're very welcome."

After he disconnected the call, Marcus realized his hands were shaking and his forehead was covered in a thick sheen of sweat. He took in a deep breath of air and released it slowly, doing his best to relax.

A round of applause broke out in the center.

"Well done," Leo said, patting Marcus on the shoulder.

"What?"

"You broke Titanic's dispatch record," Rudy called out from across the room.

Rudolf Eisenhauer was a skinny man in his early forties. He'd moved from Germany to Canada about twenty years ago with his parents. All Marcus really knew about the man was that he had an IQ so high that no one could figure out why he hadn't been gobbled up by Microsoft or Donald Trump. Maybe it had to do with the fact that he rarely spoke unless asked something.

Marcus frowned. "I broke Shipley's record?"

Rudy nodded.

"What was Shipley's time?"

"Forty-eight seconds," Leo interjected. "From the beginning of the 911 call to the time Fire picked up his dispatch."

Shipley poked his head out of his office. "What's going on?"

Leo beamed him a smile. "Marcus broke your record."

"Yeah, right."

"Forty-six seconds," Leo said. "He shaved two seconds off your record."

Shipley lumbered toward them, his face set in stone and his eyes trained on Marcus. "Is this right?"

Marcus shrugged. "I guess. I wasn't really looking at the clock."

"No," Leo said. "But I was."

Shipley didn't crack a smile. "Any casualties?"

"Not sure," Marcus said.

"Don't celebrate until you *do* know."

Shipley turned on one heel and was swallowed up by his office, the door closing behind him.

"Forget about him," Leo said.

"It's hard to forget about someone who's on a collision course with me." Marcus stood and stretched. "I need a coffee. Want one?"

Leo nodded.

In the break room, Marcus rinsed his mug. He filled it with fresh coffee and added extra cream and sugar. Leo took his coffee black. The thicker the sludge, the better.

He returned to the cubicles as Leo was taking a call.

"Heart attack," Leo mouthed, grabbing the mug from Marcus's hand. He took a gulp, wiped his mouth and said, "Sir, can I have your name please?"

Marcus returned to his desk.

The hours passed quickly. That's how it usually went when business was booming. And the night definitely boomed. Five hours into his shift, there were already two car accidents, one heart attack that ended up being a case of bad gas, two domestic disputes and the house fire.

"Good God," Leo said, groaning. "What a night. Is there a full moon out?"

"That's what sucks about this job. We either sit here for hours twiddling our thumbs, thankful that no one was hurt—"

"Or we're bombarded by emergencies and don't have time to twiddle anything."

Marcus nodded. "That about sums it up."

"You know, you're starting to look like Grizzly Adams. You ever gonna shave?"

Marcus stroked his bristly chin. "Why should I bother?"

"You ain't gonna catch a lady looking like that," Leo said, eyes narrowing. "You look like you've got something to hide."

"Maybe I do."

Leo stood up and hiked his jeans over his bulging stomach. "It's time to stop hiding, Marcus. Get out. Go on a date."

"A date. With who?"

"I'd date you," Carol called out. "Except my partner might be pissed."

"Gee, thanks, Carol." Marcus turned back to Leo. "You could at least wait until we're out of the office before talking about my personal life."

"What personal life?"

Leo was right. Ever since Jane's and Ryan's deaths, he spent his time either at work or at home wishing he was at work. He'd tried dating a half-dozen times. Some were even nice women. But none of them were Jane.

"Sorry, man. I know it's tough on you. I hate seeing you so…alone."

"Maybe I like being alone, Leo." He knew it was a lie as soon as the words were out of his mouth.

"Listen, here's an idea…"

Uh-oh. Whenever Leo had an idea, it usually ended up with Marcus passed out on a floor somewhere. It didn't happen often, but when it did, it usually meant trouble. With a capital *T*.

"I'm not going bar hopping with you, Leo."

"That's not what I had in mind." Pause. "However…"

"No strip club either."

Leo scowled. "You're no fun. But that wasn't my idea." His eyes gleamed. "We could set you up on one of those matchmaking sites. The online kind. You know, like that one they advertise on TV."

"I'm not that desperate."

One of Leo's brows arched.

"Okay, maybe I am that desperate." Marcus shrugged. "It's not my thing."

"So what is?"

"I don't know. Something more…normal. You know, you meet someone at a bookstore or a coffee shop and start up a conversation."

Leo snorted. "When's the last time you went to a bookstore? Or a Starbucks for that matter? You don't go anywhere."

Thankfully the phone rang and Marcus was saved further humiliation. If there were a Starbucks in Edson, he didn't know where the place was located. And the fact that he hadn't been inside a bookstore in months would've proven Leo right. He didn't get out enough.

While Leo took the call, Marcus stared up at the suspended ceiling tiles. He probably should make an effort to have a life. It was getting more and more difficult to recall the softness of Jane's skin and the musical tone of her voice. Or her laugh. And Ryan? Sometimes Marcus thought of him as a young child, sometimes as a teen.

The fact was, Jane and Ryan were disappearing from his life. What would he do when they were gone completely? Sure, he'd always remember them, always love them. He'd *never* forget his wife and son. But that didn't mean he had to stay in limbo. He just wasn't sure how to get out.

Getting out meant altering his life in ways he couldn't even begin to imagine. Change meant risk. Risk meant possible failure. He was deathly afraid of failure. It could send him crashing back to rock bottom. He had to prevent that at all cost.

I feel so goddamned trapped.

That feeling lingered with him for the rest of his shift.

After his shift, he drove home, walked Arizona and wolfed down a roast beef sandwich with horseradish mayonnaise. Then he walked Arizona again and polished off Andrew Gross's latest thriller. Finally, he climbed into bed and tried to sleep.

He kept thinking about the wooden box with the medical insignia on it. The one with the hypodermic needle inside and a small vial of clear liquid. Why the hell had he kept them?

Fight it, Marcus.

He focused on his breath. In…out…in…out.

"Daddy…"

Ryan stood at the foot of his bed.

Marcus swallowed. "Don't leave me."

"Daddy?" Ryan held out a small hand, but as Marcus reached for it, his son began to fade. "I love you, Daddy."

"Love—"

But Ryan was already gone.

Marcus got up, walked Arizona for the third time that evening, then settled on the couch for a long night of television.

"Insomnia's a bitch," he muttered. He glanced at Arizona, who was already half asleep. "But what do you know about it, you lucky dog?"

Chapter Eight

Friday morning, Rebecca dropped the kids off at school. They were hyped up on thoughts of their trip to Auntie Kelly's and already fighting over what they'd be doing. All Colton wanted to do was go swimming in the pool, while Ella wanted to pick wildflowers and play with the "Trips," as everyone called the triplets.

Rebecca let out a happy sigh. "Vacation, here I come!"

She'd taken the day off to get ready for the trip. She planned to drop the kids off at Kelly and Steve's after dinner and pick them up Monday afternoon. Then she'd have three nights in a B&B in Cadomin and two full days of relaxation.

The thought of leaving the kids made her stomach churn, but she pushed aside her fear. Her sister and brother-in-law could handle anything that came up. Besides, she really needed some alone time.

She glanced down at the checklist in her lap. *Snacks for the drive. Coloring book and crayons for Ella. Gas for car. Laundry. Pack the kids' bags. Clean kitchen and house. Charge cell phones (pack charger). House key to*

Heidi next door, in case of emergency. Water the plants.

She drove to the Save-On and picked up two bags of salt-and-vinegar chips, and two bottles each of green iced tea and cola. The drive to Cadomin was long, and she'd need the distractions of snacks.

Next, she stopped off at Wal-Mart and picked out a Sleeping Beauty coloring book and a large box of glitter crayons. They would keep Ella well occupied and out of Kelly's hair, especially while the Trips were napping. It would help keep her calm too—less chance of an asthma attack.

Rebecca gasped, then scribbled *PUFF!* on her list. How could she forget?

The last time they'd driven a long distance and forgotten Puff, it had almost ended in tragedy. Since Wesley refused to go, she'd driven to Calgary with the kids to see her father, who was in the hospital, recuperating from a triple bypass. The surgery hadn't gone well. The doctor stated that there were a multitude of complications. For a while it looked like her father might not make it. That thought had eaten at Rebecca for days. She and her father had unresolved issues. Being an adult child of divorce didn't make it hurt any less.

The drive back from Calgary had started off uneventful. They were about forty minutes away when Ella started coughing in the back seat.

"Can you take care of it, Colton?"

Like usual, her son balked at the extra responsibility. "Ella knows what to do, Mom."

"Help her."

With an exaggerated sigh, Colton dug around in Ella's backpack. "Puff's not here, Mom."

"What do you mean, Puff's not there?"

Colton dumped the contents of the bag on the seat.

"Mommy, I can't breathe," Ella cried.

Rebecca's heart raced as she signaled to pull off the busy highway. "Try to take a slow, deep breath."

The coughing from the back seat grew hoarse. Then the wheezing started.

"Mom?" Colton said, his voice scared. "It's not in her bag."

Rebecca eased onto the shoulder, parked the car and jumped out. When she opened the back door, she nearly fainted at the sight of Ella's gray face and hollow eyes.

"Oh, Jesus." She shoved aside the assortment of barrettes and markers from Ella's open backpack. Then she checked the floor of the car. Nothing.

Ella gasped. "I…can't…breathe."

Rebecca ripped off her daughter's seat belt and gathered her in her arms.

"Found it!" Colton shouted. He held up the inhaler.

"Thank God." Rebecca released a panicked breath.

Minutes later, Ella's asthma attack receded, and the color returned to her cheeks. "I was sitting on Puff," she said, oblivious to Rebecca's fear.

Rebecca had kept her eye on Ella all the way home. It had been a long drive.

"We don't want a repeat of that," she muttered now as she took a detour to the pharmacy.

Get refill of Puff, she mentally added to her list.

A half hour later, with the extra inhaler safely tucked in the glove compartment of the car, Rebecca drove home and unpacked the travel supplies. She threw a load of laundry into the washing machine. In Ella's room, she stacked folded socks and underwear on the Barbie comforter. Ella would want to pick out her own outfits.

Rebecca meandered down to the basement. It was her least favorite place in the old home, and she made a point of avoiding it when she could. With its stale air and unfinished walls and ceiling, the dingy basement was the catch-all for everything they couldn't fit elsewhere.

She wove through the piles of boxes and bins until she found the luggage set her mother had given her when she'd married Wes. Had this been her mother's subtle way of saying Rebecca's marriage wouldn't last?

She heaved the luggage up the stairs, then inhaled deeply. "I want a new house. With a finished basement."

Wesley always said she was a dreamer.

The phone rang, and she picked it up. "Hello?"

"I'm glad I caught you," Kelly said, panting as if she'd run a marathon.

Rebecca's heart sank. "Uh-oh. What's wrong?"

"Measles."

"Which one?"

"All of them. The Trips."

"Oh God, Kelly."

Her sister tried to laugh. "I know. It doesn't rain here. It pours."

Rebecca glanced at the clock above the kitchen sink. "I have to pick up the kids soon."

"That's why I'm calling. I really hate to do this, but with three kids with the measles—"

"Kel, don't worry about it. I wouldn't expect you to take Ella and Colton now. Besides, Ella hasn't had the measles vaccine."

"I remembered that. That's why I wanted you to know." Kelly paused. "So what'll you do? Mom can't take them. She's in Yuma."

Rebecca groaned. "I'll think of something."

"I'm so sorry, Sis."

"No worries. If worse comes to worst, I'll take them with me."

She sure as hell wasn't leaving them with Wesley.

"That's what I thought you might do," Kelly said. "I know Wesley is a no-go."

Kelly always could read her mind. They might as well have been twins for the connection they shared.

"You worry about the Trips," Rebecca said. "I'll

have no problems adjusting my plans. The hotel can always add a cot."

Kelly snickered. "I guess it's a good thing you weren't planning a romantic getaway with a handsome stranger."

"Yeah, I guess."

The thought made Rebecca sad. She missed having someone to snuggle up to at night. She missed having someone to talk to, share her day with. Sure, she had the kids, but it wasn't the same.

"One day a handsome stranger will sweep you off your feet," Kelly said.

Rebecca laughed. "I see you're still living in fantasy land."

"Always, Sis. Fantasies make the world go 'round."

After they hung up, Rebecca stared at the small bag of snacks she'd purchased. She'd need a few more if Ella and Colton were coming with her.

On the way to her bedroom, she passed the hallway mirror. Pausing, she stared into it and thought about her sister's words.

If a handsome stranger were going to make an appearance, she hoped to God it was on a day when she'd had time to shower and brush her hair.

Today wasn't that day.

After a late lunch, she finished the laundry. Then she went to work on packing clothes for the trip, including a sleek black dress she hadn't worn in over a year.

"In case I meet that handsome stranger," she murmured.

This made her laugh. She was going to Cadomin, a town so small that if you blinked you'd drive right past it. "Yeah. What are the odds?"

Catching sight of her cell phone charger on the

nightstand, she unplugged it from the wall. *Suitcase or purse?* With a shrug, she tossed it in the suitcase. Her phone had more than enough battery power to last the trip. Anyway, she had a car charger in the glove compartment, though she'd never used it.

She headed downstairs and spent the next half hour preparing snacks for the road. She'd have the kids pack them in their backpacks, and she'd keep a small cooler up front.

"Ah, water bottles."

They usually kept a case of bottled water in the refrigerator in the garage, but when she opened the fridge door, she found the plastic and cardboard wrapping for the case and no water.

"Great."

She glanced at her watch. It was time to pick up the kids. She'd stop at the store on the way home, all the while dreaming of the perfect vacation—the peace, the freedom, no stress.

By six o'clock that evening all hell had broken loose. Ella had dissolved into temper-tantrum mode because she couldn't bring her bike on the trip, and Colton was busy in his room sulking because he had to finish all his homework before they left.

"I don't get why I can't do it there," he yelled down the stairs.

Because we both know you'll get distracted as soon as you step out of the car. "Colton, just get it done, please."

Her patience was wearing thin. She released a sigh of frustration. This wasn't how she wanted to start their weekend getaway.

Chapter Nine

Edson, AB – Friday, June 14, 2013 – 2:05 PM

"Looks like today's going to be a slow one," Marcus said.

Leo hovered over his shoulder. "Slow is always good in our line of work."

"Yeah, it is." Marcus sighed.

It was days like this that made him yearn for the adrenaline rush of the old days. When he was a paramedic, he never knew what to expect. Every call was different. Different people, places, conditions, traumas. As soon as the alert would sound, his entire body would speed into overdrive.

Leo handed him a mug of coffee.

"Thanks."

"Don't thank me yet, Marcus."

"Why not?"

"It's decaf."

"You trying to kill me?"

"I was thinking that you drink too much coffee. Maybe that's why you aren't sleeping."

I'm not sleeping because when I try, I see Jane and Ryan.

"I get enough."

Leo snorted. "You don't get enough. Of *anything*."

"Please don't start."

Leo shrugged. "I'm worried about you, man." He paused and shuffled his feet. "Val wants you to come to dinner on Sunday."

"She does, does she? Who else is coming?"

Leo's face reddened. "Who said anyone else was coming? Why can't it simply be the three of us enjoying a good meal together? We're all friends."

Marcus cocked his head to one side. "Uh-huh…"

"Jesus, Marcus, you're always so…untrusting."

Marcus said nothing, his gaze locked on Leo's.

Leo let out a huff. "Okay, fine. Val invited one of her girlfriends from work. Marcy. She's smart and very attractive."

"Leo, my good friend, you've gotta stop trying to hook me up."

"It wasn't me. It was—"

"Val?" Marcus finished. "So it's all Val's fault, huh?" He picked up the phone.

"What are you doing?"

"I'm calling your wife. It's time I set her straight on my love life."

"What love life?"

Marcus scowled. "The one I'm supposed to be in control of."

Leo leaned forward and disconnected the call. "Okay, it was my idea. Not Val's." He sighed as if the whole world were on his rugged shoulders.

"I knew that." Marcus grinned.

"Shipley's heading your way," Carol called out as she passed them.

"Lucky me," Marcus muttered.

Leo ducked down behind the partition.

"Coward."

"I doubt he's coming to talk to me," came Leo's

muffled reply.

Seconds later, Pete Shipley appeared. "You messed up on yesterday's reports, Taylor."

"Great. What did I forget this time? To dot the i's?"

Shipley slapped the papers on Marcus's desk. "The dates are wrong."

Marcus glanced at the top report, taking in the dateline. It should have read *June 13th*. Instead it read *12th. What the hell?*

He picked up the paper and held it closer. The *1* was darker than the *2* and it slanted to the right. He tended to write his numbers vertically. Someone had deliberately sabotaged the form. And there was only one person motivated to do something that vindictive.

He gave Shipley a bland look. "Wite-Out will take care of this."

Shipley shook his head. "I'd like you to retype the forms."

The man was looking for a fight. He'd do anything to goad Marcus into making a move that would land him in jail.

Marcus smiled. "Sure. No problem."

Shipley's face flickered, shifting from arrogance to confusion, then back to arrogance. "This is going in your file. Too many mistakes like this and we may think you're not doing your job effectively enough to satisfy your rehab agreement."

We? Had Shipley just cloned himself?

"Who else have you mentioned my *mistake* to, Pete?"

"The powers that be have asked me to report in to them. They take your rehabilitation very seriously."

"As do I."

They locked eyes again. Shipley was the first to back down.

"Get to work, Taylor." Shipley looked at the

partition. "And Leo, enough socializing with our addict here. Do what we pay you to. Work." He marched off in the direction of his office, puffing and primping along the way.

Leo's head appeared above the partition. "What a pompous peacock."

Marcus chuckled. "You have a way with words, Leo."

"Maybe that should be his nickname. Pompous Peacock."

"Nah. Titanic suits him better. He's heading for disaster and doesn't even know it."

"Yeah, and one day he's gonna go down with his ship."

The afternoon passed uneventfully after that. Marcus retyped the reports. When he handed them in to Shipley, he said, "I've decided to make copies of my reports. In case we have another issue with the dates."

Shipley squirmed in his chair, his face slightly pink.

Marcus's message was clear. He wouldn't put up with sabotage.

The guilt-ridden part of him knew he deserved Shipley's disdain. But hell, he was clean now. He worked hard, ate well and did everything to prevent that other Marcus from showing up.

Except you still have that box.

Why the hell was he still holding on to it?

Because it's a reminder of everything you've lost.

Jane had given him the wooden box with the medical insignia on it when he'd been hired by EMS. She hadn't thought about what he'd store inside it. He supposed she figured he'd use it for his cufflinks, watch and his father's ring. It had started off that way. He'd even kept his passport inside.

Until he started using drugs and needed a place to hide them.

The box had been a safe place. After all, why would Jane need to look at his few pieces of jewelry?

Stupid.

He recalled the night he'd come home after work and found Jane sitting at the dining room table, the open box in front of her. Her eyes were swollen. She'd been crying.

"Jane, what are you doing?"

"That's what I was going to ask."

He approached with slow steps, his mind churning over all the lies he could tell her. His stomach churned with each step closer.

"Marcus?" She looked up at him, tears welling in her eyes. "Why are there drugs in this box?"

He leaned over and closed the lid. He shut his eyes, ignoring the magnetic pull of his old friend. "Don't worry about it, hon."

"Are you doing drugs?"

His eyes flared open. "Why would you ask me that? Am I not providing for you, working hard, taking care of everything?"

"Of course you are, but—"

"But what? You've got nothing better to do than snoop through my things?"

"I wasn't snooping."

"No? Then why in hell were you looking in this?" He waved the box at her.

"I was going to surprise you on our anniversary."

He snorted. "Surprise me?"

She wiped the back of her hand over her eyes. "I was going to get your father's ring sized. So you can wear it."

He clenched his teeth, fighting back the rising anger. He wasn't simply pissed off at Jane. He was mad at his father for giving him a ring that didn't fit. At himself for lying to Jane. At the drugs for making him so weak.

"You didn't answer my question," she said in a subdued tone.

"What question?"

She stared into his soul. "Are you doing drugs?"

"Only to manage my back pain. It's no big deal." He snatched his hand away. "I know what I'm doing."

"Do you? There's no prescription label on the bottle. Where did you get it?"

"From work. We don't need prescriptions—merely someone to okay it."

She gave him a doubtful look.

"Look, I'll stop taking anything except ibuprofen. I promise."

"So you'll get rid of this?"

He took a deep breath and prepared for his biggest lie. "I'm not an addict, Jane. I don't need this. It was a quick fix. A *temporary* fix."

He walked over to the kitchen, opened the cupboard beneath the sink and tossed the box in the garbage can. "See? Gone."

Jane stood and made a beeline for him, her hands shaking as she reached to touch his face. "I was so worried, Marcus. I thought…well, you know what I thought."

He smiled, then kissed her lips. "Don't worry about me. I'm fine."

In the early morning, he had rummaged through the garbage until he found the box. After wiping it down, he hid it behind some tools in the garage.

Now it was in his brother's footlocker.

It called to him. *Use me. You'll feel so good. You'll be free. No more pain.*

He took a long swig of coffee. It was cold.

During the dinner break, he pulled Leo aside. "I need to go to a meeting."

Leo patted his arm and nodded. "We'll go together."

Carol entered the break room, and they moved away from each other.

"You two whispering secrets over there?" Carol asked.

"Wouldn't you like to know," Leo said with a grin.

The woman let out a dramatic sigh. "There are a lot of things I'd like to know, Leonardo. Like why your wife lets you out in public wearing corduroys. Didn't you know that went out in the '80s?"

Marcus laughed. "She's right about that, my friend." He'd teased Leo about his cords for the past few months, but Leo liked to be different.

"What are you two—the fashion police?" Leo waved a hand in the air. "You two know nothing about fashion. Everything comes back eventually."

"So you're saying you're *ahead* of the times?" Marcus asked.

All three started laughing. Well, if you could call Carol's *"snort, snort"* a laugh.

Footsteps.

"Shit!" Leo muttered. "It's probably Titanic."

They erased all signs of laughter from their faces the second Shipley rounded the corner. He headed for the coffeepot without saying a word to any of them.

With a small wave to Carol, Marcus headed back to his desk. Leo was right behind him.

"The man has a radar for anything remotely like fun," Marcus said.

"Maybe he's bugged the break room."

"Your inner mobster is showing again, Leo."

The phone rang and they went back to work.

The early evening crept by with fewer than normal calls. Marcus handled a store fire and one suspicious call that turned out to be a crank call by a couple of bored teens. The police were on the way to their home, and Marcus could only imagine the parents' reactions when they discovered what their sweet little boys had been up to. The officers would give them a warning. Maybe the parents would ground the boys. Who knew in today's age of parenting?

He wondered if Ryan would've been so mischievous had he lived. Marcus had missed out on time with his son. Work had gotten in the way at first. And then the drugs. One thing he could always say: he had never used around Ryan. Usually he snuck out into the garage late at night. Or right before his shift. Not too responsible.

But he'd hidden that box where no one would find it. Especially Ryan.

Stop it! Don't think about that damn box. He clenched his fists. *Focus!*

The report swam in front of him. He blinked. Then he double-checked the facts, recorded the date and signed his name.

He rose from the chair, grabbed the form and headed to the copy room, where he made a copy of the report. Back at his desk, he shoved the copy into a folder in his briefcase. He'd be damned if he'd allow Shipley to set him up again.

Of course, he had no proof his supervisor had changed the dates on the other forms, but that didn't matter. Who else would have done it? Leo? Carol? Hell, even with her pinched expression and disapproving eyes, Carol was professional. He couldn't say the same about Pete Shipley.

I've got my eye on you, Shipley. Make a fool of me once, shame on you. Make a fool of me twice and you'll regret it.

Chapter Ten

It was almost seven o'clock by the time she pulled out of Edmonton and veered onto the highway heading toward Cadomin.

The kids pouted in the backseat. Ella was tired of the long wait, and Colton was upset because Rebecca refused to leave the house until he'd completed the last page of homework. Since math wasn't his strong suit, it took longer than either of them had thought. Then he'd insisted on bringing his hockey stick and duffel bag with all his gear, except for skates, which she'd made him leave behind.

He held the stick across his lap, while the bag lay wedged between his feet. "Stop kicking my stick, Ella."

"Mommy, Colton's being mean," Ella said.

"You're such a baby," Colton snapped.

"Colton!" Rebecca admonished.

From the back seat a small voice said, "Mommy, am I being a baby?"

"No, honey. Why don't you have a nap?"

"I'm not sleepy."

"Want to read my Kindle? I downloaded some

books for you."

"All right."

Rebecca kept one hand on the steering wheel while she rummaged around in her purse on the passenger seat. "Here." She held the eReader behind her seat and released it when she felt Ella grab hold. "There's a night light if it gets too dark. Colton can show you how to turn—"

"How long until we get there, Mom?" Colton interrupted.

"Not long. We'll be there before you know it."

With her mouth firmly set and both hands clenching the steering wheel, Rebecca concentrated on the road ahead. Every now and then she flexed her fingers, trying to ignore the nagging feeling that she'd forgotten something.

She hated night driving, especially when the highway was busy or it was raining. Tonight it was both.

She turned on the radio. Glancing in the rearview mirror, she was relieved when she saw Ella's eyes drift shut. Colton was playing with his iPod. Probably Angry Birds.

Oh, to be an innocent child with no worries other than which game to play.

She longed for a time when she could relax and enjoy her children, instead of working long shifts and shipping them off to a sitter. Kelly often babysat for her when she worked the later shifts. At least she had that. But being a single parent wasn't an easy feat.

She tried to focus on their family vacation. Though it hadn't started out that way, she was now enjoying the thought of sharing her adventures in Cadomin with her kids. It might be their last truly happy time together for a while.

Because when we get back, I have to tell them about the divorce.

Ella and Colton knew their family had problems.

That's why their dad had moved out. But they thought it was temporary, that he'd come home. Even though they visited Wesley in his new apartment, they still thought he was coming home.

She bit her bottom lip. *How do I tell the kids?*

She was a child of divorce, though she'd been an adult when her parents had split. It had left her feeling hurt and betrayed. By both parents. How could they split when they'd been married so long? She'd always known their marriage had been anything but perfect. But still…

And now she was going to do the same to her own kids. Hurt them.

They'll heal over time.

She knew that was true, but it didn't make things any easier.

When they returned home from this trip, she and Wesley would sit the kids down and explain to them as gently as possible why Mommy and Daddy couldn't stay married. She couldn't give them all the facts. Ella and Colton needed to know that they were loved. Nothing would ever change that.

Then she and Wesley would head to Carter's office and sign the final papers. Wesley would most likely put up a bit of a fight, but even he had to know deep down that their marriage was over. There was no salvaging something so damaged and broken.

Driving down the highway, she listened to the drumming of the rain and tried to convince herself that Wesley would see reason and sign the papers. Then they each would be able to go about their lives, separately. No more drama. No more angry, bitter words. No more accusations. No more beatings or late night hospital trips.

Her life would become…hers.

She smiled. *My life, my rules.*

Rebecca had been driving almost two and a half hours when she spotted the signs for Edson. Cadomin was about an hour and a half from there.

"Anyone need to go to the bathroom?" she asked.

"I do," Colton said.

"Me too," Ella chimed in.

She took the Edson exit and found an Esso station. She parked in front of the washroom doors, then got out. Ella and Colton followed her inside the station, where they picked up the washroom key.

"Me first," Colton said, squeezing past her as she unlocked the door. He went inside, locked the door and she heard the toilet seat bang.

"I really need to go, Mommy," Ella whispered.

Rebecca groaned. "Hurry up, Colton. Your sister has to go badly."

A minute later she heard the toilet flush, then the tap running. *Good boy!*

"Wait in the car," she told him when he emerged from the washroom. "And don't forget to lock the doors."

As Ella ran into the washroom, Rebecca remained outside until Colton was safely in the locked vehicle. She took a cautious survey of the gas station parking lot. Four vehicles were parked nearby—three cars getting gas and a dirty truck that was idling near the car wash. No one lurked outside. It was far too cold, due to the rainstorm.

"I can't reach the sink, Mommy," Ella called out.

With a quick glance over her shoulder, Rebecca opened the washroom door and stepped inside. She kept the door ajar so she could keep an eye on Colton. Once Ella had finished washing up, they returned to the car and climbed inside.

"I'm going to tape my stick while we're driving," Colton said, grabbing a roll of white hockey tape from his bag.

"Just be careful you don't accidentally hit Ella,"

Rebecca replied.

It was darker when they left the gas station and headed out of Edson. Within seconds, Mother Nature unleashed a torrent of wind and rain. Rebecca slowed the car and stayed in the right lane so faster traffic could go around her. Two cars passed her, an unusually slow day for the area. Visibility was so bad she could barely make out the brake lights on the vehicle in front of her. Then it disappeared. Except for one vehicle behind her, she was alone on the road.

Damn. Why couldn't the rain wait until after our trip?

She'd been on the road for about a half hour when a bright light flashed in the rearview mirror. "Ella? Put the Kindle down, please."

"She's asleep, Mom," Colton replied.

She squinted at the light in the rearview, then took a quick look in the side mirror. Someone trailed behind her in a large vehicle. The rain and dark sky made it hard to see whether it was a van or a truck. Every now and then the driver would inch up on her back bumper, far too close for comfort.

The light reflected in her rearview mirror was blinding. She blinked twice to clear her vision. "Go around me," she muttered beneath her breath.

Though there were a handful of vehicles in the lane to her left, they were further up the highway. The idiot behind her had plenty of room to cross over and drive past her. Maybe the rain was messing with his vision.

She cranked up the wipers and checked her speed. "I'm doing the limit, buddy. Go around."

"Mom, who you talking to?"

She eyed Colton in the rearview mirror. "Myself."

Behind her son's head, the headlights flared. The guy was right on her tail.

Back off, buddy. You're not going to make me go

faster.

From the high position of the lights, she guessed he was driving a truck. Should she pull over and let him pass? She couldn't see much ahead. No signs to indicate an off -ramp.

She racked her brain. *What was the last sign we passed?*

God, she hated driving at night.

She opted to pull over at the first exit. It was pitch black outside. The highway lights did little to illuminate a road or wide shoulder where it would be safe to pull over. From what she could recall last time they travelled the highway, the next main exit was a ways down the road. They were in the middle of nowhere.

She drove another five minutes. The truck stayed on her bumper. It was unnerving to have someone so close behind her. What if she had to slam on the brakes?

And why is this driver so persistent?

The thought niggled at her. Being followed like this made her think of those horror movies in which the unsuspecting friends are harassed by a trucker, then tortured and killed.

Don't pull over until he's gone.

Rebecca slowed the car to under the speed limit. Hopefully the guy in the truck would give up on following her. It wasn't as if her little Hyundai was sheltering him from the onslaught of rain.

Go past me, asshole.

Yes, Mr. Truck Driver had now graduated from *buddy* to *asshole.*

"Are we there yet, Mom?"

"Not quite, Colton."

"I wish it wasn't raining."

"Me too, honey." *More than you know.*

Up ahead a highway light illuminated a gravel road. It probably led to private property, but that didn't matter. It was a perfect place to pull over, providing there wasn't a chain across the road.

She blew out a pent-up breath. *Yes! Finally!*

She signaled right and reduced her speed. The truck slowed with her, and her heart skipped a beat. "Go around us."

She pulled onto the gravel road, the tires kicking up water. The truck pulled in right behind her. She slapped the steering wheel and muffled a curse. Of all the roads to choose, she'd picked the one belonging to the owner of the truck. Really?

She attempted to pull over on the dirt road, but it was barely wide enough for one vehicle. She had no choice but to keep moving. Somewhere ahead there must be a place where she could turn around. She hoped the truck driver wouldn't be too annoyed that she'd turned off on his land. Some people were very protective of their property.

There was a dull thud and the car lurched.

What's this guy doing?

"Mom?" Colton cried out. "What was that?"

"It's okay, honey. The road's a bit rough."

It wasn't the road that had made the sedan lurch. The bastard truck driver had hit the back bumper of her car.

Rebecca's pulse raced with fear. She thought about all the horror movies she'd watched growing up. The ones with the psychopathic truckers who hunted down innocent victims with their big rigs.

Jesus!

Checking the mirror, she watched in horror as the headlights from the truck behind her grew larger. He was taking another run at her. She pressed her foot to the gas pedal, weaving along the unpaved road until they were enclosed by bushes and trees. She had the high beams on her car to guide her along the rough road, but the rain made visibility almost nil.

She was lost. There were no signs. No houses. No streetlights.

"Mommy, why are you driving so fast?" Ella asked.

"I want to get to the hotel," she said in a faux cheerful voice.

God, how she wanted to get to a hotel. Or a gas station. Anywhere there were people. And a phone.

She thought about her cell phone. It was in her purse, which had landed on the floor of the passenger's seat when she'd veered around the last wild corner.

"Mom, there's someone behind us," Colton said in a nervous voice.

"I know."

"How come he's so close?"

"He wants to pass us, but there's no room."

The truck loomed closer. With the trees and brush around them keeping away much of the rain, she could make out a row of lights on the top of the truck, the kind hunters used. With these and the truck's headlights on high, the light converged into one eye-piercing beam.

She tilted the rearview mirror so the light wouldn't be in her eyes.

The truck hit them again, harder this time.

In the back seat Colton let out a yelp. "Mom?"

"Sit back, honey. I'll find a place to turn around."

Branches whipped at the side of the car as she steered it deeper into the woods. She wanted to cry. Scream. Turn around and go home. But those weren't options. All she could do was follow the road to God knows where and pray that there'd be help at the end.

What did the trucker want with them?

She glanced in the rearview mirror. Ella was awake now, playing with her Barbies, oblivious to the danger that was hot on their trail. Colton wore a fearful expression. *Oh God. He knows.*

"It's okay, honey. We're—"

The truck slammed into them. She heard Ella and

Colton scream. There was nothing she could do except scream with them as the car pitched forward toward a dense wooded area and branches scraped along the outside of the vehicle.

The front end slammed into a solid mass, the impact knocking the breath from Rebecca's lungs. As rain climaxed into a crescendo on the roof, she was thrown into the steering wheel. Pain rippled through her chest and ribs, and she fought to stay conscious. Her vision wavered, distorting everything in front of her.

Colton...Ella...

Darkness engulfed her.

Chapter Eleven

Edson, AB – Friday, June 14, 2013 – 10:30 PM

Marcus had a mere hour and a half left on his shift. For some reason he was feeling antsy. He blamed his edginess on all the coffee he'd had during his shift. Tiredness had crept into every joint of his body, and caffeine was one of few stimulants he could use nowadays.

Leo had given him a hard time this shift, telling him he should cut back on the caffeine so that maybe Marcus would finally sleep.

Marcus stared into his empty mug. *Maybe Leo's right.*

He definitely felt jittery. Last time he'd felt like this he'd been injecting himself with codeine. Stronger drugs had followed.

Look where that got you.

Quitting hadn't been easy. He still had cravings. He remembered quite clearly the sense of ethereal peace he'd felt while flying high. Nothing had bothered him. Until he found he couldn't function without it. Without the rush that burned through his veins.

He'd almost lost Jane as a result of his addiction.

The phone rang, and a small light on it flashed. It was an inner office call. Shipley.

"Need something, Pete?"

"Time for your weekly piss."

Marcus sighed. This game was getting old.

"Fine. I'll be right there."

As he headed for the men's washroom, he wondered what in God's name had possessed him to promise a weekly drug test.

You needed the job. That's why.

Besides, Leo had suggested it was the only way Pete Shipley would welcome him to the center, and it wasn't like Marcus had a lot of options. His very public and humiliating suspension from EMS had limited his choices. Since he could no longer work as a paramedic, 911 was the closest thing to the rush he'd once felt working the job. He'd whizzed through the training in no time.

Now he was whizzing in a cup on command.

Suck it up, Marcus. You made your bed.

He pushed open the washroom door.

"Here," Shipley said, handing him a sealed plastic cup. "Make it fast. I've got work to do."

"Urine my way."

Shipley gave him a tight smile. "Good one."

Marcus headed for the closest stall.

"Keep the door open," Shipley said.

"Yeah, yeah, I know the drill." Marcus glanced over his shoulder. "Wanna watch?"

Shipley's face turned beet red, and he shifted uncomfortably. "Hurry it up."

Marcus had to go, but he held it in and whistled one of Ryan's favorite songs. *This is the song that never ends...* It was from a TV show his son had watched when Ryan was a preschooler. The song was a never-ending loop. Fun for kids, but irritating as hell to adults.

It had the same effect on Shipley.

"Jesus Christ, what's that garbage you're whistling?"

Instead of answering, Marcus continued whistling and finally filled the cup halfway. As an added bonus, he splashed a little on the side.

What's a little urine between friends?

"Hurry up. And can you quit with the whistling?"

"I could," Marcus said, "but then I'd have to kill you."

"Ha ha. Very funny. You done?"

"What, this little pissing contest? Yeah. I think I won."

Shipley's mouth was pinched tighter than a Scotsman's wallet. "Pass it to me."

Marcus planted the cup in Shipley's palm. The man's eyes flared when he realized the cup was wet. Shipley used his fingertips to pick the cup up by the lid. He set it on the counter, washed his hands thoroughly, then picked up the cup with a piece of paper towel.

"Same time next week?" Marcus asked innocently.

Shipley clenched his jaw but said nothing.

Marcus smiled. "Nice doin' business with ya."

The fury that raged in Shipley left no doubt in Marcus's mind that his supervisor was imagining various methods of tortuous payback. He'd better watch his back.

Shipley exited the washroom, leaving Marcus alone and somewhat dissatisfied. He washed his hands, stared at his reflection for a few minutes and tried to ignore the twinge of fear.

He enjoyed goading Pete Shipley, but one day he'd go too far. And where would that leave him? Without a job. With no one to be accountable to except maybe Leo. *Without a life…or a reason to keep living.*

Marcus shook his head. "Enough of that."

He leaned in close, noting the bags under his eyes had deepened. There were craters in the craters, and no amount of Prep H would change that fact. He needed to sleep.

"No rest for the wicked," he reminded his reflection.

Then he went back to work.

Ten minutes later, all hell broke loose.

While Marcus finished dispatching emergency crews to the scene of an overturned oil truck, Leo was handling a fire.

"Okay, ma'am," he heard Leo say. "What's the address of the fire?" There was a pause. "An apartment building? Is anybody inside?"

Marcus flew into dispatch mode, connecting to the fire department, while the casuals contacted Ambulance and Police. All the while, Leo kept the caller on the line, relaying information to Marcus and Shipley as it came in.

The call was a bad one—a gas fire in a large four-story apartment building in downtown Hinton. The building was engulfed in flames, and an unknown number of people were trapped inside. Others, visibly wounded and in shock, sat in the grass across the street and watched their lives as they knew it go up in flames.

"There's one fire truck in the immediate area," Marcus said to Shipley, who was hanging over his shoulder.

"How many of ours are available?"

"Edson is down to two trucks. The others were sent to the overturned rig between here and Hinton."

"And one was sent to a barn fire over an hour ago," Leo interjected, one hand muffling the microphone of his headset.

Shipley stood with hands on hips. "Fine. Taylor, send both our trucks."

A shiver teased Marcus's spine. "Maybe we should hold one back in case we have another emergency."

"Things'll slow down after this."

"We don't know that."

"Well, aren't you little Miss Doom-and-Gloom."

"I have a feeling—"

"A feeling?" Shipley snorted with derision. "You want me to make a call on a *feeling*?" His eyes narrowed. "What are you on, Taylor? You should know by now that we're not Edmonton. We rarely see this much action in one night. I think we've filled our quota."

Marcus opened his mouth to argue, then shut it. Shipley *was* his supervisor, and that trumped a weird premonitory feeling, something he'd never experienced before, though he did see ghosts. Jane. Ryan. The children in the woods in Cadomin. He'd first seen them a few days before his wife and son had been killed. He'd never told a soul about those kids. Not even Leo.

"You still with us, Taylor?"

Marcus blinked back the memory of pale faces staring at him through the cabin window. "Yeah. I'm on this."

He relayed the address of the fire to the station in Edson, then connected to EMS. Seconds later, two ambulances were on their way. A third was being sent from Edmonton.

"There are two STARS helicopters on standby to take the most critical burn victims to the U of A Hospital," Leo stated.

A niggling sensation crawled over Marcus's skin.

Leo frowned. "You okay?"

"I think I've had too much coffee."

Whatever it was, it burned in the pit of his stomach and began rising in his throat until he thought he'd puke.

"I need to step out," he said, flagging down one of the casuals. "I'll be back in a couple of minutes."

"Where you going?" Shipley demanded.

"Break room. I need some water."

His supervisor eyed him with suspicion. "Long as that's all you're drinking."

"Wanna test me for that too?" Marcus snapped. "Fine. Go ahead."

"I'm just saying."

"Well, don't."

Marcus stalked off in search of a clean glass.

Chapter Twelve

Near Cadomin, AB – Friday, June 14, 2013 – 10:49 PM

Rebecca first became aware of the drumming. It filtered through her consciousness, sounding an alert in her brain like a blaring home security alarm. Except there was no sound, merely a growing sense of danger.

Wherever she was, it was dark. And cold.

Something pressed against her chest. It was difficult to breathe. She tried to open her eyes, but something wet dripped into them. She groaned and fire coursed through her chest, making it hard to breathe.

What happened?

Was she ill? Did she have the flu?

The pressure on her chest eased off a bit, and she raised her head, blinking back the wetness. She tried to wipe away the...sweat? A knife-sharp ache rippled through the fingers of her right hand. She glanced down, but she couldn't see a thing. She tried to flex her hand and almost passed out. At least two fingers were broken.

She moaned. *Where am I?*

It took a few minutes before reality hit her.

She was in the car. The faint light in front came from lights on the half-obscured dashboard, which she could now make out. Still, it wasn't bright enough to take a full inventory of the damage. She reached for the interior light and turned it on. Her eyes skimmed across the dashboard and windshield. Both were intact.

She gasped. *I was in an accident.*

Then it hit her. She hadn't been alone.

"Colton?" she cried out. "Ella?"

There was no reply. Had they been thrown out of the car?

Oh God…

"Colton! Answer me!"

Fighting panic, she attempted to turn in her seat, but a searing pain in her chest and ribs made her cry out. The steering wheel was lodged against her ribcage, pinning her in the driver's seat. She reached down for the side lever, hoping to tilt the seat back and give her room to breathe.

The lever was broken.

She stretched out her left hand, trying to reach beneath the seat for the other lever that would slide the seat backward, but there was no way she could reach it.

Rebecca was trapped.

She looked down and saw blood on her shirt. She had no idea where it had come from. She tentatively touched her chest with her left hand. She nudged her ribs and sucked in a hard breath. *Broken. Or at the very least sprained.*

She touched her forehead and her fingers came away bloody. Possible concussion? She tried to recall what all the television shows said about that, but all she could remember was not to fall asleep. She smacked her cheek with her left hand. *Stay awake!*

The dashboard lights faded, and the engine made a knocking sound, so she turned off the ignition.

"Ella? Colton? It's Mommy. Are you all right?" Tears trickled down her cheeks. "I need you to say something."

Again, no answer.

A wave of nausea swept over her.

"Do not get sick," she whispered repeatedly.

Throwing up would weaken her further. She needed every bit of strength to get her children out of the car and back to safety.

Oh Jesus...the truck.

Was it still behind her, waiting? Was some maniac going to stroll over to the car, rip open the door and haul her outside? Why was he doing this to them?

She saw no sign of the truck in the rearview mirror, and she couldn't make anything out beyond the windshield. The rain was too heavy. Surely if he was still out there, she'd see the lights from his truck.

He's gone. He hit us and then left us to die.

Her feet were numb. The steering wheel was probably cutting off her circulation. That couldn't be a good thing.

The interior light flickered. *Please don't go out.*

She peered through the side window. She couldn't even make out the moon or stars in the sky. They must be in the middle of some dense brush and trees.

She jiggled the handle, but the door wouldn't open. "Shit."

A low moan sounded behind her.

"Colton? Ella? Are you okay?"

She angled the rearview mirror so she could see more of the back seat. In the dim light, she could make out two shadowed lumps on the back seat, but she couldn't tell who was who.

She started to cry.

Something rustled behind her.

"Mom?"

It was the barest of whispers, but she heard it. "Colton?"

"What happened?"

"We were in an accident." She hoped she sounded brave and calm. "Can you see your sister?"

"No, but I feel her. She's—" Colton gasped.

Oh God…Ella's hurt. "What? What's wrong?"

"It's wet back here, Mom. On the seat." He sounded dazed, scared.

"Maybe your drink spilled."

She had to get her children out of the car. Now!

"Mom, you need to call 911."

"I know, Colton." She closed her eyes, trying to remember whether she'd put the cell phone in her purse or if it had been in the cup holder. Had she used it while they'd been on the road? No, she was sure she hadn't.

Her gaze swept across the front seat and down to the passenger seat floor, where her purse lay, some of the contents scattered about like pieces of shrapnel. "I think my phone's in my purse, on the floor."

"Can you get it?"

She reached out, ignoring the shooting pain in her fingers. After a few tries, she gave up.

Ella let out a whimper.

"Ella? Are you awake, sweetie?"

No answer.

"Colton, check your sister again."

A few seconds later Colton said, "I think she's bleeding."

"Where?"

"Her face."

Rebecca muffled a cry with her good hand. "Wake her up. Right now."

"Ella," Colton said, his voice breaking. "Ella, wake up."

"Ella, honey," Rebecca called. "Wake up, please."

"She won't wake up, Mom."

"Okay, as long as she's breathing, she's fine. Do you know where Puff is?"

Colton rummaged around in the back seat for a few minutes, long enough for Rebecca to start panicking again. If Ella woke up and realized what was going on, she'd have a major asthma attack. They needed that inhaler.

"Found it, Mom."

She blew out a pent-up breath. "Keep it in your pocket."

"Now what do we do?"

"Can you climb into the front seat?"

"I'll try."

She could hear her son moving, the seat belt releasing, then a sharp yelp.

"What's wrong, honey?"

"My leg's stuck. I can't get it out from under my hockey bag because the seat in front is pushing on it."

She surveyed the front passenger seat. It had shifted, slid back toward Colton. At some point during the rough ride, his hockey bag had slid toward the back door, lodging between the front passenger seat and his legs, trapping his right foot beneath it. There was no way she'd be able to reach the lever to move it forward and release Colton.

Dizziness rolled like a wave over her body. She couldn't help the small moan that escaped her lips.

"Mom, are you okay?"

"I'm a bit sore, but don't worry about me."

"We have water at least," Colton muttered. "I saw on a survival show that we have to have water or we'll die—"

"We're not going to die, Colton."

"—so we have to ration the water bottles until we're rescued," he continued as if she hadn't interrupted.

She wondered if he was going into shock. "We can do that, honey. Ration the water."

"And any food."

"Okay. Now let me think for a minute."

She was pinned behind the steering wheel with possible broken ribs and a useless hand. Colton couldn't move because his leg was trapped. Ella was unconscious, maybe with a concussion. And Rebecca's cell phone was either in her purse on the floor or somewhere else in the car.

The phone was their only answer. She had to find a way to get it. But how? She would need something long, something she could hook her purse with.

The hockey stick!

"Colton, can you reach your hockey stick?"

"Yeah."

"Good. Pass it to me."

She had to take the stick with her injured hand and gasped at the agony this caused. Stretching her left arm over the steering wheel, she transferred the stick to her good hand and stretched as far as possible, ignoring the throbbing in her ribs. The tip of the stick rested on her purse.

"You can do it, Mom," Colton said.

She hoped to God he was right.

Another wave of faintness swept over her. Her head felt thick, and the hand holding the hockey stick shook. How long could she hold out before she passed out?

The purse slid inches closer. She prodded the handle, attempting to slide the tip of the stick underneath. "Got it!"

From the back seat, Colton let out a relieved breath. "Careful not to drop it."

She pulled the purse up from the floor and over the passenger seat. With a deep breath, she reached out with her other hand. "Damn." She couldn't reach the purse. The window blocked the other end of the hockey stick, and there was no way she could maneuver it enough. "I can't reach my purse."

"Hold the stick up more so your purse can slide

down it."

She smiled. "You're a genius, Colton."

There was hardly enough room in the front for Rebecca to hold the stick out and tip the end up. With a few light flicks of her wrist, the purse began to slide down the stick. When it was close enough, she switched hands and slipped the purse off the stick.

"Got it." She let out an exhausted sigh.

Since she was pinned by the steering wheel, she had to change hands again, although her right hand was numb. With her good hand, she opened the zipper and reached inside. She felt her bank book, credit card holder, lipstick tubes. *Come on. Where's my phone?*

"Check on your sister again," she said, wanting to keep him busy.

She shoved her hand deeper into her purse. No cell phone.

When she was sure she'd checked every inch of the purse, she muffled a small cry. Where was her phone?

She swallowed hard. "My phone's not in my purse. It must be on the floor somewhere. I'll check up front, and you try to wake Ella so you can give her Puff."

While Colton called his sister's name, she leaned forward as far as she could. On the floor of the passenger seat was an assortment of empty bank envelopes and a notebook. She grabbed the hockey stick and poked at the envelopes. Nothing underneath them. She pushed aside the notebook. Her cell phone lay underneath.

"Found it."

"Mom, Ella's wheezy, and she's still sleeping."

"Try to give her a puff anyway."

She wasn't sure that would do much since Ella wouldn't be inhaling the medication like normal, but they had to do something to keep her breathing under control.

She tried to ease the tip of the hockey stick beneath the phone, but it only pushed the phone farther away.

What she needed was something tacky.

She stared at the tape wrapped around the blade of the hockey stick. It was something the players did to give the blade extra support. Something Wesley had shown Colton. One of his good fatherly deeds.

"Colton, where's your hockey tape?"

"I had it." A few seconds went by before he shouted, "Found it!"

"I'm going to hold your hockey stick out toward you, and I want you to put some tape on the end. But as you wind it, twist it so the sticky part is facing out. Understand?"

"No problem, Mom."

She maneuvered the stick toward him once more. Minutes later, the task was completed and she drew the stick back and over the passenger seat. Then she carefully held it out so the tip of the blade hovered over the floor of the passenger seat.

Her vision swam and she paused. *Please, God, not now.*

"Did you get it?" Colton asked.

"Not yet."

A few more inches and the stick made contact with the phone. Now all she had to do was navigate it so the sticky part of the tape would rest on the cell phone.

"Almost got it. There!"

With the phone securely stuck to the tape, she rolled the stick slowly until the phone rested on top of the blade. "I've got it, but I can't reach it because the stick's too long, so I'm going to pass it to you."

She took slow, even breaths as she moved. Her hand vibrated as she raised the stick over the passenger seat and then aimed it at her son.

"That's good, Mom." Colton grabbed the phone and peeled it from the tape.

"Give the phone to me."

She stretched out as far as possible, and Colton did the same. Her fingers just grazed the cell phone in his hand, and she bit her bottom lip when it bumped her swollen fingers. "Got it."

As soon as the phone was in her hand, she flipped it open, praying it wasn't damaged in the crash. The screen lit up as a surge of dizziness sizzled through her body. Transferring the cell phone to her good hand, she thumb-dialed 911.

"Nine one one," a warm male voice said. "Do you need Fire, Ambulance or Police?"

Rebecca opened her mouth to answer and gasped in agony.

Then she blacked out.

Chapter Thirteen

Edson, AB – Friday, June 14, 2013 – 11:10 PM

Marcus was deep into the eBook on somniphobia when the phone rang. "Nine one one," he said. "Do you need Fire, Police or Ambulance?"

A pitter-patter medley was followed by a soft whimper. Then the line went dead. *What the hell?*

"We've got a dead line," he called to Leo, giving him the cell phone number.

Leo immediately went into action, activating the number search and tracking. "It's a cell phone registered to a...Rebecca Kingston, 1832-12th Street, Edmonton. I'm calling the house number now." Pause. "No answer."

Marcus called the cell phone. "No answer on her cell either."

"The home address is registered to a Mr. and Mrs. Wesley Kingston," Leo said. "Wait! Here we are. A tower outside Edson picked up her last call."

"Not a very nice night for travelling." Marcus tried the number again. "She's not picking up, and I don't think this is a crank call. Dispatch police and EMS to the tower area. Maybe they'll see her vehicle. I'll keep trying her cell phone."

"Done."

Marcus swallowed hard. These were the calls he hated. Someone out there needed help, but without a location everyone was blind. He prayed Rebecca Kingston needed *minor* assistance.

He called the cell phone again. No one picked up.

"Marcus, we have another problem." Leo's voice was grim.

"What?"

"Police are sending a squad car to the highway, but EMS and Fire have no available vehicles. They're still working that apartment fire in Hinton."

"Shit."

"Maybe the Kingston lady ran out of gas."

"Let's hope."

He dialed again. One ring…two rings…three—

"Hello?" a woman said in a faint voice.

Marcus stood up and snapped his fingers at Leo. "Mrs. Kingston? Rebecca Kingston? This is 911. You called us a few minutes—"

"Car accident," came the reply.

"Where are you?"

"I'm not sure exactly." The woman started crying.

"Okay, Mrs. Kingston, take a breath. We're going to help you."

"Rebecca," she said. "Call me Rebecca."

"Okay, Rebecca. Here's what I need. I need you to tell me how many people are in your vehicle."

"Three. Me and my son and daughter."

"Is everyone okay?"

He heard another sob. "No. Colton's leg is trapped. I don't know if it's broken. He says he's not in pain. He's in the back seat. Ella too. She's unconscious and won't wake up. She has asthma."

"We have police heading to your area, so hold on. Can you or your son get out of the car?"

"No. My door won't open. And Colton has the door

that sticks in the back."

"Were you hit on your side of the car?"

"I don't think so. I recall hearing a grinding sound though. Like my door had crashed against something. I think that's why I can't open it."

"Can you get to the passenger door?"

"No. I'm pinned between my seat and the steering wheel." She lowered her voice. "I have two broken fingers on my right hand and I think a couple of my ribs are broken."

Marcus swore beneath his breath. Broken ribs could lead to a punctured lung. "Can you move the seat back?"

"No. I can't reach the lever. And the one on the side is broken, so I can't tip the seat back."

"Did the airbags inflate?"

"No. We were hit from behind."

"What kind of vehicle do you have?"

"A red Hyundai Accent."

"Four-door sedan?"

"Yes."

"Power door locks and windows?"

"Yes."

He took down all the information and relayed it to police dispatch.

"I want you to take small breaths and don't drop the phone. Do you have an inhaler for your daughter?"

"Yes, Colton gave it to her, but she's still not moving, not waking up. I don't know what to do."

"It's important you remain as composed as possible, Rebecca. You need to stay calm for your children. Okay?"

"Okay."

"I need more information. Can you tell me where you were heading?"

"Cadomin. I needed a vacation."

He could hear self-recrimination in her voice. "I'm

sure this isn't the vacation you planned. Now how close to Cadomin were you before the car accident."

"I don't know. It's all a blur."

He shook his head. They had one tower to go by. That left a lot of ground to cover.

"Were any other vehicles involved in the accident?"

"It wasn't an accident," Rebecca whispered.

Marcus flinched. "What do you mean?"

"We were intentionally run off the road. By someone in a truck."

A chill swept down his spine. "You sure he didn't hit you by accident?"

"I'm sure." There was a long pause. "He was behind us for at least twenty minutes. Right on my bumper. There was lots of room for him to pass, but he didn't." Sob. "I don't understand why he did this to us."

"Is he gone?"

"I think so. I can't see anything outside. It's raining hard, but I can't see his lights."

Marcus motioned to Leo. "Hit and run." To Rebecca he said, "Can you give me a description of the truck?"

"It was a dark color and had lights on the top of the roof. Really bright ones."

"Hunters' spotlights? On top of the cab?"

"Yes, I think so."

"How many lights?"

"I don't know. It was so bright I couldn't tell."

He heard a child call out, "Mom, Ella feels cold."

"Is she wearing her jacket?" Rebecca asked, the terror in her voice apparent.

"No. It's on the floor in front of her and I can't reach it," came the boy's reply. "I'll give her mine."

"It's important you keep Ella warm," Marcus said. The girl could be going into shock. "Turn the heat on and your headlights and emergency lights. And whatever you do, try to get Ella's temperature up."

"I understand. Colton, if you can reach your backpack, tuck your jersey around Ella."

"Good," Marcus said. "We have police looking for your vehicle. It shouldn't take them long to search Highway 47 between the towers."

Another sob. "But we're not *on* the highway."

Marcus's pulse raced. "I thought you said you were heading to Cadomin."

"We were. But when the guy in the truck started following too close, I pulled off onto a side road. I thought he'd drive past us. Then we could get back on the highway. But he didn't. He turned down the same road. Initially I thought it was just sheer bad luck, that he was the property owner. But then he hit us—a bump at first. Then he hit us hard." She lowered her voice. "That's when I knew he wanted to hurt us."

"Was there a sign for the road you turned down?"

"No. Nothing. It's a dirt road, gravel maybe."

Marcus flagged down Leo again. "They turned down a side road."

"Shit," Leo said. "There are quite a few turnoffs between the tower and Cadomin, and some before that."

"Rebecca, do you have a GPS system in your vehicle?"

"No."

"What about your cell phone?"

"It's old. No apps, no GPS."

"Okay." He paused, thinking hard. "How far down the road did you drive?"

"I'm not sure. I was terrified. I couldn't see where I was going. Then we got into the trees, and I could barely even see the road. I think I drove a few minutes, maybe ten."

Marcus let out another curse.

"What?" Leo asked.

Marcus muffled the microphone so Rebecca

wouldn't hear. "Police won't see her from the highway. She's ten or fifteen minutes in."

"Good God, without a helicopter, they'll have to go down every road to find her."

Marcus nodded. *And by the time they did, it could be too late.*

"I'm feeling really dizzy," Rebecca whispered. "I'm not sure how long I can stay alert."

"Listen to my voice, and keep taking small, even breaths," he said. "Rebecca, I need you to check your phone and tell me how strong the charge is."

"Oh God…" Pause. When she came back, her voice was hoarse. "I have one bar left. Why didn't I charge it before we left? How stupid could I be?"

"Rebecca—"

"I thought I'd do it when we reached the hotel. I don't even have the charger on me. It's in my suitcase. And that's in the trunk. And the car charger is in the glove box, which I can't reach."

"What about your kids? Do either of them have a phone?"

"No." Sob. "I told Wesley they didn't need cell phones."

He knew she was blaming herself. "None of this is your fault, Rebecca. Besides, one bar is good. That's still a lot." He hoped to God he was right.

"But what if you can't find us? What if my phone dies?"

"We'll find you before that happens."

"Do you promise?"

Marcus swallowed the lump in his throat as he flashed on Jane's face. "I promise. We'll find you. We're also trying to locate your husband. I'm going to patch you through to Detective John Zur from the Edson Police Department now."

"I don't want you to hang up." Soft sobs drifted in from the other end. "You're all we have right now."

"I'll call you again in five minutes. And then every five to ten minutes after that until you're found."

"But what if I can't answer? What if I pass out?"

"Is Colton alert?"

"Yes."

"If you feel like you're going to pass out, give him the phone."

"Okay."

"I'm patching you through to John. But I'll call back in *five* minutes."

"Wait! I need to know something."

"What?"

"Your name."

Marcus bit his lip and looked over his shoulder at Leo, who gave him a questioning look. It wasn't usual protocol to give out their names. There were rules the 911 operators had to follow, and one of them was anonymity.

"Please," she whispered.

To hell with the rules.

"Marcus," he said. "My name's Marcus."

Chapter Fourteen

Near Cadomin, AB – Friday, June 14, 2013 – 11:17 PM

Rebecca gave Detective Zur as much information as she could, then closed the phone and wiped away the tears. "They're coming to find us, Colton."

"How'll they know where we are?"

"They can track my phone call. There's a cell tower close by, so they know we're in the area."

She scrunched her eyes and tried to make out their surroundings. The rain was still coming down, but it had lessened somewhat. Minutes earlier, when she'd tried the engine, it sputtered to life as if it were on its last breath. Only one headlight lit up, and it revealed that they'd crashed into a copse of trees. With the headlights on high and the emergency lights flashing, she kept the interior lights turned on and fiddled with the switches on the dashboard.

Don't kill the battery.

After the heat inside reached sweat-mode, she turned the engine off and put it back to accessory mode. She'd turn it on again once the air cooled.

She tried to ignore the intense fear that raced through her. She'd never be able to drive out of here.

That meant they'd have to sit and wait for someone to find them. What if no one did?

She glanced at the phone. In five minutes Marcus would call back.

"While we're waiting, I want you to do some exercises, Colton."

"Exercises?"

"I need to know you're okay."

Behind her Colton let out a huff. "I'm fine, Mom. My leg doesn't even hurt."

"Do this for me, okay?"

"Fine. What do you want me to do?"

"Raise your arms above your head and tell me if anything hurts."

He did. "Nothing."

"Does your head hurt or your neck?"

"Nope."

"What about your good leg? Can you move it?"

"Yup." Colton nudged the back of her seat with his uninjured foot in response, oblivious to her quiet gasp of anguish.

"What about your other leg?" she said between breaths. "Is it bleeding?"

"Don't know. I can't see much except for my knee."

"Does your knee hurt?"

"Nope."

"What about when you touch it?"

Colton let out a sigh. "My knee's fine, Mom."

Rebecca held her breath, then blew it out slowly. "Can you wiggle your toes on both feet?"

There was a pause that made her heart stop.

"Yes."

Relief flooded her. "Okay, good."

"You want me to do jumping jacks next?"

She laughed. "Very funny, tough guy."

"And you can do push-ups."

She grinned. One thing about Colton, he always knew how to make people laugh. And right now she needed anything to distract her from the predicament they were in—even if laughing hurt.

"Now check on your sister," she said.

"She's the same."

"Try to wake her up."

She heard rustling in the back of the car and Colton's soft voice urging Ella to open her eyes.

"She's still asleep," Colton said in a glum tone.

Frustration and panic made Rebecca push her hands against the steering wheel, praying for even an inch of space so she could slide out. She screamed silently. *Let me out of here! I have to help my children!*

But she was still stuck.

Two more minutes until Marcus's call.

She thought about the faceless man who had answered her distress call. It must be difficult to listen to calls like hers every day. She could imagine some of the calls he'd get. Accident victims…battered wives…children. He couldn't possibly save them all. How did he deal with that?

Her phone rang.

"Marcus?" she said.

"How are you all doing?"

"As good as we can. Colton can wiggle his toes."

"That's a good sign."

"So what's the plan?"

"We're still looking for you. Unfortunately we have a few calls we're handling right now."

"What does that mean?"

"Means it could take some time to find you."

"What do we do until then?"

"Keep monitoring Colton and Ella. How's she doing?"

"The same."

"How are you doing?"

She took in the blood on her shirt. "Ask me that when we're out of here."

"We've tried to reach your husband at home, but there's no one there. Is he at work?"

"He doesn't live with us." She hesitated, then added, "We're separated."

"Where can we reach him?"

"He went to Fort McMurray for a job interview. Wesley has a cell phone though." She gave him the number.

"We'll let you know when we reach him."

"Thank you." She closed her eyes and took a long breath. "Marcus, are you married?"

There was an awkward pause.

"I was. Once."

"Sorry, I don't mean to pry. I don't want you to hang up again."

"I can stay on for a few minutes. Keep checking that bar."

"I will." She moistened her dry lips. "Were you married for a long time?"

"Long enough, I guess."

"Kids?"

She heard muffled sounds before he replied, "I had a son. Ryan."

Had.

"I'm sorry. I shouldn't be asking you these things."

"Don't worry about it. You need to stay calm, and if talking helps you, we'll talk."

"But your son…"

"Died. With his mother."

"How?" she whispered.

There was a long pause before he said, "In a car accident."

"Oh God…"

"Rebecca? Don't go there. That's not going to

happen to you and your kids."

She glanced over her shoulder at Colton. He was reading.

"Do you live alone?" As the words left her mouth, she cupped a hand against her lips and tried not to laugh at her inquisitiveness.

"No. I live with Arizona. And a specter called guilt."

"Arizona? Pretty name. Is she your girlfriend?"

Laughter filled the receiver.

"You could say that," Marcus said, chuckling. "Arizona's my dog. A red setter."

His answer made her smile. "What was your wife's name?"

"Jane."

"Tell me about her. What was she like?"

"She was smart, funny, quirky sometimes."

"How so?"

"She had a thing for numbers. Numerology. It was a hobby of hers. Threes and sevens, her favorite numbers. Jane planned everything around them."

"I don't know much about numerology, but I do know that thirteen is supposed to be a very unlucky number. Yesterday was the thirteenth, and last night when I realized that, I almost cancelled my trip." She gave a self-derisive laugh. "I guess I should've. Look where I am now."

"At least it wasn't Friday the thirteenth," he offered.

She snickered. "Yeah, because how much worse would *that* have been?"

Marcus was silent.

Talk about something else, Rebecca. "Was your wife a stay-at-home mom, or did she have a career?"

"She was a software designer for BioWare."

Rebecca frowned. "Didn't they make Jade Empire?"

"Yeah, among others."

"My son plays that game. Did your wife create it?"

"No."

Rebecca checked on Colton, then said, "It's kind of uncanny, don't you think?"

"What is?"

"Colton was playing Jade Empire before we left. And now I'm talking to someone whose wife worked for the company. I think that's weird."

She was rambling now. Anything to keep him on the line.

Marcus let out a soft chuckle. "I guess it *is* weird. It's a small world."

"That it is." Pause. "So you're a 911 operator."

"That's me."

"Superhero."

"Pardon?"

She smiled. "A 911 superhero."

She heard him laugh, a pleasant sound.

"You're picturing me in tights and a cape right now, aren't you?" he said. "With 911 blazed across my chest?"

"Something like that. Tell me more about your wife. How did you meet?"

"We started dating in high school. Proves that opposites do indeed attract. Jane was an introverted computer geek, a petite elf of a girl, barely five feet tall. I was the rebellious bad boy who towered over her at six feet."

"She must have felt very protected."

"I guess so."

"What did you do after you graduated?"

"We found a small apartment near the University of Alberta and moved in together—to save money for a wedding five years down the road, after I was well underway with my medical career and could support a wife."

"Sounds like a good plan."

"I thought so too. But even the best of plans can hit

a detour."

Someone said something to Marcus, but she couldn't make out the words.

"I have to hang up now," he said.

Dread seeped into her bones. "Can't you stay on for a few more minutes?"

"Sorry. I'll call back in ten minutes this time."

"Marcus, I hear rushing water. Really close by. Do you think we're in the water?"

"Is there water on the floor?"

She peered down. "No."

"If you see water on the floor, call me. I have to go now."

"It's going to seem like forever," she said with a moan.

"I know. But I'll call. I promise. Before I go, I have one last question. Does your husband or anyone else you know own a truck like the one that hit you?"

"No."

They disconnected.

It took a minute for Marcus's last question to sink in. *Wesley?*

"Aren't they here yet?" Colton asked.

"Not quite."

"Why were you laughing?"

"The 911 man said something funny."

"After you called him a superhero."

She smiled over her shoulder at her son. "He's going to help rescue us. That makes him a superhero in my mind."

"You're so lame, Mom."

She laughed. "Maybe. But you still love me."

Colton grinned. Beside him Ella stirred. "I think she's waking up, Mom."

Rebecca strained to see her. "Ella? Ella, honey. Time to wake up."

Ella gave a soft moan.

"She still feels kinda cold, but she's not wheezing so much now," Colton said.

"Thank you, honey. You're doing a great job taking care of Ella."

"Ella-Bella," he said in a sad tone.

She saw him reach out and stroke Ella's face. Colton was a caring big brother. When he wanted to be. When she *needed* him to be. For all their sibling rivalry, her children loved each other, and Rebecca couldn't ask for more than that.

She shut her eyes. Total exhaustion was setting in.

"Mom, you want some water?"

"Sure."

He passed her a plastic bottle. She took one sip and gave it back.

She closed her eyes again. Fatigue sent her imagination into overdrive.

They were sailing along the coastline of Southern California. The boat swayed and rocked gently. Up…down…up. She could almost feel the warm wind. And the cool mist of seawater against her face.

She drifted on the sea.

Chapter Fifteen

Edson, AB – Friday, June 14, 2013 – 11:22 PM

"What the hell do you think you're doing?" Shipley hovered over Marcus's desk, his mouth curved into a furious scowl.

"I'm helping an accident victim stay calm."

"You gave her your name and your personal information. Not very professional of you."

Marcus clenched his fists. He'd never wanted to hit someone so badly. "You want me to be professional? Rebecca Kingston is trapped inside her car with her two children. She's pinned behind the steering wheel, for Christ's sake. Her son may have a broken leg and he can't move. Her daughter is asthmatic and unconscious. And to top that off, *no* one has a goddamn clue where they are. Yeah, I'll be professional. I won't hit you. That's how professional I'll be."

"Are you threatening me?"

"Back off, Pete. There's a time to be professional and a time to be a human being." He scowled at Shipley. "But you wouldn't know anything about the latter, would you?" He stood up and Shipley backed away.

Leo stepped forward. "Marcus…"

"I need a coffee. I'm going to the break room." He glared at Shipley. "Yes, I know it's not a scheduled break. Don't be here when I get back."

Shipley shrugged. "This isn't over, Taylor. You crossed a line here."

Marcus whipped around. "No. You crossed a line when you decided to interfere with my call. We have limited resources. We're in a Code Red situation. No EMS, no Fire, no rescue vehicles of any kind and only one squad car. Even STARS is busy, so no helicopters. The clock's ticking. If we don't find Rebecca, Colton and Ella soon, this won't be a rescue operation. It'll be a body recovery operation."

With that he stormed off toward the break room. Leo trotted behind him, saying nothing.

Marcus grabbed a fresh mug, filled it with coffee and took a long swig before he realized he'd forgotten to add cream and sugar. He strode to the fridge and retrieved the cream. His hands were shaking so badly he slopped most of the cream on the counter.

"You need to calm down," Leo said.

"That man is an ass. Why is he even doing this job? He doesn't give a shit about anyone besides himself."

"That's not true," someone said.

Marcus turned and saw Carol in the doorway.

"Haven't you heard the story about his wife?" she asked.

Both Marcus and Leo shook their heads.

Carol grabbed a cloth and began cleaning the counter. After a minute she said, "Peter Shipley's wife was killed seven years ago. Right before Christmas."

"That doesn't explain why he's got such a hate-on for me."

"Marcus," Carol said, handing him a clean mug, "his wife was shot during a convenience store robbery. The man who killed her was looking for money. So he could buy drugs." She gave him a piercing look.

Marcus blinked. "He was an addict."

"Yes."

"Well, that explains why Shipley's hate radar is focused on Marcus," Leo said.

"I'm surprised you didn't know this," Carol said.

She left the break room as quietly as she'd entered it.

"You didn't know about Shipley's wife?" Marcus asked Leo.

"I'd heard rumors."

"Why didn't you ever tell me?"

Leo shrugged. "I guess it never came up."

"Because I was always too busy hating him back."

"This isn't the time to worry about Shipley. I suspect you'll have lots of time to think about him later." Leo motioned toward the doorway. "We should head back to our desks."

"He's still an ass."

"I agree."

"You're frowning, Leo. How come?"

"I've never seen you get so worked up from a call."

"Someone tried to kill a woman and her kids. She's doing her best to keep calm. She can't even hold her children right now."

"I can't imagine how she must feel," Leo said.

"I can. I know exactly how she feels. Helpless. Hopeless. Alone."

"So you did your best to help her, give her hope and make her feel less alone. There's nothing wrong about that."

"Tell that to Titanic."

Leo patted Marcus's arm. "They'll find her in time."

"I hope so."

"Until then, we have some work to do."

Marcus stepped into the hall, then stopped. "Did you try the husband's cell phone?"

"Yeah, no answer."

"Rebecca said they're separated and that he went to Fort McMurray for a job." Marcus's brow rippled.

"What's wrong?"

"I keep thinking about this truck, the one that hit her. It ran her off the road intentionally. Someone wanted to kill Rebecca. I can't wrap my head around someone being so coldhearted that they'd attempt to kill a woman and her two children."

"There are a lot of evil people out there, Marcus."

"I know. But still…he's willing to kill two children. That makes him a monster."

"I know what you're thinking."

"Do you?"

"You're wondering if the husband had anything to do with this."

"Well, he is conveniently away on *business* at the exact time someone tries to kill his wife."

"Does he own a truck?"

"His wife says no." He strode down the hallway. "But maybe he rented one. Let's find out."

Leo followed him back to his desk. "You know, if we're right and the husband tried to kill her, he may not be done. We should probably tell someone our theory."

"Not Titanic." Marcus chewed on his lip, thinking. "I'll call John Zur. He's a detective friend and a good guy."

"You know we're breaking a hundred rules now."

"Why stop now, Leo? Let's go for a hundred and one."

He dialed the number. When Zur answered, Marcus told him about Rebecca Kingston and the mysterious truck. "I'm wondering if the husband, who is conveniently away, had something to do with the hit and run."

"I'm on the road," Zur said. "I've been called out to

that apartment fire in Hinton. Suspicious circumstances. But I'll call in and let the captain know about the husband."

"I was hoping you could check him out."

"I'll do what I can, but we're spread thin right now. Must be a goddamn full moon. Too much going on tonight."

"I understand."

"Have they found the wife yet?"

"No."

There was a pause. "I'm sure they'll find her."

"What if they can't find her in time, John? We've got one police vehicle looking for her along a good stretch of highway. That's it. And Rebecca and Colton are injured. Her daughter, Ella, is asthmatic."

"Marcus." Zur's voice held a thread of warning. "Stay focused and objective."

"I am focused. I want to find this woman and her kids. That's my objective."

"Do not get emotionally invested."

"How the hell do I avoid that?"

Zur let out a light chuckle. "I hear you. Believe me, it's not easy. I battle that every day. In the end, we have to remind ourselves these are cases. And we're nothing more than a temporary fix to whatever the problem is. Eventually they go on with their lives and we go on with ours."

"I think this Wesley Kingston may be a danger to his wife."

"He'll be investigated, Marcus. By me. I was assigned the case." Zur sighed. "You know as well as I do that the spouse is usually our first suspect. Until we rule the husband out, we'll be looking at him very closely."

"You do that, John."

"Listen, I'll call you if I hear anything back on Kingston."

"I'll be waiting." Marcus said good-bye and hung up the phone.

Minutes later Leo tapped his desk. "I've got nothing. No other vehicles are registered to Wesley Kingston except an SUV. A Buick Rendezvous. You sure she saw a truck? An SUV's hefty enough to do some real damage."

Marcus shook his head. "She saw a truck with hunting lights."

"Maybe he rented it."

"We're still not a hundred percent sure it's the husband."

"You need to find out more about her. Where does she work?"

"I don't know." Marcus gave him a glum look. "I didn't ask. Where are we on emergency vehicles?"

"Nothing's changed."

"Shit."

Marcus jumped to his feet and began pacing around his cubicle. He glanced at his watch. Time trudged along, each second ticking by with relentless precision.

"I've gotta do something, Leo."

"You are. You're doing your job."

"Screw the job."

Over his shoulder he spotted Shipley leaning against the doorway to his office as if he had no cares in the world.

"Problem, Taylor?" Shipley called out.

Marcus ignored him and returned to his seat. Then he picked up the phone and dialed. "John, any word on Rebecca Kingston?"

"We're still looking for her," Zur said. "We may have some free vehicles in an hour or so."

"An hour will be too late." Marcus didn't know how he knew this, but he did.

"If we had more manpower, we'd send someone out

in another car," Zur added. "Sorry, Marcus. This is a Code Red situation. No emergency services available. We're doing our best."

"What about the truck that ran her off the road? Anyone see it, report it?"

"We've got no eye-witness reports. Her husband never rented a truck. At least not in his name."

"And you still haven't been able to reach him?"

"No. Kingston's not answering."

"How convenient."

"Look, as soon as I know anything, I'll call you."

Marcus checked his watch. "Call my cell phone."

"Will do."

As soon as Marcus hung up, Leo nudged him and passed him a sheet of paper.

"This is the time the rain hit the area?" Marcus asked.

"Yeah."

"So if she was a half hour past Edson, that would put her about here." Marcus pointed to a spot along Highway 47 on the map on his monitor. He consulted the sheet Leo had given him. "It started raining about here."

"How long did she drive in the rain?"

"Maybe fifteen or twenty minutes. But she was forced off the highway, and we have no idea how long she was passed out before she called us." He did a rough calculation. "That would put her somewhere in this area." He drew a circle with his finger around an area of the map.

"The McLeod River runs near that stretch of the highway," Leo said. "And it has a number of tributaries. That could be what she heard. The river."

"At least now we know where to look." Marcus pushed away from the desk, stood and grabbed his jacket off the back of the chair.

"What are you doing?"

"The one thing I can do. I'm going to look for

them."

"Marcus!" Leo hissed. "Are you crazy? You can't just up and leave."

"Watch me." He patted Leo's shoulder. "Look, my shift's nearly over. We have limited resources and no one else can go look for her. We know she's not far from here." He strode to the window and looked outside. "The rain's slowing. I might be able to see where she went off the highway."

"What about Shipley? You know he's gonna be pissed."

"I'll deal with him later. Right now we have a mother and two kids counting on us. We're their only hope, and I can't sit by waiting for emergency vehicles to come available when I know she might be twenty minutes away."

"She said at least half an hour from here."

Marcus grinned. "Not the way I drive."

"Be safe, man. I'll do what I can from this end to smooth things over."

"You make sure you stay by the phone."

Marcus headed for the door, but not before flicking a look toward Shipley's office. The man was nowhere in sight. *Finally, a stroke of luck.* "If he says anything to you, you be sure to tell him this was *my* idea and you tried to stop me."

"Hold on!"

Leo rushed down the hallway and through the stairwell door. He returned a few minutes later, face flushed and panting. In his hands were an emergency kit and two oxygen tanks.

"I borrowed the rebreathers from the training room," he said between breaths. "You might need them."

"Borrowed? You know this is for paramedic training. Shipley'll be pissed."

Leo shrugged. "You just have 'em back before

Titanic even notices they're missing."

"Thanks, Leo."

"Don't thank me yet. I may have to 'fess up, and you might not have a job to come back to."

"There are other jobs."

Strange. For the first time, Marcus felt a sense of liberation at the thought of pursuing some other career. Sure, there was a slim chance he could go back to being a paramedic once he'd kicked the drugs and passed his probation period. But did he even want that? He wasn't sure anymore.

Leo followed him out into the hall. "Call me as soon as you find 'em. And, Marcus?" He hesitated and chewed his bottom lip.

"Spit it out, Leo?"

"You know this isn't part of your job description."

"I know."

"You may not find them in time. They might not all make it. Are you prepared for that?"

"I won't fail, Leo. Not this time."

"Marcus—"

"Funny how things come full circle sometimes. Fate?"

Leo grunted. "Or destiny. Go get 'em."

Marcus raced from the center with two thoughts in his head. One, he was going to find Rebecca and her kids. Two, he would get them out—*alive*.

Chapter Sixteen

Near Cadomin, AB – Friday, June 14, 2013 – 11:42 PM

Rebecca opened her eyes slowly, blinking a few times to clear her vision. She was assaulted by images of the crash, Ella unconscious in the back, Colton with his leg pinned between the seats.

Her forehead felt tight. She touched it. Dried blood. That was a good sign at least.

She inhaled carefully and flinched when a sharp dagger of pain shot through her ribs. Definitely broken. She wondered how long she could remain conscious.

What if I die here, with Ella and Colton in the back seat? She shook her head. *No! I can't think like that.*

"Mom, are you awake?"

"Yes, Colton."

"I was scared you wouldn't wake up." She heard his voice tremble. "You didn't drop the phone, did you?"

She had a moment of trepidation when she thought she had, but she found her cell phone securely tucked between her chest and the steering wheel. "No, I have it." *Thank God!*

She glanced at the phone. The man from 911 should be calling her soon.

Marcus.

She thought of his voice, how soothing and comforting it was. There was kindness in his tone. And something more. Sadness. His wife was dead. And his son. *What were their names? Jane and...Ryan.*

This made her think of Wesley. She flipped open her phone and punched in his number. No answer. If he was still on the road, he wouldn't pick up the phone.

She left a message. "Wesley, we've been in a car accident. Ella and Colton are fine, I think. I've called 911. They're looking for us now." She checked the battery. "I can't call you again. My battery's too low. I'll call you when we're safe." She hung up.

"We're gonna get rescued, right, Mom?"

She pressed the phone against her cheek. "Yes, honey. Soon."

The phone rang.

"Marcus?" she said.

"Yes, it's me. How are you doing?"

"The same." She lowered her voice. "I'm sure I've broken a couple of ribs, and I'm afraid of internal damage."

"We're trying to locate more vehicles to search for you." His voice sounded tight. "I'm sorry, Rebecca."

"Why are you sorry? You didn't do anything."

"I'm feeling a bit helpless here."

She bit her lip. "You're thinking of your wife, aren't you?"

Pause. "Yes."

"And your son."

"Ryan. He was a good kid."

"I bet you were a good dad."

"I tried. We didn't have an easy time getting pregnant. Ryan was a gift."

He told her how, when he was into his second year of medical school, Jane had become pregnant. Without a second thought, he'd quit medical school—much to his parents' dismay—and got a job as a lab assistant. Then he married Jane in a quiet family-only service in his parents' backyard. Four months into the pregnancy, Jane had a miscarriage."

"That's awful," Rebecca said. "I'm very sorry."

"I submerged myself in work, while Jane mended. We tried for three years. I didn't think it would ever happen."

"And then it did."

"Yes. Ryan was born and everything changed."

"Children do that to you, don't they?"

"Listen, Rebecca, while we're searching for you, we need to get as much information as possible on the hit and run. Edmonton is sending up some squad cars to help chase down this truck."

"What do you need?"

"Do you know anyone who would do this to you? Anyone you've annoyed or ticked off?"

"I should be offended that you'd think I'd have such enemies, but I've been wondering the same thing. Honestly, I can't think of anyone who would try to run me off the road."

"You mentioned you and your husband were separated. How has that been?"

"As good as can be expected, I guess. We're not enemies, if that's what you're thinking. Wesley has a temper, sure. But he'd never do something like this." A glimmer of doubt flickered through her. "Especially to his kids."

"You said he's in Fort McMurray. When did he leave?"

"I'm not sure. We're supposed to get together when he gets back, to talk about things. The divorce."

"And he's okay with cutting the ties?"

Rebecca took a small breath. "I haven't let him know that I've proceeded with the divorce already."

"But he's expecting it, right?"

"I think so. But sometimes I think Wesley still wants to get back together."

"And you?"

"My marriage is over. It's been over for a while. I need to move on. So does Wesley."

"Do you know where's he staying in Fort McMurray?"

Her heart sank. "No. Damn. I never asked."

"Does your husband have access to large trucks, maybe a friend's?"

"No. I'm telling you, Wesley has nothing to do with this."

"Probably not. But the police will want to look at everything." She heard him clear his throat. "Tell me about your marriage."

"What do you want to know? We got married, had two kids, busy jobs, busy lifestyle, grew apart and now here we are."

"Did he ever threaten you?"

She swallowed hard. "He's not a horrible person. Not really."

"Rebecca, I need you to be honest. Did he ever hurt you physically?"

She looked over her shoulder at Colton. He was listening to her every word.

"Yes, but I can't go into details. Understand?"

"I do. So you're saying your husband was physically abusive."

"Yes."

"Verbally?"

"Sometimes."

"Sexually?"

"No."

"Did he abuse Ella or Colton?"

"No!" she said, a little too strongly. "I'd never allow that. It's one of the reasons I want the divorce."

"You fear for your kids?"

She sighed. "Wesley isn't all bad. He has a very sweet side to him. That's why I fell in love and married him. But he has issues. And not only what we're talking about." She cupped a hand by her mouth and whispered, "Gambling problems."

"Are you in financial distress because of it?"

"Some. He's lost big over the past year, so our funds are a bit depleted."

"Bankruptcy issues?"

"No, not yet. And hopefully never. He got a small loan from his father."

"What do you do, Rebecca?"

"I work for Alberta Cable. I'm a CSR—customer service rep. My job's stable, so that's one good thing."

"Do you recall anything else about the truck that hit you?"

His question came out of left field. She'd been lulled into a sense of security with his other inquiries.

"Nothing new."

"What about the road you took off the highway? Was there anything? Even the smallest detail may help us pinpoint your location."

She closed her eyes and visualized the road she'd turned off onto, but nothing particular came to mind. "The road was open at first. Nothing much around except fields. Then seconds later, trees and bushes were on both sides."

Something twigged at her memory. Then it disappeared.

"If you think of anything," Marcus said, "call 911 immediately. Don't wait for my call."

"Okay, I will."

"Is Ella awake?"

"No." She turned with caution. "Colton, check Ella."

A few seconds went by, then Colton said, "She's feeling cold again."

"Ella's cold," she said into the phone. "We don't have anything else to warm her up with."

"Damn," Marcus muttered.

She glanced down at the phone. "And we have another problem."

"What?"

"The battery on my phone shows half a bar."

There was a long pause on the other end of the line. "Marcus?"

"I'm here." She heard him breathe in deeply. "We need to conserve that battery, so we'll have to hang up."

She bit back a sob. This man, this stranger, was her lifeline. *He may be the last voice I hear.*

"Wait!" she said. "Will you call back in ten minutes?"

"Yes, but we'll keep it short." *Click.*

Chapter Seventeen

Outside Edson, AB – Friday, June 14, 2013 – 11:48 PM

The hammering rain had let up, but the roads were still wet, and puddles on the highway caused Marcus's SUV to drag. A gust of wind had worked its way into the region, and he could feel the pull on his vehicle. He'd been driving for about five minutes when he dialed Rebecca's number on his Bluetooth device. It rang four times before she picked up. Not a good sign.

"Sorry it took so long for me to call back," he said.

"I expect you're very busy," Rebecca replied.

He scrutinized the interior of the SUV. *Yeah, I'm busy.* "How are you doing?"

"Not so good."

"What's wrong?"

He heard her sigh. "I'm dizzy…sleepy."

"Do not go to sleep, Rebecca. You have to stay awake. Stay on the line with me." He gripped the steering wheel until his knuckles turned white.

"I'm going to try to back out of these trees. Maybe I can find my way back to the road or highway."

He waited, listening to the sounds of her breathing and the engine as she revved it.

"I've moved back," she said, "maybe about ten feet. But there's another problem. One of my headlights is broken and the other is so dim I can't see three feet in front of me."

"Put it in *park*. Don't worry about trying to get back to the road. It's too dangerous if you can't see where you're going. Last thing you want to do is drive blind out there."

She lowered her voice. "I tried turning the steering wheel a bit, but it's pressed so tightly against me that it was sheer torture."

"You've done fine, Rebecca. Take a break. Rest."

"At least my adrenaline's kicked in," she said with a short laugh. "I'm awake now."

"That's good. Listen…I have to go now. But I'll keep calling every five minutes or so. Okay?"

"Okay."

"I know you're scared, but you have to be brave for Colton and Ella. Can you do that?"

"I'll try."

He tapped the GPS screen and brought up a map of the area. She could be anywhere. "I need you to try to remember some landmarks."

"I can't remember anything. It was raining too hard and dark outside."

"Sometimes we think we don't remember, but it's right there, behind a veil. So think back, Rebecca. You left your house and got on the highway heading to Cadomin."

"Yes. I wanted to take the kids to see the cave." Her voice broke.

"Did you stop along the highway for gas?"

"No. I filled up earlier."

"Did you stop for a bathroom break or to buy snacks?"

"Yes, one stop in Edson. The kids needed to go to the bathroom. We were there less than ten minutes. Then we got back out on the highway heading south to Cadomin."

"How long did you drive before you noticed the truck behind you?"

"I'm not sure. I think I was on the road for maybe ten minutes, but it could have been longer. Once it started pouring, I didn't notice the time. I was too busy focusing on the road."

"Listen, Rebecca, I think we can narrow down your location."

"Oh God…please help us." She let out a sob.

"I'm working on it. How long did you drive in the rain for?"

"I haven't got a clue. Maybe fifteen, twenty minutes."

"You're doing great. But I have to go now. I'll—"

"Wait!" she shrieked. "He's back!"

"What?"

"I see lights behind me," she sobbed. "He's coming for us, Marcus. I'm starting the engine."

"Rebecca, try to stay calm. It could be someone—"

He heard the engine of her car rev up.

"I can't outrun him," Rebecca cried.

The squeal of metal on metal made Marcus cringe. "Rebecca?"

She screamed. "We're going over a cliff! Marc—"

Silence.

"Rebecca?"

No reply.

"Rebecca!"

The line was dead.

He called Leo's direct line at the center. "The bastard didn't leave, Leo."

"What?"

"He rammed the car again. Rebecca said he pushed her car off a cliff."

"But there aren't any cliffs in the area."

"I know. It doesn't make any sense."

Nothing did.

"There aren't any cliffs," Leo said in a quiet voice, "but there are some steep embankments along the McLeod River."

Marcus flinched. "The river? Oh hell."

Chapter Eighteen

Near Cadomin, AB – Friday, June 14, 2013 – 11:56 PM

The interior lights were still on, and Rebecca took stock of her surroundings. Though she couldn't see anything beyond the windows, she guessed they were at the bottom of a ditch or a quarry. Thankfully, the car hadn't flipped or rolled, but they *had* landed with a resounding crash. The front end of the car tipped down slightly, the steering wheel putting more pressure on her ribs.

"Is he coming back?" Colton cried out.

She took in a few ragged breaths and tried to calm her racing pulse. "No, honey. He's gone now."

"Are you sure?"

"Yes, Colton. He's won't be back."

She didn't know if this were true or not. All she saw in the rearview mirror was total blackness. The truck could still be out there, waiting.

She was cold, and her fingers and toes felt numb. She wiggled them, trying to force the circulation back into her hands and feet. She tried to push the steering wheel away, but that only sent daggers into her chest and made her dizzy.

"Mom, Ella's wheezing again," Colton said behind her.

"Give her another shot of Puff."

Rebecca wanted to scream, cry, lash out. Every fiber in her being was enraged by her situation. Her children needed her and she was helpless.

"Is the 911 guy calling back soon?" Colton asked.

"Any minute now, honey."

"Good."

She tried to start the car, but the engine was dead. She jiggled the door, but it held fast. "Try your door again, Colton."

She heard him grunting and straining, and she mentally kicked herself for not getting the damned door fixed.

"It won't budge," he said.

Every now and then, the car made small, subtle tremors. Somewhere in the fog of her mind, she knew it wasn't a good thing, even though this time the movement was gentler, almost peaceful. At times the car would shudder, as if the ground beneath it had given way. And she swore she heard a sharp crack.

"My feet are freezing," Colton said.

"Try to prop your good foot up behind my chair. Maybe you can massage it to get it warm."

"Mom, I think our water bottles spilled on the floor."

She shifted her feet and heard soft splashes. She glanced down at the floor near the brake. *Water.* She scowled. *An awful lot of water.*

That's when it finally hit her. Water! The car had landed in water.

Panic rose in her chest and up her throat. *Oh my God! The car's sinking!* A whimper escaped her mouth.

"What's wrong?" Colton asked, his voice tinged with fear.

"Nothing," she lied, her mind racing to recall

everything she'd ever heard about submerged vehicles and how to escape them. "My ribs hurt a bit."

Stay calm. Try not to let him know what you're thinking. Not until he has to know.

She turned on her phone and dialed 911. A stranger picked up.

"I need to speak to Marcus," she said, struggling to keep the panic from her voice.

"Rebecca?" the man said. "Marcus is going to call you from his cell phone."

"He said I should call in if—" she lowered her voice, praying that Colton couldn't hear her, "there was water on the floor of the car."

"And I take it there is," the man said in a calm voice.

"Yes."

"Rebecca? Here's what we're going to do. You hang up. I'll call Marcus and tell him to call you right away. Okay?"

"Okay."

"And by the way," the stranger said, "my name's Leo."

"Thank you, Leo." She hung up.

Please, Marcus, call me and tell me what to do.

The phone rang. "Marcus?"

"I'm here, Rebecca."

"You know what you asked me to look for? It's on the floor. And the car keeps moving every now and then."

"Tell me about the motion."

"At first it was an occasional movement, but now it's constant."

"Describe it."

"It's like we're balancing on a teeter-totter. And every now and then it feels like we're sliding forward, and sometimes it feels like we've dropped a few inches.

It's probably my imagination."

Marcus swallowed hard. "You could be hung up, rocking on an embankment of some kind, a small hill." He dreaded the thought that her car might be nose-first in the river.

"Don't try to open the doors," he said.

She moaned. "They won't budge anyway."

"Can you tell if water's coming in quickly?"

She wiggled her foot. "It's almost to the top of my foot, but it's not gushing in."

"Good. Keep me posted on how high the water is. Let me know if it gets halfway up your calf."

She shuddered at the thought. "We're in a river or lake, aren't we?"

"If you'd landed in deep water, the car would be sinking fast. We do know you're not far from Edson. You did an awesome job at helping us narrow down your location."

"But you still don't know exactly where we are."

"No." She could hear the frustration in his voice. "How are the kids doing?"

"Colton is still pinned behind the seat. Ella has barely moved."

"Keep administering her medication."

"What happens when it runs out?"

"We'll find you before that occurs."

"I'm scared," she whispered, clenching the cell phone.

"I know."

"Talk to me. I need a distraction so I won't lose it in front of Colton. Why are you a 911 operator? What made you do this job?"

"I wanted to help people."

"Because you couldn't help your wife and son?"

"I guess. And because I couldn't do the job I was originally trained for."

"What was that?"

"I was a paramedic."

"Not too far of a stretch from that to what you're doing now." She massaged her icy fingers. "Why did you leave that job?"

"I didn't have a choice."

"You were fired? Why would they fire a good person like you?"

She heard a sigh. "I wasn't such a good person back then. I made some bad choices."

"What kind of choices?"

"I had a shoulder injury after a mountain rescue. My doctor prescribed some heavy-duty painkillers. After a while, they stopped working. Some nights the pain was unbearable, but I still had to do my job."

"Why didn't you take time off so you could heal?"

"We were short-staffed, and I couldn't afford to take time off."

"So you took prescription drugs? Why would that be a problem if a doctor prescribed them?"

"When the drugs stopped being effective in managing the pain, I tried to get a stronger prescription but was told I wouldn't be able to work if I took it."

"So you tried to ignore the pain?"

"I wish I had. No, I made a decision that has haunted me ever since."

"What decision?"

She heard him inhale deeply. "I took drugs from our paramedic supplies."

"And you became addicted," she guessed.

Marcus cleared his throat. "Yes."

"So they fired you."

"They called it a temporary suspension. Said I could find another job until I had kicked my habit. Then I could come back to EMS. Leo helped me get a job at the center."

She swallowed. "Did your wife know about the

addiction?"

"She suspected. But she never knew the extent of it. I tried to shelter her from that part of my life."

"When your wife and son were killed, were you—?"

"I was shooting up in a cabin in Cadomin."

There was such intense bitterness in his voice that she flinched at his words.

"I got out of the cabin as soon as I heard, but by the time I made it to the accident scene…*it was too late.*" The last four words came in a strained whisper.

A tear slid down her cheek and she left it there, soaking in the trickle of heat it emitted before it cooled.

"How did they die exactly?" As soon as the words left her mouth, she wished she could take them back.

"Jane's car hit a patch of ice on the highway and rolled into a ditch."

Something in his voice suggested he wasn't telling her everything. "Do you want to talk about it? I've got nothing better to do than listen."

"I'm not really supposed to be telling you my life story."

"I need a distraction, Marcus. I can't keep thinking about where I am, where my kids are. Talk to me. About anything."

"I took off on them," he began. "I was holed up in that cabin in the woods, near the bat cave. I convinced Jane that I needed some time to think, to clear my head. I insisted that I wanted a week of fishing, nothing more. But I lied. I went there with drugs. I planned to stay in a fog of oblivion."

"So did you?"

"For four days I was stoned out of my mind. I started imagining things, seeing things."

"What kind of things?"

"Children. In the woods around the cabin. They were wearing pajamas, even when it was freezing outside."

"Did they say anything to you?"

"Not at first. But they left me signs that they were there. Strange gifts on my doorstep."

Rebecca shivered. "And this was all imaginary?"

"Except for the gifts. They were real. Fruit, candy…I can't explain it."

"Maybe someone was playing a prank on you."

"I thought that too. So I asked the cabin owner if there were any kids in the area."

"What did she say?"

"She gave me a weird look, shook her head and walked away. I figured she knew I was on drugs. Probably thought I was hallucinating. I'm not sure I wasn't."

"So what did you do?"

"The next time I was in Hinton getting groceries, I hunted down a dealer in the park and bought two Vicodin tablets. To numb the weird visions, I told myself. Figured I'd be back to normal after that and wouldn't need anything else."

"But it didn't work," she guessed.

"Yeah. I kept seeing those children. Two days later, I bought a vial of heroin and a package of hypodermic needles from a kid in the park. I don't remember much. I spent two days lying on the couch in a dazed stupor. Then I got the call that Ryan and Jane had been in a car accident. I got into my car and drove. But I didn't get there in time."

"I'm so sorry, Marcus. I can tell you loved them very much."

"They were my world. Until drugs took over my life. They died because of me."

"It wasn't your fault," she argued.

"Yes it was. Jane was driving out to see me, probably to bring me home."

"Still…" She paused, searching for the right words. "It wasn't your fault. It was an *accident*. An awful twist of fate."

She heard more noises on the other end. Then a horn blared. *Since when did they have horns like that in an office building?* "Marcus, where are you?"

"I'm on the highway."

She was instantly filled with hope. "You're looking for us?"

"Yes."

She blinked back the tears. "I thought you were at the 911 center."

"I'm calling you from my cell phone, so just hit *redial* if you need to call me back."

"Don't you have others looking for us?"

"I'm going to be honest with you, Rebecca. We have too many rescue vehicles already in the field at other locations. When you called in, we were down to our last police car."

"No!" she cried out, then muffled a sob. "So other than one police car, no one else is looking for us?"

"I am." His voice was firm this time, full of resolve. "I'll be there soon. You have to hang up now. I'll call you in five minutes."

"You really are a superhero," she said with a whimper.

She disconnected the call and slipped the phone between her bra and her skin. "Colton? How are you doing back there?"

No answer.

She strained to listen and heard the familiar sounds of soft snoring. Colton was okay. It was probably better that he was sleeping. At least that way he wasn't feeling the cold.

Speaking of cold…

She wiggled her toes in her shoes. She could barely feel them, or the cheap leather of her last Payless splurge. But she did feel something. Water on her ankles.

The interior lights flickered on and off like a strobe light. She didn't want to think of what would happen once the lights turned off and they were plunged into complete darkness. The mere thought made her body quake.

Plucking the phone from her bra, she shone the light from it toward the floor. Murky brown water covered her ankles completely.

If she wasn't found soon, hypothermia would set in. If it hadn't already.

She thought about Colton. His leg was trapped, which meant his foot was sitting in freezing water too.

She shone her phone toward the back seat and angled the mirror so she could see him. He'd managed to find his hockey gear and had a sweatshirt draped across Ella. His leggings and other gear were piled on top of him, not much of a barrier to the cold.

"Oh, Colton…Ella…" she sobbed.

One of Colton's shoulder pads rolled off him and landed on the floor.

Marcus had made her promise to call if the water rose.

She pointed the soft light from her cell phone at the windshield, but could see nothing beyond the glass. Just black oblivion.

What if we're already underwater?

Bile rose in her throat, and she battled to keep it at bay. Her stomach clenched, then lurched. Grabbing the steering wheel for balance with her good hand, she leaned as far as she could toward the passenger seat and threw up. The smell was overwhelming, a combination of sourness and sulfur. Fear and death.

She opened her phone, saw Marcus's phone number and hit *call*.

Chapter Nineteen

Near Cadomin, AB – Sat., June 15, 2013 – 12:03 AM

It had been about twenty minutes since Marcus had left Edson and the rain had finally let up. But still no sign of Rebecca's Hyundai. He hadn't seen any fresh tracks leading to any of the side roads. Had he already passed the area where Rebecca had been forced from the highway?

He was about to turn around when a shiver slid over his body. All the hairs on his arms stood up. The sensation made him think of the cabin in Cadomin, the one he'd stayed in before Jane and Ryan's accident. The one with the ghostly children in the woods.

The headlights of his SUV swept over something in the middle of the road.

He slammed on the brakes. *Jane?*

He blinked, but the vision of his dead wife remained. She stood in the middle of the road, pointing ahead as if telling him to keep driving.

Then she vanished.

"Keep driving!" he snarled. He'd deal with Jane's ghost later.

The phone rang.

"Everything okay, Rebecca?"

"Yeah, if you call being trapped in a car in the river 'okay.'" There was a hint of dry humor in her voice, but worry quickly followed. "The water's rising, Marcus."

Shit! That was the last thing they needed. "Are you still moving?"

"Yeah, but not as much."

His bad feeling turned rancid. Rebecca had driven off the highway, into the trees, for God knows how long. There were a few lakes in the area, and the McLeod River with all its tributaries. The second attack from the mysterious truck driver could have pushed Rebecca's vehicle into the river.

"Are you sure you didn't see anything before you left the highway?" he asked. "Something in the woods or along the highway, maybe? I need to figure out where you went off the road."

"All I saw were trees. I'm not even sure I turned down an actual road. It could've been a damned footpath for all I know."

Marcus gazed out the window as his SUV sped down the highway, his eyes darting from side to side. There were numerous unpaved roads and dirt trails that led into the bushes on either side. This was quad country.

"What about Colton?" he said suddenly.

"He's sleeping." She sounded like she was on the brink of crying.

"Maybe he saw something. You were driving, trying to see the road ahead. Maybe he saw something you missed. Ask him."

"Colton?" she called, her voice stronger. "Wake up, honey. I have a question for you. Did you see anything when we went off the road?"

Marcus couldn't make out Colton's answer.

Seconds later, Rebecca came back on the line. "He

says he saw pigs. Flying pigs." She let out a sob. "Oh God, he's hallucinating. I think Colton's going into shock. I think you're too late."

"Don't say that. I'm still here, still looking."

"If you're too late, I want you to promise me something."

"Hey," he said, trying to sound jovial, "we're not doing this right now. None of this kind of talk."

"Marcus, listen to me. Please." He heard her inhale. "If we don't make it, I'd hate it if you blamed yourself. You've done everything anyone could ask for and more. Fate, remember?"

"Fate's a mean bastard," he said between gritted teeth.

"I agree. So promise me, no blame."

Marcus cursed under his breath and slammed a fist on the wheel. Then he took a deep breath. "I promise. No blame."

"My feet are so numb I can't feel my toes."

He could almost taste her fear. "Hold on, Rebecca. Hold on."

"I'm afraid to hang up. This might be my last call to you."

He barely heard her words as something flashed up ahead. A sign! One he'd forgotten about. And carved into wood was a picture of two robust pigs with wings.

"Oh my god," he said, elated. "Flying pigs."

"What?"

"I found the pigs, Rebecca. Colton wasn't hallucinating. It's a sign on the side of the road for a pig farm. It closed down a few years ago. I'm close."

A second later, Rebecca said, "Colton says he saw the pigs in the sky, above the trees. But that makes no sense if it's a sign on the side of the road." She was sobbing uncontrollably now.

"I think there's a sign on the building. That must be what he saw. Hold on."

A few yards ahead, Marcus spotted the dirt road that led to the pig farm. He'd been down that road before. With Jane. They used to buy meat here. If his recollection was accurate, the road wove down to the river and circled back to meet the highway about a mile south.

"I know where you left the highway," he said. "I can see the road."

"Hurry, Marcus! The water's up to my knees."

"Mom!" he heard Colton shout. "The car's filling up with water! We have to get out!"

"I know, honey, help's on the way," Rebecca cried. "Marcus! Help us!"

Deep ruts were carved into the mud ahead of him. Two sets of vehicle tracks—Rebecca's and a wide-based truck tire with heavy treads.

Marcus stomped on the gas pedal and sped down the road. He swerved, barely missing an uprooted tree that had fallen across the road. "I'm almost at the farm. I see your tire tracks. I'm almost there."

The SUV bumped and jerked as he whipped down the road at breakneck speed. "I see the farm!"

Above the building was a silver weathervane that was lit by a soft light. The flying pigs again.

"Flying pigs in the sky," he murmured. That's what Colton had seen.

"Can you see us?" Rebecca pleaded. "The water's halfway up my calves."

"I'm almost to the river."

On the other end he heard Colton crying. "Try to stay calm."

Rebecca's voice was thick with terror. "The water's coming in faster, Marcus."

The tree line broke, and the river appeared to his left, swirling and churning. But no car. He followed the road alongside the river as fast as he could, his tires bouncing in and out of mud-filled ruts. *Don't let me get stuck in the mud now!*

Though he wasn't sure he really believed in a God, he found himself praying desperately to a higher being. *Please let me get there in time. Please, God.*

He pressed the Bluetooth tightly to his ear. "Rebecca, I'm nearly there."

"I have to get out. I have to get my children out."

As Marcus rounded another corner, the headlights of his car swept along the side of the road, illuminating the river. Still nothing.

"Rebecca, honk your horn."

He rolled down the window and leaned out. In the distance he heard something. "Honk again!"

Then he heard it, clear as a bell. "You're up ahead."

"Really?" Rebecca cried. "Can you see us?"

The first things he saw were two pairs of muddy tracks that led toward the river. He slowed the SUV and noticed a small but sharp ridge of ground that lined the riverbank. A burly tree had a gouge on one side and what could only be red paint was scraped into the bark.

It only took him a second to put the pieces together. This was the spot where Rebecca's car had gotten hung up. It had been pushed up to the top of the ridge, where it had teetered, while rubbing against the tree that had blocked her door.

He maneuvered the SUV as close as possible so the headlights lit up the edge of the bank. This was where the truck had rammed her once more, sending her car shooting through the air toward the water.

"I should see you any minute now, Rebecca."

He parked and jumped out of his vehicle. With the cell phone tucked in his pocket and Bluetooth activated, he approached the edge. His flashlight swept over the area. There was about an eight-foot drop to the water, and to his right, concrete steps led down to a rugged wood dock that extended twenty feet into the river directly in front of him. Something at the end of the dock glowed with a soft light.

And there it was—Rebecca's car.

While attempting to escape the truck, she had driven toward the river, and the final impact of the truck had propelled her vehicle into the air. After a short flight, the Hyundai had landed midway on the dock, splintering some of the thick planks. It was now almost a quarter submerged, the front end lower than the back.

Damn it all to hell.

It wouldn't be long before the dock collapsed entirely and the car slid beneath the water. He was running out of time—and so were Rebecca and her kids.

"I see your car," he said, his heart sinking.

"You're here?"

"You should be able to see the light from my flashlight. Behind you." He waved.

"I see the light. Marcus, please hurry."

Lightning rippled in the night sky. Thunder boomed about ten seconds later.

"What was that?" she shouted.

"Another storm is moving in."

Last thing they needed was another downpour of rain. Water was now almost halfway up the driver's window on the outside.

He quickly explained where she was and how the dock was the only thing keeping them from going under. "The next part is going to be hard. You have to be extremely brave and do everything I tell you."

"I will. What do you need me to do?"

Opening the hatch of the SUV, he grabbed the rebreathers and the kit. "Tell Colton to move Ella into his lap. He has to keep her head up above the water."

He heard her repeat his words to Colton. "Good. Now listen carefully. The water pressure on the outside of your car makes it impossible to open the doors. So you're all going to have to escape through the windows."

"But the power isn't working. We can't roll them down."

"I'm going to break them. One at a time. Yours first."

"But won't that just make the car sink faster?"

He closed his eyes. "Yes, but you're already sinking, Rebecca."

"Oh God…"

"How high is the water on the inside?" he asked, checking the oxygen levels on the tanks. They were both full.

"Up to my waist." She said something to Colton. "Colton says the water's up to his knees. He has Ella, thank God. Colton, you have to prop Ella up. Keep her head above the water."

"I have to hang up," he said, "and when I do, I want you to call Leo at 911 and tell him we're at Angelo's Pork Farm. Can you do that?"

"Yes."

Marcus ensured the emergency flashlights were secured to the straps of the rebreathers. "I'm going to swim out to the car in a second."

"Hurry."

He dug around in the kit until he found a bright blue ResQMe keychain. The rescue tool was used by numerous emergency organizations for quick vehicle rescues, and even the public could buy them. One push on vehicle glass would release a spring-loaded spike that would shatter a side window. There was also a seat belt cutter concealed beneath the plastic clip.

He shoved the ResQMe into his jeans pocket. "Tell Leo I'm going in after you."

"How will you rescue all of us by yourself?"

"Can you all swim?"

"Yes. I made the kids take lessons."

"What about you?"

"I was a life guard when I was sixteen. But I'm wedged in pretty good."

Then he asked the one question that made his gut wrench. "How long can you hold your breath?"

"I don't know. A minute, maybe more. I've never timed myself." There was dread in her voice.

"What about Colton?" he asked.

"He can pick up a half-dozen weights from the bottom of the pool in one passing. That's probably more than a minute, right?"

"Probably." He strode to the edge of the river. "Okay…you're not far from shore. Maybe six yards. All you have to do is keep your mouths above the water until I get there."

"We'll do that."

"I have two rebreathers—small oxygen tanks. Each one is set up for two people, so we have enough air for everyone. Now listen. The water will submerge you first because of the angle of the car, so I'll give you the first tank. Then I'll move to the kids."

"What about Ella? She's still unconscious."

"She'll have a mask that'll cover her nose and mouth. All of us will. The kids will share one tank. We'll share the other. Once I get you out, we'll all swim to the surface together. I'll carry Ella. Make sure you tell Colton exactly what will happen and what I'll be doing."

"He's going to be terrified when the water comes in," she whispered.

"I know." He massaged his forehead. "I have to hang up now."

"Good-bye, Marcus."

"Remember to call Leo."

"I will."

"And remember to breathe, Rebecca."

After he pushed the disconnect button, he cried out, "Jane! Help me help them!" *Please let me reach them and get them out of the car in time.*

Chapter Twenty

Rebecca placed the call to Marcus's friend Leo.

"He's going to swim out to us," she said as she quickly explained their situation.

"Marcus is a good swimmer," Leo said. "He knows what to do. How high is the water inside your car?"

"Past my waist. My kids are in the back, where the water is lower."

"Hold on." A heartbeat later, Leo returned. "I have good news."

She blew out a breath. "I could use that right about now."

"We have an ambulance and two patrol cars on their way. They're fifteen minutes out."

"I doubt we have fifteen minutes."

"Stay calm. Help is on the way. And, Mrs. Kingston?"

"Yeah?"

"I'm praying for you and your kids."

"Thanks, Leo. We could use that too."

She disconnected the call, then looked over her shoulder and caught sight of her son's terrified expression. She gave Colton a shaky smile. "When Marcus breaks my window, I want you to grab your sister and hold your breath if the car fills up." The fear in her son's eyes nearly choked her, but she pressed on. "Marcus is going to rescue us. Understand?"

"Okay. I'll hold on to Ella, and I promise I won't let go of her."

"Marcus says we're really close to shore. Do you think you can swim with your sore leg?"

Colton nodded and swiped at the tears on his cheek.

The car shuddered, and they shrieked as they were jerked forward.

She took a deep breath. "The car's going to fill up with water really fast, Colton. You're going to have to hold your breath, but not for long. Marcus has oxygen tanks. You know, like scuba gear. He's going to give me the first tank as soon as the door opens. Then he'll give you and Ella one."

"Scuba tanks? Cool. What about you, Mom? You're stuck. How will you get out?"

"Don't worry about me. I'll take care of myself."

"And we have the superhero," Colton said with a wide grin.

"Yeah." She winced as a heat flared in her chest. "Just promise me you'll be brave."

"I promise."

"I love you, honey," she said, gulping back a sob.

"Love you too, Mom."

"I am so proud of you, Colton. You are so strong and—"

They were thrown into utter blackness.

Colton let out a screech. "Turn the lights back on!"

Rebecca slammed her hands against the dashboard controls. "Come on!" she cried between gritted teeth. "Turn back on!"

The lights blinked on, off, then on again.

She covered her mouth with one hand. She was

afraid to move or breathe. If she was this frightened of being left in the dark, she could only imagine her son's fear. *Get it together, Rebecca.*

"Colton, I'm going to give you my cell phone. If the lights go out, you can open it and turn it on. Okay? I'm going to have to throw it to you."

"I'll catch it." The brave resolve in his voice made her smile.

Turning, she stared into Colton's eyes. Her hand trembled as she gripped the phone. It had been her lifeline. Literally.

You can do this.

She tossed the cell phone and breathed a sigh of relief when he caught it.

"When we get out of here, maybe you should take up baseball," she said, trying to inject some humor into an otherwise bone-chilling situation.

"Can I call Dad?" Colton asked, his voice trembling.

"You can try."

She bit her bottom lip to keep from crying. There was no point in saving the battery power now. Colton needed to hear his father's voice. To say good-bye.

She gave her head a sharp shake. *No! We're going to survive.*

"Dad's not picking up," Colton said.

"Leave him a message." Her voice cracked on the last word.

There was silence in the back seat.

"Colton?"

"I hung up. I didn't know what to say."

"That's okay, honey. He knows you love him. And Daddy loves you."

Colton began sobbing.

"Please stop crying," she said, wishing she could hold him in her arms. "I know you're scared, honey. So am I. But we have to have faith. We have to believe that we'll be out of here soon."

"Do you really think so?"

"Yes, I do. Be brave, honey."

Hearing his sobs made her angry. Not at him, but at her own uselessness.

Seething with frustration, she grabbed the steering wheel and pushed it up with all her strength. With her children's faces in her mind, she attempted to wriggle free. But every movement sent severe knife-pains through her ribs.

Her eyes streamed with tears, and she was drained of all energy. As her emotions collapsed, she cried as inaudibly as possible so that Colton wouldn't hear. There was nothing more she could do except pray for a miracle.

Chapter Twenty-One

Another jagged flash of lightning streaked across the sky, and a sharp crack came about five seconds later.

"Damn," Marcus muttered. The storm was getting closer.

He opened the car door, ripped the Bluetooth off his ear and tossed it on the passenger seat next to his cell phone. Stripping off his shirt, he slung the straps from the tanks over his shoulder. With a flashlight in hand, he waded into the river. The water was frigid, but he pressed on. The ground sloped sharply. He dove in and swam toward the car. It took less than five minutes.

As he reached for the driver's door, the boards beneath the front end gave way and the car slid further into the river.

Shit!

He rapped the flashlight on the top of the car and heard a muted reply.

How much water is inside?

The door handle was out of reach, so he dove below. He didn't bother with the mask. This was a reconnaissance dive. Plus, he needed to conserve the air in his tank, in case he couldn't get Rebecca out right away and had to leave it with her.

The door didn't budge. He shone a flashlight into the window. The sharp angle of the car had forced Rebecca over the steering wheel.

"Hurry!" she mouthed.

He gave a nod, then swam to the surface and shone the light inside the rear window. Colton had pushed an unconscious Ella up onto the top of the back seat, against the rear window. The water was up to the boy's chest.

When Colton noticed the light, the terrified boy pressed his face against the window and screamed something. It was heartbreaking to witness.

Marcus gave Colton the OK signal, then held up a finger. *One minute, and I'll have you all out.* He prayed the boy would understand.

Correct timing was essential. Marcus knew he had to get the first tank to Rebecca as soon as he broke the window. They'd be holding their breath as the car filled. He'd have to open the back door, secure the kids' masks and get them to shore.

Then he'd go back for Rebecca.

The question was, could he get everyone out alive?

Chapter Twenty-Two

Near Cadomin, AB – Sat., June 15, 2013 – 12:15 AM

Rebecca let out a victorious whoop as soon as she spotted the faint light moving in the water toward them.

"Marcus is here. Outside the car." She turned her head and saw Ella lying on top of the back seat. "You are brilliant, my son. That's the perfect place for your sister."

The car jerked and shifted forward, and they each let out a scream.

"What's happening, Mom?" Colton cried.

"Just a bit of movement. Keep calm."

Rebecca knew what had happened. The car had moved further into the river.

Colton groaned.

"Are you all right, honey?"

"I'm almost out, Mom! The seat's moved forward. My leg's almost free."

"That's awesome, honey. Keep working at it. How's Ella doing?"

"She's breathing real loud."

"Give her another dose."

"I lost Puff," he said in a forlorn tone. "It's in the

water somewhere."

She took a fortifying breath, thinking of the backup inhaler that was locked in the glove compartment. "That's okay. Marcus is here now."

"I'm out!" Colton shouted seconds later.

When he half walked, half swam toward her, Rebecca held up a hand and shook her head. "No! Stay where you are. We don't want the car to shift any more than it has. Stay back and keep your head above the water. Ella's too."

"But what about you? Maybe I can get you out."

"No, honey. We have to trust Marcus. He'll know what to do."

Something banged against the car. Rebecca knocked on the window in response.

The light moved closer. Then she saw Marcus. His face was distorted from the dirty water and faint light, but she'd never felt so glad to see someone in all her life.

She released a heavy sigh. "Hurry!"

He swam toward the rear, and a minute later, he vanished.

"Help us!" Colton sobbed, banging on the window.

"Honey, I know you're scared, but we have to stay calm."

"I want out, Mommy! Get us out!"

"I know."

She cried openly now, rocking back and forth, hugging her chest. Her heart ached for her son, for Ella. *God, please…if you can't save all of us, save my children. Save Ella and Colton. Please…*

She couldn't imagine life without her babies. Couldn't contemplate never holding them again.

"What if we die here?" Colton asked.

The question sent icicles down her spine. "We're not going to die."

"But what if we drown?"

"Marcus won't let that happen."

She didn't know why she was relying so heavily on a stranger to save them, but there'd been something in Marcus's voice—something that made her feel calm, made her believe they would all come out of this nightmare, alive.

She glanced down at the steering wheel that immobilized her. *Or at least some of us will survive.*

With a high probability of internal damage and definite broken ribs, she doubted she'd have the strength to swim, much less get out of the car. Marcus would be busy with the kids. By the time he got them to shore and came back for her, she could be dead.

But Colton and Ella will be alive.

She smiled, imagining their lives as they grew. Would they be rebellious teenagers? Would Wesley be able to handle them? What would they do with their lives? What would they become?

The water had risen to her breasts. Though the majority of her body was numb with cold, she kept her hands above her head and flexed her icy fingers every now and then. Breathing hurt her ribs, and she tried to slow each uneven breath. A surge of nausea rippled through her body. Her vision swam in and out, and all the blinking in the world wouldn't bring things into focus.

Please, God, don't let me faint now.

But God wasn't listening.

Chapter Twenty-Three

Near Cadomin, AB – Sat., June 15, 2013 – 12:17 AM

With his mask in place, Marcus dove down alongside the car. He could see brownish light coming from the headlight. The interior lights were flicking on and off. Reaching the driver's side, he gripped the slim flashlight in one hand and waved it over the window.

Rebecca wasn't moving. She had passed out, her mouth an inch from the water.

He had to move fast.

He shone the light into the back seat and waved at Colton. The boy moved to the window and pounded on the glass. That's when Marcus noticed Colton was no longer trapped in the back. He was free.

Thank God for that!

Colton pointed at his sister, grinned back at Marcus and gave the thumbs-up. The kid was ready.

Now came the difficult part.

Marcus returned to the driver's window and pulled the ResQMe tool from his pocket. Holding it in one hand, he positioned the cutter in the middle of the window. He pushed down, feeling the hard spring within the device. A web of cracks appeared and water seeped inside the car.

A second later the window caved in from the pressure. He pushed the fragments of glass aside and shoved a tank through the hole. Securing the mask over Rebecca's mouth, he flushed the water from it, all the while trying to ignore the flailing movements in the back of the car and Colton's shrieks.

Hold on, Colton! I'm coming!

Marcus glanced toward the back seat and saw the children pressed up against the rear window where there was a small pocket of air. It would last maybe thirty seconds.

He moved to the back door. *Okay, here's where timing is everything.*

One quick snap of the ResQMe and the rear side window was shattered. He wedged his body inside the window to slow the water flow and so he could reach the children. With his added weight, the car slid further into the river. He took a deep breath, held it and removed his mask. With no time to waste, he slipped it over Ella's face and flushed it. Seconds later, river water filled the interior of the car and it sank, landing on the river floor with a soft thud.

Out of the corner of his eye, he saw Colton take one last breath of air. The boy grabbed his arm and pointed at his mouth, his eyes widening with alarm. Marcus fastened the secondary mask around the boy's head, pushed the flush button. A second later, Colton nodded and held up a thumb.

Brave boy.

In seconds he had the tank strapped to the boy's back. But now Marcus needed air. Moving to the front of the car, he wedged his body between the driver and passenger seat, then secured the secondary mask from Rebecca's tank over his face. Gulping in a few breaths of air, he examined Rebecca. She was still unconscious, her hair drifting like strands of seaweed around her face. He felt her chest. Her breathing was spasmodic. Not a good sign.

He looked over his shoulder at her children. They were sitting in the back seat. Colton had strapped them in, to keep them from floating up against the ceiling of the car. The boy didn't realize how dangerous his actions were. The seat belt could jam.

Marcus felt for the ResQMe tool in his pocket. He still had it. Worst-case scenario, he'd cut the belt from the kids.

Evaluating the situation, he realized there was only one thing he could do. He had to get the kids to safety and come back for Rebecca afterward. What alarmed him was the possibility that Rebecca would regain consciousness and discover her kids were gone. If she panicked, she could do serious damage to herself, especially if a broken rib had pierced her lung, as he suspected.

He took a deep breath, held it, then removed the mask and moved to the kids. The seat belt released easily, and he pulled Colton and Ella toward him. He pointed out the door and started outside, but Colton tugged on his hand and pointed to his mother.

Marcus shook his head and pointed up. Then he dragged both kids out the door and started swimming to the surface. With Ella tucked under his arm, he held on to Colton and used the opposite hand to pull them upward.

It took a few strokes and they broke the surface.

Colton ripped off his mask. Panting, he cried out, "You have to go back for my mom."

Marcus removed his mask. "I will. As soon as I get you to shore."

"I can take Ella back."

Marcus shook his head. "Sorry, son, but I'm taking you to shore first. Your mom would never forgive me.

Now swim!"

It seemed to take forever before they reached the shallows. Colton removed the tank, handed it to Marcus and raced for the shore. Marcus followed closely behind, swinging Ella into his arms. When they reached the car, he set her down in the back seat and removed her mask. He felt for her pulse. It was faint but regular.

"Get in," he said to Colton.

The boy climbed in beside his sister. He was shivering violently, and Marcus turned on the engine and cranked up the heat. Retrieving two emergency blankets from the kit, he draped them around both children.

"Colton, stay here with your sister. Do not move! Got it?"

"Got it." The boy's teeth were chattering.

Marcus reached for his cell phone on the dash. "Here's my phone. Call 911 and ask for Leo. Tell him you and Ella are safe, but we need an ambulance."

Colton nodded.

Marcus ruffled the boy's wet hair. "I'm going back for your mom now."

Tears flowed down the boy's cheeks. "She said you would save us."

As he ran toward the river, Marcus hoped to God he wasn't too late.

Chapter Twenty-Four

Near Cadomin, AB – Sat., June 15, 2013 – 12:20 AM

Rebecca felt an unusual pressure on her face. Fighting waves of dizziness, she opened her eyes and blinked twice. Her surroundings were hazy.

Where am I?

She reached up to wipe her eyes, but her hand floated in slow motion, then connected with something hard. Her fingers grazed the object, tracing its outline.

A mask.

That's when her memories came rushing back. *I'm in the car. We're in the river, underwater. Oh God... Ella and Colton.*

She blew out a breath and twisted in her seat. The back of the car was empty. Fear slithered up her throat, and her heart thudded in her chest. She tamped down her horror when she noticed the back car door was open.

And you have an oxygen mask on. Marcus! He has the kids.

The interior light dimmed and was extinguished. Blackness swallowed her.

She felt the cold tank beside her. Marcus had jammed it between the seats. She ran her fingers over the straps and discovered something long and sleek attached to it. A flashlight.

Carefully, she pulled it toward her and turned it on. She groaned with relief. That transitory gloom of darkness had made her feel she'd been buried alive.

Stay calm. He's coming back for you.

All she could do was listen to the sound of her breathing, as erratic as it was.

She'd never been so cold in all her life—not even the time Wesley had taken her skiing in Whistler, BC, and she'd landed in a snow bank at the bottom of the bunny hill. She'd told him she couldn't ski, but he'd made it sound so damned easy. She recalled how they'd gone back to the resort afterward and she'd soaked in the hot tub for over an hour to get the chill out of her bones.

I'll need more than an hour in a hot tub now.

She coughed and cried out in misery. Where was Marcus?

She aimed the flashlight out the broken window. Nothing moved.

It was getting harder to breathe. *Is the tank out of oxygen?*

She shone the light on the tank. The meter showed a nearly full tank. So then why was it so hard to breathe? Was she having a panic attack?

Something caught her eye. A sparkle in the water.

Marcus was coming for her.

She let out a wheezy cough and tried to catch her breath. A viselike undulation wove around her chest and ribs, squeezing her as though she'd been gripped by a monstrous boa constrictor. It wrung each breath from her body and left her gasping for air and shuddering with nausea.

She dropped the flashlight.

Whipping her head around, she searched for Marcus. His light beamed closer. He was almost there.

Another minute maybe. She could hold on that long. She had to.

Seconds ticked by with a merciless slowness.

Then she saw him.

Marcus swam to the window and motioned with his flashlight and a small tool toward her seat belt. She nodded and pointed to her mask, hoping he'd decipher that she was having trouble breathing. The look he gave her made her realize he knew exactly the danger she was in.

He tugged on the car door. Once it was open, he sliced through the belt and eased it from her body. He jiggled the side lever for the seat, but nothing moved. Then he reached under her legs for the lever that would push her seat back.

She closed her eyes and tried not to think about the pain. She focused on Colton and Ella instead. They were safe. Maybe in the ambulance. They'd be warmed up and cared for, and that's all that mattered.

She felt a small *pop* near her ribs. When she opened her eyes and glanced down, she realized Marcus had slid her seat back. She was free.

He wrestled the tank from between the seats. Sliding his arm through the strap, he anchored her tank next to his. Then he reached for her. She put her arms around his neck, clinging to him and crying as he pulled her from the car. With one arm around her waist, he dragged her through the murky water.

When they reached the surface, her eyes were drawn to multiple beams of bright light coming from the shore. Headlights. An ambulance and two police cars, lights flashing on all three, were parked next to a car. And all headlights pointed toward the river.

Treading water, Marcus removed his mask, then hers.

"The ambulance is here," he said, his voice filled with relief.

"Yeah, your friend Leo said to tell you it's on its way. I would have called you to tell you, but you were already in the water."

He gave her a radiant smile. "Let's get you to shore, Rebecca Kingston. Your kids are waiting for you."

Chapter Twenty-Five

Near Cadomin, AB Sat., June 15, 2013 – 12:32 AM

Accompanied by a flash of lightning and the crash of thunder, Marcus carried Rebecca from the river. He was greeted by Ashton Campbell and Gabbie Gros, two paramedics he'd known from his days in the field.

"Hey, Ash," Marcus called out.

"What've you got?"

"She's got at least one broken rib." Marcus set Rebecca on the gurney.

The paramedics flew into immediate action, checking her vitals and assessing her injuries before wrapping an emergency blanket around her. Gabbie gave a blanket to Marcus too, and he draped it over his shoulders, shivering as his body fought to regain some warmth.

"My kids," Rebecca murmured, her eyes delirious.

"Your daughter suffered an acute asthma attack," Gabbie said. "We gave her oral prednisolone, oxygen and nebulized salbutamol."

"Is she stable?" Marcus asked.

Gabbie nodded. "She's out of danger. We have her and her brother on oxygen. Minor hypothermia." She patted Rebecca's arm. "And your son's leg is sprained but no break. Other than that, there's nothing to worry about. Your children will be fine."

"You're the one we need to worry about now, Mrs. Kingston," Ashton said as they moved the gurney into the ambulance. "Marcus, we have to get moving. The storm is picking up, and we need to get her to the hospital."

"Which hospital?"

"Hinton. Edson doesn't have any beds. Cutbacks."

Ashton motioned for Marcus to step aside.

"Wait!" Rebecca said, gripping Marcus's arm. "You have to come with us. You saved us."

"I can't go in the ambulance. It's not protocol." Even as he said this, Marcus counted all the rules of protocol he'd already broken. *There'll be hell to pay later.*

"I'll meet you at the hospital," he said. "I promise."

Inside the ambulance, Ella and Colton lay side by side on a second gurney. With blankets piled high, their small faces were barely visible.

Colton raised a hand and waved. "You *are* a superhero."

Marcus waved back. "Take care, buddy. I'll see you at the hospital."

"Taylor!" someone called out.

Marcus spun around. John Zur stood a few yards away, and the detective didn't look very happy.

"Shit," Marcus muttered beneath his breath.

He walked toward Zur, thinking of all the excuses he could use for his blatant disrespect for the rules. But there was just one excuse he could think of that made any sense. Rebecca and her kids had needed someone to help them, and Marcus had been the only "someone" available.

Zur studied him, seconds extending into minutes. "So what happened, Marcus?"

"You can see what happened, John." *I saved a woman and her kids. They're alive because of me. I didn't let them die like Jane and Ryan.*

When Zur was finished lecturing him, Marcus glanced at his watch. 12:39. He couldn't believe how his life had changed in the past twenty-four hours.

"Marcus!"

He returned to the ambulance. Inside, Rebecca was arguing with Ashton and Gabbie.

"Hey, don't give them such a hard time," he said with mock sternness. "You need to let them take care of you."

"I needed to speak with you," she said, lying back down.

"I'll see you at the hospital. We can talk all you want then."

She peered up at him, then smiled. "Your voice fits your looks."

"What?"

"You look exactly as I pictured you."

"What, soaking wet, shivering and chattering teeth? That's what you pictured?" He laughed.

"You look like a decent man. A bit on the rugged side."

The smile she gave him sent intense heat through his body. "Gee, I'm not sure if that's a good thing or not."

"It's a good thing," she said. "On the phone your voice made me think of Russell Crowe."

He batted a hand in the air. "Nah. I've been told I look more like Gerard Butler. *Before* he started working out."

She laughed. "You're not in that bad of shape. Otherwise you wouldn't have been able to do what you did tonight."

"Well, you're even prettier than I pictured you. Even if you are sopping wet and your hair is scraggly."

She touched her hair. "I'm not at my best, am I?"

He grinned. "Guess I'll have to wait and see how you clean up. Now go."

As he turned away, she shouted, "One more thing."

"What's that?" he asked, peering over his shoulder.

"Thank you! For finding us."

"You're welcome. Now lie down."

"Yes, sir."

"Hey, Marcus!" Gabbie called out.

"Yeah?"

"We miss you. When are you coming back?"

"I don't think I am. My paramedic days are over." And for once, he was okay with that thought.

"Get some rest," he called to Rebecca. "Your kids need you to be okay." So did he.

He watched as Gabbie and Ashton closed the doors, and the ambulance took off down the road. Zur and the other patrolman followed in their respective vehicles, lights flashing, no sirens.

Marcus climbed into his car. First, he took in a long gulp of air, releasing it slowly. Then he stared out the window at the river, trying to extinguish the images of a terrified boy trapped underwater. Colton had more strength than he knew. And Rebecca? She was a fighter too.

He glanced into the rearview mirror. A face stared back at him.

Jane.

For some reason, he wasn't surprised to see her, even though the rational side of his brain said it was impossible. He was afraid to turn around, in case she vanished. "Hi, Elf."

She smiled. "You did it. You saved them."

His shoulders quivered as he began to sob. "I'm sorry I didn't save you and Ryan." He covered his face with his hands.

"I know you are."

"I can't handle the accusation in your eyes. Or knowing you feel I failed you both."

Jane's expression was filled with love. "Marcus, don't you know I would never accuse you of that. Look at me."

He raised his gaze back to the mirror.

"What do you see there?" she asked.

What he saw made his heart lurch. Love, forgiveness, acceptance—they were all there in her eyes.

"I want you back," he whispered hoarsely. "Both of you. I miss you so much, Jane."

She looked stunningly beautiful, her hair glistening, her skin flushed with color and…life?

"We miss you too." She leaned forward, and her cool hand stroked his cheek. "But it's time for you to move on."

He kissed her fingertips. "I love you, Jane."

"I know."

"I'll never forget you."

"I know that too."

He stared into the mirror, willing her to stay.

"Remember what you always used to tell me after you came home from a really brutal day?" she asked.

He shook his head.

Jane smiled again. "You said, 'life is for the living.' And it is. You have a lot to live for. You're a good man with a good heart. People need you. Especially now."

"No one needs me."

"She does. And her kids."

"Rebecca needs *me*—another addict in her life? No, I doubt that very much."

Jane nodded. "She still needs rescuing."

"What do you mean? She's safe now."

"Someone tried to kill Rebecca and her kids. Someone ran her of the road intentionally." She paused and stared deep into his eyes. "You *know* what that means."

Did he?

"Shit!" he said. "They're going to try again."

Marcus shoved the car into reverse and spun it around, heading for the road. Thunder cracked nearby, and he felt the earth quiver beneath the car.

Time to get the hell out of here.

A quick look in the mirror convinced him that his passenger was gone. He'd deal with his apparent mental break later. Right now he had to get to the hospital.

As he sped down the rough road, he searched the seat next to him for his phone. Where the hell was it? Last time he had it was when…

I gave it to Colton.

He slapped the steering wheel. "Shit! Shit! *Shit!*"

Once reporters picked up the story, whoever wanted her dead would know he'd failed. And Marcus bet ten-to-one the guy would be back to finish the job. Rebecca would need a guard on her door. The kids too. If he hadn't lost his cell phone, he could've called Zur and warned him. But Zur knew the driver had come back. He'd know Rebecca was still in danger.

Wouldn't he?

Chapter Twenty-Six

Near Hinton, AB - Saturday, June 15, 2013 -12:48 AM

In the ambulance, Rebecca turned her head and watched her children sleep.

"They'll be fine, Mrs. Kingston," the female paramedic said.

"What's your name?"

"Gabrielle. Gabbie." The woman jerked her head toward the other paramedic. "That's Ashton."

Rebecca smiled. "You have kids, Gabbie?"

The woman nodded. "One."

"I almost lost mine tonight."

"But you didn't."

"No." *Thanks to Marcus.*

"We'll be at the hospital in about an hour," Ashton said. "Try to get some rest."

"Easier said than done," she muttered.

Truth was, she was afraid to fall asleep. Afraid this was all a dream and she'd wake up and find herself still trapped underwater in the car. The thought made her muscles compress, and she struggled to take a breath.

Breathe…

Rebecca had no idea how long they'd been driving, but at least now she could feel her feet again. She was also so warm that she had started to sweat, but the paramedics didn't want her to remove the blanket.

She reached out and touched Colton's hand. It was warm now. He looked so small and vulnerable with the oxygen mask over his face. Ella too.

"We're almost there," Ashton said. "Let us know if you feel any discomfort."

She nodded. "I'm fine."

"Are you okay to talk?" Gabbie asked, picking up a clipboard and pen.

"Yes."

"Detective Zur asked us to take down a quick report while we're en route to the hospital, providing you're up to it. Is that okay?"

"Yes."

"Do you remember anything that you haven't told the police?"

Rebecca shook her head. "No."

"And you don't know anyone who owns a truck like the one that hit you."

"No."

"Anyone have a grudge against you? Former friend, coworker…lover, maybe."

Rebecca blushed. "Not that I know of. And to clarify, I don't have a former lover. I've been with Wesley for years. And only him."

Gabbie's brow arched. "You told Detective Zur you were sure your husband had nothing to do with the attempt on your lives, yet medical records show you've had a number of injuries that are conclusive with abuse."

"The detective knows about this. I told him. It's one of the reasons I'm getting a divorce. The main reason. Yes, he has hurt me in the past, but Wesley is not the kind of person to outright murder someone."

Gabbie and Ashton exchanged skeptical glances.

"I'm telling you," Rebecca said, "he would never try to kill me and his children. He loves Ella and Colton."

"He know you were going away with them?" Ashton asked.

She blinked, trying to remember her conversation with Wesley. Dread washed over her. "Well, no, not exactly. He knew I was going away. The kids were supposed to be with..." Her voice trailed away. *No! It couldn't be Wesley!*

Was she in denial? Could Wesley have orchestrated the murder attempt? Was he really that eager to be rid of her?

Gabbie checked her pulse. "Supposed to be where, Mrs. Kingston?"

"With my sister."

Wesley had known she'd planned to go away and the kids were supposed to stay with Kelly.

"You and your ex fight recently?" Gabbie asked.

"Not really."

Rebecca thought about the missing money. Wesley was a gambler, an out-of-control, desperate addict.

And desperate people do desperate things.

"What is it, Mrs. Kingston?" Gabbie asked.

"I...he...he needed money. He always...needs money. He...gambles."

The ambulance hit a pothole, and she was overcome by a fit of coughing. When it subsided, she said, "It's getting harder...for me...to breathe."

"We need to give you more oxygen," Ashton said.

As he set a mask over Rebecca's nose and mouth, another episode of lightheadedness surged over her. "Don't...let me...drown."

The paramedic's face swam into view. "Her lung's collapsed."

"Hold on, Mrs. Kingston," Gabbie said, her face fading in and out.

More words drifted by. *"Pneumothorax...chest tube..."*

In a blink, the lights went out.

Chapter Twenty-Seven

Hinton, AB – Saturday, June 15, 2013 – 2:10 AM

Marcus parked close to the emergency entrance of the hospital. He noted the two patrol cars nearby. Both were empty.

That's a good sign. They must be inside.

He strode through the doors and made his way to the intake desk.

"Fill out this form and take a seat in the waiting room," the receptionist said without looking up.

"I'm not a patient," he said. "An ambulance brought in a mother and her two kids. I need to know where they were taken."

The woman scrunched her face and peered over wire-rimmed glasses. "And you are?"

"Marcus Taylor. The guy that pulled them out of the river."

"One moment, please." The woman picked up the phone, dialed, said something into the receiver, then hung up. "The boy and girl are on the third floor, room 312."

"And their mother?"

"She's in surgery. Collapsed lung."

"Damn it."

"Mr. Taylor, the police are with the children. They want to talk to you."

"Detective John Zur?"

The receptionist nodded. "And another officer."

Marcus sprinted to the main elevators. He stabbed the button, watched the numbers slowly tick down from *4* to *3*. It stopped at *2*. With a frustrated groan, he spun on one heel and headed for the stairs. He took them two at a time.

On the third floor, he followed the signs to room 312.

A police officer stood guard outside the room. Another good sign.

Marcus flashed his ID at the man. "Marcus Taylor. I work at the 911 center in Edson. I found the mother and kids."

The officer nodded and opened the door. "They're waiting for you."

The first thing Marcus saw was two kids propped up against starched white pillows in the beds. Both were grinning, their faces flushed and healthy.

When Colton saw him, the boy's face lit up like it was Christmas. "It's Marcus!" he said to his sister.

Marcus moved toward the beds. "Hey, you two. Enjoying the hospital food, I see."

"The nurse gave us green Jell-O," little Ella said.

Even though he'd only seen her briefly in the ambulance and had spent a small amount of time with Rebecca, he could tell Ella was the spitting image of her mother—all blonde hair, blue eyes and pretty face.

John Zur was seated in a chair next to Colton's bed. "They're both doing fine, Marcus. They've polished off a plate of chicken and fries." He let out a short grunt. "And they've been talking my ears off about some *superhero* dude who saved them. Don't suppose you know anything about that, do you?"

Marcus grimaced. "I didn't see anyone in tights and a cape."

"We meant *you*," Colton said, laughing.

"Yeah, thanks, buddy." Marcus ruffled the boy's hair. It was dry this time. "Listen, I have to talk to Detective Zur. We'll be right outside in the hall."

After he closed the door, Marcus nodded at the guard, then turned to Zur. "We have a problem, John."

"You mean the driver?"

"Exactly. It's unlikely this was a random hit and run. On the way here I realized that whoever wants Rebecca dead isn't going to be happy when he discovers he failed."

"And he'll most likely try again," Zur said with a nod. "I thought the same thing. We'll keep a guard on her room once she's out of surgery."

"Hear anything about that?"

"They said it'll be a few hours. Meanwhile, I've been questioning the kids. The daughter doesn't remember much."

"She had an asthma attack and was unconscious for the whole ordeal." Marcus shook his head. "Probably a good thing. Did Colton recall anything?"

"Nothing other than those flying pigs." Zur let out a chuckle. "Angelo's Pork Farm?"

"Angelo Pucelli. Guess he thought he was an angel—hence, the logo. Moved to Calgary about seven years ago, after his wife was diagnosed with leukemia."

"The place has been closed since then?"

"Yeah." He stared Zur in the eye. "Jane and I used to go there."

"Weird coincidence."

Marcus thought of Jane's ghost in the back seat of his car. "You don't know the half of it."

"Why, what's going on?"

"I'll tell you later maybe. It doesn't really relate to

this case." He leaned against the wall and peered down the hallway, looking for anyone who seemed suspicious. "You think he'll be stupid enough to come here?"

"Maybe. Rebecca's going to be here for a few days, recovering."

"What about the kids? And their father?"

"We contacted the RCMP in Fort McMurray, where her husband allegedly went to find a job. They're looking for him."

"You think it's the ex?"

"Usually is. But he's a sick bastard if he's willing to kill his kids too."

"Rebecca said that was a last-minute decision. Her sister was supposed to look after them so she could go away on her own. That's what she told the ex."

"So he thought she was alone?"

"Yeah, but the sister bailed, and Rebecca took Colton and Ella with her. Very last-minute. Wesley Kingston didn't know."

"He's looking more and more like our number-one suspect."

"You going to arrest him?"

"There's not enough evidence against him. We *will* bring him in for questioning though." Zur's cell phone buzzed. "Yeah…okay…tonight? No problem…thanks."

After Zur hung up, Marcus said, "They find Wesley Kingston?"

"Yeah. Exactly where he said he'd be. He was in interviews earlier, then went to a bar. Left his phone at the hotel. He's driving back. He'll be here in about eight hours."

"I'd like to be there when you interview him."

"Marcus…"

"Please, John. I want to hear what he has to say. You do all the asking. I'll keep my mouth shut."

Zur grunted. "Is that even possible?"

"Ha ha."

An attractive doctor in her forties approached. "Are you Mr. Kingston?

Marcus shook his head. "He's about eight hours away."

The doctor paused with one hand on the door. "Are you a detective?"

"Superhero."

"He's the guy that rescued them," Zur said. "The kids are calling him a superhero, and now he thinks he can fly."

The doctor smiled. "They've got drugs for that."

Marcus gave Zur an exaggerated grimace, but said nothing. The woman didn't know he was a recovering addict.

"Any word on the mom?" Zur asked the doctor.

"Last thing I heard, all was going well. The surgery could take two to six hours." She cracked open the door, then looked over her shoulder. "We're moving the patient in the room next door. We'll put the mom there so she can be close to her kids."

Zur gave a nod. "We'll have guards on both doors."

"Thank you," Marcus added.

She went into the room and the door swung shut. Marcus stared at it and chewed his bottom lip.

"Dr. Burns has already been checked out," Zur said. "As have the day nurse, the night nurse and Dr. Monroe, the surgeon operating on Mrs. Kingston."

"I figured as much."

"Then why do you look so worried?"

"Some guy's got it in for Rebecca and her kids. And she's in surgery fighting for her life yet again. Why shouldn't I be worried?"

"She'll be fine, Marcus."

"I sure hope so."

"Make sure this guy gets in to see Rebecca Kingston once she's out of surgery," Zur said to the guard. "Access to both rooms, anytime." He smiled at Marcus. "Now go visit the kids."

"Thanks, John."

"You might regret those words." Zur cocked his head toward the door. "Those two are hyped up on chocolate pudding and Jell-O. Have fun. I have to check in at the station and file my initial report. I'll be back later to check on everyone."

"See you."

"Oh, I almost forgot." Zur hunted around in his jacket pocket. "The boy gave me your cell phone. Said you lent it to him."

"Yeah." Marcus tucked the cell phone into his back pocket. "Thanks."

"That's a really nice picture of Jane and Ryan."

It took a second for Marcus to realize what he meant. "The screen saver."

Zur nodded, then gave a quick wave and vanished down the hallway.

Marcus waited for the doctor to leave before he entered the room. Inside, he was greeted by wide smiles and giggles.

"What are you two up to?" he asked, suspicious.

"Dr. Burns said we get to have more pudding after supper," Ella said.

Marcus laughed. "She did, did she? Lucky you."

"When's Mom going to be here?" Colton asked.

"What did Dr. Burns say?"

"She said Mom had to have an operation." The boy stared up at Marcus, while nervously plucking the blanket. "Is she going to be all right?"

"Definitely. She's a tough one, your mom."

"Will you wait here until she comes?"

Marcus nodded. "Got nowhere better to be. Besides, I wanted to ask you some questions."

"Aw," Colton groaned. "I already told that police

guy everything I remember."

"Sometimes memories are sneaky things." Marcus made a face and curled his hands into claws. "They hide out of sight. Until something makes them come out." He moved closer to the beds, and the kids shrieked with laughter.

He grinned, hoping no one would come and tell them to quiet down. There was nothing better than the sound of laughing children. God, how he missed that sound.

He perched on the side of Colton's bed. "So tell me, were you excited to go on this trip with your mom?"

Colton shook his head. "Not at first. We were supposed to stay at Auntie Kelly's, but my cousins got sick." He grinned. "I was happy about that. Not that they were sick, but that we didn't have to go there."

"You don't like staying at your Auntie Kelly's?"

"Colton doesn't like playing with babies," Ella interrupted. "But I do."

"Babies can be fun," Marcus said, ignoring the sneer that crossed Colton's face. "But maybe not for Colton. You like doing other things. Guy things, right?"

"Yup," Colton said with a nod. "I wanted to go to see the bat cave at Cadomin."

"So when your mom said you got to go, you were happy."

Another nod.

"Did you tell your dad where you were going?"

"I tried calling him when we were in the car." His mouth quivered. "Underwater. But he didn't answer."

"So you never let him know you were going to Cadomin."

"No."

"When you were driving, did you see anything strange?"

"Those flying pigs."

Marcs laughed. "You've got good eyesight, kid.

That's how I knew where you were." He patted the boy's arm. "When you were driving, did you stop anywhere?"

"At a gas station."

"And you all went to the bathroom there?"

"Yeah."

"Was the door unlocked?"

"We went inside for the key," Ella cut in.

"Did either of you see or talk to anyone inside?"

"No," they said.

"Did you see anyone outside?

Ella shook her head. So did Colton, but then he crooked his head to one side as if he were thinking.

"What?" Marcus prodded.

"When my mom was getting the key for the bathroom, I saw a man outside."

"What was he doing?"

"Watching me. Like he thought I was gonna steal something."

"Did you tell your mom about the man?"

Colton shook his head. "I didn't want *her* to think I was gonna steal something."

"Did you tell Detective Zur about the man?"

"No. I forgot until now."

"What did the man look like?"

Colton shrugged. "I guess he looked like a normal guy."

"What color hair did he have?"

"Don't know."

The boy's fingers gripped the sheets so tensely that Marcus knew he'd get nothing out of him if he remained this tense. He needed to lighten the mood.

"Okay…did the man have clothes on, or was he naked?"

The boy's eyes widened and he let out a snort. "Clothes on, silly."

"Did he have pants on, or a skirt?

Ella giggled. "A skirt."

Colton shook his head. "Pants. Jeans. Really old and dirty ones, like my dad's work jeans for when he fixes the car."

Marcus nodded. "Now we're getting somewhere. Do you remember what color his jacket was?"

"He wasn't wearing one. He had a T-shirt on."

"A plain one, or did it have words or a design?"

"Both." Colton scrunched his eyes, trying to remember. "It had…a car on it. And maybe a street name…I think." His eyes flared open. "And he had a baseball cap on. Edmonton Oilers. That's why I couldn't see his hair." His voice grew excited. "Did I do a good job remembering?"

"Excellent job. Did you tell the detective all this?"

"I just remembered now, except for the jeans."

Marcus took out his cell phone and called Zur. He relayed the info about the man at the gas station. "Oiler's cap, old, dirty jeans and a T-shirt with a car and a street name on it."

"I'll get one of our guy's on it," Zur said. "We'll bring in some photos of T-shirt logos later tonight. Maybe we'll get lucky and someone else saw this guy."

"What about a security camera? Does the gas station have one?"

"Yeah, we had a tech guy on it already. We did see one guy near the door when Mrs. Kingston and her kids went inside. But we couldn't identify him."

"What about his vehicle?"

"He parked out of view of the cameras."

"Shit." Marcus gazed at the kids, who were smirking at him. "I mean, shoot."

"You said a bad word," Ella mumbled as soon as he hung up.

"Yeah, I did. Sorry."

"That's okay," Colton said. He lowered his voice so Ella couldn't hear him. "My dad says the F-word sometimes."

Marcus didn't know what to say to that.

Chapter Twenty-Eight

Hinton, AB – Saturday, June 15, 2013 – 6:46 AM

When Rebecca opened her eyes, the early morning sun lit her hospital room with an orange glow. She didn't have a clue what time it was, but she realized where she was—and why.

Her head swam as she tried to move it.

Someone patted her hand. A young nurse. "Everything's okay, Mrs. Kingston. Your surgery went well, and your kids are right next door."

"Can I see them?" Rebecca rasped.

"Dr. Monroe wants you to rest awhile first. You don't want your kids to see you all groggy, do you?"

"No, I guess not."

"Besides," the nurse said, moving to the door. "You have another visitor. Are you up for it?"

"Who is it?"

"A man. Police maybe. Sorry, I didn't get his name. Should I go ask?"

"That's okay. Let him in."

Rebecca licked her lips. Her mouth was dry and her throat hurt. But the pressure she'd felt around her ribs and chest was gone.

She lifted the covers.

"I think everything's where it's supposed to be," someone said.

She dropped the sheets and saw a man standing in the doorway. His face was grizzled but attractive, and his pale gray-blue eyes twinkled.

She blinked. "Marcus, I can't believe you're still here. I figured you'd gone home."

"And miss this happy reunion? Not likely." He crossed the room and stood by the bed. "I promised to meet you here, and I'm a man of my word."

"Yes, you are. But I didn't expect you to wait here for hours."

He shrugged. "Who said I did? Maybe I went out for dinner, or went shopping."

She chuckled. "The doctor said there was a man pestering everyone for status updates on me every fifteen minutes, while I was in the operating room. I know that wasn't Wesley."

"How are you feeling?"

"Like I was run off the road by a maniac."

Marcus's face drooped.

"Sorry. Bad joke." She gingerly touched her stomach. "I'm pretty banged up."

"That's what you get for driving into a river."

She tried to smile, but it made her head hurt. "Wasn't exactly done on purpose."

"I know." He studied the soft contours of her face. "You do clean up well."

"That's good to know. So do you."

He offered her the glass of water that was beside her bed, and she took a sip before saying, "How are my kids?"

Marcus pulled a chair to the side of her bed and sat down. "Your son and daughter are enjoying their sugar high at Hotel Hinton."

She frowned, then realized he meant the hospital. "I hope they're behaving."

"They're fine. Right now they're watching *Shrek*." He paused for a minute. "I hope that's all right."

"Yeah."

She couldn't take her eyes off his face. This was the man who had saved her. And her children. Those eyes and smile belonged to the man who had talked to her when she wanted nothing more than to scream and cry. He'd kept her sane when her world was pure insanity.

"Uh, do I have pudding on my face?" he asked.

She smiled. "Sorry for staring. It's just that you…" She didn't know what to say next.

"I know. You're trying to figure out how a guy with such a sexy voice like mine could look like this." He rubbed his bristly chin.

She held back a laugh. "Not exactly what I was thinking. But yeah, you could use a shave."

Marcus shrugged. "I've been a little busy. You know, being a superhero and all." He leaned back in the chair and stretched his legs beneath her bed.

"Wow. You're quite modest."

He grinned. "I'm repeating what you called me."

The man was more than charming. He was flirting with her. She couldn't recall the last time a man had done that. It felt kind of good.

"Feel up to talking about the truck?" he asked.

"I see. First you get me all comfortable and unsuspecting, and then you bring on the questions."

"Sorry. It can wait."

"I was teasing." She released a long sigh, then added, "I didn't see much. A truck with those hunting lights. The truck was a dark color. That's all I remember."

"And Wesley doesn't own a truck like that."

She eyed him. "No. And he'd never hurt his kids." She could tell when he squinted down at the floor that he

Cheryl Kaye Tardif | 207

didn't believe her. "He wouldn't, Marcus."

"Colton saw a man outside the gas station when you stopped."

"Really? I didn't see anyone."

"You were busy getting the key. The guy wore an Oilers cap, a T-shirt with a car on it and dirty jeans."

She shut her eyes, willing herself to remember. "I didn't see him."

"You said you saw a couple of cars and a truck in the parking lot. Where were they exactly?"

Opening her eyes, she nodded. "The cars were near the pumps. The truck was…" She sucked in a sharp breath.

Marcus jumped to his feet. "Are you okay? Want me to call the doctor?"

"No. I'm fine. It's not that." She licked her lips again. "I remembered something."

"What?"

"That truck had lights on the top, like the one that ran me off the road."

"Are you sure?" Marcus asked, sitting again.

"I didn't think of it before because they weren't turned on at the gas station. The truck was idling, but the lights were off. Even the headlights." She caught his gaze. "That's weird, isn't it? Usually if you stop and idle the engine, you don't turn off the headlights."

Marcus nodded. "I think that's your truck."

"It was blue!" she blurted. "That shiny metallic blue. Navy blue."

"You sure?"

"Positive. The lights around the gas pumps lit it up."

"Anything else?"

She smiled. "When I drove away, I passed the truck. I wasn't really paying attention, but I did look in my rearview mirror."

208 |

"What did you see?"

"Balls." She blushed. "You know, those metal bull balls some guys hang on the hitch of their trucks."

Marcus chuckled. "Ah, those *cool* cowboy wannabes."

"Rednecks."

They both laughed.

"So," he said, "you saw a navy blue metallic truck with hunting lights on top and bull balls on the hitch."

When he put it like that, she had to grin. But her smile faded fast. "Why would someone do this?"

"We're not sure. My friend Detective Zur is working on it. They're looking at the security footage from the gas station."

"But you all think Wesley had something to do with this."

"Do *you* have any enemies?"

"No. Not that I know of."

"Has Wesley pissed anyone off lately?"

"Probably."

"That's why the police are considering him a suspect." Marcus leaned forward and picked up her hand. "We have a guard on your door, Rebecca. The kids too. Whoever did this might come back."

"Because I'm still alive," she said in a small voice.

"Yes."

"Are you going back to work?"

He released her hand. "I've taken a...leave of absence."

She sat up on her elbows. "It wasn't a voluntary leave, was it?"

Marcus's gaze shifted to the wall, then the window. "I'm on suspension. Until an investigation is completed. It's the price you pay when you break the rules."

"I'm sorry."

His eyes snapped back to hers. "Hey, don't be. I'm not. I could use a little break."

"I guess being a 911 operator isn't easy."

"Some days."

"And this was one of them," she said dryly.

He shrugged. "It was a challenging day." Then he grinned. "But I'd be kind of a lame superhero if I didn't face challenges."

"Well, I'm your number-one fan."

"Speaking of numbers," he said. "Remember when I told you about Jane's habit of adding dates?"

"Yeah."

"And you said the thirteenth was an unlucky day to plan your trip?"

Where's this leading? "Uh-huh."

"According to Jane you have to add up all the numbers and boil them down to a single digit. So June is six. Plus thirteen. That's nineteen. Then you add the one and nine, which equals ten. Then you add the one and zero, which equals—"

"Sounds pretty convoluted," she said with a laugh.

"I'm not done. One and zero equals one. Then add the numbers in the year 2013, which equals six. Then add that to the one, and voila!"

She grinned. "Seven. A lucky day. Really?"

He shrugged. "You're still here."

"You're right. That's pretty lucky, all things considered."

She yawned and he clambered to his feet. "I'll let you rest."

"For a bit," she agreed. "Then I want to see my kids."

Marcus walked to the door. "Sweet dreams."

"Wait!"

He turned back.

"Today's June fifteenth, 2013," she said. "What does that add up to?"

"Nine," he said after a moment.

"What's a nine mean?"

He smiled at her. "I'm fairly confident it means 'out with old and in with the new.' Means you've completed a cycle, and tomorrow you can start anew."

As the door closed behind him, she contemplated his words. Could she really start fresh? Was tomorrow the beginning of a new life? And would Marcus Taylor be part of that life?

To all three questions, she thought, *I sure hope so.*

Chapter Twenty-Nine

Hinton, AB – Saturday, June 15, 2013 – 7:12 AM

While Colton and Ella visited with their mother, Marcus sat in the kids' room and probed Zur for information. "She remember *anything* else?"

"Nothing. And we've checked the husband out thoroughly. His alibi checks out. Witnesses state he was in the bar in Fort McMurray when all this went down."

"Maybe he hired someone and paid cash."

"We found no large withdrawals that couldn't be accounted for."

"The guy's a gambler, John. Maybe he won some money and used that to finance the trucker."

"We're looking into every possibility."

"You check her past?"

"Rebecca Kingston's?"

Marcus nodded.

"She's clean. No priors, no arrests. Not even a speeding ticket."

"No weird religious affiliations?"

"You mean like a cult?"

"Wouldn't be the first time a cult went after a mother."

"No, she's Presbyterian."

"Really? Your investigation went that deep that it looked at her religion?"

Zur grinned. "It was on her hospital chart, Marcus."

"Oh."

There was silence in the room.

Marcus scratched his head. *Who the hell wants Rebecca dead? Who benefits?*

"You still think it's the ex?" Zur said.

"It's almost always the ex." When Zur squinted at him, Marcus added, "I watch a lot of *Law & Order*."

"Believe me, we're still looking into Wesley Kingston. He's rubbed shoulders with some wrong people over the years because of his gambling debts. Maybe Mrs. Kingston wasn't the target. Maybe her husband was."

"You think maybe someone was trying to send him a warning?"

"Makes sense. He rakes up debts and can't pay, and they go after him. Maybe they thought he was driving the car. Or they decided to get at him via his wife and kids. Would give most guys incentive to pay up."

Marcus rubbed his face. "Addictions, hey. Screws everyone's life up."

"Unless they make a choice to get help." Zur patted his arm. "How are you doing?"

Marcus shrugged. "You know how it is. Go to meetings, feel guilty, want to use, go back to meetings, feel guilty. It's a vicious circle."

"But you're doing it. You made the right choice." Zur released a heavy sigh. "Last thing I want to do is get called to a scene and find you dead. You're too good of a guy to go down that path. Remember that. People need you."

Like Rebecca and her kids?

Marcus thought about them, how it would be a whole other outcome if he hadn't picked up the phone last night and taken her 911 call. Sure, Leo would've done his best to help her, but he played by the rules. Most of the time.

"Listen," Zur said. "I have to leave. I'm going to swing by some of the casinos, talk to the people there. Maybe we'll get a break."

"You have to catch this guy, John."

"We will. Count on it."

Marcus watched his friend move down the hallway. As soon as Zur stepped into the elevator, Marcus turned to the guard and said, "I'll be back in an hour or so. If Rebecca or the kids need me—"

"I'll tell 'em."

There was someplace Marcus needed to be. Badly.

When he entered the small hall twenty minutes later, Marcus tried to be inconspicuous. With some hesitation at being in unfamiliar surroundings, he scanned the room, took note of the strangers there and sat down on a chair in the back row.

"My name is Bert," the man at the podium said, "and I'm an addict."

"Welcome, Bert," Marcus murmured with the group, as he fought to control the overwhelming need that raced through every nerve in his body.

He was so focused on his breathing that he didn't notice when someone sat next to him. But he did notice when his arm was nudged. He looked up.

Leo grinned. "I knew I'd find you here."

"What are you doing here?" Marcus whispered.

Leo lowered his voice. "Came to see you."

"I'm okay, Leo."

"Yeah, I can see that. That's why you're sitting at an NA meeting."

"I'm not going to use."

"That's good to hear."

A woman in front of them swiveled her head and glared. "Shh…"

Like a scolded schoolboy, Marcus folded his hands in his lap. Leo followed suit. They sat quietly for the duration of the meeting, each fighting their own personal demons.

Afterward, Leo said, "Let's grab a bite to eat."

Marcus followed him outside. "Take one car?"

"Sure. I'll drive."

Marcus followed Leo to his car and climbed in the passenger seat. Leo settled in behind the wheel, but didn't start the car.

"What's up?" Marcus asked.

Leo shook his head slowly. "Thought I was gonna lose you, man."

"Well, you didn't. You're stuck with me."

Leo squinted at him. "Was it worth it?"

"You mean breaking the rules, getting suspended and finding Rebecca and the kids?"

"Yeah."

"Worth every second. I'd do it again."

Leo sighed. "That's what I'm afraid of."

Marcus grinned. "Hey, don't worry about me. Really. I've never felt better. Feels like my life is finally falling into place. Like a burden's been lifted off my chest. I'd never realized how hard it was to breathe before."

"So tell me, how exactly did you find them?"

"Divine intervention."

"What, you seeing ghosts again, or did God speak to you this time?"

Marcus chuckled. "You wouldn't believe me if I told you."

"Ghosts or God?"

"Maybe a bit of both. Hell, I don't know. Maybe I imagined it all."

"Who'd you see—Jane?"

Marcus's smile faded. "So clearly I could almost touch her. And this time I wasn't dreaming."

"How do you know?"

"Because I was driving. Last night I saw Jane standing in the middle of the road, then sitting in the back seat of my car. It's not the first time either."

"You've seen Jane's ghost before?"

Marcus nodded. "And Ryan's."

Leo's mouth gaped open, but he remained silent.

"You don't believe me, Leo?"

"I believe you believe."

"Then I should probably tell you about the first time I saw ghosts. Remember when I went out to that cabin near Cadomin Cave? While I was there, I was using, but that doesn't explain everything that happened."

"Like what?"

"Like the gifts I started receiving on my doorstep. Or the children I saw in the woods."

Leo shrugged. "You probably weren't the only one renting a cabin."

"Actually, besides me and maybe three oil workers, there was no one else except Irma, the owner of the cabins."

"And no kids."

"Not a one. In fact, Irma said the last kids who'd been in the area had died in a fire."

"You think you saw their ghosts?"

"What else could they have been? I didn't know anything about those kids before I saw them. And nothing else explains the bizarre things I found outside my cabin." He frowned and scratched his chin. "I was there right before that mother—you know, the one whose son went missing back then. He was kidnapped by The Fog."

"That was a scary time for parents."

"I know."

"What were you going to say about the mother?"

"I read in the *Edmonton Journal* that she'd stayed in the same cabin I'd rented. The mother…Sadie something. I left so fast I had no time to clean up. She would have seen the needles." He looked away. "Newspapers said she admitted she'd gone there to kill herself, but said something stopped her. I wonder…"

Leo let out a snort. "Okay, buddy, you're starting to sound a little whacko. Either we get some food into you, or we go shopping for one of those special jackets that tie up in the back."

"I wonder if maybe she saw them too. The ghost kids."

Leo started the car. "Montana's? I could go for some barbecue ribs and fries. And while we wait, you're gonna tell me all about these ghosts, including Jane's. I wanna know everything."

Chapter Thirty

Hinton, AB – Saturday, June 15, 2013 – 1:20 PM

By afternoon, Rebecca was feeling a bit better. The medication they'd given her made her somewhat groggy, but she was so happy to see Ella and Colton that even drugs couldn't keep the cheerfulness from her voice.

"I hope you're being really good for the doctor and nurses."

The kids sat in chairs, their oversized hospital housecoats wrapped around them to keep them warm. Dr. Monroe had allowed them to sit in her room and watch television with her for the afternoon.

The door opened, and the police officer poked his head inside. "There's going to be a shift change in a half hour, Mrs. Kingston. I thought you should know."

"Thank you."

Having a guard on her door made her feel safe, but it didn't keep her from worrying about the truck driver. Would he make another attempt? Why?

Whenever she closed her eyes, she'd see flashes of memory and her muscles would clench. She recalled the bitter coldness of the water…and her absolute certainty that she was going to die there in the dark, alone.

"And then Marcus swam into the car," Colton was telling Ella for the one hundredth time, "and gave us scuba masks. But you were asleep, so you didn't see anything."

"And he rescued us," Ella said with a firm nod.

"Mom says he used to be, like, a doctor or something."

"A paramedic," Rebecca corrected.

"Yeah, one of those guys." Colton frowned. "You think he was ever in one of those STARS helicopters?"

"You'll have to ask him next time he visits."

The thought of Marcus Taylor coming to visit gave her butterflies. Nice ones. There was no denying they had a connection because of all that had happened.

But it's more than that.

She wanted to know more about him. Last time she'd seen him, there had been a glimmer of vulnerability in his rugged but handsome face. While they'd talked, she watched as a wave of emotions swept over him—grief, guilt, relief, joy…and anger. When she'd admitted more about their financial state and Wesley's gambling, she saw anger brimming in his eyes.

She was relieved, however, to hear that her husband was off the police's radar as a suspect. He'd never do something so hideous. Marcus had said they were looking into some other leads, that maybe Wesley's gambling was to blame. But she couldn't deal with that thought right now. All she wanted to do was hold her children…and breathe.

"Mommy needs a gentle hug," she said.

Colton and Ella were eager to obey. As they wrapped their arms around her, mindful of all the tubes and wires, she gathered them close and listened to their hearts beating in their chests.

Life. It was something worth fighting for. And damned if she was going to let anyone hurt her children ever again. Not Wesley. Not anyone.

She had called Kelly as soon as she was feeling up to talking. She'd tried to dissuade her sister out of immediately heading to Hinton.

"I'm okay," she'd promised Kelly. "The doctors are looking after me, and I have a police guard on my door. The kids too."

They'd talked about the "accident."

"I should've taken the kids," Kelly said.

"None of us knew what was going to happen, Sis. I mean, would you ever in your wildest dreams have thought some truck driver would run me off the road?"

"No. But who would want to kill you?"

Rebecca couldn't tell her about Wesley's gambling. Or that the police suspected someone wanted to send Wesley a message—through Rebecca's imminent death. She didn't want to scare her sister.

"They'll catch him," she'd said to Kelly.

Her sister had been more than determined to look after her once Rebecca was released from the hospital in a day or two. Kelly had already arranged to stay with her for a few days, but the thought made Rebecca very nervous. If someone still wanted her dead, then her house wasn't going to be safe for any of them.

She could ask Wesley to move back in. The thought made her cringe. She knew what would happen if she did that. Wesley would take advantage of the situation, of her weakness, and the next thing she'd know he'd be moved in permanently. And if there was one thing she was absolutely sure about it was that she was done with him. The divorce couldn't happen soon enough.

She thought of his gambling addiction. *He may not have tried to kill me and the kids directly, but his actions could be responsible.*

She glanced at the clock by the door. Wesley would be here soon.

"Mommy, I'm tired," Ella said.

"How about you and Colton go have a nap in your room? I think I need one too."

"I'm not tired," Colton grumbled.

"Watch TV then. But don't have the volume up too loud. Let your sister sleep."

When they were gone, she picked up the hospital phone and the business card next to it. "Marcus?" she said when he picked up. "I know you're probably busy, but..."

"What do you need?"

His voice had become an instant comfort. "To talk to you."

"Want me to come to the hospital?"

"If it's not too inconvenient."

"I'll be right over."

When Marcus entered her hospital room, the first thing Rebecca noticed was that he'd shaved. He'd also put on aftershave, something earthy—sandalwood and musk.

"You shaved," she said, biting her lip at the absurdity of her comment.

He rubbed his smooth chin. "Yeah, Leo advised me to clean up a bit. Said I looked like I'd been on a three-day bender."

"But you haven't." It was a statement, not a question. "Leo sounds like a good friend."

He dragged the chair to the side of the bed. "The best."

"How long have you known him?"

"Seems like forever." He laughed. "I met Leo on the job, back when I was a paramedic."

"Did he work with you?"

"No. At that time, he was in no condition to work for anyone." He paused as if summoning up the right words. "I was called out to a situation about fifteen years ago. Unconscious male passed out in a bar."

"Ah, and that was Leo."

He nodded. "I can't go into all the details—confidentiality and all—but I will say he was in rough shape. Even came close to dying that night."

"But he didn't, and now you're friends."

"We have a lot in common, Leo and I. Both of us have much to atone for."

She glanced out the window, thinking about Marcus's drug addiction. It had affected his career and marriage. Just like Wesley's gambling addiction. She knew the toll that had taken on her and the kids.

So why was she even considering bringing Marcus Taylor into her life?

Because you like him. Because he's not Wesley.

"Did Leo know Jane?" she asked.

"Yeah. We used to have weekend dinners with him and his wife—before they were married."

"So, technically, you saved him too."

He blushed. "I was part of a team who responded to the call."

"But you visited him afterward."

Marcus shrugged. "I went to check on him at the hospital. We got to talking, and before I knew it, we were friends."

She smiled. "Sometimes that's how fast it happens."

There was a long pause.

"How have you been, Marcus?"

"I think I should be the one asking *you* that question. You look better."

"I look like crap."

He leaned over her, examining her face. When he touched the small scar on her chin, she flinched. She'd been self-conscious about the scar for so long—not because of what it looked like but what it represented.

"Childhood accident?" he asked.

"Not exactly."

"Your husband?"

She nodded, and he opened his mouth as if to say something, but then shut it quickly.

"He hasn't…hit me in a long time."

The muscle in Marcus's jaw twitched. "He shouldn't have hit you at all."

"I know."

"Did you report him?"

She shook her head. "I couldn't. The kids…"

"He needs to know it's not right to hit a woman. Or anyone for that matter."

"You're right. I know that. But I had to give him a second chance. For Ella and Colton's sake."

He sighed. "I guess I understand second chances better than anyone."

"After the last time Wesley hurt me, I let him know I wanted a divorce. I went to Carter, my lawyer, and told him everything. And we had hospital records to back up my story. When we met with Wesley, Carter told him I wouldn't press charges if he'd agree to an amicable divorce. And he had to agree that I'd have sole custody of the kids."

"That must not have gone over too well."

"He didn't like it. But he didn't argue."

"Possibly we're all looking at this from the wrong point of view. Maybe it's not about the money. Maybe it's about the kids."

"He'd never get custody of them, even if I died. Carter took care of that too. Kelly and Steve are named as guardians, and Wesley would have the same arrangement as he does now. He agreed to everything."

"Otherwise you'd charge him for the abuse."

"Yes. And there's no way he'd give up his freedom to fight me in court. That's why I don't think he hired that guy to kill me."

"It's not the sole possible explanation. The police do have other suspects. But no one else has as strong a motive."

"The money, you mean."

"Who else would benefit from it besides Wesley?"

"No one." She let out a soft groan. "I keep going over everything in my head. Nothing makes sense. I do not understand why someone would do this. What would they gain if they'd killed me?"

"Police think maybe it was supposed to be a message. For your husband."

"*Ex*-husband-to-be. And what message would that send exactly?"

Marcus shrugged. "Maybe that they could hurt him anytime, anywhere. Perhaps they meant to scare you. Scare him."

"But the guy ran me off the road and into a river."

"It could be that things went a bit too far."

"But you still think this guy might come after me again."

"Perhaps. We can't rule that out." He leaned forward. "Better to be safe than sorry, don't you think?"

"What about when I go home? They may let me out tomorrow or the day after."

"I'm sure they'll have a police guard on your house."

"The kids are going to stay with my sister. I haven't told them yet."

"Why won't you stay there too?"

She shook her head. "I can't take the chance that whoever did this won't follow me there. I won't put Kelly and her family in harm's way."

"So you're going to stay in your house alone?"

"Kelly said she'll stay with me. I don't want her to. It's too dangerous. And I'd never forgive myself if something happened to her." She took a deep breath. "I wanted to know…if you would, uh…maybe consider…staying with me. For a few days, until they catch this guy. I could even pay you. Like a bodyguard."

His eyes widened in surprise. "I'm thinking that's not such a good idea."

"Why not?"

"I'm not really the bodyguard type. I'm no hero."

She cocked her head to one side and stared at him. "Really? You saved us already once."

"That's different."

"How? You came after us when there was no one else who could. If it hadn't been for you, we'd all be dead. You're the perfect choice for one main reason."

"What's that?"

"I trust you, Marcus." She saw doubt in his eyes. "With my life."

"You shouldn't. I have a bad habit of letting people—"

"Just say yes," she cut in. "Please. I need to know I won't be alone when I'm released from the hospital. And I need to tell Kelly I have someone else I can trust who'll be with me." She sighed. "I know it's a lot to ask. I really do. But I have a feeling they're going to catch this guy—soon. So maybe it'll be a few days. Maybe a week." She reached out and touched his hand. "Since you're not working right now, you can't tell me you've got better things to do."

And she couldn't tell him she was worried he'd relapse. Because of her. If he used again because of the stress of being suspended, she'd never forgive herself.

"You forget I have a dog," came his mumbled reply. "Arizona."

"I love dogs. Bring her along."

"She's not small."

Rebecca smiled. "I have a big house, big backyard."

They stared at each other.

Finally Marcus nodded. "If that's what you want."

"Yes."

"Okay then."

Grinning, she nudged her head in the direction of

the locker. "My purse is in there. Can you get it for me?"

When he brought her purse to her, she rummaged around until she found her keys, a pen and a notebook. "I'll write down my address for you. This key is for the front door. There should be a light on outside. It's on a timer, so it should be on by the time you get there."

"You want me to go today?"

She made a face. "Yeah. If that's okay with you. I really need some clothes for me and the kids. I forgot to ask Kelly. Everything we have here is either ripped or bloody."

Marcus's face reddened. "And you want *me* to do it?"

"Yes. Whatever you can find in the kids' rooms will do. And jeans and a shirt for me. They're in my bedroom closet in a drawer. Um...bra and underwear," she was blushing now, "in the drawer above it. And jackets from the front hallway."

"You sure you don't want to ask your sister?"

She shook her head.

When she didn't offer an explanation, he nodded and said, "Ah, you're afraid to have her go into your house, in case someone's waiting there."

Now she felt like crap. What gave her the right to ask him to put himself in danger for her—yet again? "I shouldn't be asking you to do this. I'm sorry. You've already done so much for us."

He smiled. "Consider it taken care of, Rebecca. I'm sure Detective Zur already has a car on your house. And officer will check your house before you return. But you're right. You can't be too careful."

He gave her a nod, then headed for the door.

"Marcus?"

He looked over his shoulder. "Yeah?"

"Thank you. For everything."

"Don't thank me yet. I might eat you out of house

and home. I'm starving!"

Chapter Thirty-One

Hinton, AB – Saturday, June 15, 2013 – 1:42 PM

Rebecca's laughter followed Marcus down the hall.

He entered an empty elevator and shook his head in bewilderment. "What the hell did I agree to?"

Uh, you're going to sleep in the same house as a beautiful woman, whom you are strongly attracted to, and try to pretend you're there only to protect her.

Marcus banged the heel of his hand against his forehead. "You idiot. And now you're going to rummage around in her underwear?" *What the hell?*

The elevator stopped on the second floor, but no one got on. When the doors closed, his thoughts drifted back to Rebecca. She deserved someone better than Wesley Kingston in her life. And that someone wasn't Marcus.

"She's still officially married," he reminded himself. *And drop-dead gorgeous.*

His offer to stay with her was strictly professional courtesy. She had no one else. It was a business arrangement. That's all it was. Even if he didn't accept a penny from her, which he wouldn't. Like doing an old friend a favor.

Except she's not really an old friend. More like a new one.

The elevator took him down to the main level, and he made a beeline for the emergency wing. The ER was bustling with action, but he veered toward the outside exit, weaving through the crowd of broken legs, coughs and a very pregnant woman with a brood of six kids around her.

In the parking lot, he found his car, climbed inside and glanced at the address Rebecca had written down. *Edmonton...right. Damn it!*

It would take about three hours to get there, maybe twenty minutes to grab the clothes and another three hours to get back to the hospital. Being away from her for so long didn't sit well with him.

He picked up his cell phone and called John. "I'm heading to Rebecca's house to pick up some clothes for her and the kids. You got a car watching the place?"

"Yeah. I'll let them know."

"Thanks, John. Any news on the truck or driver?"

"Actually, there is. We finally caught a break. There's a computer store across from the Esso station. They have cameras in the windows, and one of them is on 24/7, filming the street. We're going through the tape now."

"I hope you catch this guy."

"Me too. Listen, Marcus, what are your plans for the next few days? I heard you got suspended."

"I'm going to stay at Rebecca's for a bit. Until you nab this guy."

"Really?" Zur's voice was more than a little stunned.

"She didn't want to ask her sister. Doesn't want to put her in any danger. And the ex is out of the question, since you still think he's connected." Marcus paused. "You do still think that, don't you?"

"Nothing else makes much sense. It couldn't be a

random hit and run. He was waiting for her, followed her, made sure she'd end up in the McLeod River."

"Anything pan out at the casinos?"

"Nothing so far. We're still asking questions. All we need is the right answer."

"Okay, I'll be back in about six and a half hours. You'll check in on Rebecca and the kids for me?"

"Definitely. We still have a few questions for her. And the ex."

"Have you searched his place yet?"

"Can't get a warrant. Not enough evidence."

"Shit. Can't you even look at his phone records or e-mails?"

"Nope. Not until we get the warrant."

Marcus gritted his teeth. "By then he could dump everything. Especially if anyone threatened him in a voice mail or e-mail."

"I know. But we have to do this by the book. We've got a request in for a warrant. Should have it by tomorrow, maybe the next day."

Marcus massaged his temples. "Tomorrow could be too late. If Wesley Kingston has anything to connect him to the attempt on his wife's life, it'll be gone by the time you get there."

Zur let out a huff. "People think it's easy to erase files and information from a computer. It's not. Our tech guys can pull data that was deleted years ago. There's almost always a trace. I promise you, if Kingston's got anything incriminating, we'll find it." He let out a snicker. "Now let's talk about you and Mrs. Kingston living together."

"It's not like that, John."

"Isn't it?" Another chuckle. "I think it's *exactly* like that. But do yourself a favor. Wait until the ink's dry on her divorce papers before you make your move."

"I don't have a move."

"Then you'd better get one. She's into you."

Marcus blinked. "You think so?"

More laugher sounded, then Zur said, "Bye, Marcus."

Marcus started the car and pulled away from the hospital. Securing the Bluetooth over his left ear, he called Leo.

"You headed home?" Leo asked.

"No, I'm going to stay in Edmonton for a few days."

"So you can keep an eye on that Kingston woman?"

"Good guess. Actually, I agreed to stay at her house for a few days."

"Why would you do that?"

Marcus sucked in a deep breath. "She's petrified that whoever tried to kill her will come back and try again. Even the police think it's a possibility."

"What about her kids?"

"They're staying with their aunt. That leaves Rebecca alone in her house with no support other than a patrol car outside."

"If she's got police watching her, she's more than likely gonna be fine."

"Why are you giving me such a hard time about this, Leo? I'm trying to be a nice guy."

"Sorry, man. I can't help it if I worry about you. It strikes me as very unusual for you to take such an interest in one of our callers."

"Rebecca's not merely a caller. Not to me. Not after all this."

Leo sighed. "I know you feel some kind of connection to her. I won't argue with that. But I do think you're rushing into things, not considering the consequences."

"What's there to consider? I'm going to sleep on her couch so she's not alone, not sleep with her."

"You sure about that?"

Marcus clenched his jaw. "You've been telling me

for months to get out more, meet someone. Well, guess what? I did. Okay, granted I met her on the job, but who's to say there's anything wrong with that? I like her. I think she likes me. Right now, all that's important is that she feels safe. I can do that for her."

"I'm not sure about this, Marcus."

"I know what I'm doing is a bit…unorthodox. But she asked me to stay, and I couldn't say no. Hell, it's for a few days. It's not like I'm moving in with her permanently."

There was a long, uncomfortable pause.

Then Leo said, "Fine. Do what you gotta do."

"Thank you."

"It's not that I don't trust your judgment. It's just that I—"

"Don't trust my judgment."

Leo chuckled. "I worry about you. You can't blame me for that."

"I know, Leo. And I appreciate it. Really. But I'm fine. For the first time in a long time I feel like I've got my life back."

"Something else happen to you out at the river?"

"What do you mean?"

"I mean…you sound like you've had a near-death experience or something. You know, seen the light and all. Maybe you drowned and then came back to life."

Marcus laughed. "You should write books with that imagination. No, I didn't drown. No near-death experience either. No tunnel or bright light, except from the flashlight."

"So this woman. Rebecca. She hot?"

The question took Marcus by complete surprise. "Uh…I guess."

"You guess? That's lame, man. She's either hot or not."

"Fine. She's hot." *Sizzling hot.*

"You bring her over for dinner one night."

Marcus wiped a hand across his brow and focused on the road.

"Marcus, you there?"

"Yeah, Leo. I heard you. And the invite. I won't promise anything. She may not be that into me. I'm rusty at reading signals."

"But there were signals?"

"I think so."

"Well, you are her *superhero*."

Marcus sat up. "What? Where did you hear that?"

Leo erupted into laughter. "Oh man. Word got out in the hospital and went everywhere. I heard Carol's making you a cape."

"Shit."

"Hey, don't sweat it. You did good, Marcus. Real good. I'm proud of you."

"Thanks."

"Now, what do you want me to do about Arizona?"

"I'll pick her up before we leave for Rebecca's. And Leo? I've really appreciated you looking after Arizona for me."

"No problem. Except you're gonna have to talk my wife out of getting a dog now. That's all on you, buddy."

Marcus laughed. "I'll do my best, but I know that once someone looks into Arizona's big brown eyes, she's got them hooked."

"I'm *not* getting a dog."

"Okay, Leo. You keep saying that. Bye." *Click.*

On the long drive to Edmonton, Marcus mulled over the attempt on Rebecca's life and every possible scenario.

He kept hearing John Zur's voice in his head. *"She's into you."*

Could he be right?

Chapter Thirty-Two

Hinton, AB – Saturday, June 15, 2013 – 1:57 PM

When Carter Billingsley walked into her hospital room, Rebecca gave him a smile. "You didn't have to drive all the way here to see me."

"Yes, I did. It's the least I could do. You know your father and I go way back." Carter leaned down and kissed her forehead. "You're like a daughter to me."

"So the kids can call you Grandpa then?"

His frowned. "Let's stick with Uncle Carter, shall we?"

"I'm glad to see you," she said with a sigh. "It's been a rough few days."

He dragged the chair closer. "I hear it's going to be rougher."

She squeezed back tears and nodded, not trusting her voice.

"Rebecca, I want you to know that the extra bills have been paid for from your grandfather's money. Yours too." He held up a hand to silence her. "I know he specified it was to be spent solely on the children, but you and I both know he'd do this for you. He'd want you to have the best care and not have to worry about paying bills later."

A tear escaped and she wiped it away. "Thank you."

"Is there anything I can do for you or the children?"

"Get Wesley out of my life. I know he'll be in theirs, but I want this divorce finalized. The sooner, the better."

Carter's mouth thinned. "I can certainly help with that. I have the divorce papers here with me. All I need is Wesley's signature. Where can I find him?"

"I'm not sure."

Carter inhaled deeply. "Do the police believe he had anything to do with this?"

"They're checking him out, but I'm sure that Wesley did *not* try to kill me and the kids."

"Did he ever tell you he called me to ask about the terms of your inheritance?"

She shook her head.

"He wanted to know if he could borrow from it and pay it back later."

"But you advised him that he couldn't."

"Yes. And he wasn't too happy about it, Rebecca. He called me a few choice names. You too, if I remember correctly."

"Did the police talk to you?"

"Not yet. That's the other reason I'm here. I had a call from a Detective Zur. He wants to see your file, go over the inheritance. Do I have your permission to show him?"

"You give him anything he needs, Carter. I want this nightmare over. And that won't happen unless we get to the truth."

He leaned over and patted her shoulder. "If there's anything else you need, ask."

"I need my life back. With my children. I need to feel safe again. I need them to find the bastard that did this."

In the doorway, Carter said, "I hope they do. You

deserve some happiness in your life."

"Thank you, Carter. You're the best."

"Remember *that* when you get my bill," he said with a laugh.

She listened to his footsteps move down the hall.

Then she picked up the phone and called Kelly's cell phone. She quickly filled her in on the plan to have Marcus stay with her for a few days. Kelly wasn't at all thrilled with the idea.

"What do you mean you're letting a stranger stay with you?" Kelly demanded. "I said I'd do it."

"I need you to keep the kids safe."

"But you need to be safe too."

"I will be. Marcus won't let anything happen to me."

"Are you sure that's wise, Rebecca? I mean, you don't really know this Marcus guy. And to have him sleeping in your house…ugh…I'm not so sure about this, Sis. I think it'd be better if I stayed with you."

"No. This is what I want. No offense, Kelly, but it's not like you could do much if someone broke in during the middle of the night."

"Gee, you make me sound so helpless."

"Sorry. But the truth is, I wouldn't feel safe with you in my house. I'd worry about you getting hurt. This guy has his sights on me, and I need to know that the rest of my family is safe."

"Okay, okay. As long as you're sure about this 911 dude."

"Never been more sure about anyone in my life."

"You've gotta admit, Rebecca, it's kind of weird how he abandoned his job and came to your rescue."

"He didn't *abandon* it. He felt he had to do the right thing. And it was right for him to try to find us. Now quit your griping. You should be happy Marcus came to our rescue. We wouldn't be having this conversation otherwise."

There was a long silence on the other end.

"I'm not being ungrateful," Kelly said finally. "I'm very happy he found you and the kids. But I *am* worried about you. And this guy. He's a…" Kelly's voice trailed off.

"What? Rebecca prodded. "Spit it out."

"You said he was an addict."

"*Recovering* addict."

"Same thing. You sure he's not going to steal your medication, or money or jewelry?"

Rebecca released a pent-up breath. "I know you're worried for me, Sis, but trust me. I'm a good judge of character."

Kelly let out a huff. "Uh…and what about Wesley?"

"Okay, you got me there. Not a good choice. But really, don't worry about Marcus Taylor. He's one of the good guys. And there aren't many out there. I trust him. He won't steal from me. Besides, the only drugs I have at home are kids' aspirin and Buckley's cough syrup. I can tell you that Marcus isn't that desperate."

"Fine," Kelly said. "I'm already on my way. I'll be there in about three hours."

"I love you, Sis."

"Me too."

Rebecca hung up and thought about Marcus. He'd had a string of bad luck, especially with his wife's and son's deaths. On top of these, he was battling a drug addiction, and was suspended from a job he enjoyed. He liked helping people. She could tell. Yet, he was modest, never looking for the limelight, never seeking recognition.

Even when he'd told her about the old lady with the cat, she could tell he genuinely cared about people. Unlike Wesley, who cared about one solitary person—himself.

Two very different men. One terrified her. The

other made her feel…alive.

Kelly had been after her for weeks to start dating. Rebecca had argued with her that she couldn't date until she was legally divorced. She wouldn't betray her vows—even if Wesley had. In truth, the thought of dating terrified Rebecca. How does one go about meeting decent men at her age? Internet dating? Too many nutcases out there. Dating services? And what if she met no one other than jerks who thought two kids were excess baggage?

No, she'd much rather let fate intervene. She'd meet someone when the time was right. And that's what she'd always promised Kelly.

"Maybe fate has already intervened," she murmured.

Would Marcus welcome dating a woman with two kids?

Whoa! You're getting way ahead of yourself. So you like the guy. That doesn't mean he likes you back. Not in that way. Maybe he's not interested in pursuing a relationship with anyone.

But what if he was?

Chapter Thirty-Three

Edmonton, AB – Saturday, June 15, 2013 – 5:17 PM

Marcus pulled up in front of Rebecca's house. Spotting the patrol car across the streets, he gave the uniformed officer a nod and made a beeline for him.

"Marcus Taylor?" the officer said, getting out of his car.

"Yes."

"You got ID?"

Marcus retrieved his wallet from his jacket pocket and flashed his driver's license.

The officer gave a nod. "You're the guy who rescued them. Saw your picture plastered all over the news. Congrats, dude." The man smiled. "Way to go."

"Thanks." Marcus glanced at the house. "Anyone show up here?"

"No. Been dead quiet all day."

"Did Detective Zur say if there was any word on who did it?"

"You know Zur?"

"We go back a ways."

"You an ex-cop?"

"Former paramedic. We worked a few cases

together."

The officer smiled. "Zur's one of the best. Last thing I heard they were checking out a videotape lead. Saw some guy on it in a truck like the one the victim saw."

"Rebecca."

"Pardon me?"

"The victim's name. Rebecca Kingston."

"Oh, yeah."

"I'm here to pick up some things for Rebecca and the kids. I should be in and out within fifteen minutes." Marcus took a step away, but then paused. "When's the next shift change?"

"Midnight."

"Be sure to check around back every now and then."

"Will do, Mr. Taylor."

Inside the house, Marcus stood in the foyer and got his bearings. Kitchen to the right. Living room and formal dining room to the left. Open concept. No upper floor, so he guessed the bedrooms were at the far end of the house.

He headed down the hallway, doing his best to ignore the family photos on the wall. Ones of a happy couple and their children.

He paused midway and stared at the man in the photo. Wesley Kingston. Not a bad-looking fellow, midforties, maybe, with thinning hair.

"Did you do this?" Marcus muttered.

Of course, the photo didn't answer.

The first room he checked appeared to be a spare room. Nothing much personal in it and didn't look as though it had gotten much use. He wondered if Wesley had slept there after Rebecca had discovered his infidelity, or if he'd been kicked out on his ass immediately as he deserved.

It wasn't really Marcus's business, but still…

The next room he entered was Ella's—all pink and princesses. He found a pair of clean jeans and a flowered shirt, socks and underwear. Then he proceeded to the room across the hall. Colton's. A typical boy's room, the décor was all in grays and blues, with action figures on shelves on the walls. Sports gear and dirty clothing were strewn across the floor.

He gathered a change of clean clothing for the boy.

The third room he entered was the master suite. Tastefully decorated, it had an air of freshness, with its large windows and massive en suite bathroom. The walk-in closet was a modest size, and he scrutinized the hangers, studying the clothing that hung there.

Two dozen or so empty hangers had been shoved to one side, and Marcus suspected the man had already transported most of his belongings to his own place. There were, however, three oversized T-shirts that were far too large to be Rebecca's. Marcus wondered if she slept in them, like Jane had often done.

It was odd to be here, in this woman's bedroom, looking at her clothes and pondering such intimacies, but he couldn't keep the thoughts from rushing his brain. Was she ready for this divorce? Was she ready to move on?

He'd known other women who had forgiven their partner's sexual transgressions. They'd been able to salvage their marriages. Would Rebecca want to try? Or was she done with Wesley?

Is he done with her?

He found a pair of jeans and a warm but loose blouse. *Those should do fine.*

When he opened another drawer, he was faced with yet another dilemma—picking out a bra and a pair of panties. Everything was lace and pastels…silky.

Jesus, Marcus. They're clothes. Stop thinking like a pervert.

It was ridiculous really. Here he was, red-faced and sweating, sorting through Rebecca's intimate lingerie, and all he could think of was seeing her in them.

With a shake of his head, he grabbed a handful of lace and shoved them in the pile of kids' clothes. He left the closet, feeling like he should apologize. Luckily, there was no one there to witness his embarrassment.

He wandered around the bedroom, taking in a small display of photos that sat atop a photo album. He picked up one photo. Rebecca and Wesley, arms wrapped around each other. It had been taken at Disneyland, pre-kids. They'd been happy. Once.

He moved the other framed pictures and picked up the hefty photo album. A voice in the back of his head suggested he shouldn't, that he was now being plain nosy, but he ignored the voice. Flipping through the pages, he saw Rebecca's life flash before him. Photos from when she and Wesley had started dating. Wedding pictures. The births of Colton and Ella. Various parties and events she'd attended with her husband.

He studied one of the party photos. Rebecca looked so happy. She was staring at Wesley with such pride. A crowd of people had gathered around them. Some were patting Wesley on the back.

Marcus's gaze swept across the faces in the crowd. What had Wesley Kingston done to warrant such attention and approval?

A silver-haired man in an expensive suit stood a few feet away from the happy couple. His expression wasn't one of admiration but of contempt. One of Wesley's debtors? The guy looked vaguely familiar.

Marcus peeled back the clear cover and pried the photo from the page.

On the back, someone had written, "Summer party at Kingston, Bentley and Coombs. Gave Wesley's dad the news about Ella."

Ah-ha! Walter Eugene Kingston, the famed corporate lawyer.

That's who the older fellow was. Wesley's father. The man had his hand in all things mega-corporate. From the look on his face in the photo, he wasn't happy about something.

If looks could kill…

Could it be that Daddy Kingston wanted Rebecca out of the picture for some reason? If so, what would be in it for him?

He slipped the photo into his pocket. He'd give it to John later.

His phone rang. When he answered it, he said, "Your ears burning, John?"

"I hope you're saying good things about me," Zur said.

"Thinking them actually. So what's up?"

"We found the truck and the driver."

Marcus's heart raced. "You've got him in custody?"

"Not yet." Zur cleared his throat. "Guy's name is Rufus Delaney. Lots of priors and three outstanding warrants. Robbery, attempted rape and second-degree murder. Not the kind of guy you'd want your daughter dating."

"Or anyone else I knew."

"A patrol car brought in one of his known associates on another charge about five minutes ago. Guy cut a deal and gave up Delaney. Puts him at the Rosedale Hotel in downtown Edmonton. Edmonton Police are searching his room now. We've sent photos out to everyone at the hospital. Delaney won't get within two feet of Rebecca's room. I'll let you know when we find him. *And* if we figure out who hired him. Whoever did probably knows what Delaney is capable of."

Rape and murder. That could have been Rebecca's future.

Thank God Delaney had decided to run her off the

road instead.

Marcus went downstairs to the kitchen and found a plastic bag. Stuffing the clothing into it, he left the house, waved at the officer outside and hurried to his car. With Delaney on the loose, Marcus wanted nothing more than to be back at the hospital. He stepped on the gas pedal and sped off, praying he wouldn't get pulled over for speeding.

Chapter Thirty-Four

Hinton, AB – Saturday, June 15, 2013 – 5:19 PM

When Kelly arrived at the hospital, Rebecca broke down in huge gulping sobs. "I can't believe you're here. I'm so glad to see you."

"Can I hug you?" her sister asked, tears leaking from her eyes.

"You'd better."

Kelly wrapped her arms around her, ever so gently. "I'm afraid I'll hurt you."

"You won't. I'm stronger than I look."

Kelly arched a brow.

"That's what everyone keeps telling me," Rebecca explained. "That I'm stronger than I look."

"And here you are, crying like a big wussy baby."

"Yup. That's me."

Kelly's smile faded. "Seriously, Rebecca, you almost died. You and the kids."

"But we're all safe now."

"Thanks to that 911 operator."

Rebecca grinned. "Marcus was pretty fantabulous."

Kelly studied her face as if looking for some sign of insanity. "So what is this guy—sixty-five and bald?"

Rebecca gave her a wry look. "Uh, no."

"So he's seventy and bald?"

"I doubt he's much older than me. And he's not bald."

"You kinda like him," Kelly said in a singsong voice. "You think he's sexy."

"Oh, stop it."

Kelly perched on the edge of the bed. "You'll be happy to know Steve's mom has kidnapped my kids. So Ella and Colton won't be exposed to measles."

Rebecca snorted. "You make it sound like the plague."

"I swear it is. Between the crying, scratching, puking, picking, bathing and whining, I haven't had a second to brush my hair, much less pee by myself. You were lucky, Sis. Neither Colton nor Ella ever had measles."

"No. They had Wesley."

Kelly pursed her lips. "He's quite the bastard."

"And then some."

"I hope his balls rot off," Kelly muttered.

"Gross."

Kelly shrugged. "It's what he deserves."

"Thanks for driving down here, Sis."

"Hey, what are sisters for?"

"When I get out of here, I'm going to owe you. Big-time."

Kelly grinned. "I'm counting on that. Steve and I need a weekend away. Alone, no kids. So guess where they'll be staying?"

"Anytime."

Kelly hugged her. "I'm going to go grab us a bite to eat from the cafeteria. What do you want?"

"If you can find me a sandwich that doesn't look like it'll walk away on its own, get me one."

Ten minutes after Kelly left, Rebecca had another

visitor. Wesley.

She swallowed hard at the sight of him standing in the doorway to her room. A police officer stood next to him.

"Mr. Kingston," the officer said, "you cannot go into the room."

"But she's my wife, for Christ's sake."

The guard looked at Rebecca.

"It's okay," she said. "You can both come inside."

She wasn't stupid. The police were looking into Wesley's connections. Though she prayed they were wrong and that he wasn't involved, she wasn't willing to risk her life.

"Becca," Wesley said, approaching the bed, a red rose in one hand.

"That's far enough." She held up a hand. "Whatever you have to say to me can be said from where you're standing."

"I-I couldn't believe it when I heard." Wesley's face was pale, his eyes filled with concern. "The kids?" His voice cracked.

"They're okay. I'm okay too."

"Oh my God. When I think of how you all could've died…it makes me sick."

He sounded sincere. But he'd deceived her before.

"You know they think you had something to do with this," she said.

"Rebecca," Wesley said with a moan, "you can't believe I'd do something like this. I'd never hurt you—or the kids. I know things suck between us right now, but I'd hoped that you'd—"

"What? Forgive you? Let you move back in with us?" She shook her head. "That'll never happen."

"I swear to you, I did not have *anything* to do with what happened to you."

"Not intentionally maybe. But your actions…" She shrugged.

"I'm sorry," Wesley snapped. "But this is not my fault."

"I guess we'll see, won't we?"

When she looked at Wesley, all she felt was contempt. For his gambling, his apparent lack of judgment, even his poor attempt at an apology. He'd gotten mixed up in something that was bigger than either of them. And it had almost cost them everything.

Wesley ran a hand through his hair and glanced at the officer. "Can I see my kids?"

The officer nodded. "Same rules apply though. No contact."

"Can I come back and see you?" Wesley asked her.

Rebecca glanced at the officer. "Is Detective Zur going to question Wesley?"

"Yeah. He's on his way."

Relief washed over her. "Let's see what happens, Wesley."

"I'm glad you're all right." He handed the rose to the guard.

After the door closed behind him and she was alone again, Rebecca broke down. She cried for everything she had lost—her marriage, her faith in love. Then she cried for everything she'd almost lost—Ella and Colton. If their father had anything to do with them being run off the road, she had no idea how she would explain it to them.

Chapter Thirty-Five

Hinton, AB – Saturday, June 15, 2013 – 8:47 PM

At the Hinton Police Department, Marcus stood on the viewer's side of the one-way glass, while Detective John Zur interviewed Kingston in the adjoining interrogation room.

Wesley Kingston had a slick-looking lawyer present, probably a gift from Daddy Kingston. The lawyer was in his midthirties, and he licked his lips continually, as though he were hungry for a case that would propel him into the limelight. This could be that case—if Rebecca's husband had hired someone to take her out.

Zur had warned Marcus that they were still considering the angle that Kingston had hired someone to do the deed. The kids' inheritance was more than enough incentive. They were combing through his phone and e-mail records.

"I would never do anything to hurt my kids," Kingston protested yet again.

"But you stand to inherit some hefty cash if your wife and kids are dead," Zur said. "That's motive for a lot of people, especially those who are raking up bad debts."

"I've always been able to pay off what I owe. No one's after me or threatening me." Kingston scowled at his lawyer. "The only money being wasted right now is on this guy."

"Don't look a gift horse in the mouth," the lawyer said. "Your father wants you to have the best defense."

"For what?" Kingston roared. "I didn't do anything!" He jumped to his feet and paced in the small space behind his chair. "As I've insisted numerous times, I have no idea who would do this. I've not heard from anyone about it. I've not hired anyone to do it. I love my children. I love my wife."

"Then why did you have an affair?" Zur asked.

Kingston stopped, shrugged, then dropped back into the chair. "It simply…happened. Rebecca and I weren't getting along. We were on two different paths. I met Tracey years ago."

"This affair has been going on for how many years?"

"About five years maybe. I'm not sure. Tracey and I have been on and off."

"But you're 'on' now, living together."

"My marriage is over. It has been for a long time."

"Then why haven't you signed the divorce papers and moved on?"

Kingston crossed his arms over his chest. "I thought maybe she'd change her mind. Maybe we both would. I wanted to be sure I was doing the right thing. That's what I thought, so I mailed the papers back to her lawyer."

"Do you want to know what *I* think?" Zur asked, leaning forward. "I think you didn't sign the papers because once you did, you'd have zero access to the money that's supposed to go to your kids. I think you've been holding out for that. And I think you hired Rufus

Delaney to get rid of the three things that are standing in your way."

"You're not listening to me," Kingston said in a weary voice, "I don't know any Rufus Delaney."

Zur slid a photo toward Kingston. "You have no idea who this guy is? Never met him? Maybe you hired him blind, a recommendation from one of your gambling cohorts, perhaps."

Kingston shook his head. "No."

"This guy," Zur tapped the photo, "intentionally ran your wife and children off the road and into a frigid river, where they were submerged underwater, holding their breath, probably thinking they were going to die there."

Kingston shuddered and broke into gulping sobs. "I swear it wasn't me."

"Your son and daughter, such beautiful children, almost died."

Kingston covered his face. "I'd never hurt Colton or Ella. I love them!"

"We're done here," the lawyer said, tapping his client's arm.

"Mr. Kingston," Zur said, "you're free to leave. For now. Don't go anywhere. We may have more questions for you later." He flicked a look toward the one-way mirror and gave a subtle lift of his shoulders.

Behind the glass, Marcus clenched his jaw. "Shit."

Wesley Kingston was walking out of the station because there wasn't enough evidence against him to hold him here.

Marcus considered everything the man had said. Kingston's alibi had checked out. He'd been in Fort McMurray.

The door opened and Zur stepped inside, a manila folder tucked under one arm.

"We got nothing, Marcus."

"So if he didn't do it, we're back to the theory that

someone was sending him a message because he owed them."

John closed the door. "We checked the casinos. He has some debt, but not much. He'd recently paid off a two-thousand-dollar loan."

"The money Rebecca said was missing from their account."

Zur nodded. "We've got Delaney though. We've got him on security footage at the gas station. A search of his house nabbed us the baseball cap and T-shirt—Route 66 with a mustang on it. And paint transfer on his truck matches the paint on Mrs. Kingston's car."

"Sounds like you've got enough on him to lock him away for a long time."

"Yeah, except we're hoping he'll be ready to make a deal. Give up the one behind this all."

"What kind of deal?"

"Maybe less time in prison. Don't know yet. Prosecution is putting together a proposal."

"Jesus, John. We can't let Delaney walk. He has to pay for his actions. He tried to kill them, for Christ's sake."

"He won't walk. He'll go to prison. No doubt about it. We're going to offer him minimum security in exchange for giving us the name of whoever hired him."

"When are you questioning him?"

"He'll be here in about twenty minutes."

"Can I—?" Marcus indicated the one-way window.

"Yeah." Zur cleared his throat. "I heard you're going to stay with Mrs. Kingston for a few days. You sure that's a good idea?"

"She's got no one else."

"You seem to be getting a bit too close to this case. You're supposed to remain impartial."

"Says who? Emergency services criteria and regulations?"

"Exactly."

"If you haven't ·noticed, I'm not currently working. I've been suspended. I'm on my own time now. And technically, when I left my desk, I was minutes from being done with my shift. I went to look for Rebecca on my own time."

Zur nodded. "Stick with that story."

"It's not a story. It's the truth."

Zur stared at him but said nothing.

"Your truth radar is malfunctioning, John. And not just with me."

"What do you mean?

"Wesley Kingston."

"What about him?"

"He was telling you the truth. He didn't hire Delaney. He wouldn't hurt his kids, no matter how pissed off he was with Rebecca. And no matter how much money he owed someone."

"How do you know?"

"I saw it in his eyes."

"Saw what?"

"His love for his children. I was a father once too. Remember? He's not personally responsible for this. He'd never risk the lives of his children."

"But you heard him. He had no idea they were going with Rebecca. That was a last-minute change in her plans."

"Yeah, but Delaney saw they were with her. He would've reported back to whoever hired him, revealed that the kids were there. And that coldhearted person is the one who gave the order, with no forethought about killing two innocent children. Kingston isn't that ruthless."

"Then who is?"

Marcus released a heavy sigh and shook his head. "I have no idea."

"According to Kingston, everyone loves his wife.

She's got no enemies, been in no altercations with anyone and no one else would gain from her death. She's cleaner than a Catholic nun."

Marcus moved to the door. "I need to see her."

"What about Delaney?"

"Call me if he gives up a name?" He paused in the hallway. "And, John? I'll bet you season tickets to the Oilers that he won't name Wesley Kingston."

John smiled. "Done. I could use some downtime."

"You won't be the one going."

"Hold on a minute." John rifled through the folder, then handed him a photo of an unshaven, unsmiling man.

"Rufus Delaney?"

"Yeah. Show it to Mrs. Kingston. See if she knows him from someplace."

Marcus tucked the photo into his jacket pocket and strode away.

Something nagged at him. He was missing something too elusive to catch.

Chapter Thirty-Six

Hinton, AB – Sunday, June 16, 2013 – 9:49 PM

Rebecca checked her reflection in the handheld mirror one of the nurse's had lent her. Her blue eyes were framed by hollow valleys, but other than that, she looked presentable. She'd washed her face and brushed her hair—simple tasks normally, but not tonight. Her ribs still ached.

At Rebecca's insistence and after a three-hour visit, Kelly had headed back home to be with her kids. It had been hard to say good-bye, but Rebecca reassured her sister that she'd be home soon.

Marcus had called to let her know he was back in town with the clothing he'd promised to retrieve. He'd stopped off at the police station first, where Wesley was being questioned. She was relieved to hear her husband wasn't being locked up in a cell. There was no way Wesley had tried to kill them.

"Hi," Marcus said from the doorway.

Self-conscious, she slid the mirror beneath the covers. "Hi."

"How are you feeling?"

"Better." Then why was her stomach so twisted in

knots?

"Good. And the kids?"

"They're asleep. Supervised by a female officer."

Marcus nodded, then approached the bed. He set a plastic bag on the side table. "I hope these are okay."

"I'm sure they'll be fine. Thank you."

Conversation seemed unusually stilted, and the air felt charged with electricity. It was as though they each wanted to say something but held back out of fear.

"Someone brought you a rose," he said.

She looked at the vase in the window. It held the red rose Wesley had brought her. "A peace offering, I guess."

"From your husband?"

"Soon to be *ex*."

"I have something to show you," he said after a long silence.

"Pull up a chair."

He pulled something from his pocket. "Have you seen this man before?"

Rebecca took the photo. "Is this the man?"

Marcus nodded.

She stared at the photograph, thinking back to the times she'd gone shopping, driven to the school, gone to work. She traced a finger over the man's face. He had cruelty in his eyes and meanness in very line of his face.

This man tried to kill me and my kids.

"Does he look familiar?" Marcus prodded.

"No. I've never seen him before in my life."

"Are you sure?"

"Positive. What's his name?"

"Rufus Delaney."

She shook her head. "Never heard of him."

Marcus deflated with a soft hiss. "Damn. I was really hoping…"

"Me too."

She held out the photo. This time, their fingers made contact. They stared at each other, and Rebecca wondered what he was thinking. Had he felt the frisson of electricity in his fingertips like she had?

Marcus moved toward the window and stared at the starry sky. "Rebecca, someone hired Delaney to kill you. Someone who hates you that much has to be someone you know. Or someone you once knew. What about past relationships?"

"You mean boyfriends before I met Wesley?"

"Yeah. You hook up with anyone who was angry with you for some reason?"

"Hook up?" She smiled. "You know, in today's day that term means more than go out with someone to dinner or a movie."

"I, uh…well, I meant date."

She laughed at his obvious discomfort. "I didn't date much. And the guys I did date were decent ones. I wasn't a rebel. I didn't 'hook up' with the bad boys."

"What about casual friendships? Any of them end on *unfriendly* terms?"

"None that I can think of."

"You get any crank calls, any hang-ups recently?"

"Detective Zur already asked me that. No. No hang-ups, no strange e-mail or letters, no cars following me—that I noticed. Nothing out of the ordinary. I can't even remember the last argument I had with anyone, aside from Wesley. Oh wait, I think my sister and I argued over timeouts for her children."

She knew she sounded rather disdainful, but she was frustrated, dammit.

Marcus let out a groan. "None of this makes any sense."

"I know. But I'm telling you, unless it's a telemarketer ticked off because I set the phone on the table and walked away while they rambled on, I haven't got a clue who would be angry enough with me to try to kill me."

"I'll have to remember that table trick."

"It doesn't really work. They keep calling back."

As Marcus sat down again, there was a knock on the door.

"Come in," Rebecca called out.

Wesley poked his head inside, a smile on his face. "You up for visitors?"

She sighed. "I don't think we have anything more to say."

She saw the frown on Marcus's face. "Marcus, this is my—uh, Wesley. Wesley, Marcus Taylor is the man who pulled us out of the car."

Wesley opened the door all the way and stepped into the room, one hand outstretched. "I can't thank you enough, Mr. Taylor. If you hadn't been there…" He shook his head and looked at Rebecca. "My wife and kids are alive because of you."

Rebecca noticed that Marcus gave an abrupt nod, but didn't offer his hand.

"Becca," Wesley said, "there's someone else who'd like to see you."

Rebecca looked over his shoulder. "Ah, the other woman."

Tracey Whitaker gave her a timid smile and sniffed. "Rebecca. I hope you don't mind, but as soon as I heard what happened I asked Walter to drive me here. We knew Wesley would head straight here as soon as he heard." She inched near the bed. "I was so worried when I heard about the accident. And the kids. I couldn't believe it when Wesley told me what happened. And now here you are with police guards on your door. Oh my God!" She rambled for a few seconds, then said, "How are the kids?"

Rebecca couldn't answer. Her mind was too numb from the sparkle that resonated from Tracey's left hand.

"You're engaged?"

Tracey covered the ring. "I, uh…we…Wesley and I were going to tell you later. At a better time."

Rebecca swallowed. "There is no better time."

"I'm sorry," Tracey said, staring at the floor.

It wasn't that Rebecca hadn't seen this coming. She'd anticipated it a while ago. Hadn't she been the one who asked Wesley if he had wedding plans? And hadn't he said he'd tell her if there was?

She eyed her future ex-husband. "When's the happy day?"

"We'll pick a date as soon as the divorce is finalized," Wesley said. At least he had the decency to look shamefaced.

"Congratulations. I hope you two will be happy." She was surprised to discover she meant it.

Marcus stood. "Uh, I should be going, let you all talk."

He slipped past Wesley and had one hand on the door, when Rebecca called out, "What time will you be here tomorrow to pick me up?"

"Dr. Monroe said you'll be released at noon. I'll be here by then."

She waved. "Bye, Marcus."

After he was gone, she let out a yawn. "It's late, Wesley. We can talk another time."

"My dad wanted to come by and—"

"Not now. Later maybe. I appreciate your concern, but I'm tired."

Wesley opened his mouth as if to argue, but Tracey tugged on his arm.

"Hope you feel better soon," Tracey said.

Rebecca's lips thinned. "Me too."

"We'll go see the kids now." Wesley ushered Tracey into the hall. "Take care, Becca. Oh, we're staying in Hinton overnight. We'll come by in the morning." The door closed on his last words.

Last thing she wanted was to see Wesley again. But Colton and Ella were his children. Of course he was concerned about them.

In the back of her mind there was a small glimmer of doubt.

No. Wesley had nothing to do with this.

But what if she were wrong?

"Mrs. Kingston?"

"Huh?" She looked up. The guard stood in the doorway.

"You okay, Mrs. Kingston?"

"Yeah. But I am tired."

"I'll be right outside if you need anything."

"All I need is sleep." *And answers.*

Chapter Thirty-Seven

Hinton, AB – Sunday, June 16, 2013 – 7:30 AM

In a room at the Holiday Inn, Marcus had slept his usual two hours. Upon waking, he groaned. His body felt as though it had been through the ringer. Every movement hurt, even tying his shoelaces. But that didn't stop him from rushing to the hospital to see Rebecca.

Before going to her room, he stopped by the hospital cafeteria for breakfast.

He spotted Zur standing by the cappuccino machine.

"What are you doing here, John?"

"Well, I'm not here for the menu." Zur dropped a tray with a stale-looking sandwich with mystery meat on a table, then indicated that Marcus should join him. "You visiting Mrs. Kingston again?"

Marcus dispensed a paper cup of vanilla cappuccino. "Just about to head up."

"How's she doing?"

"Fine. Except her husband and his mistress showed up last night."

Zur cringed. "Ouch."

"Yeah, I thought it was a tacky move on Kingston's

behalf."

"The guy's not too sharp."

Marcus nodded. "I know. That's the other reason why I'm sure he didn't orchestrate the murder attempt on his wife. Guy doesn't have the balls."

"He had enough to screw around on her."

"He's engaged to the woman now. Rebecca found out last night."

"Double ouch. That's like putting salt in a wound."

"You should've seen the look on Rebecca's face. She was so hurt. But I think she realizes her marriage is now over."

"She already did. She's the one that filed for divorce."

Marcus shrugged. "Wouldn't you hold out and hope things would change if you and Lily hit a rough patch?"

"As long as I could. But not if she had feelings for another man."

Marcus mulled on that for a fleeting moment. "Kingston's been screwing around for five years." He was engulfed in a bone-tingling shiver. "What a bastard."

"But not a murdering bastard."

"Still," Marcus said, "he won't win any 'husband of the year' award."

"Maybe he'll do better the second time around. Some men do." Zur arched a brow.

"You talking about me? Whoa, there. I'm not looking to get married anytime soon."

Zur let out a lengthy sigh. "Marcus, Marcus…one of these days, you're going to have to explore your emotions more fully. Let someone in. Love again. We've been friends far too long for me to pussyfoot around with you. You need to get a life."

"You sound like Leo."

"Leo Lombardo? Your 911 buddy?"

"Yeah, you know him?"

"We met at Jane's funeral."

The air around Marcus grew thick.

"Sorry," Zur said.

"For what? Mentioning Jane's name? It's not taboo."

Zur shifted in his chair. "Isn't it?"

Marcus's gaze drifted to the French door that opened up to a terrarium full of plants. "I guess I haven't been very open about how I feel about Jane and Ryan. It's been tough. They're not here. I am."

"You deserve to be here."

"Do I?" He stared into his friend's eyes. "They had more to offer this world than I do. They should be alive. Not me."

Zur shook his head. "If you'd died instead of them, what would've happened to Rebecca Kingston and her kids?"

Neither spoke. Seconds turned into minutes.

Finally, Marcus said, "You get anything from Delaney?"

He already knew the answer. If Delaney had given up his accomplice, Zur would've filled Marcus in right away.

"We threatened the guy with solitary, and he didn't crack."

"Seems kind of unusual."

"How do you mean?"

"If Delaney had taken a job for hire and got a bit of money out of the deal, it seems he'd be happy to name whoever hired him, in exchange for maybe a lighter sentence or some perks. But he says nothing?"

"Someone has a real hold over him."

"You thinking mob? Are we back to the whole casino theory?"

"I don't know, Marcus. We're going in circles here. We—" Zur bit his lip.

"What? Spit it out?"

Zur picked something slimy out of his sandwich and wiped his fingers on a napkin. "We were hoping whoever hired Delaney would make his move while Mrs. Kingston was in the hospital."

"We're playing the idea of setting a trap."

"What kind?"

"One that involves Mrs. Kingston."

Marcus's eyes widened. "You want to use her as bait?"

"We'd have her covered. Lots of protection."

"No! You can't do this."

Zur set down the half-eaten sandwich. "Look, we're running out of options. Whoever went after Rebecca will most likely try it again. One night when she's home alone maybe, when you're not around to protect her."

"You can't put her life at risk like that. She has children who need her."

"We think we could escalate things, draw this person out into the open. Then we'd have him. They'd be locked away. Rebecca and her kids would be safe. Isn't that what you want?"

"Of course. But can't you use a double or something? Maybe an undercover agent?"

Zur let out a snort. "That's for the movies. We don't have the budget for that. Marcus, we would have someone in the washroom in her robe watching her room with cameras. We'd have officers in plainclothes positioned outside her door. And I'd be there, not far from her room."

Marcus chewed on the plan, his gut churning in rebellion. He didn't like it. Something could go wrong.

But what if they caught him? Rebecca would never have to worry.

"What's the plan exactly?" he asked.

"We'd have the doctors report a relapse in her health. Maybe she's unconscious. We'd simultaneously report on an accident somewhere, something that police would have to respond to. We'd let the news know, everyone related to the case, and we'd make it known that we had to take the guard off her door because of this faux emergency. Word'll spread fast."

"But you'll be here."

Zur nodded. "I'll be at the main station, a few doors from Mrs. Kingston's room."

"And the kids?"

"We'd move them to the fourth floor—pediatrics—to be safe."

"How many officers near Rebecca's room?"

"Four. They'd be positioned as nurses or patients. And then we'd wait."

Marcus sighed. "Are you going to tell Rebecca?"

"We already have. We needed her permission."

"Because she'll be putting herself in harm's way."

"Yeah, but you can rest easy. We'll have her well protected." Zur chugged back his coffee and wiped his mouth on his sleeve. "Marcus, I know this isn't the optimum strategy, but we're running out of leads. And ideas. If we don't try to coax this guy in, he could go underground for months."

"And resurface when no one's expecting him."

"Exactly."

"I have to see Rebecca."

Zur stood. "Let's go then. We're setting everything into place now. You'll have a few minutes before we fake her relapse. In fact, you could help make it believable."

On the way up to Rebecca's room, Zur filled him in on all the details.

Chapter Thirty-Eight

Hinton, AB – Sunday, June 16, 2013 – 7:53 AM

In a private room in the ICU, Rebecca prepared for the performance of her life. She'd already been drilled about what to expect and how to act barely conscious if anyone entered the room after it was cleared.

Marcus sat near the bed, massaging his temples. His clenched jaw and occasional huffs intimated he wasn't happy about the plan.

But she had to do it. She didn't have a choice. Not if she wanted to breathe again, or live her life without fear.

She gave Detective Zur a shaky smile. "Okay…I'm ready."

"Great. We'll be outside your door, watching every—"

"Rebecca, you don't have to do this," Marcus interrupted. "They can catch this guy another way."

"What other way?" Detective Zur cut in. "We have no leads. We haven't got an inkling who hired Delaney. If we don't get him now—"

"He'll get away and hide," Rebecca finished. "I need to do this, Marcus. So I'm not always looking over my shoulder, wondering if someone's going to come after me. Or the kids."

A nurse hovered over her, fastening an IV line to an empty plastic pouch.

"What's that for?" Rebecca asked.

The nurse glanced at the detective who gave a slight nod. "We're running a fake IV drip. It'll run into this pouch, not into your arm."

"Why would you do that?"

The nurse bit her lip. "It's in case someone tries to…uh, tamper with your IV."

"Tamper." Rebecca blinked, then glanced at Detective Zur. "You think someone will try to drug me?"

"Possibly. We think they'll try to take advantage of your 'relapse' and make your death look like an accident."

"I guess that's better than having them walk in and shoot me." She cringed. "What's stopping them from doing that?"

Detective Zur shook his head. "Whoever planned this has been very smart up until now. He'd want to get in and out as quickly as possible. He wouldn't risk gunshots."

"What if he has a silencer?" she asked.

The detective glanced from Rebecca to Marcus and back to her. "I think you two watch the same movies. Listen, Mrs. Kingston, the first attempt on your life was in a remote location away from witnesses. If you and your children hadn't survived, we wouldn't have Delaney. It might even have appeared to be an accident. Like you'd taken the wrong turn and run off the road."

"And you think whoever hired this Delaney guy still wants no witnesses and no evidence leading back to him."

Detective Zur nodded. "And a death that looks accidental."

"Plus, injecting you with a drug gives him time to get away," Marcus said. "Less chance he'd get caught."

"Exactly," the detective agreed.

"So I'm going to lie here and pretend I'm fading in and out of consciousness, and try not to fall asleep." She sighed. "I guess I can do that."

"We have two cameras set up in your room," Zur said. "One aimed at the door and the other at your bed."

"So you'll see everything."

He nodded, then beckoned to an officer standing in the doorway. "We don't have time to wire your room with microphones, so Corporal Raddison is going to secure a wire to your pillow."

Rebecca took a deep breath. "But you'll get him even if he says nothing?"

"All he has to do is make an attempt and we'll get it on tape."

"What if he tries to smother me with a pillow?"

"Every pillow has been removed from your room, except the one you're lying on. We'll be here in seconds of him making a move." Zur glanced at his watch and picked up the TV remote control. "Ah, showtime."

He flicked on a local television station, and Rebecca gasped. Her photograph was pasted across the screen. Below it, the caption read, "Hit-and-run victim suffers serious complications."

The camera zoomed in on a female reporter standing outside the hospital. "Rebecca Kingston, a victim of a vicious hit and run that included her two children, remains in serious condition at Hinton Hospital. Sources say the woman is in and out of consciousness after lung surgery setbacks. Her two children will be released into their aunt's care later this afternoon, while Rebecca Kingston continues to fight for her life."

A man's face flashed on the screen.

Rebecca shivered. *Rufus Delaney.*

She knew his face from the photo Marcus had

shown her. This was the man who'd run her off the road.

"Turn it off please," she said quietly.

The detective gave her an apologetic look, then turned off the television.

"So now all I do is lie here and wait?" she asked him.

"Yes. I'll be able to check on you once in a while, as will one of the nurses. To make sure you're okay. We don't want you panicking and having a relapse for real."

"I'm sure that's a big comfort," Marcus muttered.

She reached out. "I'm fine. And I'll *be* fine. This was my choice."

When he took her hand and squeezed it, she felt rejuvenated with energy.

"I'm sticking around too," he said.

"You can't stay on the floor," Detective Zur argued. "Your face has been plastered all over the news. For saving Rebecca and her kids."

Marcus shrugged. "Then it'll make sense why I'm hanging around."

The detective's lips thinned. "You can't interfere."

"He won't," Rebecca said. "Right, Marcus? You're going to stay at a safe distance and let them do their jobs."

"Fine."

"You can sit in the room with the recording crew," Detective Zur said. "You'll be able to see and hear everything in this room."

"There. Everything's settled." Rebecca attempted a smile.

"It will be," Marcus said. "Once we catch this bastard."

She glanced at the detective. "Can I have a word with Marcus alone, please?"

"Of course. No more than five minutes. Marcus, when you're done, meet me in the exam room across from the nurses' station?"

"Okay."

When she was alone with Marcus, her hands began to shake and her lips trembled in fear. "I'm not sure if I can do this."

"You can."

"But some guy might come in here and try to kill me."

"Might. We don't even know for sure that anyone will show. And even if he does, he won't get far. Zur will catch him." He stroked her hand, his fingers warm against her skin. "I won't let anything happen to you. I promise. And you trusted me once before, remember?"

"Kind of hard to forget."

"June sixteenth, 2013," he said.

"Pardon?"

"Today's date. It's a 'one' day. New beginnings, remember?"

She smiled. "I like the sound of that."

"Be brave. You're a strong woman, Rebecca Kingston. And when this all over, you and I will go out and celebrate."

She gaped at him in surprise. "Are you asking me out? On a date?"

"Time's up! I have to go now."

He was gone before she could argue.

A second later, she realized he hadn't answered her question.

Chapter Thirty-Nine

Geraldo and Simms, two plainclothes officers, sat at a makeshift desk—the exam table—monitoring a live computer feed and scarcely acknowledging Marcus's presence as he wandered around the room. Every now and then they'd send a status report to Zur.

"Jesus," he muttered. "How long's this going to take?"

He didn't expect an answer. And he didn't get one.

The entire floor had been cleared of nonessential personnel. Patients had been covertly diverted to other areas of the floor, while hospital security restricted all visitors. Yet there had been no action near Rebecca's room.

Come on, asshole. Take the bait!

Marcus had spent the past few hours watching the video from Rebecca's room. Only the nurse, who had been cleared by the police, and John Zur had entered the room. The latter made an imposing figure dressed in doctor's gear, a stethoscope draped around his neck and a bogus ID tag clipped to his jacket pocket.

Marcus hovered over one of the techs and listened

in.

"Need anything, Mrs. Kingston?" the nurse asked, flicking a look over her shoulder and staring into the camera. She gave the thumbs-up.

"Maybe a glass of water," Rebecca said.

The nurse disappeared into the washroom and returned a few seconds later.

After Rebecca had taken a few sips, the nurse said, "I have to empty the glass. An unconscious patient wouldn't be drinking water."

"I understand."

Marcus admired Rebecca's courage. She'd been through so much. She'd survived abuse at the hands of her husband and a murder attempt that had almost been fatal. And now she was luring in a killer.

His cell phone rang. "Hey, John. Any word?"

"Nothing yet. Security is tight, but there haven't been any reports of anyone suspicious entering the hospital. 'Course it would help if we knew who the hell we were looking for."

"I keep going over everything Rebecca told me. No one else seems to benefit from her death except—"

"Wesley Kingston. I know. We showed his picture around the hotel where Delaney was staying. No one recognizes him. We did get one interesting tidbit from Delaney though."

"What's that?"

"When we checked his bank records, we found a large cash deposit."

"How large?"

"Twenty-five thousand."

"Shit. There's no way Kingston had that kind of money lying around."

"Nope. And he didn't win it gambling. We called in a few favors, asked the casino some questions—under threat of temporary shutdown."

"Let me guess. Kingston didn't *borrow* twenty-five thousand either."

"By all accounts, Wesley Kingston was barely scraping by. Motive? Definitely. But he didn't hire Delaney."

"Then who the hell did?"

"Your guess is as good as mine, Marcus. We're still digging around, checking his debts. Seems he owes a few thousand, but unless the casinos are lying, that's it."

"Casinos aren't known for their honesty."

"Yeah, so we're back to the old theory. That someone's trying to send Kingston a message. We're going to bring him back in for questioning if nothing pans out here tonight."

The feed on the monitor wavered.

"What's going on?" Marcus asked Geraldo.

"What do you mean?"

"Didn't you see the camera move?"

"Probably a power surge. Cameras are both working. Nothing to worry about, sir."

Marcus watched the screen. The more he stared, the more he was certain there was someone in the room with Rebecca. Someone standing near her bed.

"Can't you see that?" he asked.

"See what?" Simms snapped.

Marcus was about to point out the shadow near the bed, but it was gone.

"Rewind the tape," he demanded.

Simms clenched his jaw but obeyed. The tape raced back a minute and a half, then played.

"I don't see nothin'," Geraldo said.

Simms glared up at Marcus. "Me neither."

That made three of them.

Shit...

"Marcus!" Zur shouted from the phone.

"Sorry, John. The camera in Rebecca's room flickered for a second."

"Don't worry. She's fine. They're streaming the feed to my tablet so I can see everything you see. Maybe you should go grab a coffee, take a break. This could be a long night."

Marcus hesitated. Last thing he wanted to do was leave.

"We've got her covered," Zur said. "Grab a coffee, clear your head, then go back to the exam room. We could be waiting all night."

"Fine. I'll take a short break."

Marcus disconnected the call, then grabbed his jacket from the hook on the wall. He'd get some fresh air, bring back some coffee and settle in for the long haul.

"You two want anything?" he asked, feeling benevolent.

"Coffee, double cream for me," one said.

"Black," the other replied. "And a donut if they have any."

Neither man looked up.

Marcus sighed. Seems he had a coffee run to make. Hell, at least it got him out of the room for a while. He was starting to go stir-crazy, see things that weren't there.

He thought of Jane and Ryan. He'd been seeing their ghosts for six years. They visited him at night. He'd always insisted they were merely dreams. But Jane had made an appearance yesterday near the McLeod River, and there was no way he'd dreamt that.

What did it all mean?

Means you need to sleep, dumb-ass!

Zur was right. Marcus needed to clear his head.

Chapter Forty

The lamp overhead cast soft shadows into the corners of the room as Rebecca lay in bed, staring at the tiny holes in the ceiling tiles, playing a random game of Connect the Dots. As she mentally drew the lines, her mind returned over and over again to the one thought that haunted her.

Who wanted her dead?

Her pulse raced, even though the machines beside her didn't register this. Lights flashed on it, giving the illusion that she was hooked up. But she wasn't.

There was a silence so thick it nearly choked her. It was broken occasionally by intermittent footsteps. When she heard them, she'd have a second to feign unconsciousness before Detective Zur or the nurse entered and reassured her she was doing the right thing.

She needed this nightmare to be over. She wanted nothing more than to gather her children in her arms and tell them everything was okay.

It will be. Soon.

She wouldn't even consider what would happen if Detective Zur's plan failed. Sure, Marcus had agreed to stay with her for a while, until they found whoever was doing this, but she couldn't expect him to stay forever.

Her body tingled when she pictured Marcus's kind face. His strong hands and soothing voice. She could tell he wasn't sold on Detective Zur's plan. He was afraid for her. He'd already saved her once. It was natural he'd feel somewhat responsible for her.

Is that all it is? This connection between us?

Perhaps she'd been reading the signals all wrong. It seemed rather silly to think there was anything more than a rescuer/victim relationship developing here. And maybe a little innocent flirting. They were both adults. He was single and she was almost single. Maybe he didn't think of her the way she'd been thinking of him.

At least Colton and Ella were safe. Kelly and Steve had picked them up and taken them back to Edmonton.

She pictured their sweet faces, and tears pooled in her eyes. *My babies.*

But even they couldn't keep the terror from her soul.

What if the police were too late? What if she died tonight?

A movement in the corner of her room caught her eye. She blinked. The shadows there rippled as though someone were standing there. She squinted, and for a second, she could almost swear there was a woman in her room.

But there was no one there.

The most peculiar thing was that instead of being horrified by the thought that someone was in her room, she felt this strange sense of peace. Like she was being watched over by a calm, loving presence.

She bit back a laugh. *Good grief. Now you're imagining a guardian angel?*

A breeze wafted over her, and she inhaled the scent of sandalwood.

Weird. Nurses aren't supposed to wear perfume. And I'm not wearing any.

So where was the scent coming from?

A sound interrupted her thoughts.

Footsteps.

Coming closer to her room.

The door opened and she shut her eyes, waiting for the nurse or Detective Zur to make themselves known.

Silence.

Maybe she'd imagined the footsteps too.

With caution, she slowly opened one eye. She didn't see anyone at first. She was about to open both eyes, when a voice whispered, *"Keep your eyes closed."* It was a woman's voice and not one she recognized.

Footsteps approached the bed, and Rebecca tamped down the lurching of her heart. A shiver ran down her body.

"Stay calm," the voice in her ear said.

What the heck? Why would a killer tell her to stay calm? And how would they know she was conscious? It didn't make sense.

The person standing by her bed leaned over her. Rebecca could tell because the dim light she sensed behind her closed lids became darker.

"I'm sorry, Rebecca," a second voice said.

That voice she recognized.

Chapter Forty-One

Marcus took the stairs down to the first floor and walked past the cafeteria on the way to the ER. As he moved toward the exterior doors, he noticed a man standing near the elevator, arguing with a police officer.

Marcus frowned. *What the hell is Wesley Kingston doing here?*

"I want to see my wife for a few minutes," Kingston was saying to the officer.

"Sorry, sir, but Detective Zur wants you to stay here. He'll be down in a few minutes."

"Problem?" Marcus showed the officer his ID. "Marcus Taylor, 911." He was sure by now all the officers on duty would know he had clearance. "Detective Zur can vouch for me."

"Already has," the officer said. "Mr. Kingston is insisting on seeing his wife."

Marcus turned to Rebecca's husband. "Wesley, your wife's in ICU."

"I know. I want to make sure she's okay."

"She's unconscious."

The man flinched, and a small part of Marcus took

pleasure in Kingston's pain.

"They're doing everything they can for her," Marcus said. "Let's go grab a coffee."

"Tracey is getting me one. And some dinner. I would've joined her in the cafeteria except I was detained." He glared at the officer. "By *this* man. He even searched me like I was some common criminal or something."

The officer shrugged. "I'm following orders."

"Let's sit down somewhere," Marcus said with a sigh.

As much as he didn't want Kingston's company, it appeared he wouldn't be able to escape it. Someone had to calm the man down. He could blow everything.

"I'm sure you want the best for your wife, so trust me when I say she'll be fine."

"But the news said she'd had a relapse. She was supposed to be released today."

"These things happen. They're taking good care of her." Marcus took a deep breath. "You see anyone else around the hospital that you know?"

Kingston shook his head. "It's like a morgue around here. Dead quiet."

The guy was oblivious to how inappropriate his comment was, considering where they were.

"You're probably wondering why I even care, seeing as Becca and I are getting a divorce."

Marcus shrugged. "Not my business."

Wesley Kingston stared at the floor. "I made a lot of mistakes. Too many to count. But there are two things I got right—Colton and Ella. I'm not a deadbeat dad. I love my kids. And no matter what Becca and I become, friends or foe, that'll never change."

"The police think you hired the guy that ran your wife's car off the road."

"I would never do such a thing. Besides, how could I hire someone? I haven't got that kind of money?"

"What kind?"

"Whatever it takes to hire someone." Kingston gazed into his eyes. "I swear to you, Mr. Taylor, I had nothing to do with this. I don't hate Rebecca like that. I'm moving on. I have a fiancée, and I'm cutting back on the gambling. We're not rich by anyone's standards. But eventually I'll get a better job, and until I do, Tracey's income from the old folks' home is enough to survive on."

"So you don't owe anyone money?"

"You mean like the casinos?" Kingston shook his head. "Like I told the detective, I had a few small debts, but those were paid off last week."

"From the money Rebecca had saved."

"No, Tracey got a loan."

Marcus saw Zur approaching. He stood. "I have to go, Mr. Kingston. Your date has arrived."

Wesley Kingston greeted the detective with a glum sigh. "How's Rebecca?"

Zur flicked a look at Marcus. "She's still unconscious. I'll take you up to see her in a while. First, I have few more questions."

With his jacket tucked over one arm, Marcus left them to talk and stepped through the emergency doors and out onto the sidewalk. The night air was invigorating, and he inhaled it as though it might be his last breath. After a minute or two, a chill seeped through the thin dress shirt he wore. He shivered.

He was about to put on his jacket when a rectangular piece of paper fell from the pocket and wafted across the parking lot. His initial reaction was to ignore it. It was probably a receipt. But something made him rush after the paper. He grabbed it before it blew into the bushes.

It was the photo he'd taken from Rebecca's house.

Running back to the hospital entrance, he held the

photo under the light and studied it. There was Rebecca looking happier than he'd ever seen her. Wesley appeared a bit nervous, but happy. In the background, a crowd of people gathered around them, champagne glasses raised in a congratulatory toast.

Marcus's gaze flitted across the unfamiliar faces.

Until he saw one he recognized.

Oh damn...

Warning bells blared in his head.

His eyes scoured the nearby bushes. Then the cars parked in the lot.

Nothing seemed out of place.

Then why did it feel like a current of electricity sizzled beneath his skin?

Jane?

She appeared in a fog of serene radiance, her beautiful face and melancholy gaze expressing a despondency that gripped his heart. She stretched out a hand.

As he reached for it, she whispered one word. *"Hurry..."*

Chapter Forty-Two

Hinton, AB – Sunday, June 16, 2013 – 11:12 PM

Rebecca peeked between half-closed eyes. Her suspicion was correct. The voice had come from someone she'd never have suspected. In some ways it made sense, though they'd been civil to each other, and Rebecca wasn't a threat.

So then why was Tracey Whitaker in her room, dressed in a nurse's uniform and holding a syringe?

As instructed, Rebecca feigned grogginess. "Hi, Tracey. What are y-you doing h-here?"

Tracey leaned over her. "I came to finish the job."

"W-what do you mean?" Rebecca muffled an exaggerated yawn, praying that Detective Zur was getting every word on tape. "What job? What are you talking about?"

"You were supposed to die, Rebecca. Quick and easy." Tracey shrugged. "Well, maybe not so quick. But it was supposed to be a simple hit and run, no survivor."

"But you and Wesley are getting married. I'm not standing in your way. You can have him. There's no need to do this."

Tracey shook her head. "Rebecca, you have no idea.

Of course I have to do this. For the money."

The money? This was all about the kids' inheritance?

"You know Wesley can't touch that money," Rebecca said in a faux-groggy voice.

"He can if you're dead before the divorce goes through. He'd automatically get custody of Ella and Colton, and everything that comes with them. Including the money your grandfather left them. Wesley would have signing authority."

"I'm not sure it would work that way."

Tracey smiled. "We've already consulted a lawyer. The guy insisted there's no contingency plan. If you die, Wesley gets the money."

"It's for the kids." *Where the hell is Detective Zur?*

Tracey placed her hands on either side of Rebecca's pillow, then hunched down close to Rebecca's face. "It's not difficult to make an expense look like it's for them and not us."

"I can't believe Wesley's in on this," Rebecca slurred. "I can't believe the father of my children would agree to murder. Of me or his kids. My God…"

Tracey snickered. "Wesley doesn't have the balls to do what's needed." An evil smile lit her face. "But I do."

"The police will catch you," Rebecca said. *If they ever get here!*

Tracey held up the syringe. "You don't think I know what kind of drug to use? There are dozens that won't show up in an autopsy, unless one knew what to look for. No, dear Rebecca, you'll fall asleep until your lungs stop pumping oxygen to your brain and body. The police will think you suffered complications with your lung surgery." She moved to the IV pole and injected the drug into the line.

"Please, Tracey."

The woman capped the hypodermic needle and pocketed it. Then she bent down and kissed Rebecca's forehead. "It won't hurt a bit. I promise."

"Tracey, please. Think about what you're doing."

"I've been thinking about this for months. You haven't been easy to spy on." Tracey laughed. "You almost caught me, do you know that?"

"What are you talking about?"

"Colton's last hockey game. You all went out to watch, and I convinced Wesley I had cold so I could do a little reconnaissance. When he called me after the game to tell me you were going to Cadomin, I knew exactly what I needed to do. But first I had to figure out your exact route. Thankfully, you left a map on a table for me."

Rebecca thought back to that night. *The open garage door!* "You broke into in my house?"

Tracey leaned close. "I've been in your house many times. I've even been in your bed. With Wesley."

Rebecca flicked a look at the door. "That doesn't surprise me. Wesley has a bad habit of making rotten decisions."

Tracey observed her, her forehead furrowing in confusion. After a moment, she shook her head and said, "The little cocktail I prepared for you should be kicking in any second. Why don't you just close your eyes and sleep?"

"Because I'm not tired, you stupid bitch."

Tracey grabbed Rebecca's arm and stared at the area where the IV needle should have been attached. "What the hell?" She yanked the IV bag from beneath the covers.

It was Rebecca's turn to smile. "Sorry to disappoint. Guess you've wasted those drugs for nothing."

"Then it's a good thing I brought a backup." Tracey held up a scalpel.

Chapter Forty-Three

Marcus searched the ER waiting area for Zur, but the detective was gone. So was Wesley Kingston. He ran into the cafeteria and found Kingston sitting at a table, alone.

"Where's your fiancée?"

"I have no idea. I thought she was in here, getting us dinner. I tried calling her, but she's not picking up. Maybe she went to get something from the car." Kingston frowned. "Why?"

Marcus didn't answer. Instead, he raced toward the elevators, while digging his cell phone out of his shirt pocket. In the elevator he stabbed the third-floor button and dialed Zur's number.

"What's up, Marcus?"

"I think I know who's trying to kill Rebecca, and it's not a man. It's a woman. Tracey. Wesley Kingston's fiancée."

"What makes you think that?"

"I found a photo in Rebecca's house." When Zur started to interrupt him, he said, "I had permission to be there. Don't ask. I'll tell you later. Anyways, I found a photo of a party at Kingston's father's law firm. Says on the back that they'd released the news about Rebecca being pregnant with Ella."

"What's that got to do with this Tracey woman?"

"She's standing in the crowd and doesn't look very happy about the news."

"What's she look like?"

"She's tall, maybe five foot ten. Thin. Long red hair, brown eyes. How's Rebecca doing?"

"I'm watching the feed. Mrs. Kingston is fine. But we're having a few problems with the sound. It's cutting in and out. I think she dislodged it by moving around too much."

"Is she alone?"

"No. The nurse is with her."

"The same nurse you vetted?"

There was a pause on the other end.

"Shit," came Zur's reply. "I think it's the fiancée. She's been talking to Mrs. Kingston, leaning over her." He mumbled something Marcus couldn't hear.

"What's wrong?" Marcus demanded.

"Security found our nurse stashed in a janitor's closet two minutes ago. She's unconscious, but alive. We weren't expecting a woman, Marcus, and she's wearing a uniform. We missed it."

Marcus slammed a fist into the wall of the elevator. "I'll be there right away."

"No, don't. I have enough men up here to handle this."

There was more mumbling on the other end, then Zur said, "We've got her! Tracey Whitaker just injected something into the IV. Don't worry. It's not actually attached to Mrs. Kingston. We're going in." The line went dead.

Marcus bounced on the balls of his feet. "Why did I get the slowest elevator ever made?"

There was a brash *ding* and the doors opened. Marcus ran down the hallway, cursing under his breath for not taking the central elevator, which would have exited much closer to Rebecca's room.

As he rounded the corner, he saw six plainclothes officers with their guns drawn. Zur, in his doctor gear, stood outside Rebecca's door, his weapon aimed inside.

Marcus's heart did a flip-flop. "What's going on?"

"Hostage situation," the officer closest to him replied.

Marcus couldn't breathe. *Rebecca...*

He watched in horror as Zur backed away and Rebecca appeared in the doorway. Behind her stood Tracey, though the woman's appearance had changed. Her hair was twisted into a bun, and she wore a nurse's uniform and the black-rimmed glasses she'd confiscated from the real nurse.

Tracey held a scalpel to Rebecca's neck.

"Ms. Whitaker, drop the knife," Zur said.

The woman gripped Rebecca tighter. "Get back!"

"Ms. Whitaker, I'm Detective John Zur. You're making a terrible mistake here."

"She's the one who made the mistake!" Tracey screamed, the knife nicking Rebecca's neck and leaving a thin trail of blood.

"Tell us what you want," Zur said. "What do you need?"

"I need for her to die, like she was supposed to."

Rebecca's panicked eyes found Marcus's, and he tried to mentally send her strength. *Hold on. Don't do anything. Let John handle it.*

"Rebecca Kingston has two young children," Zur said. "You wanted them dead too?"

"No!" Tracey shouted as tears flowed down her cheeks. "They weren't supposed to be there. Wesley said they were staying with their aunt."

"So Mr. Kingston didn't know they were with their

mom?"

Tracey's eyes flashed with panic. "No. *She* was the one who was supposed to die. That's the way he wanted it, planned it. He paid that guy to run her off the road. He said I had to finish it, that we'd get the money for sure then. There was no other way I could pay back the goddamn loan."

Marcus swallowed hard. He and Zur had been wrong about Wesley Kingston. The man *had* planned Rebecca's murder. *The bastard!*

"Ms. Whitaker—Tracey," Zur said in a calm tone. "If you put down the knife, you can walk away."

"Yeah, right." The knife trembled and dipped slightly lower.

"I give you my word. You can walk out those doors. We won't follow you."

"And all I have to do is let this bitch go?"

"Yes."

What happened next was a blur of motion and sound. Tracey jerked her hand upward, and a shot rang out. Someone screamed. Tracey and Rebecca toppled backward, hit the wall and landed on the floor. The scalpel clattered across the tiles, landing in a pool of blood.

"Rebecca!" Marcus screamed.

An officer held him back. "Zur has her, Mr. Taylor. She's all right."

"But I saw blood," he replied with a moan.

"The Whitaker woman. Detective Zur shot her. She's dead."

"I have to see Rebecca. John!"

Zur glanced around, saw Marcus and rushed over. "I can't let you any further, Marcus. It's a crime scene. But what I will do is bring her to you as soon as we've taken her statement. Go wait in the exam room with Simms and Geraldo."

"Kingston is in the cafeteria," Marcus said.

Zur nodded. "We got him. He's already in custody. We'll talk later, okay?"

As Zur walked away, Marcus struggled to get a glimpse of Rebecca. He breathed a sigh of relief when he saw her moving around, uninjured. She was okay. Well, as okay as she could be after Tracey held a knife to her throat.

He watched as Zur led Rebecca back to her room. With nothing left to do, Marcus wandered down the hall, replaying the night's events in his head.

Tracey Whitaker and Wesley Kingston had conspired to murder Rebecca.

He shook his head. How could he have been so wrong about Kingston?

The money.

Not the money the kids would inherit, but the money used to pay off Delaney. That's what had thrown Marcus. He'd been so sure that Kingston had no access to such a large amount of money. Twenty-five thousand dollars? But it had been Tracey who'd come up with payment. One coldhearted bitch.

And now one coldhearted *dead* bitch.

Kingston...

The guy was downstairs eating dinner, for Christ's sake. The mastermind had been right under everyone's noses.

Marcus took a detour and headed to the stairwell. Taking the steps two at a time, he was on the main floor in less than two minutes. A few patients wandered the floor, along with three interns and an ER doctor.

He strode down the hallway, hell-bent on pounding Kingston's face to a pulp. When he reached the cafeteria, he found Wesley Kingston standing near a table, his hands cuffed behind his back while an officer read him his rights.

"I had nothing to do with this," Kingston shrieked.

The officer led Kingston toward Marcus. They locked eyes as they passed.

"It wasn't me," Kingston insisted. "I swear, I didn't try to kill her!"

"Bullshit!" Marcus said, his fists clenched at his sides. "Tracey already admitted you planned it all. You're going down for attempted murder. Of your wife *and* your two kids, you son of a bitch."

"You're wrong," Kingston sobbed. "I'd never hurt them. I have no reason to want them dead."

"I can think of about eight hundred *thousand* reasons."

Kingston shook his head. "What you're suggesting is ludicrous. I'm not capable of murder."

"Money can make people do desperate things," Marcus said between gritted teeth. "Things they thought they were never capable of."

"I didn't do this," Kingston hissed. "Tracey—"

"Is dead," Marcus snapped. "That's what your plan got you. A dead fiancée and a prison sentence."

Kingston was led away amid shrieks of protest and denials.

Marcus ran a shaky hand through his hair and released a pent-up groan. He'd wasted enough time on Kingston. The man would get what was coming to him.

He walked back to the elevator and stepped inside.

Time to tell Rebecca the nightmare is finally over.

Chapter Forty-Four

Hinton, AB – Sunday, June 16, 2013 – 11:37 PM

Rebecca's hands quivered as Dr. Monroe inspected the stitches in her side.

"Everything looks good here," the doctor said before leaving the room.

Rebecca watched the clock on the wall and wondered how her life had gone so wrong. At what point had she taken this detour into hell? And what had she done to deserve such atrocities?

"I still can't believe it," she said to Detective Zur, who was seated by the bed. "Tracey Whitaker?" She shook her head slowly.

"She was a desperate woman. She wanted you out of your husband's life, so she could have a future with him. And the money."

"And Wesley agreed to it all." She stifled a sob. "I can't believe I was so mistaken about him. I was married to him, for crying out loud. How could I have misjudged his character so badly? How could I have allowed my children to be anywhere near him?"

The detective shrugged. "You didn't know."

She clenched her teeth, then said, "Well, I should've

known."

"Try not to be so hard on yourself, Mrs. Kingston. Some people are schemers and liars. They find ways to bend the truth, twist it to their realities. Your husband and Ms. Whitaker, they're both master manipulators. They wanted you to see what they presented."

"But I was so gullible."

"Unfortunately, we didn't get anything from Rufus Delaney. He's still not talking. And the little we got from Ms. Whitaker isn't really enough to say your husband absolutely knew you had your son and daughter. It's possible Ms. Whitaker gave the order to Rufus. She may have known where your children were."

She shuddered. "They almost died."

"They're alive and safe. And so are you. We couldn't have brought Delaney and Ms. Whitaker down without your assistance. So…thank you."

"I'm glad it's over."

Detective Zur nodded. "The danger's over. I'll warn you though—the next few months are not going to be easy. We're going to process your husband. He'll be charged with attempted murder. If we link him to Delaney, he could be charged with hiring a contract killer. We're still looking for hard evidence against your husband."

"You mean he could get off?"

"I'm going to do everything in my power so that doesn't happen."

"Thank you."

The detective smiled. "You can thank me by getting better and taking your family home."

"That's what I plan to do."

Detective Zur stood. "I have to get back to the station. I expect you'll see Marcus later?"

"I think so. You two go way back, isn't that right?"

He nodded. "A few years."

292 | S U B M E R G E D

"What was he like before his wife and son died?"

"He was a good guy. Trustworthy. Funny. And a great cook. Of course, that was before he made some wrong choices."

"The drugs, you mean."

Detective Zur raised a brow. "Marcus told you about that?"

She nodded. "We had a lot of time to talk. On the phone when I was in the river. He kept me calm." She stared up at him. "You seem surprised."

"I am. Astounded, actually."

"Why?"

"The Marcus Taylor I know has been rather…closed off. He talked to me a bit after the accident. Then he closed right down. Ever since Jane and Ryan died, he's become more introverted, not so funny."

"He's made *me* laugh a few times."

The detective watched her, his face brightening. "You like him?"

She blushed. "I, uh…"

"Forget I asked. It's none of my business."

"I'm still married."

Detective Zur walked to the door. "You already initiated divorce proceedings, Mrs. Kingston. If you like Marcus, let him know. He's the kind of guy who'll wait."

"Do you think people can change after years of bad choices?"

"In my line of work," he said, "I see it happen quite often. But some people have to hit rock bottom before they resurface and realize what's important in life. The hardest part for those people is figuring out exactly where their 'rock bottom' is." He released a heavy sigh. "You don't have to concern yourself with Marcus. He hit his six years ago."

"When Jane and Ryan died."

He nodded. "Things have been shaky since then, but he's coming around. I can see a difference in him already. And I have a feeling you'll be better for him than any drug."

"I'm not sure that's a compliment."

Detective Zur grinned. "Believe me, it is."

Rebecca glanced at the clock for the millionth time. It was almost midnight and still no Marcus.

Maybe he's not coming.

She wondered if he'd gone back to the hotel to sleep.

He doesn't sleep. He has somniphobia.

She flicked on the television and wandered through the channels. Nothing interested her, and her eyes drifted to the door.

She thought about Wesley. Was he in a jail cell, cursing because his plans had been blown? Was he raging because she and the kids were still alive?

She gave herself a mental kick for believing his lies.

Greed. One of the seven deadly sins.

She prayed Wesley was as cold and miserable as she had been when trapped in the car.

Then she thought about Ella and Colton. She wanted to curl up and cry for them, for what they were about to endure. In a matter of hours they would discover their father had tried to kill them—and their mother. How do children live with that?

How will I live with that?

The air in the room shifted as though a breeze had wafted in from an open window. But the window was closed.

She had the distinct sensation that someone was leaning over her. And then she heard a soft female voice say, *"You'll live with this, Rebecca, one day at a time."*

Her eyes drifted shut and a sensation of bliss washed over her.

One day at a time.

Chapter Forty-Five

Hinton, AB – Monday, June 17, 2013 – 12:44 AM

Marcus tiptoed into Rebecca's room, a bouquet of assorted blue flowers in his hand. The only ones left in the hospital flower shop, they'd had a blue balloon attached, announcing the birth of a baby boy. He'd removed the balloon and left it tied to a doorknob.

"Hi," she said from the bed.

"Hi." He surveyed the room, then spotted a vase with a wilted single red rose on the windowsill. "Want me to throw this out?"

"Please," she said with obvious relief.

"These were all they had left downstairs," he said, motioning to the bouquet.

"Blue flowers are my favorite."

They match your eyes, he wanted to say. "I, uh, wanted you to have something colorful and bright to look at."

"These walls are really sterile looking, aren't they?"

He laughed. "Hospital white."

"Remind me not to order that paint color—ever."

There was an uncomfortable second of stillness.

"When are you—?"

"Do you think—?" she said at the same time.

They grinned at each other.

"You first," he said.

"I was wondering if you think you'll come visit me sometime. In Edmonton."

His brow arched. "You want me to?"

"I wouldn't suggest it if I didn't." Her expression grew serious. "I don't play head games, Marcus. And I'm pretty sure neither do you. I'd like to get to know you."

"Without my cape, you mean."

She laughed, and it sent shivers down his spine.

"Fine. I'll come see you in Edmonton."

Her smile radiated sheer delight, and he hoped he'd never see it disappear.

"You started to say something," she reminded him.

He shrugged. "I wanted to know when you were going to get out of here."

"You make it sound like I'm in jail." She flinched.

"Are you thinking of Wesley?"

"I'm still having trouble wrapping my brain around everything he's done. I didn't see it coming. None of it."

Marcus's lips thinned. "How could you? He's the father of your children. And regardless of what he'd done in the past, you never dreamed he'd be capable of murder."

She shuddered. "I guess I'm quite the fool."

"No you're not. You were manipulated by someone you once trusted."

"What'll happen now?"

"The system will take care of Wesley, and you'll get justice for you, Ella and Colton. How are they doing, by the way?"

She smiled. "Driving Kelly insane."

Chapter Forty-Six

Edmonton, AB – Monday, June 17, 2013 – 2:19 PM

Rebecca unlocked the front door, then turned to Marcus. "I can't thank you enough for everything you've done for us."

"I'm glad I could help."

"Help?" She let out a sad laugh. "You did more than that. My children and I will never be able to repay you."

"I'm not looking for repayment."

She stepped inside her home. It felt like she'd been gone for months instead of days. "Want to come in? I could fix us some dinner."

"I should probably be going."

She cocked her head to one side. "You drove me home, Marcus. Dinner is the least I could do."

"Fine," he said, moving inside and closing the door. "But you need to rest still. I'll do the cooking, providing you've got food in the house."

She grinned. "I can't promise a stocked pantry. I didn't bothering buying much before we left. But there might be something in the fridge or freezer."

Marcus helped her ease off her jacket. She sucked in a breath when pain flared around her chest.

"See?" Marcus said. "What did I tell you? You need to rest."

She sank down on the sofa, grateful to take his advice, and there was an awkward moment of silence as he propped her feet up on the sofa, then sat in the chair across from her.

"At least I won't have to worry about Colton and Ella tonight," she said.

He nodded. "It was nice that your sister decided to keep them overnight and give you an evening to yourself."

"Kelly's good that way. She always seems to know what I need."

"My brother, Paul, was a bit like that, although he was caught up in his army career. He made a good soldier."

"That must have been really hard on you when he died."

"Yeah. It was hard on everyone. Paul's death left a huge hole in our family. Seems I have a lot of holes."

She gazed into his eyes and saw bitter grief there. "Jane and Ryan?"

He nodded. "You have any tea?"

"I think so. Herbal or regular?"

"Green tea, if you have it. And don't move. I'll get it. You just tell me where everything is." He was about to walk away, but stopped. "I quit drinking when I quit drugs, even though I never had any problem with alcohol. I thought you should know."

Admiring his honesty, she watched as he puttered around in the kitchen, gave him directions to the tea and teapot, then agreed to ordering in some salads from Boston Pizza, since Marcus couldn't find anything salvageable in the fridge.

"So tell me more about this sleep phobia you have," she said when he handed her a mug.

"Somniphobia. It sucks. I'd give anything to be able to climb into bed and sleep more than two hours at a stretch."

"What happens when you try to sleep?"

"My heart begins to pound. My palms sweat. I feel like I'm gasping for breath. As soon as I drift off, I jerk awake. Sometimes I see things that aren't there."

"What kind of things?"

He shook his head and stared at the fireplace. "Ghosts mostly. I know, crazy. I'm sleep deprived. But sometimes…" He shrugged.

"What?"

"They seem so real."

"Your wife and son?"

"Yes."

"Paul?"

"I used to see him, but it's been a long time since he visited me."

"Maybe he's at peace now."

He raised his eyes and stared at her. "You know, most women would simply laugh at an admission like this. They'd think I was nuts."

"Are you?"

He chuckled. "There are days when I wonder."

"Like recently?"

"Yeah. The past few days have been high on my list of weird."

"Gee, thanks."

He laughed. "I didn't mean you."

"It has been *beyond* strange." Her smile faded. "It's not every day that I have to fight for my life because my husband and his lover want me out of the picture." She still couldn't wrap her head around the fact that Wesley had planned everything.

"I'm really sorry, Rebecca. I can't imagine what you're going through."

"It's probably my fault the police didn't consider

her."

"What do you mean?"

"When Detective Zur asked me about Tracey, I said we were civil to each other, that there were no hard feelings."

"You thought that was true. She didn't give you any reason to think otherwise."

"They did look into her," she said, trying to recall what Zur had stated about Tracey right before she'd left Hinton. "She's not living with Wesley, and no one knew they were engaged. That happy event happened a few days ago, according to Tracey. She's never been arrested and had such nice things to tell the police about me. And since her bank records didn't show anything unusual, the police didn't consider her a suspect."

"You don't have to worry about her now."

She nodded. "I know."

The image of Tracey's body falling to the floor, taking her down with her, kept replaying in her mind. The police had pulled Tracey off her, and all Rebecca had seen was the blood.

She cringed at the memory. "Wesley has her blood on his hands."

"He almost had yours and the kids' too."

She blinked back tears. "Wesley told your detective friend that he'd mentioned the kids' inheritance to her. He still claims he had nothing to do with this. He's a good liar." She couldn't keep the resentment from her voice.

"And now he's locked up. You won't have to worry about him for a long time."

Her gaze swept over the living room. There was so much here that reminded her of Wesley. Too much. "I think I'm going to sell the house and move."

"Where to?"

"I don't know. Someplace that's quiet. That doesn't

remind me of this life I had with him."

"Housing market kinda sucks right now."

"What do you propose I do?"

"Wait a few months. See if the market improves, and if it does, sell then."

She smiled. "Ever think of going into real estate?"

"No. I've been keeping my eyes open, though. There's something Jane and I had planned to do."

"What's that?"

He shrugged. "Maybe I'll tell you one day. Right now, you should focus on what you're going to do."

She let out a small groan. "I haven't got a clue. How does one return to normal life when things have been anything but normal?"

He leaned forward, and at first she thought he was going to touch her, but he clasped his hands in his lap. "One day at a time."

"Speaking of which…" She took a deep breath. "Are you going to go to a meeting tonight?"

"I was planning on it. Unless you want me to stay here."

She shook her head. "The last thing I need is a babysitter, Marcus."

"I don't mind staying for one night. So you're not alone."

"The police car outside is gone because there's no threat. Tracey is dead and Wesley's in jail. There's nothing for me to be afraid of anymore. I'm safe. Besides, it's time for you to look after yourself for a change." She tilted her head at him. "I'd feel better if I knew you were at a meeting tonight."

Marcus's brow arched. "Are you worried that I might use?"

"If you did, I'd think it was my fault." She held her breath and waited for his reply.

"It's never anyone else's fault," he said. "When an addict uses, it's his or her choice. Always."

"Then go to a meeting. When it's over, come back here."

He gave her a surprised look and she added, "You can sleep on the couch. Or watch TV."

"Why'd you change your mind?"

She looked away. "Even though I'm no longer in danger, the thought of staying in the house by myself is a bit unnerving. I'd feel better if someone else were here. Even if just for a night."

"No problem."

She caught his arm. "Before you go, can you do me a favor?"

"Sure thing. What do you need?"

"The doctor gave me some painkillers and something to help me sleep. They're in my purse, by the front door. Can you put them in the kitchen by the sink? I think that's as far as I'm going to make it. At least until you get back."

He stared at her, his face serious and grim. "Are you testing me?"

"Huh?"

"With the drugs."

"No!" Her eyes widened in shock. "That's the last thing I'd do. I want those pills where I can reach them easily. That's all."

Marcus's face reddened. "Sorry. I-I'm so used to suspicion, I guess."

She waved a hand in the air. "Forget about it. I trust you."

He watched her, skepticism etched into his face. "You're too nice, Rebecca Kingston."

"Nice. Oh yay. Just what every woman wants to hear."

When he looked as though he were going to apologize again, she laughed. "I'm joking."

She watched as he pulled on his jacket and opened

the door.

Pausing in the doorway, he said, "You probably shouldn't, you know."

"Shouldn't what?"

"Trust me."

She pondered his words as the door closed behind him. *Too late, Marcus.*

Chapter Forty-Seven

Edmonton, AB – Monday, June 17, 2013 – 2:48 PM

Marcus found an NA meeting about fifteen minutes from Rebecca's house. It was being held in the basement of a small Pentecostal church. As much as he missed the familiar crowd of his meetings back home, there was some comfort in being in a room with complete strangers. And no pressure to speak.

Last thing he wanted to do was admit how badly he craved drugs—especially after the stress of recent events. The little devil on his shoulder tried to convince him that he could have just a little bit—enough to take the edge off. The rational side of his mind—he refused to call it angelic—reminded him of the downward spiral he'd quickly go into if he used.

Listening to one man tell his story, how he'd lost everything, including his wife, kids, job and home and was now living on the streets in downtown east Edmonton, brought home the reality of drug addiction. An addict wasn't in control; the drugs were. And there was no such thing as a small slipup. Using was using, no matter the quantity or the drug of choice.

Choices…that's what everything comes down to.

Marcus thought about Leo. His best friend had managed to turn his life around after alcoholism and cocaine nearly ruined him. Now he was married to a great woman and had a job he enjoyed. Leo had made all the right choices.

Every morning when Marcus woke up, the first thing he did was make a choice. "Today I'm not going to use drugs, no matter the temptation. Today I will say 'No!'"

"Anyone else have something to share?" the guy in charge of the meeting asked.

No one spoke up.

"What about you, sir, in the back row? You're new here, and we welcome you with open arms. Feel free to share."

Marcus nearly bolted from his chair. "I…uh…not tonight."

"That's okay. Maybe next time."

Next time. It was always "next time."

Marcus knew he had a mental block that kept him from speaking up at meetings. He'd argued with Leo over it for months. When the time was right, Marcus believed he'd know it, feel it. Leo would then give him shit and tell him it was an excuse. Nothing more.

Is it? Am I making excuses?

He thought about Rebecca. She'd been to hell and back in the last three days. He admired her inner strength. She didn't make excuses. Not for Wesley, or herself. Not for anyone. She was the first person Marcus felt he could really talk to, about anything.

He was attracted to her. There was no denying that. No excuses either. She was a beautiful woman. Inside and out. He was perplexed by her offer of spending the night, albeit on the couch. Had she done so because she was still afraid? Or did she feel something more?

Jesus, Marcus. She's grateful. That's all. You rescued her and her kids. It's common for people in these situations to feel attracted to their rescuers. But it doesn't last. It's not real.

Then again, he wasn't a very good judge of what was real. He talked to his dead wife's ghost. How real was that? She came to him during times of intense stress. When he'd had very little sleep. Obviously she was a figment of his exhausted mind. Ghosts weren't real.

But she led you to Rebecca.

And she'd warned him to hurry in the hospital.

Natural intuition. Nothing more than that.

He listened to the final speaker, all the while rationalizing Jane's recent "appearances." He fought back a yawn as people shuffled to their feet, all promising to hold on for one more day.

On his way to the door, he bumped into the leader of the meeting.

"Excuse me," the guy said, "but is your name Marcus Taylor?"

"Uh, we're supposed to maintain anonymity here."

"I know. My apologies. But your picture was in the newspaper. You rescued that woman and her kids." The man smiled. "You're a hero. Not many of us in this room can say that."

"I prefer to think of it as doing the right thing."

"You're a 911 operator. Physically searching for someone is beyond your job description, isn't it? That's a hero."

Marcus didn't know what to say.

"You did the right thing," the man said. "You showed extreme courage."

Marcus shrugged. "Like I said, it was right thing to do at the time."

"Doing the right thing isn't always easy. That's why we're here in this church basement. But you're on the right track." The man patted him on the back. "Hopefully one day you'll show that same kind of courage and share your story."

"Perhaps."

"Good-bye, Mr. Taylor. It was an honor meeting you."

Driving away, Marcus replayed the man's words in his head.

A block from Rebecca's house, he slowed the car as a peculiar tingling went through his body. He glanced in the rearview mirror, half expecting to see Jane sitting behind him. But the seat was empty.

"Jeez, Marcus. Overactive imagination much?"

A sensation of foreboding crept over him, one he couldn't shake.

"Get it together," he muttered beneath his breath.

He pulled over once Rebecca's house came into view, parked and shut off the engine. There was no way in hell he was going to let Rebecca see him like this. He needed to calm down.

He twisted in his seat. "Okay, Jane. If you're going to make an appearance, please do. I'll wait for you."

Then he settled back and waited for his wife's ghost to appear.

After ten minutes, Jane hadn't shown up.

He was about to get out of the car when a sleek black town car pulled up to the curb ahead of him. He didn't pay it any mind at first, until a tall, silver-haired man climbed out and made his way across the street. The man glanced over his shoulder in Marcus's direction. Sunlight caught the angles of his face—the bushy eyebrows and piercing stare. He strode to Rebecca's front door, knocked and then went inside.

The man looked familiar, but Marcus couldn't quite place him. The guy wasn't one of the detectives. Their pay scale didn't supply them with Lincoln town cars.

"The lawyer," he mumbled. That's who it must be. Carter something.

Not wanting to interrupt them, Marcus remained in his car.

Chapter Forty-Eight

Edmonton, AB – Monday, June 17, 2013 – 4:16 PM

Returning from the washroom, Rebecca heard the knock on her door and let out a relieved sigh. Marcus was back. The past hour and a half had ticked by so slowly, and though she knew there was no longer any threat to her life, she didn't like being alone. She'd jumped at every noise, every shadow.

"Come on in, Marcus," she called out. "The door's unlocked."

She moved down the hallway and heard the soft creak of the front door. Rounding the corner, she smiled. "So how did your meeting—" She blinked.

Walter Kingston stood in her living room.

"Hello, Rebecca," he said stiffly.

"Walter. What are you doing here?"

"I came to apologize. For the behavior of my son and his…well, you know."

She nodded, thankful her racing heart was slowing. "That's very kind of you, considering the circumstances. Thank you."

He took a few steps, then said, "You're expecting someone?"

"Uh…yes. Marcus Taylor, the man who found us."

"I expect you're very grateful he did."

She frowned. "Of course. We wouldn't be alive if it weren't for him."

"So he'll be here soon?"

"I think so. He had a…meeting to attend."

Walter's eyes grew shadowed. "Then I guess I'd better do what I came here to do."

"There's no need to apologize, Walter. Wesley made some awful choices. I don't hold you responsible for your son's actions."

Walter ambled forward and opened his arms wide. "I'm so happy to hear that." He gathered her up in his arms. "But I'm still sorry."

"How about a glass of wine or some tea?" she asked, slipping out of his grasp. "Come on in, take off your gloves and stay a while. You can meet Marcus when he gets back."

"Oh, I'm not planning to stay long. But tea sounds like a plan. Let me get it for you. You don't seem to be moving too quickly."

She smiled. "Thanks, Walter."

As he puttered around in the kitchen, he called out, "Honey or sugar?"

"Honey, please." She settled back onto the sofa and propped a pillow behind her. "There's herbal tea in the cupboard and regular too."

"Found it. Let's try the strawberry pomegranate. Lots of antioxidants."

She almost laughed, wondering when Walter had become such a connoisseur of teas.

When he handed her a mug, she nodded in thanks. "It really is very nice of you to stop by."

He set the teapot on the coffee table. "You *are* my daughter-in-law." He peered over her shoulder. "Are the kids sleeping?"

"They're at my sister's."

"Perfect."

She raised a brow. "How so?"

"I mean, dear, that you need some time to heal, and running after two active children can't be easy right now."

He had a point, and she let out a sigh. "The past few days have been very difficult."

"And Wesley and Tracey didn't make it easy."

She was touched by his understanding. They'd never been that close. She'd always found Walter a little standoffish. Yet here he was, drinking tea in her living room.

"I wish things had gone differently," she said.

"Me too."

She cradled the mug in her hands and took a sip of tea. It had a bitter aftertaste, and she made a face.

"Too sweet?" he asked. "I wasn't sure how much honey you take, so I put in a good spoonful. Can't hurt. It's good for you."

"It's fine." She drank a bit more, hoping to get the sickening sweet taste out of her mouth. "I still can't believe it…" She shook her head. "I'm sorry. It's probably best we don't talk about everything that happened." She yawned. "It's been a long day."

"I'm sure it has."

"I hope we can remain…friends. For the kids' sake. You're their grandpa."

"You need fluid and lots of rest."

She chuckled. "You sound like a doctor. Dr. Kingston, MD."

"There was a time when I thought I'd go into that profession. But law suited me better. I have a deep need to right wrongs."

She blinked. "You're a good lawyer."

"I don't hate you, Rebecca. I want you to know that. Sometimes we have to make hard decisions."

Walter's response wasn't what she'd expected.

In their shared silence, she listened to the ticking of the clock in the kitchen. It made her want to go to sleep. All she had to do was close her eyes.

Stay awake!

She nearly fell off her chair at the voice in her ear. A woman's voice. The same voice she'd heard when Tracey had tried to kill her.

Rebecca's eyes wandered over Walter's face. His smile was gone, replaced with a frown. "What's wrong, Walter?"

"Besides everything?"

She tried to sit up, but her limbs felt suddenly weak. "I know you must be upset because—"

"Upset?" His voice sounded distorted as he reached out, taking her mug and setting it on the table. "Your pathetic husband can't get a grip on his spending, and you think I'm upset?"

"I meant because of…the accident…the kids."

"I told Wesley he needed help," Walter said, as if he hadn't heard a word she'd said. "He needed to get that damned gambling under control."

"You knew?"

"Of course I knew. I knew everything. Do you think I'm an idiot? Besides, who do you think has been bailing him out all this time?"

"Tr…Tracey." Why was the room spinning?

"That stupid twit? She couldn't even follow simple instructions. All she had to do was get the drugs into your IV. But no, she had to talk to you, waste time."

"W-what? What are y-y-you talking about?"

"She came to me, begging for another loan to give to Wesley. But they'd been sponging off me far too long. She couldn't pay off the last loan. And when I found out about the money you got from your grandfather…" He let out a mocking laugh. "You couldn't even bail out your own husband?"

"The money's for the k-kids."

"So it's okay for Wesley to keep taking my money?" His voice was dripping with bitterness. "It's okay to make me look like a fool? Well, no longer."

"I d-don't understand."

"It's simple. Wesley is an embarrassment. I ordered him to clean up his mess. I gave him precise instructions to get the money from you, pay off his own debts for a change. But he's too much of a wimp and couldn't follow directions if someone stamped them on his forehead."

Walter's words made no sense. And why was he still wearing his gloves?

"You think Wesley set this all up?" he asked, his lips twisting into an ugly jeer. "You're as stupid as he is. When Tracey told me about the money you'd inherited, I said I'd do one last thing. Help them get the money. What they did with it was their problem, but there'd be no more loans from me. With one exception. I hired someone I could trust that could get the job done."

"You?" Rebecca shuddered. "Y-you paid off…that…Delaney g-guy? You hired him…to k-kill me—us?"

"I had no idea the kids were with you. Until Rufus called me from the gas station. I am sorry about that. But there was no other way. With the three of you out of the picture, Wesley could clear his debts and move on—out of my life. That was deal I made with Tracey."

"Deal?"

"I'd pay Rufus and help them get the money, and they'd leave Edmonton. I couldn't afford the rumors about Wesley affecting me any longer. Even his blasted affair with Tracey was office fodder. Oh, and Rebecca?" He stared into her bleary eyes. "They'd been having an affair far longer than you think."

She swallowed hard and fought back tears. "How long?"

"Since you were pregnant with the girl."

Ella. Sweet Ella.

She recalled how nervous Wesley had been when she'd said she was pregnant again. She'd thought it was because his job situation was so precarious. Now she knew better.

But still…Walter?

"Drink some more, Rebecca. You'll feel better. It's special tea." The mug shifted, splitting into two and then three.

Her breath froze in her chest, and her pulse raced. "'Special tea'?"

The malevolent look in Water's eyes told her he'd drugged it.

With a flick of her wrist, she dropped her mug, spilling tea down her legs.

Oh God. He's going to kill me.

Chapter Forty-Nine

Edmonton, AB – Monday, June 17, 2013 – 4:32 PM

Marcus's cell phone rang. It was Zur.

"Hey, John. What's up?"

"Just thought you should know we're getting nowhere with Kingston. He still claims he's innocent."

"Don't they all?"

"Yeah, except we can't find any evidence against him."

"What about the confession from the Whitaker woman?"

"She didn't specifically name Wesley Kingston. We'll hold him, but unless we find something concrete…"

"You may have to let him walk." *Shit!*

"We'll have no choice. He has a solid alibi. So while he may have motive, we can't pin him to the crime scene. Nor can we find any link between Kingston and Rufus Delaney."

"What's Delaney have to say, now that Tracey is dead?"

"He still won't admit she hired him. And we haven't found a trace of the money."

"He's probably got it stashed somewhere."

"We're still checking him out. Something tells me we're missing the connection between Delaney and Kingston."

Delaney and Kingston…

Marcus stared out the windshield, his eyes resting on the license plate of the vehicle in front of him. JU5T1C3—an odd combination for an Alberta plate.

He narrowed his eyes. *JUST…once…three?*

Then it came to him. *JUSTICE.*

His gaze jerked toward Rebecca's house as the pieces slipped into place.

Walter Kingston, Wesley's father, was a lawyer. And what did lawyers usually want? Justice.

The man was wealthy, respected and in a position of power.

Marcus redialed John's number. Three rings and his friend picked up.

"Did you ever check out Walter Kingston?" Marcus asked.

"The lawyer?"

"Yeah. He's Rebecca's father-in-law."

"We interviewed him after Mrs. Kingston was found, but he didn't know anything about his son or the Whitaker woman's plans. And he seemed to have a decent relationship with Mrs. Kingston. Even she said so." Zur cleared his throat. "You think he had something to do with this?"

Marcus groaned and rubbed a hand over his face. "I don't know. I'm probably grasping at straws here."

"Hold on. Let me check something."

Seconds later, Zur came back on the line. "We missed it. It was there all along, but we didn't dig far enough."

"What?"

"Back a few years, when Walter Kingston worked

criminal law, he represented someone we both know."

"Let me guess. Rufus Delaney."

"The one and only."

"Shit…" Marcus turned off the ignition.

"Listen, Marcus, as soon as I get off the phone and get a warrant, I'm going to have one of our tech guys check out his bank records."

"You think he's the one who paid off Delaney?"

"Tracey said someone loaned her the money. We know Wesley Kingston doesn't have any. Daddy Kingston's the next best thing. We're going to send a car to Kingston's place and pick him up."

"He's not there."

"What? Where the hell is he?"

Marcus climbed out of the car and quietly closed the door. "He went into Rebecca's house over twenty minutes ago. I'm going in."

"No, stay where you are. In your vehicle. I'll have cars be there with backup in less than ten minutes."

Marcus crossed the street. "He's in there with her now."

"Stay in your car!"

"Sorry, John. I can't do that. Rebecca's in danger."

"Wait!"

But he was no longer listening.

Tucking the cell phone into his pocket, Marcus strode up the sidewalk. At first, he figured he'd rush through the front door, but common sense kicked in. What if Walter Kingston had a gun? No. His best chance of saving Rebecca was bringing the element of surprise.

He crept up to the living room window. Lights from the kitchen and a lamp near the door illuminated the room. There was no sign of Walter Kingston. Or Rebecca.

He moved to the front door, turned the knob and let out a soft breath when it opened. Slipping into the house, he eased the door closed. Then he listened. Someone moved at the far end of the house.

With cautious footsteps, he proceeded into the house. From his previous visit, he knew the floor plan. The bedrooms were in the back. That's where he'd find Kingston and Rebecca.

Passing through the kitchen, he spotted a pill bottle on the counter. It rested on its side, a pile of small blue pills next to it. A kettle next to both.

Shit! He's drugged her.

As he tiptoed down the hall, Marcus caught sight of Colton's bedroom. It was exactly like he'd last seen it, with clothing and sporting equipment spread out across the floor—including a worn-out hockey stick.

That'll do.

He strode into the room, grabbed the stick and continued down the hall, hockey stick raised.

"What are you doing?" he heard Rebecca say from inside her bedroom.

The sounds of her slurred voice combined with running water made Marcus shiver. *I'm coming, Rebecca. Hold on.*

"Relax, Rebecca," Walter Kingston replied.

Marcus muffled a curse. Then he stepped up to the bedroom door, which was cracked open an inch, and peered inside. The room was empty, but dancing shadows came from the open doorway into the en suite.

He moved swiftly into the room. He scrutinized his surroundings, desperate to find a way to catch Kingston off guard. He had to get him out of the bathroom, away from Rebecca. How?

A laptop sat on the bed, its screen glowing. Had Kingston caught her in bed checking e-mails?

Marcus approached the laptop, and when he read the document displayed, his stomach clenched. It was a suicide note. From Rebecca. Either Kingston had typed it, or he'd made Rebecca do it.

Splashing sounds came from the bathroom.

"No!" Rebecca cried. "Stop!"

Marcus spun toward the hallway, nearly knocking over the laptop. Forgetting his previous plan to lure Walter Kingston back into the bedroom, he darted toward the doorway.

What he saw made his heart stop.

Rebecca was in the bathtub, fully clothed, while Walter Kingston held her head underwater with one hand. In his other hand, he held a straight blade.

Marcus would have taken a slap shot at the man's head, but at the sound of footsteps, Kingston whipped around, his eyes locking on Marcus's, the knife against the back of Rebecca's neck.

"Let her go!" Marcus shouted. "It's over, Mr. Kingston. The police are on their way."

Rebecca's head was still beneath the water.

"Let Rebecca go," he said again, moving closer.

Kingston raised the blade. "Stay back! I don't know who you are, but this isn't your concern." He yanked Rebecca's head up, and she gulped for air. "It's all *her* fault."

Marcus lowered the hockey stick and held his other hand up to stall him. "Listen, Rebecca didn't do anything other than marry your son."

"Wesley?" The man sneered. "He's no son of mine. He's a weakling."

"The police know everything. They'll be here any second. If you step away from her and put the blade down, things won't get any worse for you."

"Worse? Tracey is dead. Wesley's in jail. And that bastard Rufus is probably singing like a fucking canary." Kingston's lips thinned. "So, yeah, how could things possibly get worse?" He drew the straight blade underneath Rebecca's chin and a thin line of blood appeared.

Marcus flinched. "Let Rebecca go, Walter. The kids

need her."

"It's too late, Mr. Whoever-You-Are."

"S-superhero," Rebecca slurred.

Marcus frowned. *Kingston must have drugged her first.*

As Kingston's head swiveled toward her, Marcus lunged forward, but Kingston must have heard him because the man twisted around and swiped at him with the knife. The blade slashed across Marcus's arm, tearing through the fabric of his jacket and slicing through skin. Blood gushed from the wound.

Marcus growled a curse and batted the blade from the man's hand. It skittered across the floor. Kingston let out a roar and rushed at Marcus, tackling him with startling agility. The hockey stick flew out of Marcus's hand, and they rolled across the bathroom floor, each struggling to get the upper hand.

Marcus landed a punch to Kingston's left cheek.

The man went down, but he didn't stay down. Without warning, Kingston grabbed Marcus and pinned him to the floor.

Before Marcus realized what had happened, the man was on top of him, his hands wrapped around Marcus's throat, squeezing.

Marcus gasped, and his vision became distorted. *Oh God, Rebecca...*

He blinked and saw movement by the bath tub.

Then he saw the hockey stick slice through the air. It made a sickening sound as it connected with the back of Kingston's head. The man's eyes rolled back and his mouth gaped as if he wanted to say something. Then he slumped forward, his face resting inches from Marcus's.

Marcus scrambled out from beneath Kingston. Pressing two fingers to the man's neck, he felt a faint pulse.

"Is he dead?" Rebecca said in a shaky voice.

"No."

He heard her blow out a pent-up breath. Her shoulders slumped and he reached her as she collapsed on the bloody floor. Sweeping her up in his arms, he strode out of the bathroom and set her down on the bed.

"You think you'll ever be done rescuing me?" she asked in a groggy voice.

"Probably not—if you can't kick this drug habit you've got." When she stared at him in confusion, he added, "That's twice now that someone tried to drug you." He grinned, then gathered her close and kissed her hair. "I thought you were dead."

"Apparently, I'm not that easy to kill," she slurred.

They heard shouts coming from the front of the house. The cavalry had arrived.

"Marcus?" someone yelled.

"John Zur," Marcus said to Rebecca. Then he hollered, "We're back here! Kingston is down."

As footsteps thundered down the hall, Rebecca stared at the broken hockey stick on the floor. "I owe Colton a hockey stick."

He grinned. "We'll buy him all new gear."

"You're bleeding," she said with a gasp.

He looked down at his arm. A thick trail of blood oozed down his sleeve and dripped onto the floor. "It's a flesh wound. You aren't afraid of a little blood, are you?"

When she shook her head, he said, "Good." Then he hugged her.

Chapter Fifty

Edmonton, AB – Monday, June 17, 2013 – 5:28 PM

After Walter was taken into custody and the house was cleared, Rebecca changed into some warm clothes, then joined Detective Zur and Marcus at the kitchen table. Marcus had already made coffee, and she grabbed a mug and sipped it, fighting back the tears that simmered in her eyes.

"Thank God you didn't finish the tea," Marcus said, shaking his head slowly.

Still lightheaded, she glanced at him but said nothing. She knew how close she'd come to death. A few sips more and it would have been lights out. Walter would've succeeded in drowning her.

Detective Zur sat down across from her. "Your father-in-law will be going away for a long time, Mrs. Kingston."

"Please. Call me Rebecca. That name…" She shivered.

"Of course." The detective placed a hand over hers. "Rebecca."

"Seems like Walter Kingston went through an awful lot of trouble just to get back the money for loans he gave Tracey and Wesley," Marcus muttered.

"That's why we never considered him a suspect. The guy was loaded."

"What I can't comprehend is why Walter would go to all this trouble to get me out of the way," she said. "He didn't need the money. And he had no personal reason to see me…dead."

"There *is* another reason," Detective Zur replied.

Rebecca frowned. "What?"

"This is what we've been able to piece together. Walter Kingston was working on a major merger deal with two very well-known eBook retailers—one from Canada, the other from the US. It would've been huge news, especially for the Canadian company, which Walter represented. He'd spent thousands on research, all of which would have been recouped once the merger went through. Not to mention, he'd earn a hefty sum for closing the deal."

"But what's that got to do with me?"

"Everything started with Wesley."

"His gambling," she guessed.

"Wesley had borrowed money from his father to repay his gambling debts, then incurred more debt. That's when Tracey Whitaker went to Walter and relayed what Wesley had told her about the inheritance you received from your grandfather."

"The *kids'* money," she corrected.

"Yes. She convinced him that, with you out of the picture, Wesley could get his hands on that money, clear his debts and repay the loans to Walter. He knew he had to do something to help Wesley because if word got out about his son's gambling, the companies would pull out of the merger and—"

"And the Canadian company would dump Walter as their lawyer," she finished.

Detective Zur nodded. "Exactly. Kingston would lose millions in the deal."

"So he's the one who hired Rufus Delaney to run me off the road."

"Yes. And when that failed, he paid Tracey to drug you in the hospital."

Rebecca recalled Tracey's words. *That's the way he wanted it, planned it. He paid that guy to run her off the road. He said I had to finish it, that we'd get the money for sure then. There was no other way I could pay back the goddamn loan.*

"At the hospital," she said, "right before she was shot, we thought she was saying that Wesley had been her partner in crime."

"But all along it was his father," Marcus said.

Rebecca thought of Wesley, of her marriage, of all the lies. Her children had almost paid the price for his behavior. *Never again!*

"Life isn't all sunshine and roses, is it?" Marcus said.

She shook her head. "Maybe it's time to get a new life." She gazed into his eyes. "Both of us."

"Time for me to go," the detective said. "You two can come down in the morning, and I'll take your statements then. You both look like you've been through hell."

"And back," Marcus agreed.

"You should stop by the hospital and get checked out. You're going to need stitches in your arm."

"Later. Right now, John, I want to sit awhile and relax."

Detective Zur looked at Rebecca and rolled his eyes. "He's such a tough guy. Make sure he gets checked out. Don't take no for an answer."

Rebecca grinned. "I won't. I'll drive him there myself."

Marcus let out a snort and she whipped around. "What? Are you suggesting I'm not a good driver?"

"Look where your last trip got you."

"Ha ha, Mr. Big Shot."

He smiled at her, and it lit his eyes. "I thought I was Mr. Superhero."

"I think I'm going to regret that comment."

"Okay, okay," he said waving his hands in the air. "You can drive my car. I know I'll never get any peace from you unless I go."

Rebecca glanced over her shoulder to say something to the detective, but he was already gone. "Give me your keys," she said to Marcus. "I promise not to drive us into a river."

Chapter Fifty-One

Edmonton, AB – Monday, June 17, 2013 – 8:23 PM

Marcus left the hospital exam room, feeling a strange lightness in his step and a weightlessness to his body. He hadn't even realized he'd been holding his breath until he released it, slowly, evenly.

Everything had checked out. An ER doctor had ordered some X-rays on his hands and face, but she said nothing was broken. She'd patched up the cuts, stitched his arm and warned him he'd feel worse in the morning.

Great. With nothing stronger that Tylenol, tomorrow was going to be one nasty day. Except for seeing Rebecca.

He smiled and dialed her cell phone. "I'm all done."

She'd wanted to wait with him, but he'd insisted that the long wait and subsequent tests wouldn't be much fun, and he suggested she visit her kids. He figured her sister would take care of her for the few hours he'd be at the hospital.

"My sister wants to meet you," she said.

"I'm not very good with families."

She laughed. "You'll do fine. Kelly's already got you up on a gold-plated pedestal."

"You sure know how to put a guy at ease," he said wryly.

"Come on, Marcus. It'll be fun. We'll have lunch tomorrow with the kids, Kelly and Steve after we see Detective Zur."

He grinned. "Sounds like a date."

There was a long pause on the other end of the line.

"Lunch tomorrow is fine, Rebecca."

"See you in twenty minutes."

"Actually, I have someplace I need to be. I'll take a cab to your place afterward so I can pick up my car." After she agreed, he hung up.

During the examination, all he could think about was Rebecca and how close they'd all come to death. It put things in perspective. Life was short. Death could come knocking any time.

After Walter Kingston attempted to drown Rebecca, Marcus realized something had changed in his own life. He could finally breathe. It was like he'd been submerged, lost, but now a switch had been flipped. Like he'd been given a new lease on life…and more. A new relationship—one he'd never expected but wanted very much to explore.

However, he had to clean up his old life first. He'd left too much unfinished.

Time to burn the wooden box.

This time, he knew he'd do it. He'd watch the damn thing burn until all that was left was a pile of ashes. He was done with holding on to the past. Done with drugs. Done with ghosts. As soon as he got home, he'd light a fire in the fireplace.

Dust to dust, ashes to ashes…

In the hallway near the nurses' station he spotted a public phone. Should he make the call?

"Time to get a new life," Rebecca had said.

Before he could do that, he needed to say farewell to the old one.

He grabbed the receiver and dialed. When his former mother-in-law picked up, he took a deep breath. "Mom—uh, Wanda? It's Marcus. I wanted to let you know that I *will* be coming to Jane's memorial."

"That's wonderful," Wanda said.

"I, uh…I'll be bringing a guest, if that's all right."

"Of course. Anyone I know?"

"No. It's someone I…met recently."

"A woman?" There was surprise in Wanda's voice, and something that sounded like joy.

"Yes," he said. "Rebecca."

There was a long pause. Was Wanda upset with him?

"Marcus," she said, "I'm so relieved to hear you're finally ready to move on."

"What?"

"Jane would want you to be happy, dear. So would Ryan. Neither of them would want to see you all alone in this world."

Wanda's response was nothing like he'd expected.

"Thank you…Mom."

"You'll always be my son, Marcus. In my heart. You gave my daughter the best years of her life."

"And some not so good ones," he reminded her.

"Jane never dwelled on that stuff. She loved you. You loved her. You just went missing for a while. And you've been lost ever since she and Ryan died."

Marcus lowered his head and turned his back to the nurses' station, while wiping away a wayward tear. "So you forgive me?"

"Of course, dear. I forgave you years ago. So did Jane and Ryan. The question is, Marcus, do you forgive yourself?"

"I do."

As he hung up, Marcus realized he'd stated the truth to Wanda for the first time in six years. He *did* forgive himself. Another realization hit him. His new life had finally begun.

But first there were a few loose ends that needed to be tied up.

"My name's Marcus," he said, following the decades-old ritual, "and I'm a drug addict."

He took a moment to examine the faces of the people who understood him, although all were strangers except for Leo, who sat in the front row. These people had come from all walks of life. Some young, some old. Male, female, it didn't matter. Addiction didn't discriminate.

"Until today," he said, "I've mainly listened while others have shared their stories. I've admired you for your courage, something I've been lacking in for far too long." He thought of the NA group in Edson. "I've selfishly listened while you've laid bare your souls, not once giving you the same respect. And for that I am deeply sorry."

He bowed his head and took a deep breath. Then he lifted his eyes and stared into the faces of the bravest men and women he knew, drawing upon their strength and remembering Leo's wise words: *"Admission is good for the soul."*

"The first time I used," Marcus began, "it was an excuse to stay alert, stay awake. I rationalized my behavior, telling myself I'd save lives. I was a paramedic. I stole drugs to feed my habit. I forged signatures on prescription pads I stole from doctors I'd worked with. I betrayed their trust—and everyone else's—all the time telling myself I could stop any time. That it was no big deal."

His audience was transfixed, each identifying with the rationale that all addicts turn to—excuses.

"I tried to quit after my wife and son died. I killed them, or at least that's what I'd always thought."

There were gasps from some of the new members.

"I didn't kill them with my hands, but it doesn't matter. My actions—using drugs—led to their deaths. At the time, I convinced myself I had it under control, that the drugs weren't affecting my life. I was fooling myself. I honestly believed I could quit anytime and that I was using so that I could be on top of my game. Alert. Quick to act."

He caught Leo's eye. His friend knew the game. How common it was for paramedics and other high-stress career people to take something to keep them alert. Most started with high-energy drinks. When these stopped working, they moved to the small stuff—codeine/caffeine combinations usually. Then the stealing would begin. Leo and Marcus had been resourceful thieves.

"I was cocky and stupid," Marcus said. "I tried to separate myself physically from Jane and Ryan, thinking they'd be safer that way. That was a mistake. One I can never, *ever*, take back."

A young woman in the front row nodded in understanding.

"My wife was worried when I took off to clear my head," he continued. "She tried calling me, but I didn't answer my phone." His voice cracked. "If only I'd picked up. Maybe I could have convinced her to stay home. But instead, Jane and Ryan drove from Edmonton to Cadomin in a torrential rainstorm, with almost zero visibility."

As he gathered his courage, Leo gave him a slow nod. In that instant, Marcus knew it was time to let go of the terrible burden he'd been keeping close to his heart. The secret that kept him from living. His guilty soul passenger.

"They hit a patch of ice and water," he said in a subdued voice. "The car spun out of control and flipped.

There were no other vehicles in sight when they flipped upside down and landed in a ditch filled with about four feet of freezing water."

Murmurs of compassion filled the room.

"Keep going," Leo urged him from the front row.

"Jane and Ryan drowned. They were dead when rescuers found them." Marcus's voice turned bitter. "Dead because they were coming to save *me*."

For a long time after, he'd thought his life wasn't worth saving, and if it hadn't been for Leo, he'd probably be dead. And with Jane and Ryan. That thought teased him day and night. In his dreams. In his waking thoughts. Some days he yearned for it to be true.

"They died six years ago," he said, staring into Leo's eyes. "And for a long time I wanted to die too. But someone reminded me that life is for the living."

He saw Leo blink back tears. So did some others in the group.

"It hasn't been easy," he said with a heavy sigh. "I still think about using. I still crave it. And I've slipped sometimes. I still carry the weight of guilt, but I'm trying to grasp the concept that I *didn't* kill them. It was an accident, a terrible tragedy. They could have died going for groceries." Closing his eyes, he pictured Jane's sexy grin and twinkling emerald eyes. "If nothing else, Jane taught me how to live. And I'm still alive. I'm here and they're not. I survived. I was given the gift of life, and I can't waste that gift."

His gaze swept across the sober faces, faces that now knew exactly where he'd been, what he'd done. He'd expected to find condemnation in their expressions, but what he found was forgiveness and understanding.

"One day at a time."

His words were softly echoed by the group, and he stepped away from the podium.

"You did good, man," Leo whispered as Marcus sat down.

"I survived, Leo." His voice was thick with emotion, and tears flowed freely down his cheeks.

When Marcus showed up at Rebecca's house, she took one look at his red-rimmed eyes and hugged him.

"You can tell me later," she said. "For now, just relax. It has been a long few days. Come on." She tugged on his hand.

"Where are we going?"

"To my room."

Though his mind was a mess of jumbled thoughts, he didn't argue when she led him into the house. His body felt like mush, like it would fold in on itself any moment. Each step felt like a lead weight had been strapped to his ankles. With the light from the hallway to guide them, they reached the bedroom.

Rebecca turned on a lamp, then pulled back the comforter and sheets.

"Are you trying to get me into bed?" he said with a sardonic smirk.

She arched a brow. "Your talent for deduction is mind-boggling. Come here."

He maneuvered around the side of the bed, and she began to unbutton his shirt, careful not to disturb the bandages around his arm.

She kissed his chest. "Tonight you will sleep like a baby."

With careful movements, she unbuttoned his pants, which seemed to propel him out of the fog he was in. He stripped off the jeans and his socks, then reached for her. But she pushed his hand away.

Confused, he said, "Aren't we gonna…" He wiggled his brows.

"Nope."

"Really?"

"Really."

"So we're just gonna—"

"Sleep, yes. We have plenty of time for the other, once your arm has healed. And my ribs."

"But that'll take weeks. What'll we do on our other dates until then?"

She nudged him down onto the bed. "Sleep. Or there won't be another date."

He grinned. "You drive a hard bargain, woman."

Dressed in his boxers, Marcus climbed beneath the sheets. They felt cool, satiny. He'd forgotten that sensation.

Rebecca stripped to her bra and panties, her own injuries hidden by bandages.

"We make a great couple," he said wryly.

She laughed, then climbed in beside him. He tugged her close, his hand resting on her hip.

She watched him, a worried expression in her eyes. "Sleep, Marcus."

She combed his hair with her fingers and he shivered. Her touch was comforting and he sighed. He stared at her for a long time, watching her pale eyelids close, her lips part and the lines across her forehead soften and disappear.

He listened to her slow steady breaths. In…out…in…out. The sound of life.

He closed his eyes.

This time, no haunting images visited him. He was free from tormented memories of the past. Free of the bloodsucking, energy draining weight of guilt that had submerged his life so completely. It was as if he had broken the surface and could now, finally, breathe.

And for the first time in over six years, Marcus slept.

Epilogue

Edson, Alberta – Friday, July 19, 2013 – 7:30 PM

There was a knock at Marcus's front door.

Arizona let out a bark and a whimper.

"Arizona," Marcus warned. "I expect you to behave like the lady you are." The dog cocked her head to one side as if considering his words.

He sucked in a deep breath and squared his shoulders as if preparing for battle. He walked to the door, opened it and his voice left him as he gazed at the ethereal image on his doorstep. Strands of blond hair were swept up by a light breeze, then fluttered to Rebecca's shoulders.

They'd been dating for a month now, each time in Edmonton, in public places. At first they'd gotten together for coffee. Then lunch. They talked about everything—Rebecca's husband and their looming divorce, the pending court case against Walter Kingston, and life with Jane and Ryan.

Marcus had been more than a little surprised at the warm welcome he and Rebecca received at Jane and Ryan's memorial, especially after he stood up in front of the family and told them about his addiction. He found forgiveness there, something he hadn't expected.

"Hi," he said, dazed.

There was an awkward pause, before she said, "Are you going to let me in?"

"Of course." Wanting to kick himself, Marcus pushed the door open and ushered her inside. "Sorry. It's been a long time since I…since I've…you know."

Rebecca raised a brow. "What? Cooked dinner?"

"Had someone over. On a date."

"Is that what this is?" Her blue eyes were luminescent.

He laughed. "We do have problems defining that word, don't we?"

"I'm starved." She took his arm. "Lead the way."

Arizona whined.

"This is Arizona," he said. "The other female in my life."

"Hey, Arizona," Rebecca said, pulling a rawhide stick from her pocket. "I have a treat for you."

Arizona pushed her nose under Rebecca's hand, a silent demand for attention. Funny thing was, Arizona didn't normally do this with strangers.

The meal Marcus had prepared turned out perfectly. Marinated steaks grilled on the barbecue, pan-fried jumbo shrimp in Cajun spices, butter and lemon juice for dipping, and a Caesar salad. For dessert, he'd cheated though. He'd picked up a raspberry custard pie from the deli.

After dinner, they relaxed on the couch in the living room. Sipping a non-alcohol Saskatoon berry wine, they talked about their dreams and goals. Rebecca shared her excitement about starting her own business—a bed and breakfast somewhere in Alberta. He shared his thoughts of finding something different, something challenging but less stressful. But he still had doubts about his future.

"Do you believe someone like me can find redemption?" he asked.

"Yes."

Her words caused his armor to shatter. Could it be true?

"Have you found peace with Wesley? With your marriage?"

She nodded. "He left me a long time ago. In spirit, anyway."

"Wesley didn't value what he had. I will."

"I know."

In that moment Marcus knew exactly what he wanted for his future. Rebecca. He wanted the whole package—Ella and Colton too. The thought made his heart leap.

"Come with me," he said, tugging on her hand. "I have something to show you."

"What?"

"You'll see." He went to the closet and took out her jacket. "It's a little cool outside."

"We're going for a walk?"

Arizona let out a bark.

"Uh-oh," he said, grinning. "You said the magic word."

He leashed Arizona and they headed outside.

"This way," he said. "Last house on the left."

She gave a nervous laugh. "Sounds ominous."

They strolled arm in arm until they got to the end of the road.

"What's down there?" she asked, eyeing the woods.

"A ravine with a creek. It's quite pretty in the daylight. Not too safe at night though. Teens hang out there, smoking, doing drugs—unless I kick them out. I've been trying to clean up the riffraff."

"Does that tempt you—the drugs?"

"Some days."

She watched him with great intensity. "You're a very honest man, Marcus."

"I'm getting there."

"So what's this surprise you're talking about?"

He pointed to the Victorian house with the lush gardens. "What do you think?"

"It's beautiful. Very well kept. Charming." She faced him, still looking unsure. "Do you know the owner?"

"I did. Mrs. Landry died a few weeks ago. The house is for sale. What comes to mind when you look at it?"

She smiled. "That's easy. It's close to the highway, but near a ravine. It would make a perfect bed and breakfast."

"That's what I was thinking."

He stared into her eyes, caught up in the churning emotions he saw there. Happiness. Excitement. Doubt.

"I don't know, Marcus…"

"I do." He grabbed her hands and kissed them. "For the first time in a long time, I know exactly what I want."

They stood in silence, too afraid to speak. Too scared they'd ruin the moment—and all the possibilities.

"Don't you think we're rushing things?" she asked.

"Do you?"

"Strangely…no." She lifted her face and he kissed her.

"I saw Jane and Ryan a few nights ago," he said. "In my dreams."

She hugged him tight. "Was it terrible?"

"No. They came to say good-bye. She said they're both at peace now and want the same for me."

"Marcus?" Rebecca said in a hesitant voice. "There's something I haven't told you. About Jane."

"What?"

"Right before Tracey Whitaker visited my hospital room, I heard a woman's voice. She was comforting me, telling me to stay calm. That same voice visited me when Walter came to my house and tried to kill me."

"You think it was Jane?" he said.

"Who else could it be? You said you keep seeing her, so why would it be so weird if I *heard* her?"

He didn't know what to say.

They strolled back to his house in quiet reflection. Instead of going inside, he led her around to the backyard. "Wait here. I'll be right back."

Inside, he retrieved the wooden box from its hiding place. Then he headed outside, where he opened the box and showed her its contents. The drugs, the needle. His shame, his guilt. The latter two poured from the box, invisible yet potent.

"It's time for me to let go of this," he said.

He set the box in the fire pit. Removing a lighter from his pocket, he lit the kindling beneath the box and they stood a few feet away, watching it smolder, sizzle and burn.

"I spent a long time hiding from the truth," he said. "I was good at that. Hiding things. Submerging myself in guilt."

Rebecca took his hand. "You never have to hide from me."

He kissed her again, pondering the complexity of fate. In his search to find Rebecca and her children, she had found him. And now the world opened to him with all its infinite possibilities.

~ * ~

If you enjoyed this book, please consider writing a short review and posting it on Amazon, Goodreads, etc. Reviews are very helpful to other readers and are greatly appreciated by authors, especially me. When you post a review, drop me an email and let me know and I may feature part of it on my blog/site. Thank you. ~ Cheryl

cherylktardif@shaw.ca

And now here's an excerpt from Cheryl's international bestselling thriller, CHILDREN OF THE FOG...

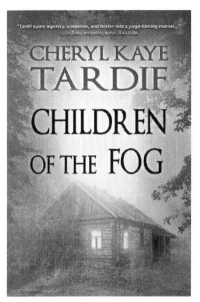

prologue

May 14th, 2007

She was ready to die.

She sat at the kitchen table, a half empty bottle of Philip's precious red wine in one hand, a loaded gun in the other. Staring at the foreign chunk of metal, she willed it to vanish. But it didn't.

Sadie checked the gun and noted the single bullet.

"One's all you need."

If she did it right.

She placed the gun on the table and glanced at a pewter-framed photograph that hung off-kilter above the mantle of the fireplace. It was illuminated by a vanilla-scented candle, one of many that threw flickering shadows over the rough wood walls of the log cabin.

Sam's sweet face stared back at her, smiling.

Alive.

From where she sat, she could see the small chip in his right front tooth, the result of an impatient father raising the training wheels too early. But there was no point in blaming Philip—not when they'd both lost so much.

Not when it's all my fault.

Her gaze swept over the mantle. There were three objects on it besides the candle. Two envelopes, one addressed to Leah and one to Philip, and the portfolio case that contained the illustrations and manuscript on disc for Sam's book.

She had finished it, just like she had promised.

"And promises can't be broken. Right, Sam?"

A single tear burned a path down her cheek.

Sam was gone.

What reason do I have for living now?

She gulped back the last pungent mouthful of Cabernet and dropped the empty bottle. It rolled under the chair, unbroken, rocking on the hardwood floor. Then all was silent, except the antique grandfather clock in the far corner. Its ticking reminded her of the clown's shoe. The one with the tack in it.

Tick, tick, tick…

The clock belched out an ominous gong.

It was almost midnight.

Almost time.

She drew an infinity symbol in the dust on the table.

∞

"Sadie and Sam. For all eternity."

Gong…

She swallowed hard as tears flooded her eyes. "I'm sorry I couldn't save you, baby. I tried to. God, I tried. Forgive me, Sam." Her words ended in a gut-wrenching moan.

Something scraped the window beside her.

She pressed her face to the frosted glass, then jerked back with a gasp. "Go away!"

They stood motionless—six children that drifted from the swirling miasma of night air, haunting her nights and every waking moment. Surrounded by the moonlit fog, they began to chant. *"One fine day, in the middle of the night..."*

"You're not real," she whispered.

"Two dead boys got up to fight."

A small, pale hand splayed against the exterior of the window. Below it, droplets of condensation slid like tears down the glass.

She reached out, matching her hand to the child's. Shivering, she pulled away. "You don't exist."

The clock continued its morbid countdown.

As the alcohol and drug potpourri kicked in, the room began to spin and her stomach heaved. She inhaled deeply. She couldn't afford to get sick. Sam was waiting for her.

Tears spilled down her cheeks. "I'm ready."

Gong...

Without hesitation, she raised the gun to her temple.

"Don't!" the children shrieked.

She pressed the gun against her flesh. The tip of the barrel was cold. Like her hands, her feet...her heart.

A sob erupted from the back of her throat.

The clock let out a final gong. Then it was deathly silent.

It was midnight.

Her eyes found Sam's face again.

"Happy Mother's Day, Sadie."

She took a steadying breath, pushed the gun hard against her skin and clamped her eyes shut.

"Mommy's coming, Sam."

She squeezed the trigger.

1

Sadie O'Connell let out a snicker as she stared at the price tag on the toy in her hand. "What did they stuff this with, laundered money?" She tossed the bunny back into the bin and turned to the tall, leggy woman beside her. "What are you getting Sam for his birthday?"

Her best friend gave her a cocky grin. "What *should* I get him? Your kid's got everything already."

"Don't even go there, my friend."

But Leah was right. Sadie and Philip spoiled Sam silly. Why shouldn't they? They had waited a long time for a baby. Or at least, *she* had. After two miscarriages, Sam's birth had been nothing short of a miracle. A miracle that deserved to be spoiled.

Leah groaned loudly. "Christ, it's a goddamn zoo in here."

Toyz & Twirlz in West Edmonton Mall was crawling with overzealous customers. The first major sale of the spring season always brought people out in droves. Frazzled parents swarmed the toy store, swatting their wayward brood occasionally—the way you'd swat a pesky yellowjacket at a barbecue. One distressed father hunted the aisles for his son, who had apparently taken off on him as soon as his back was turned. In every aisle, parents shouted at their kids, threatening, cajoling, pleading and then predictably giving in.

"So who let the animals out?" Sadie said, surveying the store.

The screeching wheels of shopping carts and the constant whining of overtired toddlers were giving her a headache. She wished to God she'd stayed home.

"Excuse me."

A plump woman with frizzy, over-bleached hair gave Sadie an apologetic look. She navigated past them, pushing a stroller occupied by a miniature screaming alien. A few feet away, she stopped, bent down and wiped something that looked like curdled rice pudding from the corner of the child's mouth.

Sadie turned to Leah. "Thank God Sam's past that stage."

At five years old—soon to be six—her son was the apple of her eye. In fact, he was the whole darned tree. A lanky imp of a boy with tousled black hair, sapphire-blue eyes and perfect bow lips, Sam was the spitting image of his mother and the exact opposite of his father in temperament. While Sam was sweet natured, gentle and loving, Philip was impatient and distant. So distant that he rarely said *I love you* anymore.

She stared at her wedding ring. *What happened to us?*

But she knew what had happened. Philip's status as a trial lawyer had grown, more money had poured in and fame had gone to his head. He had changed. The man she had fallen in love with, the dreamer, had gone. In his place was someone she barely knew, a stranger who had decided too late that he didn't want kids.

Or a wife.

"How about this?" Leah said, nudging her.

Sadie stared at the yellow dump truck. "Fill it with a

stuffed bat and Sam will think it's awesome."

Her son's fascination with bats was almost comical. The television was always tuned in to the Discovery Channel while her son searched endlessly for any show on the furry animals.

"What did Phil the Pill get him?" Leah asked dryly.

"A new Leap Frog module."

"I still can't believe the things that kid can do."

Sadie grinned. "Me neither."

Sam's mind was a sponge. He absorbed information so fast that he only had to be shown once. His powers of observation were so keen that he had learned how to unlock the door just by watching Sadie do it, so Philip had to add an extra deadbolt at the top. By the time Sam was three, he had figured out the remote control and the DVD player. Sadie still had problems turning on the TV.

Sam…my sweet, wonderful, little genius.

"Maybe I'll get him a movie," Leah said. "How about *Batman Begins*?"

"He's turning six, not sixteen."

"Well, what do I know? I don't have kids."

At thirty-four, Leah Winters was an attractive, willowy brunette with wild multi-colored streaks, thick-lashed hazel eyes, a flirty smile and a penchant for younger men. While Sadie's pale face had a scattering of tiny freckles across the bridge of her nose and cheekbones, Leah's complexion was tanned and clear.

She'd been Sadie's best friend for eight years—*soul sistahs*. Ever since the day she had emailed Sadie out of the blue to ask questions about writing and publishing. They'd met at Book Ends, a popular Edmonton bookstore, for what Leah had expected would be a quick coffee. Their connection was so strong and so immediate that they talked for almost five hours. They still joked about it, about how Leah had thought Sadie was some hotshot writer who wouldn't give her the time of day.

Yet Sadie had given her more. She'd given Leah a piece of her heart.

A rugged, handsome Colin Farrell look-alike passed them in the aisle, and Leah stared after him, eyes glittering.

"I'll take one of those," she said with a soft growl. "To go."

"You won't find Mr. Right in a toy store," Sadie said dryly. "They're usually all taken. And somehow I don't think you're gonna find him at Karma either."

Klub Karma was a popular nightclub on Whyte Avenue. It boasted the best ladies' night in Edmonton, complete with steroid-muscled male strippers. Leah was a regular.

"And why not?"

Sadie rolled her eyes. "Because Karma is packed with sweaty, young puppies who are only interested in one thing."

Leah gave her a blank look.

"Getting laid," Sadie added. "Honestly, I don't know what you see in that place."

"What, are you daft?" Leah arched her brow and grinned devilishly. "I'm chalking it up to my civil duty. Someone's gotta show these young guys how it's done."

"Someone should show Philip," Sadie muttered.

"Why—can't he get it up?"

"Jesus, Leah!"

"Well? Fess up."

"Later maybe. When we stop for coffee."

Leah glanced at her watch. "We going to our usual place?"

"Of course. Do you think Victor would forgive us if we went to any other coffee shop?"

Leah chuckled. "No. He'd start skimping on the whipped cream if we turned traitor. So what are you getting Sam?"

"I'll know it when I see it. I'm waiting for a sign."

"You're always such a sucker for this *fate* thing."

Sadie shrugged. "Sometimes you have to have faith that things will work out."

They continued down the aisle, both searching for something for the sweetest boy they knew. When Sadie spotted the one thing she was sure Sam would love, she let out a hoot and gave Leah an I-told-you-so look.

"This bike is perfect. Since his birthday is actually on Monday, I'll give it to him then. He'll get enough things from his friends at his party on Sunday anyway."

Little did she know that Sam wouldn't see his bike.

He wouldn't be around to get it.

"Haven't seen you two all week," Victor Guan said. "Another day and I would've called nine-one-one."

"It's been a busy week," Sadie replied, plopping her purse on the counter. "How's business, Victor?"

"Picking up again with this cold snap."

The young Chinese man owned the Cuppa Cappuccino a few blocks from Sadie's house. The coffee shop had a gas fireplace, a relaxed ambiance and often featured local musicians like Jessy Green and Alexia Melnychuk. Not only did Victor serve the best homemade soups and feta Caesar salad, the mocha lattés were absolutely sinful.

Leah made a beeline for the washroom. "You know what I want."

Sadie ordered a Chai and a mocha.

"You see that fog this morning?" Victor asked.

"Yeah, I drove Sam to school in it. I could barely see the car in front of me."

She shivered and Victor gave her a concerned look.

"Cat walk over your grave or something?" he asked.

"No, I'm just tired of winter."

She grabbed a newspaper from the rack and headed for the upper level. The sofa by the fireplace was unoccupied, so she sat down and tossed the newspaper on the table.

The headline on the front page made her gasp.

The Fog Strikes Again!

Her breath felt constricted. "Oh God. Not another one."

A photograph of a blond-haired, blue-eyed girl sitting on concrete steps dominated the front page. Eight-year-old Cortnie Bornyk, from the north side of Edmonton, was missing. According to the newspaper, the girl had disappeared in the middle of the night. No sign of forced entry and no evidence as to who had taken her, but investigators were sure it was the same man who had taken the others.

Sadie opened the newspaper to page three, where the story continued. She empathized with the girl's father, a single dad who had left Ontario to find construction work in Edmonton. Matthew Bornyk had moved here to make a better life. Not a bad decision, considering that the housing market was booming. But now he was pleading for the safe return of his daughter.

"Here you go," Victor said, setting two mugs on the table.

"Thanks," she said, without looking up.

Her eyes were glued to the smaller photo of Bornyk and his daughter. The man had a smile plastered across his face, while his daughter was frozen in a silly pose, tongue hanging out the side of her mouth.

Daddy's little girl, Sadie thought sadly.

Leah flopped into an armchair beside her. "Who's the hunk?"

"His daughter was abducted last night."

"How horrible."

"Yeah," Sadie said, taking a tentative sip from her mug.

"Did anyone see anything?"

"Nothing." She locked eyes on Leah. "Except the

fog."

"Do they think it's *him*?"

Sadie skimmed the article. "There are no ransom demands yet. Sounds like him."

"Shit. That makes, what—six kids?"

"Seven. Three boys, four girls."

"One more boy to go." Leah's voice dripped with dread.

The Fog, as the kidnapper was known, crept in during the dead of night or early morning, under the cloak of a dense fog. He wrapped himself around his prey and like a fog, he disappeared without a trace, capturing the souls of children and stealing the hopes and dreams of parents. One boy, one girl. Every spring. For the last four years.

Sadie flipped the newspaper over. "Let's change the subject."

Her eyes drifted across the room, taking in the diversity of Victor's customers. In one corner of the upper level, three teenaged boys played poker, while a fourth watched and hooted every time one of his friends won. Across from Sadie, a redheaded woman wearing a mauve sweatshirt plunked away on a laptop, stopping every now and then to cast the noisy boys a frustrated look. On the lower level, one of the regulars—Old Ralph—was reading every newspaper from front to back. He sipped his black coffee when he finished each page.

"So…" Leah drawled as she crossed her long legs. "What's going on with Phil the Pill?"

Sadie scowled. "That's what I'd like to know. He says he's working long nights at the firm."

"And you're thinking, what? That he's screwing around?"

Leah never was one to beat around the bush—about anything.

"Maybe he's just working hard," her friend suggested.

Sadie shook her head. "He got home at two this morning, reeking of perfume and booze."

"Isn't his firm working on that oil spill case? I bet all the partners are pulling late nights on that one."

Sadie snorted. "Including Brigitte Moreau."

Brigitte was her husband's *right-hand-woman*, as he'd made a point of telling her often. Apparently, the new addition to Fleming Warner Law Offices was indispensable. The slender, blond lawyer, with a pair of breasts she'd obviously paid for, never left Philip's side.

Sadie wondered what Brigitte did when she had to pee.

Probably drags Philip in with her.

"It could be perfectly innocent," Leah suggested.

"Yeah, right. I was at the conference after-party. I saw them together, and there was nothing innocent about them. Brigitte was holding onto Philip's arm as if she owned him. And he was laughing, whispering in her ear." She pursed her lips. "His co-workers were looking at me with sympathetic eyes, pitying me. I could see it in their faces. Even *they* knew."

Leah winced. "Did you call him on it?"

"I asked him if he was messing around again."

Just before Sam was born, Philip had admitted to two other affairs. Both office flings, according to him. "Both meant nothing," he had said, before blaming his infidelities on her swollen belly and her lack of sexual interest.

"What'd he say?" Leah prodded, with the determination of a pit-bull slobbering over a t-bone steak.

"Nothing. He just stormed out of the house. He called me from work just before you came over. Said I was being ridiculous, that my accusations were hurtful and unfair." She lowered her voice. "He asked me if I was drinking again."

"Bastard. And you wonder why I'm still single."

Sadie said nothing. Instead, she thought about her marriage.

They'd been happy—once. Before her downward spiral into alcoholism. In the early years of their marriage, Philip had been attentive and caring, supporting her decision to focus on her writing. It wasn't until she started talking about having a family that things had changed.

She flicked a look at Leah, grateful for her loyal companionship and understanding. Fate had definitely intervened when it had led her to Leah. Her friend had gone above and beyond the duty of friendship, dropping everything in a blink if she called. Leah was her life support, especially on the days and nights when the bottle called her. She'd even attended a few AA meetings with Sadie.

And where was Philip? Probably with Brigitte.

"Come on, my friend," Leah said, grinning. "I know you really want to swear. Let it out."

"You know I don't use language like that."

"You're such a prude. Philip's an ass, a bastard. Let me hear you say it. *Bas...tard.*"

"I'll let you be the foul-mouthed one," Sadie said sweetly.

"Fuckin' right. Swearing is liberating." Leah took a careful sip of tea. "So how's the book coming?"

Sadie smiled. "I finished the text yesterday. Tomorrow I'll start on the illustrations. I'm so excited about it."

"Got a title yet?"

"Going Batty."

Leah's pencil-thin brow arched. "Hmm...how appropriate."

Sadie gave her a playful slap on the arm. "It's about

a little bat who can't find his way home because his radar gets screwed up. At first, he thinks he's picking up radio signals, but then he realizes he's picking up other creatures' thoughts."

"That's perfect. Sam'll love it."

"I know. I can't believe I waited so long to write something special for him."

A few months ago, Sadie decided to take a break from writing another Lexa Caine mystery, especially since her agent had secured her a deal for two children's picture books.

"It's been a welcome break," she admitted. "Lexa needed a year off. A holiday."

"Some break," Leah said. "I've hardly seen you. You've been working day and night on Sam's book."

"It's been worth it."

"Is it harder than writing mysteries?"

"Other than the artwork, I think it's easier," Sadie said, somewhat surprised by her own answer. "But then, Sam inspires me. He's my muse. Kids see things so differently."

"Wish I had one."

Sadie's jaw dropped. "A kid?"

"A muse, idiot."

Sadie grinned. "How's the steamy romance novel going?"

"I'm stumped. I've got Clara trapped below deck on the pirate ship, locked in the cargo hold with no way out."

Since the success of her debut novel, *Sweet Destiny*, Leah had found her niche and was working on her second historical romance.

"What's in the room?"

Leah gave her a wry grin. "Cases of Bermuda rum."

"Well, she's not going to drink it, so what else can she do?"

"I don't know. She can't get the crew drunk, if that's

what you're thinking. "

"What if the ship caught on fire?"

Excitement percolated in Leah's eyes. "Yeah. A fire could really heat things up. Pun intended."

They were silent for a moment, lost in their own thoughts.

"Hey," Sadie said finally. "I've been tempted to cut my hair. What do you think?"

Leah stared at her. "You want to get rid of all that beautiful hair? Jesus, Sadie, it's past your bra strap." In a thick Irish accent, she said, "Have ye lost your Irish mind just a wee bit, lassie?"

"It's too much work," Sadie said with a pout.

"What does Philip think?"

"He'd be happy if I kept it long," she replied, scowling. "Maybe that's one reason why I want to cut it."

Leah laughed. "Then you go, girl."

Half an hour later, they parted ways—with Leah eager to get back to the innocent Clara and her handsome, sword-wielding pirate, and Sadie not so thrilled to be going back to an empty house. As she climbed into her sporty Mazda3, she smiled, relieved as always that she had chosen practical over the flashy and pretentious Mercedes that Philip drove.

She glanced at the clock and heaved a sigh of relief. It was almost time to pick Sam up from school.

Her heart skipped a beat.

Maybe there's been some progress today.

2

The instant Sam saw her standing in the classroom doorway, he let out a wild yell and charged at her, almost knocking her off her feet.

"Whoa there, little man," she said breathlessly. "Who are you supposed to be? Tarzan?"

"We just finished watching Pocahontas," a woman's voice called out.

"Hi, Jean," Sadie said. "How are things today?"

Jean Ellis taught a class of children with hearing impairments.

"Same as usual," the kindergarten teacher replied. "No change, I'm afraid."

Sadie tried to hide her disappointment. "Maybe tomorrow."

She studied Sam, who could hear everything just fine.

Why won't he speak?

"Did you have a good day, honey?"

Ignoring her, Sam pulled on a winter jacket and stuffed his feet into a pair of insulated boots.

"It was a great day," Jean said, signing as she spoke. "Sam made a friend. A real one this time."

Sadie was astounded. Sam's first real friend. Well, unless she counted his invisible friend, Joey.

"Hey, little man," she said, crouching down to gather him in her arms. "Mommy missed you today. But I'm glad you have a new friend. What's his name?"

When Sam didn't answer, Sadie glanced at Jean.

"Victoria," the woman said with a wink.

Grinning, Sadie ruffled Sam's hair. "Okay, charmer. Let's go."

With a quick wave to Jean, she reached for Sam's hand. She was always amazed by how perfectly it fit into hers, how warm and soft his skin was.

Outside in the parking lot, she unlocked the car and Sam scampered into the booster seat in the back. She leaned forward, fastened his seatbelt, then kissed his cheek. "Snug as a bug?"

He gave her the thumbs up.

Pulling away from the school, she flicked a look in her rearview mirror. Sam stared straight ahead, uninterested in the laughing children who waited for their parents to arrive. Her son was a shy boy, a loner who unintentionally scared kids away because of his inability to speak.

His lack of desire to speak, she corrected.

Sam hadn't always been mute.

Sadie had taught him the alphabet at two. By the age of three, he was reading short sentences. Then one day, for no apparent reason, Sam stopped talking.

Sadie was devastated.

And Philip? There were no words to describe his erratic behavior. At first, he seemed mortified, concerned. Then he shouted accusations at her, insinuating so many horrible things that after a while even she began to wonder. During one nasty exchange, he had grabbed her, his fingers digging into her arms.

"Did you drink while you were pregnant?" he demanded.

"No!" she wailed. "I haven't had a drop."

His eyes narrowed in disbelief. "Really?"

"I swear, Philip."

He stared at her for a long time before shaking his head and walking away.

"We have to get him help," she said, running after him.

Philip swiveled on one heel. "What exactly do you suggest?"

"There's a specialist downtown. Dr. Wheaton recommended him."

"Dr. Wheaton is an idiot. Sam will speak when he's good and ready to. Unless you've screwed him up for good."

His insensitive words cut her deeply, and after he'd gone back to work, she picked up the phone and booked Sam's first appointment. She didn't feel good about going behind Philip's back, but he'd left her no choice.

By the time Sam was three and a half, he had undergone numerous hearing and intelligence tests, x-rays, ultrasounds and psychiatric counseling, yet no one could explain why he wouldn't say a word. His vocal chords were perfectly healthy, according to one specialist. And he was right. Sam could scream, cry or shout. They had heard enough of *that* when he was younger.

Sadie finally managed to drag Philip to an appointment, but the psychologist—a small, timid man wearing a garish red-striped tie that screamed *overcompensation*—didn't have good news for them. He sat behind a sterile metal desk, all the while watching Philip and twitching as if he had Tourette's.

"Your son is suffering from some kind of trauma," the man said, pointing out what seemed obvious to Sadie.

"But what could've caused it?" she asked in dismay.

The doctor fidgeted with his tie. "Symptoms such as these often result from some form of...of abuse."

Philip jumped to his feet. "What the hell are you saying?"

The man's entire body jerked. "I-I'm saying that perhaps someone or something scared your son. Like a fight between parents, or witnessing drug or alcohol abuse."

Sadie cringed at his last words. The look Philip gave her was one of pure anger. And censure.

The doctor took a deep breath. "And of course, there is the possibility of physical or sexual—"

Without a word, Philip stormed out of the doctor's office.

Sadie ran after him.

He had blamed her, of course. According to him, it was her drinking that had caused her miscarriages. *And* Sam's delayed verbal development.

That night, after Sam had gone to bed, Philip had rummaged through every dresser drawer. Then he searched the closet.

She watched apprehensively. "What are you doing?"

"Looking for the bottles!" he barked.

She hissed in a breath. "I told you. I am *not* drinking."

"Once a drunk..."

She cowered when he approached her, his face flushed with anger.

"It's *your* fault!" he yelled.

Guilt did terrible things to people. It was such a destructive, invisible force that not even Sadie could fight it.

She looked in the rearview mirror and took in Sam's

heart-shaped face and serious expression. She wondered for the millionth time why he wouldn't speak. She'd give anything to hear his voice, to hear one word. *Any* word. She'd been praying that the school environment would break through the language barrier.

No such luck.

Suddenly, she was desperate to hear his voice.

"Sam? Can you say Mommy?"

He signed *Mom*.

"Come on, honey," she begged. "*Muhh-mmy.*"

In the mirror, he smiled and pointed at her.

Tears welled in her eyes, but she blinked them away. One day he *would* speak. He'd call her Mommy and tell her he loved her.

"One day," she whispered.

For now, she'd just have to settle for the undeniably strong bond she felt. The connection between mother and child had been forged at conception and she always knew how Sam felt, even without words between them.

She turned down the road that led to the quiet subdivision on the southeast side of Edmonton. She pulled into the driveway and pushed the garage door remote, immediately noticing the sleek silver Mercedes parked in the spacious two-car garage.

Her breath caught in the back of her throat.

Philip was home.

"Okay, little man," she murmured. "Daddy's home."

She scooped Sam out of the back seat and headed for the door. He wriggled until she put him down. Then he raced into the house, straight upstairs. She flinched when she heard his bedroom door slam.

"I guess neither of us is too excited to see Daddy," she said.

Tossing her keys into a crystal dish on the table by the door, she dropped her purse under the desk, kicked off her shoes, puffed her chest and headed into the war zone.

But the door to Philip's office was closed.

She turned toward the kitchen instead.

The war can wait. It always does.

Passing by his office door an hour later, she heard Philip bellowing at someone on the phone. Whoever it was, they were getting quite an earful. A minute later, something hit the door.

She backed away. "Don't stir the pot, Sadie."

Philip remained locked away in his office and refused to come out for supper, so she made a quick meal of hotdogs for Sam and a salad for herself. She left a plate of the past night's leftovers—ham, potatoes and vegetables—on the counter for Philip.

Later, she gave Sam a bath and dressed him for bed.

"Auntie Leah came over today," she said, buttoning his pajama top. "She told me to say hi to her favorite boy."

There wasn't much else to say, other than she had finished writing the bat story. She wasn't about to tell him that she had ordered his birthday cake and bought him a bicycle, which she had wrestled into the house by herself and hidden in the basement.

"Want me to read you a story?" she asked.

Sam grinned.

She sat on the edge of the bed and nudged her head in the direction of the bookshelf. "You pick."

He wandered over to the rows of books, staring at them thoughtfully. Then he zeroed in on a book with a white spine. It was the same story he chose every night.

"My Imaginary Friend again?" she asked, amused.

He nodded and jumped into bed, settling under the blankets.

Sadie snuggled in beside him. As she read about Cathy, a young girl with an imaginary friend who always got her into trouble, she couldn't help but think of Sam. For the past year, he'd been adamant about the existence of Joey, a boy his age who he swore lived in his room. She'd often catch Sam smiling and nodding, as if in conversation. No words, no signing, just the odd facial expression. Some days he seemed lost in his own world.

"Lisa says you should close your eyes," she read.

Sam's eyes fluttered shut.

"Now turn this page and use your imagination."

He turned the page, then opened his eyes. They lit up when he saw the colorful drawing of Cathy's imaginary friend, Lisa.

"Can you see me now?" she read, smiling.

Sam pointed to the girl in the mirror.

"Good night, Cathy. And good night, friend. The end."

She closed the book and set it next to the bat signal clock on the nightstand. Then she scooted off the bed, leaned down and kissed her son's warm skin.

"Good night, Sam-I-Am."

His small hand reached up. With one finger, he drew a sideways 'S' in the air. Their nightly ritual.

"S…for Sam," she said softly.

And like every night, she drew the reflection.

"S…for Sadie."

Together, they created an infinity symbol.

She smiled. "Always and forever."

She flicked off the bedside lamp and eased out of the room. As she looked over her shoulder, she saw Sam's angelic face illuminated by the light from the hall. She shut the door, pressed her cheek against it and closed her eyes.

Sam was the only one who truly loved her, trusted her. From the first day he had rested his huge black-lashed eyes on hers, she had fallen completely and undeniably in love. A mother's love could be no purer.

"My beautiful boy."

Turning away, she slammed into a tall, solid mass. Her smile disappeared when she identified it.

Philip.

And he wasn't happy. Not one bit.

He glared down at her, one hand braced against the wall to bar her escape. His lips—the same ones that had smiled at her so charismatically the night they had met— were curled in disdain.

"You could've told me Sam was going to bed."

She sidestepped around him. "You were busy. As usual."

"What the hell's that supposed to mean?"

She cringed at his abrasive tone, but said nothing.

"You're not going all paranoid on me again, are you?" He grabbed her arm. "I already told you. Brigitte is a co-worker. Nothing more. Jesus, Sadie! You're not a child. You're almost forty years old. What the hell's gotten into you lately?"

"Not a thing, Philip. And I'll be thirty-eight this year. Not forty." She yanked her arm away, then brushed past him, heading for the bedroom.

Their marriage was a sham.

"Doomed from the beginning," her mother had told her one night when Sadie, a sobbing wreck, had called her after Philip had admitted to his first affair.

But she'd proven her mother wrong. Hadn't she? Things seemed better the year after Sam was born. Then she and Philip started fighting again. Lately, it had escalated into a nightly event. At least on the nights he came home before she went to sleep.

Philip entered the bedroom and slammed the door.

"You know," he said. "You've been a bitch for months."

"No, I haven't."

"A *frigid* bitch. And we both know it's not from PMS, seeing as you don't get that anymore."

Flinching, she caught her sad reflection in the dresser mirror. She should be used to his careless name-calling by now. But she wasn't. Each time, it was like a knife piercing deeper into her heart. One of these days, she wouldn't be able to pull it out. Then where would they be? Just another statistic?

Philip waited behind her, flustered, combing a hand through his graying brown hair.

For a moment, she felt ashamed of her thoughts.

"Are you even listening to me?" he sputtered in outrage.

And the moment was gone.

She sighed, drained. "What do you want me to say, Philip? You're never home. And when you are, you're busy working in your office. We don't do anything together or go any—"

"Christ, Sadie! We were just out with Morris and his wife."

"I'm not talking about functions for the firm," she argued. "We don't see our old friends anymore. We never go to movies, never just sit and talk, never make…love."

Philip crossed his arms and scowled. "And whose fault is that? It's certainly not mine. You're the one who pulls away every time I try to get close to you. You know, a guy can only handle so much rejection before—"

"What?" She whipped around to confront him. "Before you go looking for it elsewhere?"

He stared at her for a long moment and the air grew rank with tension, coiling around them with the slyness of a venomous snake, fangs exposed, ready to strike.

When he finally spoke, his voice was quiet, defeated. "Maybe if you gave some of the love you pour on Sam to *me* once in a while, I wouldn't be tempted to look elsewhere."

He strode out of the room, his footsteps thundering down the stairs. A minute later, a door slammed.

She released a trembling breath. "Coward."

She wasn't sure if she meant Philip…or herself.

Brushing the drapes aside, she peered through the window to the dimly lit street below. It was devoid of any moving traffic, just a few parked vehicles lining the sidewalks. The faint rumble of the garage door made her clench the drapes. She heard the defiant revving of an engine, and then watched as the Mercedes backed down the driveway, a stream of frosty exhaust trailing behind it. The surface of the street shimmered from a fresh glazing of ice, and the car sped away, tires spinning on the pavement.

Philip always seemed to get in the last word.

She watched the fiery glow of the taillights as they faded into the night. Then the flickering of the streetlamp across the road caught her eye. She frowned when the light went out. One of the neighbors' dogs started barking, set off by either the abrupt darkness or Philip's noisy departure. She wasn't sure which.

And then something emerged from the bushes.

A lumbering shadow shuffled down the sidewalk, a few yards to the right of the lamp. It was a man, of that she was sure. She could make out a heavy jacket and some kind of hat, but she couldn't distinguish anything else.

The man paused across the street from her house.

Sadie was sure that he was staring up at her.

She shivered and stepped out of view, the drapes flowing back into place. When her breathing calmed, she edged toward the window again and took a surreptitious peek.

Gail, a neighbor from across the street, was walking Kali, a Shih Tzu poodle. But other than the woman and her dog, the sidewalk was empty.

Sadie locked all the doors and windows, and set the security alarm…

Want to keep reading?
CHILDREN OF THE FOG is available at your favorite retailer in ebook and trade paperback editions.

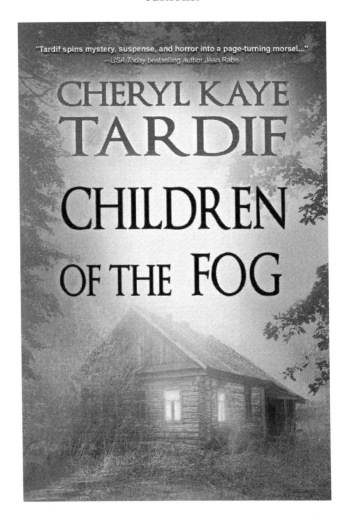

"Tardif spins mystery, suspense, and horror into a page-turning morsel..."
—USA Today bestselling author Jean Rabe

CHERYL KAYE TARDIF

CHILDREN OF THE FOG

**STEM CELL RESEARCH, CLONING, AND
WORLD DOMINATION--WITH AN EXPLOSIVE
TWIST...**

*The South Nahanni River area of Canada's Northwest
Territories has a history of mysterious deaths,
disappearances and headless corpses, but it may also
hold the key to humanity's survival—or its destruction.*

Del thought her father was long dead. But someone from
her past says otherwise. Now she and a group of near
strangers embark on a perilous mission…

CFBI agent Jasmine McLellan leads a psychically gifted team in the hunt for a serial arsonist—a murderer who has already taken the lives of three people.

Jasi and her team members—Psychometric Empath and profiler Ben Roberts and Victim Empath Natassia Prushenko—are joined by Brandon Walsh, the handsome but skeptical Chief of Arson Investigations. In a manhunt that takes them from Vancouver to Kelowna, Penticton and Victoria, they are led down a twisting path of sinister secrets…

Book 1 in the Divine Trilogy

Works by Cheryl Kaye Tardif

Novels:
SUBMERGED
CHILDREN OF THE FOG
WHALE SONG (Includes WHALE SONG: School
Edition [with discussion guide for schools and book
clubs] and Large Print edition)
DIVINE INTERVENTION
DIVINE JUSTICE
DIVINE SANCTUARY
THE RIVER
LANCELOT'S LADY

Anthologies or Collections:
SKELETONS IN THE CLOSET & OTHER CREEPY
STORIES
WHAT FEARS BECOME
SHADOW MASTERS
A FEAST OF FRIGHTS FROM THE HORROR ZINE
25 YEARS IN THE REARVIEW MIRROR: 52 Authors
Look Back

Bundles & Trilogies:
DIVINE TRILOGY

Short Stories:
EAGLE E.Y.E. (Qwickie)
E.Y.E. OF THE SCORPION (Qwickie)
INFESTATION (Qwickie)
DREAM HOUSE
REMOTE CONTROL

Children's Books:
THE ELFLING PRINCESS
MY IMAGINARY FRIEND

Foreign Translations:
SUBMERGÉS
SUMERGIDO (Spanish – Submerged)
I BAMBINI DELLA NEBBIA (Italian – COF)
LOS NINOS DE LA NIEBLA (Spanish – COF)
VERSUNKEN (German - Submerged)
LES ENFANTS DU BROUILLARD (French - Children of the Fog)
DIVINE: Blick ins Feuer (German - Divine Intervention)
WILDER FLUSS (German - The River)
DES NEBELS KINDER (German - Children of the Fog)
DIE MELODIE DER WALE (German - Whale Song)
DIE MELODIE DER WALE: Schulausgabe (German - Whale Song: School Edition)
LANCELOTS LADY (German - Lancelot's Lady - soon to be released)
GIZEMLI NEHIR (Turkish - The River)
2 Chinese titles (Out of print - WHALE SONG and CHILDREN OF THE FOG)

Non-Fiction:
HOW I MADE OVER $42,000 IN 1 MONTH SELLING MY KINDLE eBOOKS

Audio Books:
CHILDREN OF THE FOG
SUBMERGED
DES NEBELS KINDER (German – Children of the Fog)

About the Author

Cheryl Kaye Tardif is an award-winning, international bestselling Canadian suspense author published by various publishers. Some of her most popular novels have been translated into foreign languages. She is best known for CHILDREN OF THE FOG (over 150,000 copies sold worldwide) and WHALE SONG.

When people ask her what she does, Cheryl likes to say, "I kill people off for a living!" You can imagine the looks she gets. Sometimes she'll add, "Fictitiously, of course. I'm a suspense author." Sometimes she won't say anything else.

Inspired by Stephen King, Dean Koontz and others, Cheryl strives to create stories that feel real, characters you'll love or hate, and a pace that will keep you reading.

In 2014, she penned her first "Qwickie" (novella) for Imajin Books™ new imprint, Imajin Qwickies™. *E.Y.E. of the Scorpion* is the first in her E.Y.E. Spy Mystery series.

Residing in West Kelowna, BC, Canada, Cheryl is now working on her next thriller. Booklist raves, "Tardif, already a big hit in Canada…a name to reckon with south of the border."

Cheryl's website: www.cherylktardif.com
Blog: www.cherylktardif.blogspot.com
Twitter: www.twitter.com/cherylktardif
Facebook:
https://www.facebook.com/CherylKayeTardif

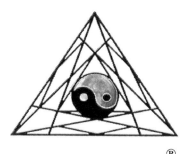

IMAJIN BOOKS ®

Quality fiction beyond your wildest dreams

For your next eBook or paperback purchase, please visit:

www.imajinbooks.com

www.imajinbooks.blogspot.com

www.twitter.com/imajinbooks

www.facebook.com/imajinbooks

IMAJIN QWICKIES ®
www.ImajinQwickies.com